VARIETIES OF FEMALE GOTHIC

VARIETIES OF FEMALE GOTHIC

General editor:
Gary Kelly

Volume 6

Orientalist Gothic

LONDON
PICKERING & CHATTO
2002

Published by Pickering & Chatto (Publishers) Limited
21 Bloomsbury Way, London, WC1A 2TH

2252 Ridge Road, Brookfield, Vermont 05036, USA

www.pickeringchatto.com

BRITISH LIBRARY CATALOGUING IN PUBLICATION DATA
Varieties of female gothic
1. Gothic revival (Literature) – Women authors 2. Gothic revival (Literature) – History
and criticism
I. Kelly, Gary
823'.08729'0907

ISBN 1851967176

LIBRARY OF CONGRESS CATALOGING-IN-PUBLICATION DATA
Varieties of female gothic / general editor, Gary Kelly.
    p. cm
    Includes bibliographical references
    Contents: v. 1. Enlightenment gothic and terror gothic – v. 2. Street gothic – v. 3.
Erotic gothic – v. 4–5. Historical gothic – v. 6. Orientalist gothic.
    ISBN 1-85196-717-6 (set : acid-free paper)
    1. Horror tales, English. 2. English fiction – Women authors. 3. Gothic revival (Liter-
ature) – Great Britain. I. Kelly, Gary.

PR830.T3 V28 2001
823'.08729089287–dc21   2001021814

This publication is printed on acid-free paper that conforms to
the American National Standard for Permanence of Paper in Printed Library Materials.

Typeset by
P&C

Printed and bound in Great Britain by
Cromwell Press, Trowbridge

CONTENTS

INTRODUCTION

John Drew, in his comprehensive examination of 'India and the Romantic Imagination', describes Sydney Owenson's *The Missionary: An Indian Tale* (3 vols, 1811) as 'oriental Gothic'.[1] Here I will argue that a more apt definition would be 'Orientalist Gothic', and that, as such, Owenson's novel, like the others in this set, addresses particular as well as general issues in the literature, culture and politics of its time. Some idea of the location of *The Missionary* in its historical moment can be gathered from the fact that negotiations between its author and publisher were managed by a leading politician and concluded in his coach. The politician was Castlereagh, momentarily out of office over failures in British campaigns against Napoleon, but soon to return to office as foreign secretary the year after *The Missionary* was published. At that moment Sydney Owenson (1776–1859) was already famous, for four related reasons. She was personally attractive, with a number of socially well-placed admirers. She had developed a public identity as the female embodiment of a liberal Romantic idea of Ireland. This role she performed for the titled and powerful of Ireland and England in the drawing rooms of their country mansions and town houses, and particularly the Dublin and London houses of her patrons, the Marquis and Marchioness of Abercorn. Lastly, she also embodied this role in fiction as the author of a series of successful novels in the new genre of the 'national tale', or story dealing with a region's or nation's culture, history and identity through familiar plots of love and courtship. This introduction will first describe Sydney Owenson's social formation as a promoter of liberal Romantic nationalism, then relate her work to the aristocratic reform movement within the governmental and imperial administration of the late eighteenth and early nineteenth centuries and to the Romantic Orientalism that was part of it. It will then go on to survey the development of her fiction up to *The Missionary*, and consider *The Missionary*, in particular, as an example of Orientalist Gothic.

Owenson let on that she was born on board ship between England and Ireland, thereby suggesting that she had a particularly 'British' identity for an age

1 John Drew, *India and the Romantic Imagination* (Delhi: Oxford University Press, 1987), p. 241.

that saw the emergence of new models of nation and empire.[1] Owenson's father, Robert (originally MacOwen or MacEon) was an Irish singer and actor who specialised in stock Irishman roles, in which he larded his speeches with bits of Gaelic. His wife, Jane (Hill) was an Englishwoman, the daughter of a merchant in Shrewsbury, and disliked Ireland. Robert Owenson was taken by an English gentleman to London for education in music and other subjects. Though given a Protestant education, Owenson claimed extensive Irish kin, including Oliver Goldsmith, and he had picked up a vast store of Irish song, anecdote and legend. Jane Owenson was resolutely pious and respectable, and gave her daughters Sydney and Olivia a thorough training in the Bible and domestic craft. After Owenson quarrelled with his employer Richard Daly, the notoriously licentious Dublin theatre proprietor, he opened his own theatre in Fishamble Street, Dublin, strongly supported by the Anglo-Irish landed and professional classes who were at that moment claiming greater independence for Ireland from its colonial ruler, Britain. Art and politics would always be linked for the Owensons. The loyalist-dominated Irish parliament suppressed the theatre, and Owenson had to return to Daly's company. The Owensons' infant son died, and they informally adopted a gifted ragamuffin, Thomas Dermody, who became the Owenson sisters' companion. When Jane Owenson died, the sisters were placed in a Huguenot Calvinist boarding school at Clontarf, now part of Dublin, and after three years, in a finishing school in Dublin, to prepare them for the marriage market. Owenson fell out with Daly again, and some aristocratic friends helped him set up a theatre in Kilkenny, in the south, which opened in August 1794, but quickly failed. Now educating herself, Sydney studied literature and science, and took up writing. She also spent a lot of time with her father in the west of Ireland, where he had a theatre at Sligo.

It, too, failed, in 1798, and a family friend procured Sydney a position as governess with the Featherstonehaugh family of Bracklin Castle, Westmeath, in the centre of Ireland, where she continued reading, and writing verse and fiction. While staying at the Featherstonehaughs' Dublin house, Sydney and her sister met Thomas Moore, rapidly becoming the most popular Irish poet, who would become a leading literary spokesman for Irish identity, culture and rights. Soon Sydney Owenson published her own book, *Poems* (1801), dedicated to her father's friend and Thomas Dermody's one-time patron, Lady Moira. The Moiras were members of a new generation of aristocrats promoting economic and social modernisation, reform and the professionalisation of government and its administration. Like the Moiras, many of these progressive aristocrats were

1 I am indebted for biographical details to *Lady Morgan's Memoirs: Autobiography, Diaries and Correspondence* (2 vols, London: W. H. Allen and Co., 1862); Lionel Stevenson, *The Wild Irish Girl: The Life of Sydney Owenson, Lady Morgan (1776–1859)* (1936; New York: Russell and Russell, 1969), which follows *Lady Morgan's Memoirs* closely, adding some details from other memoirists; and Mary Campbell, *Lady Morgan: The Life and Times of Sydney Owenson* (London: Pandora, 1988), which adds more details of the social context.

located in the Irish and Scottish peripheries of the new United Kingdom of Great Britain and Ireland, and they would transform the British state and Empire under the pressure of the Napoleonic wars. Sydney Owenson continued corresponding with Dermody, and after spending some time with her father, who now had a small theatre at Coleraine, she was engaged by the Crawfords of Fort William, Tipperary. During her many stays and visits in various parts of Ireland she had picked up a good number of Irish ways, to add to the stories, songs and pastiches of Irish culture she had acquired from her father. She also sensed the pressing need for national and imperial reorganisation circulating among her hosts and their guests in many a country mansion and elegant town house. At such aristocratic gatherings Sydney Owenson was beginning to be known for her 'Irish' songs and dances, and her ability to provide amusingly ethnic entertainment. Owenson was constructing herself as an embodiment of Irishness for the consumption of the Anglo-Irish ruling class, who were well-connected both to the British ruling class and the new colonial administrators.

Sydney's construction of herself as the epitome of Irishness for such people was timely. The Irish rebellion of 1798 had frightened the Anglo-Irish ruling class and alarmed the British government. Social and political conflicts in Britain, Europe, and its colonies threatened the break-up of countries, states and empires. Militant French Revolutionary patriotism and Napoleonic imperialism provoked development of 'national' identities and cultures throughout Europe and its colonies. The Union of Ireland with Great Britain at the end of 1800 was designed in part to answer the challenge of regionalism and nationalism within the British isles, and Sydney Owenson had been well educated, in her home and outside it, to respond to this, in person and in writing. Her achievement would be to bring together broad cultural movements in order to address the situation of the United Kingdom and its Empire in the Revolutionary aftermath and Napoleonic crisis. That ability is intimated in her first novel, *St. Clair; or, The Heiress of Desmond*, published at Dublin in 1802 and republished the following year at London, with a third edition, 'corrected and much enlarged', in 1812. Like *The Missionary*, it represents two lovers with intensely communing subjectivities set in a picturesque and sublime landscape. While this landscape validates their passion, the lovers are prevented in the end from uniting. The novel draws on European literary antecedents in the proto-revolutionary culture of Sensibility, in particular Rousseau's *La Nouvelle Héloïse* (1756–8), Goethe's *Sorrows of Werther* (1774), and Bernardin de St Pierre's *Paul et Virginie* (1787). Readers could be expected to recognise these literary antecedents, which were influential texts of the culture of Sensibility, but which were also coming to be strongly associated with liberal, reformist politics across Europe. Though the social values and politics of the literature and culture of Sensibility were widely seen as the inspiration for French Revolutionaries and their European sympathisers, by the time Owenson's novel was published, Sensibility was becoming appropriated to a post-Revolutionary and anti-Napoleonic culture that would emerge as liberal Romanticism.

There is another important dimension of literary reference in *St. Clair*. A trait of all Owenson's fiction is its use of literary reference and allusion, and here there are plentiful references to 'Ossian' – purported to be a Celtic bard of ancient Scotland, but in fact a fabrication of the clergyman James Macpherson as the voice of a once unified 'national' culture supposedly shared by all classes. Though mostly fictitious, Ossian was a central figure in what Katie Trumpener has called 'bardic nationalism'.[1] This was the tendency of certain scholars and writers to base a unifying ideology of 'national' identity, history and destiny on a supposedly original, though now fragmentary or corrupted, culture. Representing themselves as 'national' bards, such scholars and writers proposed that this original 'national' culture could and should be retrieved or restored to reconcile present social conflicts, to transform the existing order and to create a new national self-consciousness. Ossian alone had a tremendous influence throughout Europe – Ossian was Napoleon's favourite poet.[2] Figures such as Ossian and bardic nationalist texts generally draw on national topography as well as social relations and cultural forms to constitute the 'national' subject – i.e., the nation internalised in the character and consciousness of the individual subjectivity, and the individual subject as representative of the nation. Accordingly, *St. Clair* also draws on Owenson's knowledge of Irish landscape and culture, for Ireland is the setting here. What Owenson does in *St. Clair* is to place Ireland – or her version of Ireland – in the political context of the new Romantic nationalism that had absorbed central elements of the earlier culture of Sensibility. *St. Clair*'s Irish topography and cultural references, together with its Ossianism and echoes of certain leading novels of Sensibility, are designed to eclipse the realities of Revolutionary violence, including the Irish Rebellion of 1798, and transform the novel of Sensibility into a pioneering text of the new, liberal Romantic nationalism.

The novel does so through the representation of its protagonists' and especially its heroine's subjectivity. The novel's heroine, who bears the name of Owenson's sister, Olivia, embodies Ireland, and especially its culture, figured as a product of its landscape. Furthermore, this identity is distinctively feminine, and even feminist. Olivia declares that her education has not imposed on her the usual 'prejudices' – or merely social values and conventions – acquired by women subjected to the ideology and culture of fashionable, courtly society. In other words, Owenson constructs Olivia as the kind of sovereign subject that was the model for political liberals across Europe. Moreover, Olivia's subjectivity is supposedly 'natural' and Irish in a way that internalises the national landscape and the 'national' culture of the people. Yet Olivia's subjectivity is also disciplined in a way centrally important to the middle class reading public of Owenson's day, and thus brings together discourses of both middle and lower

1 Katie Trumpener, *Bardic Nationalism: The Romantic Novel and the British Empire* (Princeton: Princeton University Press, 1997).

2 Frank McLynn, *Napoleon: A Biography* (London: Pimlico, 1998), p. 256.

classes. It is the eponymous hero, St Clair, with his excessive subjectivity and indulgence in 'passion', who brings about the male competition resulting in his death at the hands of his rival for Olivia, and consequently her death from grief – another form of excessive subjectivity. Like many post-Revolutionary novels, *St. Clair* ostensibly warns against the subjective sensibility celebrated in the novels that it echoes, especially Rousseau's; at the same time it gives full and lyrical representation to that subjectivity and thus in a way celebrates it. This paradox, of the soul too beautiful to live in a world of social difference and conflict – not to mention a world of global imperial struggle – would be a central theme of Owenson's work and of both Romanticism and early nineteenth-century liberalism. The paradox is central to what I have elsewhere called the Romantic 'novel of passion' – 'passion' in the double sense of 'suffering' (the original sense) and 'powerful or overwhelming desire' (the later sense).[1] Such representations of passion obviously fascinated readers of the time, as striking figures of strong subjectivity, but also created anxiety over the issue of self-control. Not surprisingly, then, both reviewers and friends told Owenson that her glamorising representation of her protagonists' excessive subjectivities overrode the novel's warning against such extremes.[2]

Nevertheless the reception of *St. Clair* was generally appreciative. Encouraged by this, Owenson left her position as governess to follow her father again in his theatrical projects, and attempt a breakthrough to self-supporting authorship. With her sister, she joined her father at Strabane, county Tyrone, a dozen miles south of Londonderry. She published versions of two old Irish songs and a pamphlet defending the state of the theatre in Ireland. While staying with her father at Londonderry, she worked on a collection of Irish songs taken down from him; this was published in 1806 as *Twelve Original Hibernian Melodies: With English Words, Imitated and Translated from the Works of the Ancient Irish Bards*. The work participates in a wave of such works throughout Europe and elsewhere, ostensibly recovering and preserving a heritage of the 'national' culture. Owenson also worked on a long historical romance set in the France of Henri IV, published in 1806 as *The Novice of St. Dominick* (4 vols). This was the period of the bloody religious civil wars of late sixteenth-century France, which had been used throughout the seventeenth and eighteenth centuries by British political writers as a parallel to civil and religious divisions there, and as a warning against both excessive royal power and popular rebelliousness.[3] Though her friend, Alicia Lefanu, had warned her against any open display of learning and acquiring the then pejorative appellation of 'bluestocking', Owenson's new work is noticeably, perhaps ostentatiously learned. It belongs to a class of Romantic

1 Gary Kelly, *English Fiction of the Romantic Period 1789–1830* (London and New York: Longman, 1989), pp. 43–4, 184–210.

2 Stevenson, *Wild Irish Girl*, pp. 58–9.

3 J. M. H. Salmon, *The French Religious Wars in English Political Thought* (Oxford: Clarendon Press, 1959).

fiction that could be described as the 'footnote novel', with numerous references to historiographical and other works apparently designed to authenticate the fiction with fact. Critics of the time complained that mingling history and fiction would delude young readers and break down a major discursive distinction, leading ultimately to the subverting of reason and virtue – disciplined subjectivity – by delusive fantasy. Nevertheless, the reading public was showing an increasing appetite for such fictions, and as ever Owenson was quick to exploit such appetites.

In *The Novice* she takes the long-standing historical analogy between the French religious wars and British politics and adapts it to her own time in a way that would have been familiar to her readers. Any story set in times and places of historic civil discord, conflict or war could serve as a commentary on the situation of Britain and Europe in the Revolutionary and Napoleonic crisis. Ireland, however, was a special case. As in sixteenth-century France, Ireland around 1800 was the scene of often brutal and bloody conflict between a Protestant minority and a Catholic majority. After the Irish Rebellion of 1798 many of the Anglo-Irish gentry and aristocracy, including those whom Owenson knew, came to believe that only emancipation of the Catholics from their civil disabilities, or repeal of their legislated exclusion from full civil rights, civic offices, professions, and tolerance of their church and schools, would ensure security and prosperity, not only of Ireland but the United Kingdom. As the first and nearest of England's colonies, Ireland was in many ways a test case for the Empire. Ireland was also an experimental laboratory for administrative and other reforms that many felt were needed to defend the Empire against competitors and to secure the state against new claimants for participation in the political process, especially dissident and politicised elements of the lower and lower middle classes.[1] It was these classes who supported violent revolution in many places, including Ireland. In July 1803 the uprising of the so-called United Irishmen, which was led by Robert Emmett and encouraged by Napoleon, revived concern over national unity and the reliability of Catholics and other disaffected groups. The rising was abortive; Emmett was caught, tried, convicted and hung; Protestant Orangemen renewed vigilante persecution of suspect, prominent, or outspoken Catholics; and Catholic peasant secret societies continued economic violence and intimidation against Anglo-Irish landowners in the countryside.

The Novice of St. Dominick addresses this continuing crisis in several ways. It re-inscribes bardic nationalism, here by extensive references to Provençal culture. Provençal minstrelsy, language and culture are represented as the expression of a libertarian, patriotic, independent and religiously tolerant people against centuries of attempts by outsiders to suppress them and assimilate them to the religion, culture and language of powerful neighbours. In fact, Owenson intended to call her novel *The Minstrel*, but her publisher persuaded her to change to the catchpenny title that suggested Gothic dimensions – con-

1 R. F. Foster, *Modern Ireland 1600–1972* (London: Penguin Books, 1989), p. 290.

vent Gothic then being in full vogue. Certainly the parallel between Provence and Ireland was obvious enough. In fact, Provence would become an important symbol in Romantic liberalism through the early nineteenth century, largely through J. C. de Sismondi's *Littérature du Midi de l'Europe* (1813). As in *St. Clair*, Owenson builds *The Novice* around a female protagonist, here named Imogen, invoking a parallel to Shakespeare's romance *Cymbeline* which, as Carol Hart notes, 'resembles *The Novice* in its depiction of lost status, female heroism and bourgeois and aristocratic alliance'.[1] Owenson's Imogen has a complex subjectivity and many talents and in the course of the story undertakes a tour of French society and culture of the time, from which she learns the vanity, instability and treacherousness of fashionable courtly society and the evils of religious intolerance of both Protestants and Catholics. The liberal, reformist and patriotic purpose of the novel is indicated by the fact that Owenson travelled to London to get the work published by Richard Phillips, a well known English Jacobin, whose bookshop was a drop-in centre for reformist politicians and agitators, and such prominent and politically radical intellectuals as William Godwin.

Returning to Ireland, Owenson plunged into a new fiction project. This was designed to promote more directly the theatricalised version of Irish identity and culture she had taken over from her father and developed into both a literary discourse and a personal performance routine in the salons of those with direct political influence. In order to do so, Owenson again undertook formal innovation to achieve her political aims. Like the other politically motivated authors published by Phillips, Owenson understood that, though despised, the novel was the most widely read form of print, apart from newspapers and magazines, among the middle and upper classes. She would also have known that the next most widely read form of book was the travelogue.[2] At this time the travelogue was widely used to promote a combination of political, cultural and economic issues. Such travelogues often combined a distinctively individual narrating persona with a miscellany of entertaining yet politically pointed information about culture, society, politics, economic development and so on. New elements were also being absorbed into both the novel and the travelogue from the burgeoning research taking place into the historic culture of the common people, research that was appropriated or forged in texts of bardic nationalism.

These studies were called 'popular antiquities' at the time, and later came to be known as folklore. Such research had several functions. Knowledge of local

---

1 Carol Ann Hart, 'Domains of Difference: Gender, Class and Ethnicity in the Novels of Sydney Owenson, Lady Morgan c. 1802–1811' (unpub. PhD diss., University of Alberta, 1996), p. 90.

2 See Charles L. Batten, Jr., *Pleasurable Instruction: Form and Convention in Eighteenth-Century Travel Literature* (Berkeley, California: University of California Press, 1978); Percy G. Adams, *Travel Literature and the Evolution of the Novel* (Lexington: University Press of Kentucky, 1983).

plebeian lore and social practices could assist programmes of economic, social and cultural modernisation, and 'popular antiquities' were often included in studies of regional topography, economic resources and infrastructure on which public policy for development was based. This was the case especially in the peripheries of the United Kingdom, considered most in need of, or open to, modernisation, to bring those regions into economic, social, cultural and, hence, political interdependence with the metropolis – in this case, England. Another important cultural use of research on 'popular antiquities' was in fabrication of a supposedly national identity from the agglomeration of local and regional identities in complex states, such as the United Kingdom. A less obvious but perhaps more important function of 'popular antiquities' was ideological, and thus political: such studies incorporated the culture of the common people into learned discourses commanded and practised by the professional middle classes and professionalised landowning class, thereby appropriating an alternative cultural and ideological domain to the interests and aims of those classes. Associated with this kind of work were the fakes, forgeries, fabrications and imitations, ranging from Macpherson's 'Ossian' through the art ballads or imitation 'folk' ballads produced by writers such as Walter Scott, to the partly original, partly traditional songs such as those published by Owenson in *Twelve Hibernian Melodies*.

A travelogue-novel could give such materials a wider readership, and this could be especially true for a work dealing with Ireland. The Union of Ireland and Great Britain had shifted party political power, making the government at Westminster dependent on the new Members of Parliament from Ireland. William Pitt and the government, along with many officials sent to govern Ireland, favoured emancipation of Roman Catholics from their historic civil disabilities, but emancipation was vehemently opposed by many Anglo-Irish landowners, by Orangemen, or intransigent middle class Irish Protestants, and by many in England – where Catholics had long been regarded as subservient to a foreign power and thus unpatriotic. In fact, as Linda Colley has argued, 'English' national identity was partly formed as anti-Catholic.[1] Catholic emancipation was opposed with particular vehemence by George III. Yet it was clearly a desirable political option at that moment. The Rebellion of 1798, the uprising of the United Irishmen in 1803, the ensuing bloody and cruel repression of Irish peasants, parliament's rejection of a petition from Irish Catholics in 1805 and continuing fear of Napoleon's military intervention placed the 'Irish question' in the forefront of British politics. At the same time, the Union had aroused expectations among all classes of Irish Catholics, including the remaining aristocrats, and many feared that delay of emancipation would precipitate another bloody revolution.[2] Resolving the 'Irish question' had become critical to

---

1 Linda Colley, *Britons: Forging the Nation 1707–1837* (London: Pimlico, 1992).

2 Ursula Henriques, *Religious Toleration in England 1787–1833* (London: Routledge and Kegan Paul, 1961), pp. 138–43.

the government's stability, to national unity, and perhaps to imperial survival. Owenson could not be addressing a more important issue in 1805.

She prepared for her task by study of books, by field research in Connaught in the west of Ireland – long regarded as the most 'Irish' part of the country – and by consulting experts such as the Irish antiquarian Joseph Cooper Walker.[1] She described her project to Phillips, but he recommended casting the work as a series of letters in travelogue form, like Lady Mary Wortley Montagu's often reprinted *Letters ... Written during Her Travels in Europe, Asia, and Africa* (1763–7), or publishing a series of factual reports in epistolary form in his liberal periodical, the *Monthly Magazine*, followed by book publication. She stuck to the travelogue-novel, however, and finished her work early in 1806. Knowing what she had, she demanded £300 from Phillips. When he demurred, she went to the firm of Joseph Johnson. Johnson was the leading publisher of the English jacobins, including Godwin, and Revolutionary feminists such as Mary Wollstonecraft and Mary Hays. Johnson also published two of the leading Anglo-Irish promoters of modernisation – Richard Lovell Edgeworth and his daughter Maria, whose *Castle Rackrent: An Hibernian Tale* (1800) had already broken the ground in fictionalising Irish national identity and culture. Owenson intended to call her work *The Princess of Inismore*, but her friend John Wolcot, known as 'Peter Pindar' and for his verse satires on current affairs, suggested 'The Wild Irish Girl'. After a somewhat erotically suggestive correspondence, Phillips came up with the £300, exulting that '*The Wild Irish Girl* is mine, to do with her as I please!'[2] Such punning with titles was common at the time, and Phillips's freedom of expression, which might have seemed ungentlemanly to some, was a cultural marker of liberal, avant-garde circles, carried over into liberal writing, and was widely deplored by conservative critics and writers. The erotic, Owenson was aware, and as her fiction and the critical response to it would demonstrate, had powerful political resonance.

The Wild Irish Girl: A National Tale was published by Phillips in three volumes in 1806 and was an immediate sensation. This was the first of a series of fictions to receive the new generic designation 'national tale', though there were a number of eighteenth-century novels that incorporated regional colour and culture from the margins, especially Scotland and Wales, but also Ireland. The latter included novels by Sarah Butler (*Irish Tales*, London, 1716), William Chaigneau (*The History of Jack Connor*, 2 vols, London, 1752), Thomas Amory (*The Life of John Buncle, Esq.*, 2 vols, London, 1756), Frances Sheridan (*Memoirs of Miss Sidney Biddulph*, 3 vols, London, 1761, and *Conclusion* ..., 1767), Thomas Leland (*Longsword, Earl of Salisbury*, 2 vols, London, 1762) and Regina Maria Roche (*The Children of the Abbey: A Tale*, 4 vols, London, 1796).[3] There was also

---

1 Walker was a literary correspondent of another pioneering woman political novelist, Clara Reeve; see Introduction to Reeve in volume 1 of this edition.

2 Stevenson, *Wild Irish Girl*, p. 77.

3 Ian Campbell Ross, review of *The Wild Irish Girl*, ed. Claire Connolly and Stephen Copley (2000), in *Eighteenth-Century Fiction*, 14:2 (January 2002), p. 227.

Maria Edgeworth's recent and successful *Castle Rackrent* (1800), although Edgeworth aimed to show how the Irish gentry and peasantry degraded each other and therefore needed modernisation and union with Britain.

The term 'tale' had long been used as a generic label for relatively short narratives, usually fictitious, originally supposed to be derived from oral 'folk' narratives but collected in compilations of various lengths since antiquity. In the late eighteenth and early nineteenth centuries, however, the term came to be used in English to indicate a fiction different from the full-scale, multi-volume 'modern novel' or 'romance' that had many characters, incidents and settings and usually dealt with fashionable upper class society. 'A Tale' on the title page invited the reader to expect a simpler narrative, focused on a few characters in a particular location and probably dealing with common life and local, quotidian events. By 'National Tale' Owenson seems to have meant such a fiction dealing with issues and representing characters, incidents and settings supposedly characteristic of a 'nation', or people with a distinct language, culture, history and identity. Subsequent novels identified on their title pages as 'national tales' include *O'Donnel* (3 vols, 1814) by Owenson (by then Lady Morgan), *Clan-Albin* (4 vols, 1815) by Christian Isobel Johnstone, *The Matron of Erin* (3 vols, 1816) by a 'Matron of Honour', *Edgar* (3 vols, 1816) by 'Miss Appleton', and *The O'Briens and the O'Flahertys* (4 vols, 1827) by Lady Morgan. Though the designation was not used often, the form of the 'national tale' would be the characteristic genre of liberal Romantic nationalism through the nineteenth and into the twentieth century, especially as restructured by Walter Scott and his numerous imitators, around the globe.

In fact, *The Wild Irish Girl* is an epistolary novel, in which H. M., a decadent young English aristocrat, writes to his partner in fashionable dissipation, J. D. Esq., M. P., his impressions of Ireland. H. M. has been sent there by his father, the Earl of M—, ostensibly to visit his Irish estates but in fact to detach him from his dissolute associates and way of life. Arrived at M— House on the north-west coast of Connaught, H. M. is surprised by the beauty of the country, the energy, simplicity and honesty of the common Irish, and by the cultivation – without loss of 'national' authenticity – of the Irish Catholic aristocracy, represented by Glorvina, the 'wild Irish girl', and her father, the Prince of Inismore. The Inismores once owned the estates of the area and their ancestor was murdered by the Earl of M—'s forebear when Ireland was seized by the English. Even Catholicism wears a benign face in Ireland, represented by the learned, wise, and virtuous Father John, the Inismores' chaplain. The phrase 'wild Irish' was an English usage found in medieval writing to indicate the Irish living beyond the reach of English rule, and later the phrase came to mean the 'less civilised' Irish, that is, those not anglicised sufficiently, in the eyes of the English.[1] Owenson aims to turn the slur into a celebration, for the jaded English narrator finds that though the 'wild Irish girl' is certainly the embodiment of

1 *Oxford English Dictionary*.

Ireland's uncorrupted soul, or culture, spirit and 'national' character, she can quote Tasso as well as sing Irish folksongs, and that his own decadently civilised soul is refreshed, restored, and reformed by her. Posing as an artist, he undertakes to tutor Glorvina in drawing in exchange for an informal degree course in Irish language, history, topography, flora and fauna, cultural anthropology, 'popular antiquities' and political economy (including the way his father's English steward exploits the Irish tenants and defrauds his employer). Thanks to extensive footnotes, the reader is informed even more fully than is H. M.

With this kind of interchange of minds and souls carried on amidst validating picturesque nature – and in countryside that, in different senses, belongs to both the Princess of Inismore and himself – H. M. inevitably comes to desire further physical and legal union. As in literary romance and in marriages of state, such a union would echo the Union of Ireland and Great Britain. There are, also inevitably, obstacles, to which Owenson gives a Gothic shading and setting. Glorvina's first duty is to her ailing and impecunious father; H. M. fears his father's disapproval. H. M. learns that a figure of satisfactorily Gothic obscurity had appeared annually, apparently from England, and engaged in mysterious interviews with the Prince of Inismore. At the same time, H. M. learns that his father is to arrive, with H. M.'s arranged betrothed and her father, who turn out to be vulgar, shallow and mercenary. The 'Conclusion', by a third-person narrator, recounts the Gothic denouement: in a gloomy chapel H. M. comes upon the marriage ceremony of Glorvina to the obscure stranger. Rushing forward, H. M. finds that the intended bridegroom is none other than his own father who, by the marriage, intended to erase the wrongs and divisions of the past by a union in the present. With that disclosure, the happy ending unfolds, H. M. and Glorvina wed, and the novel closes with the Earl of M—'s epistolary blessing on the symbolically and exemplarily British couple. As Lionel Stevenson observes, the hero's 'falling in love with Glorvina is taken as a matter of course, and his falling in love with Ireland is the real theme'.[1] The plot represents England's desire for Ireland, in which a forcible violation in the past is repaired by a culturally, intellectually and morally validated mutual erotic desire leading to conjugal union in the present, though shadowed by a Gothic alternative possibility.

The representation of desire is reinforced by the lyrical language of the male protagonist and principal narrative voice, H. M. This lyricism has an erotic dimension that could be indicative of the eroticism of courtly decadence, widely deplored at the time as a symptom of Britain's dangerous national moral decline, possibly leading to military failures and imperial disaster. The novel opens by strongly associating H. M. with that kind of courtly eroticism and decadence, but the novel's plot aims to demonstrate that desire can be educated and reformed by 'national' culture and landscape to a politically conciliatory, culturally harmonising, socially unifying, and patriotically responsible role. The

1 Stevenson, *Wild Irish Girl*, p. 72.

erotic, or a certain form of the erotic, is thus central to Owenson's form of liberal Romanticism, redeployed in different ways throughout her fiction, from *St. Clair* on. It is a form of libertarian subjectivity, the assertion of a sovereign subjectivity but also, as here and elsewhere in her fiction and that of certain contemporaries, close to libertine subjectivity. Because of this propinquity, some of Owenson's readers and critics deplored the erotic element in her work, or saw it as colluding with libertine eroticism and thus with the courtly decadence widely seen as a major cause of Britain's domestic and international crisis. Richard Lovell Edgeworth wrote to Owenson praising *The Wild Irish Girl* for its representation of 'the lower Irish', Father John's 'sound and judicious observations', and the cleverly inserted information on Irish history, but he diplomatically criticised the lush language.[1] The two related charges of excessive eroticism and overwriting continued to be applied to Owenson's writing by critics down to the twentieth century. Such charges had been associated with reformist, then pro-Revolutionary, then liberal writing from the Della Cruscan controversy of the late 1780s, at least, and these associations were exploited by a number of women writers, including Mary Robinson in the 1790s and Charlotte Dacre in the first decade of the nineteenth century. Owenson was consciously writing in that line. Ina Ferris has noted the difficulty that Owenson/Morgan posed to her contemporaries, centred in the erotic quality of her writing: 'If Morgan's high-coloured sensibility threatened the decorum of femininity through a female excessiveness, her ambition challenged it through an assumption of masculine power.'[2] This 'excessiveness' was widely understood as an aspect of her politics, however.

These politics of theme and style were recognised at the time, and reacted to accordingly. *The Wild Irish Girl* was received enthusiastically on the whole in Ireland, but a paper war soon broke out led by John Wilson Croker, probably quietly encouraged for a time by the British-appointed administration in Dublin. At that moment this administration was following the policy of the government in London by rejecting calls for Catholic emancipation and greater autonomy for Ireland. Other readers and critics defended Owenson and her novel, declaring the work to be an accurate and overdue positive representation of Irish history, culture and society. Then the British government decided to take a more conciliatory line toward the Irish and ordered the Lord Lieutenant of Ireland, the Duke of Bedford, to demonstrate the fact. At that moment Owenson was planning to mount an opera, capitalising on her novel's textualisation of a gentrified and idealised version of Irish identity culture, dress, song and language by again staging her and her father's performative embodiment of them. *The First Attempt; or, The Whim of the Moment*, with Robert Owenson in his char-

1 R. L. Edgeworth to Sydney Owenson, 23 December 1806, in *Lady Morgan's Memoirs*, vol. 1, pp. 293–4.

2 Ina Ferris, *The Achievement of Literary Authority: Gender, History, and the Waverley Novels* (Ithaca, New York, and London: Cornell University Press, 1991), p. 48.

acteristic Irishman role, opened in spring 1807. It was attended by the Lord Lieutenant and his suite, leading garrison officers and pro-emancipation lawyers and professionals. At the same time, Sydney Owenson published *The Lay of an Irish Harp* with Phillips, hitting the market from another angle while her name was still before the public. Owenson had now become the public symbol of Irishness, for some, at least. Later in the year, she came to her subject from yet another quarter with *Patriotic Sketches of Ireland, Written in Connaught*, a travelogue of the kind favoured by reformists and liberals as a way of grounding proposals for change based on observation. The book uses anecdote to advance a wide range of detailed national and local reform proposals. Politically and discursively, then, *Patriotic Sketches* was a kind of non-fiction sequel and counterpart to *The Wild Irish Girl*.

Owenson was now playing to her main chance both socially and professionally. Aristocratic Anglo-Irish ladies ignored Owenson as a social phenomenon, but the aristocratic English ladies associated with the Irish administration turned the 'wild Irish girl' – both the fictional character and her author – into a fashion moment, demanding that jewellers create copies of the 'Glorvina ornament', while dressmakers produced a 'Glorvina mantle'. Owenson and her harp and 'Irish' items of dress and ornament were more in demand than ever in Dublin salons, while Owenson was also sought out, sometimes with a politically liberal element of flirtation, by leading cultural and political men, such as the scientist Richard Kirwan and the barrister Sir Charles Montague Ormsby. Early in 1808 she visited London and found that 'Glorvina' was the social rage among aristocratic Whig high society, though the price she had to pay for admission to these circles was to stay in role. Through a combination of public and literary self-construction she had become an important public intellectual, and she proceeded to serve those who 'employed' her to promote their cultural, social and political policies.

Another woman with a similar public role had just created a literary and political sensation with her novel *Corinne; ou, l'Italie* (3 vols, London and Paris, 1807). Germaine Necker, Baronne de Staël-Holstein, known as Madame de Staël, was the daughter of Louis XVI's prime minister at the outbreak of the French Revolution. She associated with the moderate Girondin faction in the early years of the Revolution and then, forced out of France by Napoleon, she led an international salon of intellectuals and liberals from exile. *Corinne* had an enormous impact throughout Europe, and especially on women writers. Its eponymous heroine is represented as the contemporary national bard of an Italy enslaved for centuries by foreign and despotic powers. Corinne embodies the spirit of both ancient republican Rome and a future independent Italy, and for much of the novel she gives a guided tour of the now ruined Roman glories of Italy's national and imperial past, accompanied by lectures on Italian culture, literature, and history. In these respects, she resembled Owenson's Glorvina. *Corinne* is in effect a novelised handbook of liberal Romantic nationalism across Europe. In the end, however, Corinne herself is crushed by the conflict between her public identity and patriotic responsibilities on the one hand and the personal absolute of romantic love on the other. In this, she represents the 'beautiful soul' of the European middle-class ideology of the sovereign subject who is exiled, or self-exiled, within her own country by the unreformed state of its society, culture and government. In the case of the national voice such as Corinne, this subjectivity may be fatally forced back on itself, but nevertheless disburdens its afflicted selfhood in patriotic artistic expression.

In fashionable London society Owenson discovered that, thanks to *The Wild Irish Girl*, she was called 'the Irish Corinne'. The association soon opened new opportunities for her. Owenson and her harp quickly became featured entertainment at the London soirées of the Countess of Cork and Orrery, the leading society hostess of the day. Through her, Owenson met William Gell, who suggested she apply her version of the liberal Romantic 'national tale' to Greece, then still under Turkish rule but becoming a leading cause for European liberals, enabling the expression of political views and protest that would, in many European countries, otherwise be banned. Gell supplied Owenson with information and a research plan and she went to stay with her mother's relatives in Shrewsbury to novelise her findings. She continued to write on through a busy season of socialising and celebrity in Ireland, and finished her novel in the autumn. It was published as *Woman; or, Ida of Athens* (4 vols, 1808).

In its eponymous heroine Owenson combines four female figures (at least). There is a Greek version of 'the wild Irish girl'. There is the Corinne figure. There is the figure of the intellectual woman, also known at the time pejoratively as the 'bluestocking' and positively as the 'female philosopher' (such as Mary Wollstonecraft) and already represented in Owenson's earlier novels. Finally, there is in Ida what the reading public by now would be able to recognise as a version of Sydney Owenson. This composite figure is set in a plot that reworks elements of *The Wild Irish Girl* and *Corinne*, with particular political implications. The decadent English aristocrat reappears, and a darker version of the melancholy but virtuous Lord Nelvil in *Corinne*. Unlike H. M. in *The Wild Irish Girl*, however, the foreign suitor remains unredeemed by the heroine. Ida's lover is a Greek patriot, forced into exile after an unsuccessful revolt against the foreign ruler – in this case, the Turks. Like the Irish 'wild geese' – patriot Catholic exiles – he flees his conquered native land to serve a foreign power, rising to the rank of general in the Russian army. Exiled herself, Ida nearly starves in London before coming into a fortune. Catapulted by chance from the depths to the heights of 'society', Ida, like Owenson, performs her country's culture before fashionable society. Like Imogen in *The Novice of St. Dominick*, Ida discovers the shallowness and unreliability of such people. Finally, thanks to the English aristocrat, Ida and her patriotic Greek lover are reunited.

Owenson designed her composite heroine for several effects. Ida continues to project the embodiment of the 'national' identity and culture as female and feminine, the more effectively to dramatise 'her' resistance to a masculinist regime of oppression, at the same time suggesting that the liberal nationalist revolution must include women. Like Corinne, Glorvina and Owenson the public performer, Ida is a mobilised form of the 'national' culture, and her character is constructed to suggest that the liberal Romantic nation-state will be achieved through the conventionally 'feminine' domain of culture rather than through the violent revolutions or armed movements of guerrilla warfare or national armies that were, as the novel was published, already active in various places in Europe and the New World. Ida's combination of Enlightenment ideas, culture of Sensibility, and 'national' (i.e., folk) culture suggests a programme for constructing national cultural identities. Similar programmes were in fact instituted by new liberal states in education and arts policy through the nineteenth and twentieth centuries. Not surprisingly, then, the novel contains extensive discussions of educational theory and practice, generally advocating the kind of liberal, permissive education designed to produce distinctive, individual, sovereign subjects – the model for the citizen of the liberal state. The broad invitation to the reader to identify protagonist and author (reinforced here by Owenson's highly personal prefatory apology, representing herself as a spontaneous national voice) claims the authority of personal experience for the representation of female patriot. 'Woman', embodied in Ida of Athens, is the exemplary sovereign subject of the modern liberal state which does not yet exist but – in Ida's Greece, as in Corinne's Italy and Glorvina/Owenson's Ireland – which is embodied in this subject, and waiting to be expressed in a political, constitutional reality.

Owenson changed publishers for *Woman; or, Ida of Athens*, leaving Phillips for the more politically mainstream firm of Longman, Hurst, Rees, Orme and Brown. Though her new publisher expressed concern that the liberal opinions in the book would harm sales,[1] Owenson counter-argued that controversy was more likely to boost them. Like its predecessor, her new novel certainly became a political-aesthetic bone of contention between liberals and conservatives. The leading Anti-Jacobin polemicist William Gifford, who during the 1790s had satirised the Della Cruscans and various women writers and founded the *Anti-Jacobin* magazine, attacked the novel in the first number of the new *Quarterly Review*, just established by a group of Scottish and English Tories and edited by Gifford to oppose liberal and Whig magazines such as Phillips's *Monthly Magazine* and the *Edinburgh Review*. Undeterred, Owenson soon embarked on a new fiction, combining elements of the 'national tale' and the new historical romance with aspects of the novel of passion and the Gothic romance, informed by Romantic Orientalism. At the same time, Owenson agreed to join the household of the Marquis of Abercorn and his wife as a permanent guest. The Abercorns were wealthy aristocrats with estates in Ireland and elsewhere, and with manor houses in county Tyrone, Ireland, and at Stanmore, near London. The Marquis was a Tory but the Abercorns followed the practice of the day in entertaining politicians, intellectuals, writers and artists of diverse political,

---

1 Stevenson, *Wild Irish Girl*, p. 114.

social and religious commitments. Following her usual practice, Owenson researched her novel, using the libraries of the Abercorns, Sir Charles Montague Ormsby, and other friends.

Part of her routine as resident entertainer was to read freshly drafted parts of her manuscript aloud to the Abercorns and their guests. On one such occasion at Stanmore, among the auditors was Robert Stewart, Viscount Castlereagh. Castlereagh was an Irish landowner and aristocrat, with estates in counties Down and Donegal (the latter the setting for *The Wild Irish Girl*). He had been a member of the Irish parliament and served in the Irish administration in the late 1790s. He supported the Union and Catholic emancipation as ways to ensure Ireland's loyalty and reliability in the larger struggle against Napoleon, but resigned when the King refused to allow emancipation or other measures favourable to Irish Catholics. After the Union, Castlereagh joined the British government under Addington and, while advocating strong measures to repress rebellion and dissidence, he advocated Catholic emancipation, relief of Irish Catholics from double tithes, and state payment of non-Anglican ministers. When Pitt returned as head of government, Castlereagh became secretary for war and colonial affairs, in which he supported the policies of another Irish peer, Richard Wellesley, Earl of Mornington, as governor general of India from 1797 to 1805. After the brief, Whig-dominated 'ministry of all the talents', which he could not support, Castlereagh returned to office under Portland and strongly promoted Wellesley's brother Arthur, later Duke of Wellington, as commander in Spain against Napoleon. The government's inability to defeat Napoleon was blamed on Castlereagh, however, which led to a duel with his government colleague, George Canning, and the subsequent resignation of both in 1809. This was when he met Owenson, and took it upon himself to secure publication of her new novel, presumably because he thought it promoted the same policies towards India and other colonies, including Ireland, as he did. He invited the publisher Stockdale to his office to discuss terms, and at a meeting with Stockdale and Owenson in his coach, he secured £400 for the work, published as *The Missionary: An Indian Tale* (3 vols, 1811).[1]

The novel is set in the early seventeenth century, during the Catholic counter-Reformation and Spain's occupation of the Portuguese throne. The third-person narrator recounts the life of 'the missionary', a Portuguese nobleman of royal blood who abandons the world for the church, becoming a Franciscan monk and taking the name Hilarion, after a fourth-century saint who was known for his extraordinary asceticism and performance of miracles, by which he converted many pagans. The modern day Hilarion, too, acquires a reputation for superhuman holiness and, though a Franciscan rather than a Jesuit, and ambitious to achieve wonders, he follows the example of the historical St Francis Xavier (1506–52), famous co-founder of the Jesuit order and missionary to Asia from 1542 to his death. As papal legate, St Francis operated

1 Stevenson, *Wild Irish Girl*, p. 130.

from the Portuguese bastion of Goa on India's west coast, baptised some tens of thousands of Indians, and then moved on through the East Indies, Japan and an island off the coast of China, where he died. Hilarion's mission takes place against a background of multiple usurpations by armed forces – particularly of the Portuguese throne by the Spanish monarch, and of the Mogul throne of India by the Muslim prince, Aurengzeb. There is also a background of religious conflict, as the Hindus resisted, often violently, attempts by both Muslims and Christians to proselytise them. Seeking to overcome this resistance, Hilarion is led by a 'pundit', or learned man (who seems to be more like a freethinking 'philosopher' of the European Enlightenment) to fix on converting a famous Indian holy woman, Luxima, whom he sees at Goa. 'Luxima' is a version of 'Lakshmi', name of the Hindu goddess of prosperity, beauty and love. Hilarion learns that Luxima was widowed as a bride and then became a spiritual teacher and priestess under the protection of her grandfather, a Hindu priest. Hilarion believes that converting such a figure will make the conversion of her entire people possible. He follows her across intervening torrents, deserts and mountains to the paradisal valley of Kashmir. He takes up residence in a cave near her isolated dwelling, an encounter occurs, then others, in which they debate the merits of their respective religions and values. As Martin Jarrett-Kerr puts it, 'For half the book ... they argue theology',[1] though the discussions have more to do with values and their implications for personal life and social relations in a broad context of European Enlightenment and liberal ideology. Luxima falls under the missionary's spell, but he falls in love with her. After he sees off a princely rival, Solyman Sheko, who is engaged in the family struggle over the Mogul throne, Luxima accepts Hilarion's religion without fully understanding it, out of love for him rather than theological conviction.

This means she becomes an outcast from her own people and believes she sees the spectre of one of their deities condemning her. Then, while sheltering in a vast temple of Gothic obscurity, she and Hilarion witness her ritual excommunication by her grandfather and attendants. Aware that she is an exile in her own land, and conscious of their sexual desire for one another, forbidden by both his religious vocation and by her former one, Hilarion and Luxima decide to obviate the 'crime' that may result by returning to Goa, where Luxima will be placed in a convent. Here there are extended debates between the missionary and his acolyte on the nature of faith and religion, in which Hilarion upholds the necessity of adhering strictly to principle and striving for perfection, while Luxima promotes a religion of love and acceptance of humanity. This part of the novel is also studded with quotations from, and allusions to, Milton's representation of the fall of Adam and Eve and their expulsion from Eden in *Paradise Lost*. Recrossing a desert landscape of excellently Gothic horror, the fugitives join a caravan, but Hilarion is questioned about his mission and his beliefs by

1 Martin Jarrett-Kerr, 'Indian Religion in English Literature 1675–1967', *Essays and Studies* (1984), p. 93.

some hooded Europeans and then arrested by these men, who turn out to be officers of the Inquisition. Back at Goa, Luxima is placed in a convent and Hilarion tried for heresy by the Inquisition, convicted and handed over to the state for execution at the stake. Meanwhile, however, the pundit enables Luxima to escape from the convent and secretly stirs up the Hindu populace by claiming that Luxima the priestess is being forcibly converted. At the *auto da fe*, or execution, Luxima bursts from the crowd to throw herself on the fire about to consume Hilarion. The crowd reacts with violence, Hilarion rescues Luxima, who has lost her mind, and in the confusion they escape with the pundit's help, sheltering in a seaside cave. The rebellion is suppressed by force, but the missionary and his acolyte are never seen again. Ashes and remains of ritual cremation are found soon after in the cave, and years later a European 'philosopher', who is probably meant to be the early French Orientalist François Bernier (c. 1625–88, one of Owenson's sources), leaves the suite of the Mogul emperor Aurengzeb and visits the cave in Kashmir where local legends still tell of a European missionary-hermit and his unfortunate convert.

The formal elements of *The Missionary* are similar to those in Owenson's earlier work, with some adjustments of particulars appropriate to the new subject. These elements include a third-person narrator; protagonists in a relationship of passion, sympathetically retold by the narrator; stress on the erotic as both generalised and sexual desire; a correspondingly lyrical, expressive and hyperbolic style; few other characters, and these merely sketched; much local and cultural description, bolstered by footnotes; lengthy philosophical dialogues; selected Gothic elements, somewhat modified; a simple plot of a kind of courtship, here ending fatally rather than happily, with no subplots; and broad parallels to certain earlier Sentimental and contemporary Romantic novels, especially those dealing with lovers divided by social or other 'artificial' differences yet placed in intimate proximity and isolated from the rest of society, characteristically represented as irredeemably conflicted, hostile, and even violent. This formal structure is designed, as in the novels of Sensibility and Gothic romances that *The Missionary* takes after, to foreground conflicted and hence afflicted subjectivity – that is, subjectivity divided between a personal, subjective absolute, here erotic love, on the one hand and on the other hand ideology, or the internalised values of particular societies. In this case the values are those of militantly Catholic Europe and defensively exclusionist India, for in this novel ideology is presented as false consciousness. In short, the novel focuses on ideology and passion contending in masculine and feminine subjects that seek harmony and union. In the background, and heightening the meaning of that contention, is a complex and shadowy drama of continuing and often violent institutional, dynastic, nationalist and imperial struggles, local and global, set in the past but resonating powerfully with the present of the novel's readers.

Spain rules Portugal and its empire, against Portuguese resentment, resistance and eventual resurgence. The Spanish and Portuguese seek to colonise and convert Asia, against local resistance. The Papacy tries to dominate church and state, using the infamous Inquisition to do so. The aggressive Jesuits and the famously indolent Franciscans vie for dominance among Catholic religious orders. The sons of the Muslim Mogul emperor fight among themselves for his throne. Hindus, themselves divided by caste, passively resist European and Muslim intruders alike, while maintaining strict hierarchy and religious uniformity. Owenson's readers could readily fit this backdrop to events of their own day: Napoleon's seizure of the Spanish throne and attempt to conquer Portugal against guerrilla resistance and British military intervention; the Revolution's suppression of the Catholic church and Napoleon's *rapprochement* with it; the revolts within European Catholic countries by liberal nationalists opposing the coalition of reactionary Papacy and despotic monarchies; religious revivalism in Protestant countries; revolts in Europe's American colonies. For British readers, there was, again, a further resonance with the continuing 'Irish question', which seemed to offer many parallels to the problem of how to administer Britain's empire in Asia. A novel, as Owenson's readers would know, was not expected to deal directly with such issues, but it could be expected to deal with them through the historic, conventional, generic specialty of the novel – individual life and personal relations, and especially love. Furthermore, by this time the novel's subject had increasingly become subjectivity in one or more of the forms then circulating in the culture of the novel-reading public. The linking of the public and the personal, the social and the subjective, the global and the local was by now the mainstay of much fiction, and Owenson was one of those who had helped make it so, in her earlier work. *The Missionary* nevertheless treats this subject matter in a distinctive way, one that constitutes it as Orientalist and not just oriental Gothic.

The complex interplay of the immediate and subjective on the one hand and the political and global, historical and present on the other is reinforced and nuanced by a characteristically rich use of literary and cultural reference and allusion. *The Missionary* is categorised by critics as 'Gothic',[1] but as in *The Wild Irish Girl* and other of her earlier novels, and like certain English jacobin novelists such as William Godwin, Mary Wollstonecraft and Mary Hays, Owenson adapts elements of the Gothic in *The Missionary* rather than adhering to a particular model of Gothic romance. These elements include a sympathising but moralising omniscient third-person narrator (as in Radcliffe's novels), certain kinds of protagonists (mainly after Lewis's *The Monk*), malign conspirators, a stagy or melodramatic style of dialogue, certain kinds of exotic setting, evocative landscape, portentous dreams, the supernatural or apparently supernatural and of course horrors and grotesqueries.

1 For example, Jarrett-Kerr, 'Indian Religion in English Literature 1675–1967', *Essays and Studies* (1984), p. 92; John Drew, '"In Vishnu-land what Avatar?" Sir William Jones, India and the English Romantic Imagination', in *Tropic Crucible: Self and Theory in Language and Literature*, ed. Ranjit Chatterjee and Colin Nicholson (Singapore: Singapore University Press, 1984), p. 244.

Most obviously Gothic is Owenson's use of the monk figure, made a staple of Gothic romance by M. G. Lewis. Owenson transforms M. G. Lewis's 'monk' Ambrosio into a monk turned missionary, Hilarion, and there are striking similarities. Both Ambrosio and Hilarion are unfitted to face the realities of fleshly temptation by their austere, isolated education and their monastic life, presumably teaching the reader that the world must be engaged with as it is, not held to an impossibly high standard; this is a reformist creed. Both Ambrosio and Hilarion are idolised by others for their flawless life and inspired preaching. Both succumb to erotic desire. The differences, however, are as striking and instructive as the similarities. There is no Satan in female guise to lead Hilarion to ruin, but only the reality of his own humanity, and Owenson's character is more nuanced psychologically than Lewis's. Hilarion does not succumb bodily to temptation, though the effect of desire on his body is described. In general, Owenson's holy man is represented as more human and less sublime than Lewis's, and evil in Owenson's novel is rationalised as an aspect of human character and social institutions rather than personified as an ontological other – the devil. The same is true of Owenson's heroine, who is as pure and innocent as the victim of Lewis's Monk, but whose idolisation of the hero is more fully represented and explained. The psychology of Luxima's love is much more fully represented than that of Lewis's female characters. Though the motives of Owenson's villain – Hilarion's Jesuit rival – are explained, he remains a shadowy Gothic figure and the novel's institutional villain – the Inquisition – also remains shrouded in Gothic obscurity. The narrator in each novel explicitly condemns monastic institutions – a commonplace of Gothic fiction.

There are frights, terrors, horrors and grotesqueries in Owenson's novel, such as a gloomy Hindu temple, fiery plains of naphtha, a menacing serpent, a ravaging wolf, the Inquisition and its flaming pyres and so on. These are represented less for their own sake, or as occasions for troubling the subjectivity of protagonists and readers, however, than as plausible aspects of the otherness of India, as perceived by Hilarion. The element of Gothic exoticism is amply furnished by the setting in India, with the description of Goa serving as a transplanted version of the southern, Catholic Europe favoured by many Gothic novelists. Description of the landscape of Kashmir serves the function of such picturesque passages in Gothic novels – as occasions for exercise of the protagonist's and reader's sensibility, but in *The Missionary* a further function is to furnish the earthly paradise in which Owenson's Miltonic Adam and Eve can experience their fall from superhuman to human. The dialogue is as stylised and melodramatic as a romance reader could wish, especially that between Hilarion and other characters besides Luxima. The dialogues between the missionary and the priestess bear much of the novel's burden of conflicting philosophies of religion, morality, ethics, human nature and love. These dialogues have something of the character of the 'rants' or philosophical declamations in Restoration heroic drama, such as John Dryden's *Aureng-Zebe* (produced 1675, published 1676), also set in India, also based on Orientalist scholarship, and also dealing with conflict of love and duty. The high philosophy and theology of these dialogues in *The Missionary* are, however, nicely ironised by the narrator's interspersed descriptions of the growing desire between the interlocutors. This device makes its own liberal Romantic point about the insufficiency of 'theory', 'philosophy' and religious dogma to human 'nature', including erotic desire, and the hostility to these 'natural' impulses of social, cultural, religious and other differences and conflicts. In summary, *The Missionary* uses Gothic elements in its own way for its own purposes and, like many novels by this time, gives these refashioned elements new functions in a complex structure of literary, cultural and historical reference.

This range of reference is European in scope rather than merely British, in a manner consistent with literary practice of liberal Romantics. Like many liberal Romantic texts, Owenson's novel represents love in paradisal nature, but love doomed by social, cultural and ideological difference. It does so partly by invoking a certain body of literary texts. There are explicit references in *The Missionary* to the Biblical myth of the Fall as represented in Milton's *Paradise Lost* – a major reference for Romantic writers. As in Owenson's previous novels, there are also echoes of, and parallels to, leading novels of Sensibility and Romanticism. These include Bernardin de St Pierre's *Paul et Virginie* (1787), Chateaubriand's *Atala* (1801) and Marie 'Sophie' Cottin's *Mathilde; ou, mémoires tirés de l'histoire des croisades* (1805). Literature dealing with the conflict between love as a personal absolute and social differences of class, race, or culture went back to classical antiquity. It is the central theme of the most popular literary form in history – romantic comedy – and, more recently, domestic tragedy. These highly adaptable forms expressed perduring social anxieties about the need for social stability and continuity on the one hand, formalised in social conventions, regulations and laws, and the need for renewal and innovation on the other. Conventionally, this tension is represented as a conflict between generations and centring on class and family interests. The erotic desire of the younger, relatively powerless generation is pitted against the material interests and social prejudices of the older, power-holding generation. Earlier examples range from Renaissance tragedies such as Shakespeare's *Romeo and Juliet*, through Restoration heroic dramas such as John Dryden's *Aureng-Zebe* and Augustan texts such as Nicholas Rowe's 'she-tragedies' *Jane Shore* and *The Fair Penitent* and Richardson's novel *Clarissa* to novels of Sensibility and Romanticism such as Rousseau's *La Nouvelle Héloïse* and Chateaubriand's *Atala*.

From the work of Richardson and Rousseau on, however, the emphasis shifted from adventures and vicissitudes of society-crossed lovers to love as a field of afflicted subjectivity – afflicted by 'unjust' or 'irrational' social difference and 'prejudice', but also by cultural and ideological difference. This newer form of romantic comedy or domestic tragedy became a special province of Gothic fiction and of the novels of Owenson and those who were her sources and models. This form also addressed the conditions of the Revolutionary and Napoleonic period, when ideological difference, especially in politics and religion (usually linked), disrupted or threatened to disrupt established orders of all kinds, from the family and property through the church and the state to discourse and meaning themselves.

These literary forms expressed and addressed contemporary social and political realities. The disruption that could be caused by ideological conflict was a particular concern to the revolutionary classes – those in what were called the 'middle ranks' throughout Europe and its colonies and former colonies. These groups were in the process of wresting power from the historic ruling class and state structures, but different factions among them also turned on each other in a prolonged struggle for leadership of social and political transformation. This struggle was manifested particularly in the Revolution debate of the 1790s, but also in the regional conflicts such as the 'Irish question' addressed in fiction by Owenson. In the Napoleonic and Romantic period the theme of exile, physical or psychological, became especially prominent, reflecting the fact that French Revolutionary militancy and Napoleonic imperialism and the forces that opposed them created waves of exiles of all kinds and all political and religious persuasions. *The Missionary* addresses the collision of personal absolutes and unaccommodating social structures through the figure represented in Owenson's title – a figure that supposedly mediated transformation between individuals and established institutions, discourses, and ideologies.

For part of the global dislocation of people in Owenson's time resulted from another activity characteristic of the period – 'missionary' work of various kinds. Successive French Revolutionary governments sent out *commissaires* to the provinces of France, to preach approved political and social (and usually anti-clerical and anti-ecclesiastical) doctrines of the moment; French agents were sent out into conquered territories all over Europe with similar missions. Often such political evangelisation was ignored, or resisted even to violence, as in the Vendée region of western France, or in southern Italy, Spain and so on. Many Revolutionaries, Revolutionary sympathisers and reformists represented themselves as political evangelisers, often invoking the figure of Rousseau as a model, purporting, like him, to have withdrawn themselves from the world in order to change it. A similar representation of the political evangeliser was used negatively by anti-Revolutionaries such as Edmund Burke. In his *Reflections on the Revolution in France* (1790), Burke compares English Revolutionary sympathisers to militant religious fanatics of the kind who led the parliamentary forces in the seventeenth-century civil war against the monarchy and established church. In the political controversies of Owenson's day, military and religious leaders were often compared with each other, sometimes negatively, as versions of the same disruptive and destructive individualism, and sometimes the religious evangelist was compared favourably with the military conqueror, as a man of peace and love rather than war and destruction. To take just one example, Helen Maria Williams's widely read poem *Peru* (1784) contrasted the Spanish military conquest of South America, followed by forcible conversion and enslavement of the aborigines, with the benevolent advocacy of native peoples by the priest Bartolomé de las Casas (1474–1566), and implicitly called for a similar philanthropic policy for Britain.

Hilarion himself invokes a comparison of his mission with that of a previous European with designs on India – the military conqueror Alexander the Great.[1] Since we are told that Hilarion had studied the history of India, including Alexander's expedition, he would know that, according to different narratives, once Alexander had reached India he was told that conquering the world was pointless unless he had conquered himself.[2] In other words, the subjective world is more important than the world of empire, military or religious. Certainly that is one lesson of Hilarion's expedition in the novel. There is further contemporary relevance to Hilarion's project. In late eighteenth- and early nineteenth-century Europe, and largely as a response to Revolutionary and Napoleonic political proselytising, religious evangelisation increased greatly everywhere, with several aims. One aim was to counter both Enlightenment-Revolutionary irreligion and lower class dissidence; another aim was to exercise a form of ideological social control; finally, evangelisation aimed to instil class discipline in the very middle classes who managed most of the religious evangelising. In Ireland, Protestant evangelisation of Catholics was seen by some as a way to pacify Britain's notoriously restless and rebellious, first and nearest colony. Such evangelisation was resented by Irish Catholics, however. It was seen as unnecessarily disruptive by many of those whose views Owenson shared and served, such as her aristocratic friends involved in Irish administration and in government, including *The Missionary*'s patron, Castlereagh. At the same time, Evangelicals in the Church of England were agitating to be allowed to proselytise in India, against the policy followed by both the East India Company and the British government.[3] In short, this was an era of missionaries and prophets both political and religious, from the emperor Napoleon to the working-class religious prophet Joanna Southcott, from Revolutionary agents in Italy, Spain and elsewhere to Anglican Evangelicals in Ireland and India. In the cultural domain, Romantic writers displayed a distinct enthusiasm for representing themselves as prophets and literature as prophecy dedicated to reclaiming humanity and the world. Owenson participated in that self-appointed sense of vocation, in her own picturesque and provocative way.

The position that *The Missionary* takes on the issue of evangelisation, in general and in India, is part of what makes it an Orientalist novel. For the resistance of Owenson's political friends to allowing Christian evangelisation in India was one aspect of the broad movement of Enlightenment Orientalism supported by successive governors general in India, from Warren Hastings to Lord Richard Wellesley. At that time, an Orientalist would be understood as a scholar

---

1 See p. 17 in the present edition.

2 Drew, '"In Vishnu-land what Avatar?" Sir William Jones, India and the English Romantic Imagination', p. 223.

3 See the Introduction to Mary Butt's *The Traditions*, volume 1 in this set, pp. xcix–civ.

of all aspects of what Europeans considered to be the 'Orient', from the Turkish empire to Japan, and ranging from languages to natural history.[1] Such scholarship had always been politically and ideologically driven, however, and there was therefore a broad and complex political history behind, and context for, the work of the British Indian Orientalists whose studies helped inform Owenson's novel.

Eighteenth-century political opinion in Britain was often critical and suspicious of British expansion in India, where vast fortunes could be made, by largely illicit means, at the same time exploiting and corrupting Indian rulers and peoples. Such issues were brought to a head in the long trial of Warren Hastings for allegedly abusing his position as governor general in India. Many thought that fortunes acquired in India could be taken back to Britain, and used to purchase gentry estates and status, seats in parliament and political influence and to spread a taste for 'oriental' luxury and decadence. In the opinion of those who jealously monitored the balance of powers between king, lords and commons, the wealth of the Orient was potentially a dangerous and destabilising force in Britain. Consequently the relationship of the government and the Company had to be policed and the Company's activities regulated. In response to these concerns, certain late eighteenth-century East India Company administrators tried to adapt Company practices to local conditions and cultures. In order to do so, they promoted study of all aspects of Indian topography, ecology, natural history, resources, languages, literatures, culture, history, social structure, property tenure and laws to ensure orderly and profitable administration of the Indian territories that the Company controlled. For example, Warren Hastings engaged young Company officers to study Indian languages and translate law codes, so that British magistrates could administer justice according to local conditions. Hastings believed that using Hindu and Muslim 'pundits' to advise British magistrates and officials had not worked because these advisors used their British superiors' ignorance of local languages and codes to exploit and oppress other local people and to enrich themselves.

There were other, broader factors shaping the work of the Orientalists Owenson studied for her novel. Sixteenth- and seventeenth-century Orientalists often carried out their work as part of missionary activity, especially the Roman Catholics, led by the Jesuits. The missionary Orientalists had an interest in learning local languages and customs in order to proselytise, often because resistance of local rulers and peoples to their activities meant that they had to operate discreetly and covertly. A well known example was the Jesuit Roberto de Nobili (1577–1656), originally a Roman nobleman who became fired with the ambition to follow the example of St Francis Xavier, and who may have been the model for Owenson's missionary. Nobili learned Sanskrit and local lan-

---

1 On this body of literature, see Raymond Schwab, *The Oriental Renaissance: Europe's Rediscovery of India and the East, 1660–1880*, trans. Gene Patterson-Black and Victor Reinking (New York: Columbia University Press, 1984).

guages, moved to a southern Indian city, adopted the dress, appearance, lifestyle and diet of a Brahmin and sanyassi, or holy man, and carried out a diverse range of ideological activities to further the work of conversion.[1] He passed himself off as a 'Roman Brahmin' and claimed that central Hindu doctrines resembled Christian ones. He joined learned disputations between Hindu scholars and priests, trying to suggest that Hindus could retain much of their traditional religion and still become Christians. He published a summary of Christian doctrine in local vernacular, as well as refutations of leading Hindu beliefs, such as reincarnation. According to O. P. Kejariwal, Nobili also wrote '*L'Ezour Vedam*, a clever forgery of the Vedas in which he extolled the virtues of Christianity, and which deceived Voltaire into considering it a genuine Sanskrit text'.[2] Like other, later missionaries, however, Nobili found his efforts often conflicted with the interests of the Portuguese administration at Goa, and the Papacy and the Jesuits at Rome. Some regarded Nobili as a pioneer in taking Christianity to foreign cultures and peoples, rather than imposing it on them, while others regarded him as a typically scheming and duplicitous Jesuit Catholic. Very broadly, Owenson's missionary follows a policy and a path similar to Nobili's, though heading north to Kashmir rather than to southern India. Owenson's representation of her missionary as a contradictory figure, nobly inspired but in the end wrong, also incorporates the two contrasting views of Nobili and his work.

Owenson also historicises missionary endeavour in India because, viewed from her time, any missionary endeavour became coloured by that history. Centuries-old British suspicion of Catholicism generally, and the Jesuits in particular, perhaps reinforced the desire of the British government and the Company to avoid the often violent resistance to proselytising. Historically, such resistance characterised relations between indigenous Hindu populations and their Muslim conquerors and rulers on the one hand, and the Christian missionaries on the other. The work of earlier eighteenth-century French Orientalists, who were sent out to promote French imperial interests, had more relevance to British Orientalism, and some of these French sources are cited by Owenson. By middle decades of the eighteenth century, however, France had been surpassed by Britain as a military and commercial force in India, and the East India Company was still expanding its sphere of influence. There was an obvious need for research to ensure effective rule, and this was sponsored by Warren Hastings from the late 1770s, not without resistance from some in the Company and his own governing council in Bengal. Nevertheless, Hastings accomplished a great deal. He had the ancient law codes in Sanskrit and Persian translated into English – translations which continue to be reprinted in India today. Under his administration, company officers in Bengal, led by Sir William

---

1 Vincent Cronin, *A Pearl to India: The Life of Roberto de Nobili* (London: Rupert Hart-Davis, 1959).

2 O. P. Kejariwal, *The Asiatic Society of Bengal and the Discovery of India's Past 1784–1838* (Delhi: Oxford University Press, 1988), p. 15.

Jones, translated Sanskrit texts and studied local antiquities, architecture, and flora and fauna. These Orientalists founded the Asiatic Society, which still exists and still publishes scholarly work in a range of disciplines from linguistics to the sciences. They called their association the 'Asiatic' Society because Jones felt 'Oriental' had a merely relational meaning that suggested Asia had significance only in relation to Europe. Nevertheless, Jones and his associates continued to be known as Orientalists, and 'Oriental' even came to be Jones's nick-name, in the manner of 'Monk' Lewis.

Very broadly, then, the work of the British Orientalists in India can be related to the same broad programme of reform and modernisation that informed Britain's policy in Ireland – and elsewhere. The foundation for modernisation of the economy, society, politics and government of colonies from Ireland to India, as well as of the metropolis itself, was to be study of the local topography, flora and fauna, resources, weather and human inhabitants and their languages, culture, social structure and religion. As Benedict Anderson points out, this kind of knowledge, formalised later in the nineteenth century in such practices and institutions as mapping, censuses and museums, was central to modernisation and imperialism.[1] In Owenson's day, the movement for production of such knowledge was sustained by the landed class in Britain and their followers, clients, dependents and employees among the professional and commercial middle classes, in their own interests. As C. A. Bayly argues, this movement was supported and staffed especially by aristocrats from Britain's and the United Kingdom's peripheries of Scotland and Ireland, such as Lords Moira, Wellesley, and Castlereagh.[2] These were the same people who took Owenson into their entourage – in fact, soon after the publication of The Wild Irish Girl, Owenson was described by a friend as 'a protégée of Moira House',[3] and it is clear that Castlereagh's patronage of The Missionary was no whim. Not surprisingly, the works of the Orientalists were in these friends' libraries and, even less surprisingly, Owenson used these materials, drew attention to the fact that she had done so and incorporated their central arguments into the literary form of her novel.

She was not the first woman novelist to do so – Elizabeth Hamilton, whose brother was one of those employed by Hastings to translate Indian law codes, had already given an extended summary of Orientalist research and doctrine in the introduction to her novel Letters of a Hindoo Rajah (2 vols, 1796).[4] Owenson researched the work of European Orientalists going back to the seventeenth cen-

1 Benedict Anderson, *Imagined Communities: Reflections on the Origin and Spread of Nationalism*, ch. 10, added to revised edition (London and New York: Verso, 1991).

2 C. A. Bayly, *Imperial Meridian: The British Empire and the World 1780–1830* (London and New York: Longman, 1989), pp. 119, 135.

3 Stevenson, *Wild Irish Girl*, p. 93.

4 See Gary Kelly, *Women, Writing, and Revolution 1780–1827* (Oxford: Clarendon Press, 1993), pp. 132–43.

tury, available in her friends' libraries, but it was the works of Sir William Jones and his followers in the Asiatic Society of Bengal that were her immediate sources. John Drew claims that 'not only many details but whole passages from Jones's essays are absorbed' into *The Missionary*.[1] A wide range of topics researched by the Orientalists finds its way into Owenson's novel, from archaeology and herpetology to mineralogy and musicology. The major topics, however, are social, cultural and ideological. For example, Owenson cites Henry Thomas Colebrooke's translation of a Sanskrit text on 'suttee' (sati), or ritual immolation of a widow on her late husband's funeral pyre.[2] This was a practice which the British administration of India tried over a long period to suppress; it is a fate which the heroine of *The Missionary* had been spared before assuming her function as priestess, and it is the ritual she tries to carry out at the novel's end when, believing Hilarion dead, she throws herself on the pyre which is about to consume him.[3] Owenson seems to have availed herself of Colebrooke's translation of another Sanskrit text, on caste distinctions, in his 'Enumeration of Indian Classes'.[4] Several essays by Jones provided intellectual and cultural background, including 'On the Philosophy of the Asiatics' and 'On the Literature of the Hindus'.[5] As Thomas R. Metcalf argues, to a large extent this work constructed an 'Indian' and especially a 'Hindu' culture and religion that could be used in administering Britain's – or the East India Company's – Indian territories according to a British ideal of an 'improving', paternalistic landed class.[6] At the same time, the Orientalists' researches aimed to achieve both an understanding of Indian civilisation and 'a sense of mastery over it'.[7]

It was, however, the views of Jones and the other members of the Asiatic Society on the relation of India to Europe, their accounts of the distinctive features of Indian literature and culture, and the consequences of these for colonial policy, that were most important in shaping *The Missionary*. For example, Jones's essay 'On the Mystical Poetry of the East' quotes passages from Christian writers on fundamental tenets of their religion and then adduces passages from Indian texts in Persian and Sanskrit that evince the same

1 Drew, '"In Vishnu-land what Avatar?" Sir William Jones, India and the English Romantic Imagination', pp. 219–50 (p. 244). For examples given by Drew, see the present text, statements by Luxima, pp. 20, 52, 64.

2 H. T. Colebrooke, 'On the Duties of a Faithful Hindu Widow', translated from Sanskrit, in *Asiatic Researches; or, Transactions of a Society Instituted in Bengal for Inquiring into the History and Antiquities, the Arts, Sciences, and Literature of Asia*, 5 vols (London: J. Sewell, 1799), vol. 4, pp. 209–19.

3 See p. 27 in the present edition.

4 *Asiatic Researches*, vol. 5, pp. 345–70.

5 *Asiatic Researches*, vol. 4, pp. 169–80; vol. 1, pp. 340–55; these essays have slightly different titles as published in different collections and authors' works.

6 Thomas R. Metcalf, *The New Cambridge History of India*, vol. 3, part 4, *Ideologies of the Raj* (Cambridge and New York: Cambridge University Press, 1994), pp. 10–11, 21.

7 Metcalf, *Ideologies of the Raj*, p. 9.

principles.[1] The same line is taken by Owenson throughout *The Missionary*. Jones was a man of the Enlightenment, and a similar understanding of parallels between Christianity and Hinduism circulated among Enlightenment deists and freethinkers who aimed to examine religious beliefs apart from what they saw as self-serving and oppressive ecclesiastical-state institutions.[2] Their views were taken up in turn by early nineteenth-century liberals who wished to create secular constitutional states in place of court monarchies supported by established churches. Famously, Jones's work on Asian languages was pioneering in its illustration of the common origin of Sanskrit and many European languages, and he pushed the recovery of parallels and continuities further, into the central issue of religion and theology. Jones's Enlightenment, deist and even freethinking attitude is shown in his essay 'On the Gods of Greece, Italy, and India', which practically translates the classical European pantheon of deities into Hindu terms and vice versa.[3] *The Missionary* makes similar comparisons. Jones's essay also argues that, though both Islam and Hinduism have close similarities to Christianity, Indians are so deeply committed to their religions that their conversion to Christianity is virtually hopeless, and could only be effected very slowly over a long period, by translating Biblical prophetic books into Sanskrit for assimilation by the educated and cultivated Indian classes. Again, *The Missionary* promotes a similar view.

Crucially related to these points is Jones's treatment of a certain kind of eroticism as a characteristic of Indian culture and religion, and this, too, shaped *The Missionary* in important ways. The erotic was a central theme and stylistic practice in much literature of the time with a broadly reformist or liberal agenda, such as Charlotte Dacre's 'erotic Gothic' novel, *The Libertine*.[4] This line of the erotic was predominantly literary and cultural, and though Owenson participated in it, she also seems to have drawn on the somewhat different line of 'philosophical' or scientific erotic to be found in the work of the Orientalists and other prominent Enlightenment writers. Jones's essays and translations illustrate what could be called a spiritualised or philosophised eroticism in the literatures of India, both Persian and Sanskrit. Jones presents this eroticism in terms of a continuity between earthly and divine, erotic and mystic love; in *The Missionary*, these forms of love are embodied in Luxima, and fatally resisted by Hilarion, to their cost.

Such views of the relation between body and 'soul', matter and intellect, are grounded in Enlightenment materialist philosophy. This philosophy also underwrote much of the literature and politics of Sensibility, Revolution and Romanticism, and argued that 'higher', intellectual knowledge was obtained

---

1 *Asiatic Researches*, vol. 3, pp. 165–208.

2 See John Drew, *India and the Romantic Imagination* (Delhi: Oxford University Press, 1987), p. 79.

3 *Asiatic Researches*, vol. 1, pp. 221–75.

4 See the Introduction to volume 3 in this set.

'experimentally', through the senses. Furthermore, Enlightenment materialist philosophers argued that the character of the individual and of societies was influenced, if not determined, by their circumambient material, natural, social and institutional world, including the prevailing system of government. This line of thinking motivated much of the broadly scientific impulses in the various European Enlightenments, including that of the late eighteenth-century Orientalists. There could be reformist and even democratic implications in such assumptions, producing a vision of common humanity based in bodily and material reality, though perhaps with 'innate' differences in physical organisation, degree of bodily 'sensibility', or sensitivity, intellectual powers and material and social circumstances and opportunities. Nevertheless, materialist thinking could also lead to inquiry for commonalities across individuals and societies, and for explanations of those differences that did exist – in terms of 'accidental' circumstances ranging from climate and topography through educational opportunities and social conventions to prevailing religious and political systems. Enlightenment materialism also informed much scientific inquiry and speculation on the forces that animated the natural world. One field of such Enlightenment philosophy focused on the erotic, or desire, as the force in all life – vegetable, animal, human and spiritual.

The materialist-erotic philosophy of nature went back to Lucretius, at least, but perhaps its leading proponent in late eighteenth-century Britain was Erasmus Darwin. As Donald M. Hassler observes, 'for Darwin sex works not only on the small level of animal reproduction, but also on the cosmic level of creation'.[1] Broadly speaking, this was the view Jones found in Hindu philosophy and religion. Darwin set forth his ideas in a complex series of literary-scientific texts – massively footnoted allegorical and mythological poems including *The Botanic Garden* (1791), part 1, *The Economy of Vegetation: A Poem* (1791), and part 2, *The Loves of the Plants: A Poem* (first published 1789); *Zoonomia* (1794–6); and *The Temple of Nature; or, The Origin of Society: A Poem* (1803). These works became notorious for their attribution of all changes and renewals in nature and human life, society and culture to the erotic, or desire. They also became notorious and influential for their corresponding use of form and style. In these poems Darwin enunciated a poetics based on his Enlightenment materialism; he argues in effect that form and style are designed to stimulate the senses and thus the imagination and thought of the reader, producing a new vision and a new understanding of reality, and thus a desire for a new order. In these philosophical poems Darwin tries to use form and style to this end. Put another way, Darwin aims to use form and style to educate desire in the reader, and thereby to change society. Because Darwin and those who espoused similar ideas were freethinkers and reformists, such ideas also came to be associated in the early nineteenth century with avant-garde, reformist and liberal politics – and also

1 Donald M. Hassler, *The Comedian as the Letter D: Erasmus Darwin's Comic Materialism* (The Hague: Martinus Nijhoff, 1973), p. 57.

with Revolutionary and Romantic philosophico-sexual vanguardism, denoun-
ced by conservatives and counter-Revolutionaries as libertinism. Certainly the
views of Darwin and others like him proved highly influential with liberal
Romantic intellectuals and writers, in Britain and beyond, because such views
had powerful aesthetic implications, which Darwin both argued and illustrated
by means of his poems.[1]

In certain respects the work of Sir William Jones and the Asiatic Society parallels Darwin's philosophy, poetics and literary practice of the erotic. Interested
in everything to with India, for example, the members of the Asiatic Society
may well have known the poem *Alexander's Expedition* (1792), by Darwin's 'most
fervent disciple', Thomas Beddoes, describing Alexander's attempt to conquer
India, with which Owenson's missionary compares his own project.[2] More
important, however, is the emphasis in Darwin and the Orientalists on sexuality
in natural and human life and society. The Orientalists' essays describe, and
their translations illustrate, the central place in Indian philosophy and literature of a certain form of the erotic – cycles of generation and destruction and the
affinity of all things in a universe of desire. Both the subject matter and the language and style of many of the translations, such as those in Jones's essay 'On
the Mystical Poetry of the East', would seem erotically hyperbolic and extravagant in ways long associated with Oriental literature by writers in the Occident.
To readers in Britain, the language and style of these translations would resemble the work of such controversially erotic writers as the Della Cruscans,
Charlotte Dacre, and Owenson herself, whose representations of the erotic, both
in subjectivity and social relations, was set forth in a corresponding style of ver-
bal and figural excess. Owenson's novels had already been widely criticised,
even by friends, for such stylistic traits. Because *The Missionary* is Orientalist in
ideology and reference, however, it is also necessarily erotic in theme and style.
Owenson uses the erotic much as Gothic novelists used the picturesque – to represent in the fictional character and to evoke in the reader a form of subjectivity
related to a historically particular aesthetics and politics. In *Asiatic Researches*
and other Orientalist works, Owenson would find studies and translations of
ancient literatures, conducted by respected men of affairs and science, that
expressed ideas on love and the erotic in language and style similar to her own.
Since her subject now was the collision of Orient and Occident, this Orientalist
work, too, would have particular relevance for her complex novelistic representation of cultural and ideological difference and similarity, with important and
immediately contemporary political implications.

For, as she and her aristocratic patrons and friends would be aware, other
forces in Britain were developing their own policies towards Great Britain's col-
onised peoples, from Ireland to India. These forces may be represented by Mary

1 Desmond King-Hele, *Erasmus Darwin and the Romantic Poets* (New York: St Martin's Press, 1986).

2 King-Hele, *Erasmus Darwin and the Romantic Poets*, p. 174.

Sherwood. Her attitude to, and experience of, India have been described in the Introduction to her Gothic novel *The Traditions* (1795), in volume one of this edition, with sufficient detail to provide a contrast to the representation of India in Owenson's *The Missionary*. Sherwood, too, wrote tales of India and missionaries, beginning with *Little Henry and His Bearer* (1814). Whereas Owenson's novels may be seen to represent the ideology and policies of the reformist aristocratic politicians who supported Hastings and Jones and the Orientalists, Sherwood's tales may be seen to represent and anticipate the ideology of a later, moralistic, and middle-class phase of imperial policy, which became dominant in the 1820s and 30s.[1] As ever, the Empire, from Ireland to India, was treated in terms of social and political conflicts in Britain. The crisis of the French Revolution and Napoleonic wars created in Britain movements for moral reform and social surveillance and control, associated especially with Evangelicals in the Church of England but supported by many in the commercial and professional middle classes with other sectarian affiliations. Many in these classes opposed historic upper-class hegemony and paternalism, embodied in such institutions as the mercantilist East India Company, and wanted nation and Empire opened up to a coalition of free trade and the cross. This was the movement to which Sherwood belonged. As C. A. Bayly puts it, 'People whose commitment to an individualistic moral rearmament in English society was closely connected with their advocacy of free trade and a distrust of [aristocratic] paternalism, could be found arguing that in the colonies, or even in Ireland, "the state of society" warranted benevolent British intervention in the market and indigenous customs.'[2]

As seen in the account of Sherwood's response to India, and especially in such incidents as her encounter with the nautch girls, the new, morally motivated imperialists increasingly saw colonial peoples as radically different from Britons and Europeans. The 'Orient' had long been associated in European ideology and culture with a dangerously seductive eroticism, and in the eighteenth century India was seen by many in Britain as a school of luxury, decadence and eroticism that corrupted Europeans and that Europeans brought home with them. Increasingly, then, colonial peoples and cultures, especially in Asia, were regarded as needing British intervention, of an ostensibly 'benevolent' kind to be sure, and ranging from religious conversion to greater administrative and legal control and separation from Europeans along 'racial' lines. These forces were already active in India when Owenson published *The Missionary*; they were represented by the Sherwoods and the missionaries they met and worked with, and they were opposed by the policy-makers whose views Owenson supports in her novel. As in Ireland, administrators in India sought to diminish religious friction and to ensure social order and stability, and as in Ireland, the British administration in the Indian territory of Madras did so in part by providing

1 Metcalf, *Ideologies of the Raj*, ch. 2; and Antony Copley, *Religions in Conflict: Ideology, Cultural Contact and Conversion in Late Colonial India* (Delhi: Oxford University Press, 1997).

2 Bayly, *Imperial Meridian*, p. 137.

state support for the religion of the majority, while discouraging or even banning Christian missionary activity. As Burton Stein comments, 'The caution of
the Madras government was vindicated to some extent when the mutiny of the
Company's [Indian] soldiers at its Vellore garrison in 1806 was found to have
resulted in part from resentment on the part of the rank and file over the open
proselytising engaged in by their European officers.'[1] Stein goes on to remark,
'The situation ominously anticipated the Great Mutiny of fifty years later.' Sig-
nificantly, Owenson, by then Lady Morgan, reissued her Orientalist Gothic
novel immediately after the Indian Mutiny of 1857–8, with a preface readdress-
ing it to this new crisis of empire, though retitled *Luxima*, out of respect for, or
fear of, the now powerful missionary movements in Britain, India, and throughout the Empire.

In *The Missionary*, then, Owenson addressed a continuing national and imperial crisis and conflict over imperial administration from Ireland to India by
turning to a particular body of Orientalist work – that produced by Sir William
Jones and the Asiatic Society – to support a reformed East India Company
administration dominated by elements of the modernising British landed class.
In fact, by the time Owenson published her novel, attitudes to India were changing again, influenced by Romantic liberal nationalism and a shift away from
governance through Indian elites to governance of Indian peasants. Nevertheless, the new attitudes and policies still resisted the British commercial and
religious interests inspired by Evangelicalism, active from Ireland to India, and
represented by the Sherwoods and their missionary friends. Owenson addresses
this issue in her novel by a complex amalgamation of Orientalist ideas and writings, certain historical parallels, the line of contemporary erotic literature from
the Orientalists' translations through the British Della Cruscans, and erotic
Gothic novelists such as M. G. Lewis and Charlotte Dacre, and the novel form
she had been developing for almost a decade. To modify slightly a point made
earlier: because *The Missionary* is Orientalist Gothic, it is also erotic Gothic. As
for Owenson's resort to historical analogy, this was becoming increasingly the
choice of innovating novelists, as in Jane Porter's historical Gothic *The Scottish
Chiefs*, also in this set, which was published a year before *The Missionary*. Moreover, it would have been as dangerous to represent a contemporary Protestant
missionary zealot in a novel set in India as to represent an Orangeman in a novel
set in Ireland. Eighteenth-century British reformist writers often represented
Spanish and other Catholic missionaries as cruel and repressive agents of auto-
cratic imperialism, and so Owenson turns to that stereotype for her missionary,
and to an earlier historical moment in the contact of Europe and Asia. Otherwise, she sustains the particular form of novel that she had been developing
through her career in response to the work of her contemporaries and the issues
of the day, as viewed by her social and literary patrons. In *The Missionary*, Owen-

1 Burton Stein, *A History of India* (Oxford: Blackwell, 1998), p. 216.

son, too, is a missionary – an ideological agent for a particular class formation during a particular period of national and international crisis.

Certainly her *Missionary* made its converts, especially among leading Romantic writers. Byron commented in a characteristic piece of mockingly respectful doggerel, contained in a letter to his publisher John Murray: 'I read the *Missionary*: / Pretty – very ...' – 'pretty' here has something of the sense of 'titillatingly scandalous'. Byron would learn from Owenson, however: certain character types and relationships in his Orientalist poems of the 1810s, dealing with Greece and the Levant, reformulate the relationship of Hilarion and Luxima. Byron's friend and Owenson's fellow Irish patriot writer Thomas Moore studied it in preparing for his own verse novel set in Asia, *Lalla Rookh* (1817). Percy Shelley, who was an aficionado and imitator of erotic and Orientalist Gothic, was an extravagant admirer.[1] He later reframed major elements of *The Missionary* in his early visionary-utopian poem *Laon and Cythna* (1817), republished soon after as *The Revolt of Islam* (1818). John Drew and Nigel Leask argue that *The Missionary* can also be traced in Shelley's *Alastor* (1816).[2]

The Missionary's impact on the younger generation of British Romantic liberals was only part of Owenson's public, literary, cultural and political role, however. She soon became, and would remain for several decades, a major and controversial voice of liberalism and what she called 'Europeanism',[3] or a broad, internationalist and constitutionalist culture – in Britain, Europe and beyond. Several circumstances combined in the few years after publication of *The Missionary* to provide this opportunity. The accession of the Prince of Wales to power as regent in 1811, and his decisive turn away from his long-standing association with reformist Whig politicians to Tory and conservative ones kept reform on the margins of British government policy for two decades. Major changes in Morgan's personal situation also played a role, freeing her to create her own social world, across Europe, rather than remain the dependent in someone else's. The Abercorns promoted a match between Owenson and another of their house guests – their resident physician, the widower Thomas Charles Morgan, recently knighted, and the couple were married on 12 January 1812. A few months later Robert Owenson died. After taking a year to extract themselves from the Abercorns' house and circle and become more independent, the Morgans settled in Dublin and began a public literary career as representatives of liberal literary and scientific culture with European impact. Lady Morgan's *O'Donnel: A National Tale* (3 vols, 1814) was as controversial as any of her earlier

1 Stevenson, *Wild Irish Girl*, p. 132–3; and Drew, *India and the Romantic Imagination*, p. 240.

2 Drew, *India and the Romantic Imagination*, p. 253; and Nigel Leask, *British Romantic Writers and the East: Anxieties of Empire* (Cambridge: Cambridge University Press, 1992), pp. 126–9.

3 Stevenson, *Wild Irish Girl*, p. 290.

novels, and made its author £500 from the enterprising firm of Henry Colburn.[1] The fall of Napoleon and the restoration of reactionary court monarchies across Europe left a large middle-class liberal reading public without adequate institutional and political expression. Lady Morgan stepped forward.

Following the example of Europe's best known woman author and liberal, Germaine de Staël, and her pioneering work of cultural and social studies, *De l'Allemagne* (1810), Lady Morgan decided to produce a similar book on France. The Morgans paid a prolonged visit to Paris, where they were celebrated by all levels of upper- and middle-class society, but especially by liberals, for her fiction and his scientific writing. Colburn paid £1000 for *France* (1817) and was very well rewarded. Inevitably the book became the centre of a highly political storm on both sides of the English Channel. Striking while the iron was hot, Lady Morgan published another novel, *Florence Macarthy: An Irish Tale* (3 vols, 1818), featuring a version of herself in a heroine who is a cultural and political agent for justice and change in a misunderstood and oppressed Ireland that could stand for any similar land in Europe and beyond. Coburn paid £1200 for it along with Sir Charles Morgan's treatise on materialist science, *Sketches of the Philosophy of Life*. Both works proved satisfyingly controversial, his for supposedly undermining religion, hers for the usual reasons. Mary Mitford, who would herself become one of the century's most influential literary inventors of rural England, wrote to a friend describing the main elements of *Florence Macarthy*: 'a hero, compounded of Bonaparte and General Mina [Spanish guerrilla leader and leading liberal]; a hero, *en second*, Lord Byron; a villain, Mr. Croker [leading literary critic of Morgan, her works and her politics]; and a heroine, Lady Morgan herself; a plot half made of [Morgan's own] *O'Donnel* and half [of Walter Scott's recent] *Guy Mannering* – a vast deal of incredible antiquarianism, and Ireland! Ireland! Ireland! as the one single sauce of all these viands'. [2]

Exhilarated with his author and her ability to arouse controversy and thereby increase sales, Colburn proposed that the Morgans tour Italy and Lady Morgan produce a book on it, in the style of her *France*. They wintered *en route* in Paris, enjoying their celebrity and notoriety as liberals in literature and science, respectively. Lady Morgan set up her own salon, and was even inducted into a women's lodge of Freemasonry – the organisation accused by many of spreading revolutionary ideas across Europe and beyond in the late eighteenth and early nineteenth century. When they finally left Paris, their journey across France and Italy was at times more like a triumphal progress, an occasion for local liberal intellectuals and aristocrats to express themselves publicly, and their movements and associates were accordingly watched by government spies. In Italy they went as far south as the ruins of Pompeii, and again met everyone thought worth meeting, from Catholic Cardinals and American businessmen through artists, poets and aristocrats to Napoleon's infamously libertine and

---

1 Campbell, *Lady Morgan*, p. 132; and Stevenson, *Wild Irish Girl*, p. 168.
2 Quoted in Stevenson, *Wild Irish Girl*, p. 200.

political sister Paulina, while themselves being everywhere sought after. Being a famous and infamous liberal involved circulating socially as well as textually across society and Europe. While *Italy* (2 vols, 1821) takes up a cause made centrally symbolic for European liberals since de Staël's *Corinne*, at least, it in fact condemns the entire post-Napoleonic European order of reactionary church and state, and the British government's tacit complicity with it. Not only did the book set off a barrage of conservative obloquy in Britain, France and Italy, its publication coincided with an outburst of unsuccessful revolts in southern Europe that resulted in the imprisonment of many of those liberals whom the Morgans had met, and the banning of the book itself in many states – Byron, converted into a fan by the book's uncompromisingly liberal politics, tried to smuggle it into Italy, where he was then living. The Morgans wrote brief, satirical replies to their critics, and moved on.

Another product of the Italian expedition was Lady Morgan's idea for a historical romance on the life of the Italian painter Salvator Rosa, who had been a favourite in the literature and culture of Sensibility, but after carrying out her usual programme of research, she dropped her sights to a racy biography, entitled *The Life and Times of Salvator Rosa* (2 vols, 1824). The Morgans held the only salon in Dublin, associated with reformists, the fashionable and numerous foreign literary tourists. They continued to be reviled in the Tory magazines and contributed to Colburn's liberal *New Monthly Magazine*. Lady Morgan published another Irish novel – *The O'Briens and the O'Flahertys: A National tale* (4 vols, 1827) – for which Colburn paid £1,300.[1] When a scathing review appeared in the anti-liberal *Literary Gazette*, Colburn and a partner started the *Athenæum*, which would become one of the most distinguished intellectual and literary magazines of the nineteenth century. In 1828 the campaign, for which Lady Morgan had long been the leading literary voice, succeeded in achieving Catholic emancipation, and the political movement's leader, Daniel O'Connell, praised her work for the cause, declaring, 'Her name is received with enthusiasm by the people of the country where her writings create and perpetuate among the youth of both sexes a patriotic ardour in the cause of everything that is noble and dignified.'[2] In the following years, however, she fell out with O'Connell's movement and became disillusioned with the new, predominantly middle-class reform politics. Though she kept up her promotion of Ireland's interests, the Morgans became more society figures than political intermediaries. As a celebrity, and someone who had made a career of being a public individualist and liberal sovereign subject, Lady Morgan could expect to sell books by writing directly about herself, rather than in fictionalised guise, and in 1829 published *The Book of the Boudoir* (2 vols), a compilation of reflections, observations and anecdotes which she originally intended to call 'Memoirs of Myself and for Myself'.

1 Stevenson, *Wild Irish Girl*, p. 257.
2 Quoted in Stevenson, *Wild Irish Girl*, p. 267.

To renew their political interests and friendships, the Morgans travelled again to France in 1829, and though Lady Morgan was hailed as a pioneer and prophet by French Romantic liberals, and found them espousing many of her views, she also felt out of sympathy with French Romantic literature.[1] Nevertheless, in her account of the expedition, *France in 1829–30* (2 vols, 1830), she defined the movement that had recently begun to be called 'Romanticism', in terms that indicate the connection between eighteenth-century 'old Whig' ideology and nineteenth-century liberalism:

> [Romanticism] came forth from the northern forests, rude and barbarous as the people to whom it belonged; and, like them, it overran the polished feebleness and elegant corruption which no longer served the interests or reflected the feelings of a new-modelled society. Wherever freedom waved her oriflamme, there, it fixed its standard.

She goes on to trace its progress from these 'Gothic' origins through the medieval 'free states' of Italy, into England 'under the authority of Magna Charta, with Chaucer, Spenser, Shakespeare, and Milton', and on to the Reformation, when it was subdued by 'the power of the [Holy Roman] empire, the pope, and the commercial aristocracy', with 'the unquestioned sway of classic absolutism in letters', to be revived in her own time in specifically national literatures.[2]

With such breathtaking literary swashbuckling, Lady Morgan was still considered a controversial and consequently commercial author, and she sold the work for £1,000, not to Colburn but to the rival firm of Saunders and Otley. The book had the good fortune to be in press when the July Revolution in France seemed to confirm many of Lady Morgan's political comments, as she pointed out in a 'Postscript'. Colburn revenged himself, however, by turning his formidable publicity machine against his former star author, and the book did poorly and led to lawsuits. In fact, Lady Morgan's time as a leading author of the day was over. The Morgans remained prominent literary-political social figures, however, and continued to produce books. The Morgans had always numbered many friends and contacts among reformers, and rejoiced in the Reform Bill of 1832, but Lady Morgan kept up her criticism of the exploitative social and economic structure of Ireland in 'Manor Sackville', one of three satirical texts in her *Dramatic Scenes from Real Life* (2 vols, 1833). Lady Morgan had tried to interest Byron's publisher John Murray in a book of lives of Flemish painters. When that failed, and after a trip down the Rhine and through Belgium, now a constitutional monarchy after a revolution there, and further researches, she planned to celebrate the Belgian revolution in another portrait-of-a-nation. Forestalled in that by Frances Trollope, she turned her materials into a novel, *The Princess; or, The Beguine* (3 vols, 1834), published with the firm of Bentley.

1 Stevenson, *Wild Irish Girl*, p. 271–2.
2 Lady Morgan, *France in 1829–30*, second ed. (2 vols, London: Saunders and Otley, 1831), vol. 1, pp. 228–30.

As Britons of all parties accustomed themselves to the post-Reform Act political order, the Morgans were regarded as aging pioneers of liberalism, and in 1837 recognition for Lady Morgan came from the reformed state as a government pension of £300 a year for services to literature – the first such pension awarded to a woman.

With this, the Morgans were able to settle in London, just south of Hyde Park, where they established a new literary-political salon. It flourished for years and through it passed younger generations of leaders in Victorian literature, culture, society and politics, along with many foreign visitors of all kinds. There were a number of female writers advancing the claims of women in the modern liberal state, and Lady Morgan returned to Colburn with *Woman and Her Master* (2 vols, 1840). It is a work of what would become known as 'Whig history', or historiography that viewed the historical process as one of progress and advancement. Morgan's book argues that women have made the significant contribution to the progress of civilisation by feminising the masculine forces – an idea often found in liberal writers, where masculinist forces represent ambition, despotism and destruction, and feminine forces represent social conciliation, peace, prosperity and progress. This was a process in which the author herself could claim a part, and which was implicitly argued in all of her novels, including *The Missionary*. A year later Colburn published a two-volume selection of the Morgans' magazine essays, entitled *The Book Without a Name*, but Sir Charles died at the end of August 1843, followed two years later by her sister. Lady Morgan carried on socialising relentlessly. In 1846 *The Wild Irish Girl* was republished by Colburn in his 'Standard Novels' – a formative version of a national literary canon. In 1850 Lady Morgan was enabled to appear in one last public controversy, with Nicholas Wiseman, Catholic Archbishop of Westminster, in which she unleashed her old liberal anti-clerical satire. With Geraldine Jewsbury as her amanuensis, she began publishing memoirs, starting with a diary of her trip to Paris in 1818 – *Passages from My Autobiography* (1859). The Indian Mutiny called forth a revised edition of *The Missionary* as *Luxima, The Prophetess: A Tale of India* (1859), but by the time it appeared, Lady Morgan had died, on 16 April.

BIBLIOGRAPHY

Sydney, Lady Morgan, (with Sir T. C. Morgan), *Absenteeism* (London: Henry Colburn, 1825)

Sydney, Lady Morgan, *The Book of the Boudoir*, 2 vols (London: Henry Colburn, 1829)

Sydney, Lady Morgan, and Sir T. C. Morgan, *The Book Without a Name*, 2 vols (London: Henry Colburn, 1841)

Sydney, Lady Morgan, *Dramatic Scenes from Real Life*, 2 vols (London: Saunders and Otley, 1833)

[Sydney Owenson], *A Few Reflections, Occasioned by the Perusal of a Work, Entitled 'Familiar Epistles, to Frederick J—s, Esq., on the Present State of the Irish Stage'* (Dublin: J. Parry, 1804)

Sydney, Lady Morgan, *Florence Macarthy: An Irish Tale*, 4 vols (London: Henry Colburn, 1818)

Sydney, Lady Morgan, (with Sir Thomas Charles Morgan), *France*, 2 vols (London: Henry Colburn, 1817)

Sydney, Lady Morgan, (with Sir T. C. Morgan), *France in 1829–30*, 2 vols (London: Saunders and Otley, 1830)

Sydney, Lady Morgan, *Italy*, 2 vols (London: Henry Colburn, 1821)

Sydney, Lady Morgan, *Lady Morgan's Memoirs: Autobiography, Diaries and Correspondence*, 2 vols (London: W. H. Allen and Co., 1862)

Sydney Owenson, *The Lay of an Irish Harp; or, Metrical Fragments* (London: R. Phillips, 1807)

Sydney, Lady Morgan, *Letter to Cardinal Wiseman, in Answer to His 'Remarks on Lady Morgan's Statements Regarding St. Peter's Chair'* (London: C. Westerton, 1851)

Sydney, Lady Morgan, *Letter to the Reviewers of 'Italy'; Including an Answer to a Pamphlet Entitled 'Observations upon the Calumnies and Misrepresentations in Lady Morgan's Italy*, (London: Henry Colburn, 1821)

Sydney, Lady Morgan, *The Life and Times of Salvator Rosa*, 2 vols (London: Henry Colburn, 1824)

Sydney Owenson, *The Missionary: An Indian Tale*, 3 vols (London: J. J. Stockdale, 1811)

Sydney Owenson, *The Novice of Saint Dominick*, 4 vols (London: Richard Phillips, 1806; Bodleian Library dates 1805)

Sydney, Lady Morgan, *The O'Briens and the O'Flahertys*, 4 vols (London: Henry Colburn, 1827)

Sydney, Lady Morgan, *O'Donnel: A National Tale*, 3 vols (London: Henry Colburn, 1814)

Sydney, Lady Morgan, *Passages from My Autobiography* (London: Richard Bentley, 1859)

Sydney Owenson, *Patriotic Sketches of Ireland, Written in Connaught*, 2 vols (London: R. Phillips, 1807)

Sydney Owenson, *Poems, Dedicated by Permission to the Right Honorable the Countess of Moira* (Dublin: A. Stewart; London: Mr. Phillips, 1801)

Sydney, Lady Morgan, *The Princess; or, The Beguine*, 3 vols (London: R. Bentley, 1835)

S[ydney] O[wenson], *St. Clair; or, The Heiress of Desmond* (Dublin; Wogan, Brown, Halpin, Colbert, Jon Dornin, Jackson and Medcalf, 1803; separate edition, London: E. Harding and Highley, 1803)

Sydney Owenson, *Twelve Original Hibernian melodies, with English Words, Imitated and Translated from the Works of the Ancient Irish Bards* (London: Preston, [1805])

Sydney Owenson, *The Wild Irish Girl: A National Tale*, 3 vols (London: Richard Phillips, 1806)

Sydney, Lady Morgan, *Woman and Her Master*, 2 vols (London: Henry Colburn, 1840)

Sydney Owenson, *Woman; or, Ida of Athens*, 4 vols (London: Longman, Hurst, Rees and Orme, 1809)

CHRONOLOGY

Sydney Owenson

[Because Morgan proudly concealed her age, her *Memoirs*, the main source of biographical information, is entirely free of dates for her early years]

1776   Claims to have been born 25 December on board a ship crossing from England to Ireland, probably in this year, to Jane (Hill), merchant's daughter, and Robert Owenson, actor

c. 1778–80   Sister Olivia born

1789   Mother dies

1794   Father opens theatre at Kilkenny; Sydney spends time there

1796   Probably last year at school

1801   Publishes *Poems*, dedicated to Countess of Moira, while employed as governess with Featherstonehaugh family

1803   Publishes novel *St. Clair*; with her sister, spends time with her father when he manages theatres at various places in Ireland

1805   With father at Londonderry; publishes novel *The Novice of St. Dominick* (dated 1806) publishes *Twelve Original Hibernian Melodies*

1806   Publishes novel *The Wild Irish Girl*; spends time in Connaught; novel makes her a celebrity

1807   Mounts opera in Dublin, *The First Attempt; or, The Whim of the Moment* (probably unpublished); publishes *The Lay of an Irish Harp*; summer: visits relatives in west of Ireland; publishes *Patriotic Sketches of Ireland*, book of social commentary

1808   Visits London, performs 'Irish' material in fashionable assemblies; December: marriage of sister Olivia to Dr, later Sir Arthur Clarke, physician

1809   Publishes novel on Turkish oppression of Greece, *Woman; or, Ida of Athens*; attacked vigorously in Tory press; invited to reside with Marquis and Marchioness of Abercorn

1811   Publishes novel *The Missionary*, set in India

1812   Abercorns bring about a marriage between Owenson and their personal physician, Sir Thomas Charles Morgan, 12 January; spring: death of father; Morgans take house in Kildare Street, Dublin

1814   Publishes novel *O'Donnel*

1816–17	Morgans reside at Paris, circulate in literary, political and fashionable society
1817	Publishes *France*, social and cultural commentary; arouses a vigorous debate in Britain and France; sets up salon in Dublin
1818	Publishes novel *Florence Macarthy*; long trip to Italy sponsored by publisher Colburn, to produce another book
1820	Morgans return to Dublin
1821	Publishes *Italy*; more controversy in Britain, France and Italy over her liberal opinions; she replies in *Letter to the Reviewers of 'Italy'*; Colburn offers the Morgans £2,000 for companion work on Germany, but they decline
1824	Publishes *Life and Times of Salvator Rosa*, biography originally designed as a novel
1827	Publishes another Irish novel, *The O'Briens and the O'Flahertys*; again attacked in Tory press
1828	Legislation for Catholic Emancipation passed; Lady Morgan hailed as pioneering Irish patriot
1829	Publishes *The Book of the Boudoir*, anthology of personal reflections and commentary; summer: Morgans revisit France
1830	Publishes *France in 1829–30* just after July Revolution in Paris; claims to have anticipated it; publishes more literary magazine essays
1833	Summer: tours in Germany and Belgium; publishes *Dramatic Scenes*, dealing with social issues
1834	Publishes last novel, *The Princess; or, The Beguine*
1837	Receives government pension for services to literature; moves to London, sets up salon there
1841	Morgans tour in Germany
1843	28 August: Sir Charles Morgan dies
1845	Death of sister
1850	Pamphlet controversy with Cardinal Wiseman causes her last public stir
1859	Publishes *Passages from My Autobiography*; revises *The Missionary* as *Luxima, The Prophetess*, in response to public shock at Indian Mutiny; dies 16 April

NOTE ON THE TEXT

The Missionary went through three editions in its first year of publication and was later republished as *Luxima, The Prophetess: A Tale of India* in 1859, following the Indian Mutiny, and appearing shortly after the death of Lady Morgan. As with the other texts in this collection, I have based this edition on the first published version of the text. Editorial interventions have been kept to a minimum; however obvious typographical errors have been silently corrected. Other editorial changes have been noted in the textual notes.

Sydney Owenson,
The Missionary (1811)

Ja.ᵗ Godby sculp.

Miss Owenson.

Published 13.ᵗʰ February 1811 by J. Stockdale, Pall Mall.

THE

MISSIONARY:

AN

INDIAN TALE.

———————

BY

MISS OWENSON.

———————

WITH A PORTRAIT OF THE AUTHOR.

=====

IN THREE VOLUMES.

=====

VOL. I.

===============

LONDON:
PRINTED FOR J. J. STOCKDALE,
NO. 41, PALL MALL.
1811.[a]

The Missionary.[a]
Volume 1.

CHAPTER I.

IN the beginning of the seventeenth century, Portugal, bereft of her natural sovereigns, had become an object of contention, to various powers in Europe. The houses of Braganza and of Parma, of Savoy and Medici, alike published their pretensions, and alike submitted to that decision, which the arms of Spain finally made in its own favour.[1] Under the goading oppression of Philip the Second, and of his two immediate successors, the national independence of a brave people faded gradually away, and Portugal, wholly losing its rank in the scale of nations, sunk into a Spanish province. From the torpid dream of slavish dependence, the victims of a mild oppression were suddenly awakened, by the rapacious cruelties of Olivarez, the gloomy minister of Philip the Fourth; and the spring of national liberty, receiving its impulse from the very pressure of the tyranny which crushed it, already recovered something of that tone of force and elasticity which finally produced one of the most singular and perfect revolutions, which the history of nations has recorded. It was at this period, that Portugal became divided into two powerful factions, and the Spanish partizans, and Portuguese patriots, openly expressed their mutual abhorrence, and secretly planned their respective destruction. Even Religion forfeited her dove-like character of peace, and enrolled herself beneath the banners of civil discord and factious commotion. The Jesuits governed with the Spaniards; the Franciscans resisted with the Portuguese; and each accused the other of promulgating heretical tenets, in support of that cause, to which each was respectively attached.*

It was in the midst of these religious and political feuds, that the Order of St. Francis became distinguished in Portugal, by the sanctity and genius of one of

---

* The Jesuits,[2] being charged with fraudulent practices, in endeavouring to persuade the Indians that the Brahminical and Christian doctrines differed not essentially, were openly condemned by the Franciscans;[3] which laid the foundation of those long and violent contests, decided by Innocent the Tenth,[4] in favour of the Franciscans.

its members; and the monastery, into which the holy enthusiast had retired from the splendour of opulence and rank, from the pleasures of youth and the pursuits of life, became the shrine of pilgrimage, to many pious votarists, who sought Heaven through the mediation of him, who, on earth, had already obtained the title of 'the man without a fault.'[a]

The monastery of St. Francis stands at the foot of that mighty chain of mountains, which partially divides the province of Alentejo from the sea-beat shores of Algarva. Excavated from a pile of rocks, its cells are little better than rude caverns; and its heavy portico, and gloomy chapel, are composed of the fragments of a Moorish castle, whose mouldering turrets mingle, in the haze of distance, with the lofty spires of the Christian sanctuary, while both are reflected, by[b] the bosom of one of those lakes so peculiar to Portugal, whose subterraneous thunder rolls with an incessant uproar, even when the waves of the ocean are still, and the air breathes of peace. Celebrated,[c] in the natural history of the country, for its absorbent and sanative qualities, Superstition had wrested the phænomenon to her own mystic purposes; and the roaring lake, which added so fine and awful a feature to the gloomy scenery of the convent, brought to its altars the grateful tributes of those, who piously believed that they obtained, from the consecrated waters, health in this world, and salvation in the world to come.

To the left of the monastery, some traces of a Roman fortress, similar to that of Coimbra, were still visible: to the north, the mighty hills of Alentejo terminated the prospect: while to the south, the view seemed extended to infinitude by the mightier ocean, beyond whose horizon fancy sought the coast of Carthage; and memory, awakening to her magic, dwelt on the altar of Hannibal, or hovered round the victor standard of Scipio Africanus.[d5] The mountains; the ocean; the lake of subterraneous thunder; the ruins of Moorish splendour; the vestiges of Roman prowess; the pile of monastic gloom: – magnificent assemblage of great and discordant images! What various epochas in time; what various states of human power and human intellect, did not ye blend and harmonize, in one great picture! What a powerful influence were not your wildness and your solemnity, your grandeur and your gloom, calculated to produce upon the mind of religious enthusiasm, upon the spirit of genius and melancholy; upon a character, formed of all the higher elements of human nature, upon such a mind, upon such a genius, upon such a character as thine, Hilarion![e6]

Amidst the hanging woods which shaded the southern side of the mountains of Algarva, rose the turrets of the castle of Acugna; and the moon-beams which fell upon its ramparts, were reflected back by the glittering spires of St. Francis.

To this solitary and deserted castle, Hilarion, Count d'Acugna, had been sent, by his uncle and guardian, the Archbishop of Lisbon, in 1620. The young Hilarion[f] had scarcely attained his tenth year. His sole companion was his preceptor, an old brother of the order of St. Francis.[g] History attests the antiquity and splendour of the House d'Acugna. The royal blood of Portugal flowed in the veins of Hilarion, for his mother was a daughter of the House of Braganza. His elder, and only brother, Don Lewis, Duke d'Acugna, was one of the most power-ful grandees in the state; his uncle, the Archbishop of Lisbon, was considered as the leader of the disaffected nobles, whom the Spanish tyranny had almost driven to desperation; and, while the Duke and the Prelate were involved in all the political commotions of the day, the young Hilarion, impressed by the grand solemnity of the images by which he was surrounded;[a] inflamed by the visionary nature of his religious studies; borne away by the complexional enthusiasm of his character, and influenced by the eloquence and example of his preceptor, emulated[b] the ascetic life of his patron saint, sighed to retire to some boundless desert, to live superior to nature, and to nature's laws, beyond the power of temptation, and the possibility of error; to subdue, alike, the human weakness and the human passion, and, wholly devoted to Heaven, to give himself up to such spiritual communions and celestial visions, as visit the souls of the pure in spirit, even during their probation on earth, until, his unregulated mind becom-ing the victim of his ardent imagination, he lost sight of the true object of human existence, a life acceptable to the Creator by being serviceable to his creatures.[7] Endowed with that complexional enthusiasm, which disdains the ordinary business of life, with that profound sensibility which unfits for its pur-suits, wrapt in holy dreams and pious ecstacies, all external circumstances gradually faded from his view, and, in his eighteenth year, believing himself, by the sudden death of his preceptor, to be the 'inheritor of his sacred mantle,' he offered up the sacrifice of his worldly honours, of his human possessions, to Heaven, and became a monk of the order of St. Francis.[c]

The Archbishop, and the Duke d'Acugna, received the intelligence of his pro-fession with less emotion than surprise. Absence had loosened the tie of natural affection. The political state of Portugal rendered an adequate provision for the younger brother of so illustrious an house, difficult and precarious; and the Patriarch of Lisbon well knew that, to enter the portals of the church was not to close, for ever, the gate of temporal preferment. The uncle and the brother wrote to felicitate the young monk on his heavenly vocation, presented a considerable donation to the monastery of St. Francis, and soon lost sight of their enthusiast-relative in the public commotions and private factions of the day.

CHAPTER II.

THERE is a dear and precious period in the life of man, which, brief as sweet, is best appreciated in recollection; when but to exist is to enjoy; when the rapid pulse throbs, wildly, with the vague delight which fills the careless heart, and when it may be truly said, 'that nothing is, but what is not.'[a8]

While this rainbow hour lasted, the thorny wreath, which faith had plaited round Hilarion's brow, was worn as cheerily, as if the rose of pleasure had glowed upon his temple. The vows he had made were ever present to his mind. The ceremonies of his religion occupied his imagination; and its forms, no less than its spirit, engaged his whole existence. He had taken holy orders, and was frequently engaged in the interesting offices of the priesthood. He studied, with unwearied ardour, the sacred legends and records of the convent library, and, during six years of monastic seclusion, his pure and sinless life had been so distinguished by religious discipline and pious austerity; by devotional zeal and fervid enthusiasm; by charitable exertion and rigid self-denial; and by an eloquence in the cause of religion, so profound, so brilliant, and so touching, that, even envy, which, in a cloister's gloom, survives the death of better passions, flung not its venom on his sacred character; and the celebrity of the *man without a fault* had extended far beyond the confines of his own secluded monastery.

The monks conceived, that his illustrious birth, not less than his eminent genius and unrivalled piety, threw a splendour on their order, and they daily looked forward to the hour when the Father Hilarion should wave the banner of successful controversy over the prostrate necks of the fallen Jesuits. Yet the brotherhood had hitherto but remotely hinted their wishes, or suggested their expectations. The familiar ease of the novice had faded away with the purple bloom of the youth; and the reserved dignity of the man threw, at an hopeless distance, those whom the monk, indeed, in the meekness of religious phraseology, called his superiors; but whom the saint and the nobleman equally felt unworthy to be classed with him, as beings of the same species; he stood alone, lofty and aspiring, self-wrapt and dignified; and no external discipline, no internal humiliation, had so crucified the human weakness in his bosom, as wholly to exclude the leaven of mortality from the perfection of religious excellence.

Hitherto the life of the young monk resembled the pure and holy dream of saintly slumbers, for it was still a dream; splendid indeed, but visionary; pure, but useless; bright, but unsubstantial. Dead to all those ties, which, at once, constitute the charm and the anxiety of existence, which agitate while they bless the life of man, the spring of human affection lay untouched within his bosom, and

8

the faculty of human reason unused within his mind. Hitherto, his genius had alone betrayed its powers, in deceiving others, or himself, by those imposing creations, by which faith was secured through the medium of imagination; and the ardour of his tender feelings wasted, in visions of holy illusion, or dreams of pious fraud. Yet these feelings, though unexercised, were not extinct; they betrayed their existence even in the torpid life he had chosen; for the true source of his religion, enveloped as it was in mysteries and dogmas, was but a divine and tender impulse of gratitude towards the First Cause; and his benevolent charity, which he coldly called his duty, but the extension of that impulse towards his fellow-creature! His habits, though they had tended to calm the impetuosity of his complexional character, and to purify and strengthen his moral principles, had added to his enthusiasm, what they had subtracted from his passions, and had given to his zeal, all that they had taken from his heart: but when the animated fervour of adolescence subsided in the dignified tranquillity of manhood, when the reiteration of the same images denied the same vivacity of sensation as had distinguished their original impression, then the visions, which had entranced his dreaming youth, ceased to people and to cheer his unbroken solitude; then, even Religion, though she lost nothing of her influence, lost much of her charm. While the faith which occupied his soul was not sufficient, in its pure but passive effects, to engage his life; the active vital principle, which dictates to man, the sphere for which he was created, preyed on its own existence, and he turned upon himself those exertions, which were intended to benefit the species to which he belonged: his religious discipline became more severe; his mortifications more numerous; his prayers and penance more rigid and more frequent; and that which was but the result of the weakness of human nature, conscious of its frailty, added new lustre to the reputation of the saint, and excited a warmer reverence for the virtues of the man. Accustomed to pursue the bold wanderings of the human mind, upon subjects whose awful mystery escapes all human research, intense study finally gave place to ceaseless meditation. Connecting, or endeavouring to connect, his incongruous ideas, by abstract principles, he lost sight of fact, in pursuit of inference; and, excluded from all social intercourse, from all active engagement, his ardent imagination became his ruling faculty, while the wild magnificence of the scenes by which he was surrounded, threw its correspondent influence on his disordered mind; and all within, and all without his monastery, contributed to cherish and to perpetuate the religious melancholy and gloomy enthusiasm of his character. More zealous in his faith at twenty-six than he had been at eighteen, it yet no longer opened to his view the heaven which smiled upon his head; but, beneath his feet, an abyss which seemed ready to ingulf him. He sometimes wildly talked of evil deeds which crossed his brain; of evil passions which shook his frame; and doubted if the mercy of his Redeemer extended to him, whose sinless life was not a sufficient propitiation for sinful thoughts: and this sensitive delicacy of a morbid conscience plunged him into habitual sadness, while it added to his holy fame, and excited a still higher veneration for his character, in those who were the witnesses of its perfection.[a]

He frequently spent days, devoted to religious exercises, in the gloomy woods of the monastery; and the monk, who, from kindness or from curiosity, pursued his wanderings, sometimes found him cradled on a beetling cliff, rocked by the rising storm; sometimes buried amidst the ruins of the Moorish castle, the companion of the solitary bittern; and sometimes hanging over the lake, whose subterraneous thunder scared all ears but his.

The change which had gradually taken place in the character and manners of the monk had long awakened the attention of the Prior and the brotherhood of St. Francis; but such was the veneration he had established for his character, by the austerity of his life, and the superiority of his genius, by the rank he had sacrificed, and the dignity he had retained, that his associates sought not in natural or moral causes for the source of effects so striking and so extraordinary: they said, 'It is the mysterious workings of divine grace; it is a vocation from Heaven; a miracle is about to be wrought, and it is reserved for a member of the order of St. Francis to perform it.'

These observations had reached the ears of the Father Hilarion, when those who pronounced them believed him lost in spiritual meditation; they became imprinted on his mind; they fastened on his imagination; they occupied his waking thought, and influenced his broken dream. It was in one of those suspensions of the senses, when a doubtful sleep unlinks the ideas, without wholly subduing the powers of the mind, that he fancied a favourite dove had flown from his bosom, where it was wont to nestle, towards the east; that, suddenly endowed with the power of flight, he pursued the bird of peace through regions of air, till he beheld its delicate form absorbed in the effulgence of the rising sun, whose splendour shone so intensely on him, that, even when he awoke, he still felt its warmth, and shrank beneath its brightness. He perceived, also, that the dove, which had been the subject of his vision, and which had drooped and pined during the preceding day, lay dead upon his bosom. This dream made a strong impression on his mind. The effects of that impression were betrayed in a discourse which he delivered on the eve of the festival of St. Hilarion. He took for his subject the life of Paul,[9] whom he called the first missionary. He spoke of the faith of the apostle, not as it touched himself only, but as to its beneficent relations towards others.

In the picture which he had drawn, the monks perceived the state of his own mind. They said, 'It is not of St. Paul alone he speaks, but of himself; he is consumed with an insatiable thirst for the conversion of souls; for the dilatation and honour of the kingdom of Christ. It is through him that the heretical tenets of the Jesuits will be confounded and exposed. Let us honour ourselves and our order, by promoting his inspired views.' In a few days, therefore, his mission to India was determined on. Arrangements for his departure were effected, permission[b] from the Governor of the order to leave the convent was obtained, and he

10

repaired to Lisbon, to procure the necessary credentials for his perilous enterprise.

After a separation of fifteen years, the Father Hilarion appeared before his guardian uncle, and his brother, the Duke d'Acugna; and never did a mortal form present a finer image of what man was,[a] when God first created him after his own likeness, and sin had not yet effaced the glorious impress of the Divinity. Nature stood honoured in this most perfect model of her power; and the expression of the best and highest of the human passions would have marred that pure and splendid character of look, which seemed to belong to something beyond the high perfection of human power or of human genius.[b] Lofty and dignified in his air, there was an aspiring grandeur in the figure of the Monk, which resembled the transfiguration of mortal into heavenly greatness: and, though his eagle-eye, when raised from earth, flashed all the fire of inspiration; yet, when again it sunk in holy meekness, the softer excellence of heavenly mercy hung its tender traits upon his pensive brow; his up-turned glance beaming the heroic fortitude of the martyr; his down-cast look, the tender sympathies of the saint; each, respectively, marking the heroism of a great soul, prepared to suffer and to resist; the sensibility of a feeling heart, created to pity and to relieve; indicating a character, formed upon that bright model, which so intimately associated the attributes of the God with the feelings of the man.[c]

The Duke and the Archbishop stood awed in the presence of this extraordinary being. They secretly smiled at what they deemed the romance[10] of his intentions; but they had not the courage to oppose them: they were rich in worldly arguments, against an enterprise so full of danger, and so destitute of recompense; but how could they offer them to one, who breathed not of this world; to whom earthy passions, and earthly views, were alike unknown; who already seemed to belong to that heaven, to which he was about to lead millions of erring creatures: all, therefore, that was reserved for them to effect, was, to throw a splendour over his mission, correspondent to his illustrious rank; and, in spite of the intrigues of the Jesuits, the reluctance of the Spanish vice-reine, and the wishes of the minister, Miguel Vasconcellas,[11] the united influence of the houses of Braganza and Acugna procured a brief from the Pope's legate, then resident in Lisbon, constituting a Franciscan monk apostolic nuncio[12] in India, and appointing Goa,[13] then deemed the bulwark of Christianity, in Hindostan, the centre of his mission.

Followed to the shore by a multitude of persons, who beheld in the apostolic nuncio another Francis Xaverius,[14] the Father Hilarion embarked with the Indian fleet, on board the admiral's ship, which also carried the governor-general, recently appointed to the government of Goa. The Nuncio was accompanied by a coadjutor, a young man strongly recommended by the Archbishop of Braga, a Jesuit, and the professed enemy of the Franciscans,[d] who had obtained the appointment of his protegé by his influence with the minister.

During the voyage, the rank and character of the Missionary procured him the particular attentions of the Viceroy; but the man of God was not to be tempted to mingle with the profane crowd which surrounded the man of the world. Devoted to a higher communion, his soul only stooped from heaven to earth, to relieve the sufferings he pitied, or to correct the errors he condemned; to substitute peace for animosity; to restrain the blasphemies of the profane; to dispel the darkness of the ignorant; to support the sick; to solace the wretched; to strengthen the weak, and to encourage the timid; to watch, to pray, to fast, and to suffer for all. Such was the occupation of a life, active as it was sinless.[a]

Such was the tenour of a conduct, which raised him, in the estimation of those who witnessed its excellence, to the character of a saint; but endeared him still more to their hearts, as a man who mingled sympathy with relief, and who added to the awful sentiment of veneration he inspired, the tender feeling of gratitude his mild benevolence was calculated to awaken.

Yet, over this bright display of virtues, scarcely human, one trait of conduct, something less than saintly, threw a transient shadow. He had disgraced the coadjutor from his appointment, for an irregularity of conduct almost venial from the circumstances connected with it. With him, virtue was not a relative, but an abstract quality, referable only to love of Deity, and independent of human temptation and mortal events; he, therefore, publicly rebuked the coadjutor as a person unworthy to belong to the congregation of the mission. He said, 'Let us be merciful to all but to ourselves; it is not by our preaching alone we can promote the sacred cause in which we have embarked – it is also by our example.' Even the mediation of the Viceroy was urged in vain. Firm of purpose, rigid, inflexible, he acted only from conviction, the purest and the strongest; but once resolved, his decree was immutable as the law of the God he served. His severe justice added to the veneration he inspired; but as he wept while he condemned, it detracted nothing from the general sentiment of affection he excited.

The voyage had been far from prosperous. The fleet had suffered much from repeated storms; and danger the most imminent, accompanied by all those awful appearances, with which conflicting elements strike terror into the boldest heart, had betrayed in the sufferers exposed to their rage, all the symptoms of human weakness, reduced to a feeling sense of its own insignificance, by impending destruction, under the most terrific and awful forms of divine power. The Missionary, alone, seemed uninfluenced by the threatened approach of that dreadful and untimely death, to which he stood exposed, in common with others. Calm and firm, his counsel and exertions alike displayed the soul incapable of fear; to whom life was indifferent, and for whom death had no terrors while his frame, as if partaking the immortality of his soul, resisted the influence of fatigue, and the vicissitudes of the elements. He[b] met, unappalled, the midnight storm; he beheld, unmoved, the tumultuous billows, which rushed loudly on, pouring destruction in their course, and bore, with uncomplaining firmness, the chilling cold of Cape Verd, the burning heats of Guinea, and the pestilential vapours of the line.[15]

It was on the first day of the sixth month of the voyage, that the fleet sailed up the Indian seas, and, through the clear bright atmosphere, the shores and

mighty regions of the East presented themselves to the view, while the imagination of the Missionary, escaping beyond the limits of human vision, stretched
over those various and wondrous tracts, so diversified by clime and soil, by government and by religion, and which present to the contemplation of philosophy
a boundless variety in form and spirit. Towards the west, it rested on the
Arochosian[16] mountains, which divide the territories of Persia from those of
India – primæval mountains! whose wondrous formation preceded that of all
organic matter, coequal with the globe which bears them! and which still
embosom, in their stupendous shades, a nest of warlike states, rude as the
aspects of their native regions, and wild as the storms that visit them; the
descendants of those warrior hordes, which once spread desolation over the eastern hemisphere, till the powerful genius of an individual triumphed over the
combined forces of nations, and the Affgans found, that the natural bulwark of
their native mountains was alone a sufficient barrier against the victorious arms
of Tamerlane.[17]

From the recollection of the character and prowess of the Tartar hero, the
mind of the Missionary turned towards the shores, which were rather imagined
than perceived in so great an interval of distance; and the Impostor of Mecca[18]
occurred to his recollection, with the scenes of his nativity and success. Bold in
error, dauntless in imposition, enslaving the moral freedom while he subverted
the natural liberty of mankind, and spreading, by the force of his single and singular genius, the wild doctrines he had invented, over the greatest empires of
the earth, from the shores of the Atlantic to the walls of China; his success
appeared even more wondrous, and his genius more powerful, than that of the
Tartar conqueror. The soul of the Missionary swelled in the contemplation of
scenes so calculated to elevate the ideas, to inflame the imagination, and to
recall the memory to those æras in time, to those events in human history,
which stimulate, by their example, the powers of latent genius, rouse the dor-
mant passions into action, and excite man to sow the seeds of great and distant
events, to found empires, or to destroy them.

His spirit, awakening to a new impulse, partook, for a moment, the sublimity
of the objects he contemplated, the force of the characters he reflected on, and,
expanding with its elevation, mingled with the universe. He remembered, that
he, too, might have been an hero; he, too, might have founded states, and given
birth to doctrines; for what had Timur boasted, or Mahomet possessed, that
nature had denied to him? A frame of Herculean mould; a soul of fire; a mind of
infinite resource; energy to impel; genius to execute; an arm to strike; a tongue
to persuade; and a vital activity of spirit to give impulse and motion to the
whole: – such were the endowments, which, coming from God himself, give to
man so dangerous an ascendant over his species; and such were his. For the first
time, his energy of feeling, his enthusiasm of fancy, received a new object for its
exercise. He pursued, with an eagle glance, the sun's majestic course:[a] 'To-day,'
he said, 'it rose upon the Pagoda of Brahma;[19] it hastens to gild, with equal rays,

the temple once dedicated to its own divinity, in the deserts of Palmyra;[20] to illumine the Caaba of Mecca;[21] and to shine upon the tabernacle of Jerusalem!'[22] He started at the climax. The empires of the earth, and the genius of man, suddenly faded from his mind; he thought of Him, in whose eye empire was a speck, and man an atom; he stood self-accused, humbled, awed; and invoked the protection of Him, who reigns only in perfect love in that heart, where worldly ambition has ceased to linger, and from whence human passions have long been exterminated.[a]

The vessel in which he had embarked, was among the last to reach the port of Goa; and the reputation of his sanctity, and the history of his rank, his genius, and his mission, had preceded his arrival. The places under the civil and ecclesiastical government of Goa, were filled by Spaniards, but the Portuguese constituted the mass of the people.[*] They groaned under the tyranny of the Spanish Jesuits, and they heard, with a rapture which their policy should have taught them to conceal, that an apostolic nuncio, of the royal line of Portugal, and of the order of St. Francis, was come to visit their settlements, to correct the abuses of the church, and to pursue the task of conversion, by means more consonant to the evangelical principles of a mild and pure religion. An enthusiast multitude rushed to the shore, to hail his arrival: the splendid train of the Viceroy was scarcely observed; and the man of God, who disclaimed the pomp of all worldly glory, exclusively received it. He moved slowly on, in all the majesty of religious meekness: awful in his humility – commanding in his subjection: his finely formed head, unshaded, even by his cowl; his naked feet unshrinking from the sharpness of the stony pavement; the peace of Heaven stamped on his countenance; and the cross he had taken up, pressed to his bosom. All that could touch in the saint, or impose in the man, breathed around him: the sublimity of religion, and the splendour of beauty, the purity of faith, and the dignity of manhood; grace and majesty, holiness and simplicity, diffusing their combined influence over his form and motions, his look and air.[b]

He passed before the residence of the Grand Inquisitor,[†] who stood, surrounded by his ecclesiastical court, at a balcony, and witnessed this singular procession. At the moment when the Missionary reached the portals of a Carmelite[25] monastery, where he was to take up his residence, the monks approached to receive him; the multitude called for his benediction: ere he retired from its view he bestowed it; and never had the sacred ceremony been performed with a zeal so touching, with an enthusiasm so devout, with a look, an attitude, an air so pure, so tender, so holy, and so inspired.[c] The portals

* The misfortune of Portugal being united to the kingdom of Spain after the death of Cardinal Henry, uncle to the King Sebastian, gave a terrible blow to the Portuguese power in the Indies. – GUZON, Histoire des Indes Orientales.[23]

† The power of that formidable ecclesiastic, the Inquisitor General, is very terrible; and extends to persons of all ranks – the Viceroy, Archbishop, and his vicar, excepted. – See HAMILTON'S New Account of the East Indies.[24]

closed upon the saint; and those who had touched the hem of his garment, believed themselves peculiarly favoured by Heaven.[a]

The next day he received an audience from the Bishop and Grand Inquisitor of Goa; marked by a distinction due to his rank; but characterized by a coldness, and by some invidious observations, little consonant to the enthusiasm of his own character, and unbefitting an enterprise so laudable and magnanimous as that in which he had engaged. – The Missionary, disgusted with all he saw and all he heard, with the luxury and pomp of the ecclesiastical court, and with the chilling haughtiness and illiberal sentiments of those who presided over it, and who openly condemned the tenets of the order to which he belonged;[b] quickly resolved on an immediate departure from Goa. A few days, however, were requisite to arrange the circumstances necessary for the promotion of his mission. His vow of poverty related only to himself; but his mission required worldly means, as well as divine inspiration, to effect its beneficent purpose; and the charity which became a duty towards persons of his own order in Christendom, must, in a country where his religion was not known, depend upon the casualty of natural feeling: something, therefore, which belonged to earth, entered into an enterprise which referred ultimately to heaven; and the saint was obliged to provide for the contingencies of the prelate and the man.

The route which he laid out for his mission, was from Tatta to Lahore, by the course of the Indus, and from Lahore to the province of Cashmire. To fix upon this remote and little known province, as the peculiar object of his mission, was an idea belonging to that higher order of genius, which grasps, by a single view, what mediocrity contemplates in detail, or considers impracticable in accomplishment. To penetrate into those regions, which the spirit of invasion, or the enterprise of commerce, had never yet reached; to pass that boundary, which the hallowed footstep of Christianity had never yet consecrated; to preach the doctrine of a self-denying faith, in the land of perpetual enjoyment; and, amidst the luxurious shades, which the Indian fancy contemplates as the model of its own heavenly Indra,[26] to attack, in the birthplace of Brahma, the vital soul of a religion, supposed to have existed by its enthusiast votary beyond all æra of human record, beyond all reach of human tradition, which had so long survived the vicissitudes of time, the shock of conquest, and the persecution of intolerance: this was a view of a bold and an enthusiastic mind, confident in the powers of a genius which would rise with the occasion, and superior to all earthly obstacles, which might oppose its efforts; of a mind, to be incited, rather than to be repelled, by difficulties; to be animated, rather than subdued, by danger.

The person, the character, the life, the eloquence of the Missionary, were all calculated to awaken a popular feeling in his favour; and, during the few weeks he remained at Goa, the confessional from which he absolved, and the pulpit whence he preached, became the shrines of popular devotion.

His eloquence was irresistible: it was the language of fearless genius, of enthusiastic zeal; vehement and impassioned, it ever aspired at the pathetic, or reached the sublime; and if it were, sometimes, more dazzling than judicious, more affecting than correct, still it persuaded when it failed to convince, still it was distinguished by those touches of tenderness, by those visions of enthusiasm, which blend and assimilate, so intimately, with human feeling, which ever address themselves, with such invariable success, to human passion![a]

The departure of the Nuncio from Goa was attended by circumstances which accorded not with the character of the apostle of Him, who, in approaching the spot whence he was to announce his divine mission to the rulers of the people, 'came riding on an ass;'[27] for the departure of the Missionary was triumphant and splendid. The most illustrious of the Portuguese families in Goa attended in his train, and the homage of the multitude pursued him to the shore, whence he was to embark for Tatta. He moved meekly on in the midst of the crowd; but through the profound humility of his countenance shone such magnanimity of soul, such perfect consciousness of a genius and a zeal equal to the sacred enterprise in which he had embarked, that the most favourable presages were formed of the success of a man, who seemed to blend, in his character, the piety of the saint with the energy of the hero. He embarked: – the anchor was raised; a favourable breeze swelled the sails. The Missionary stood on the deck, dignified, but not unmoved: the triumph of religion, softened by its meekness, sat on his brow! The happy auspices under which he had left the centre of his mission, promised him a return still more triumphant: his soul swelled with emotions, which diffused themselves over his countenance; and as the vessel receded from the shore, his ear still caught the murmured homage offered to his unrivalled excellence. The humility of the monk rejected the unmerited tribute; but the heart of the man throbbed with an ardour, not all saintly, as he received it; and the pious visionary, who attempted, by an abstraction of mind, to love God, without enjoying the pleasure which accompanies that love, now, with a natural feeling, superior to the influence of a stoical zeal, unconsciously rejoiced, even in the suffrages of man.[b]

CHAPTER III.

ON the evening of the day in which the apostolic Nuncio arrived at Tatta, he embarked on the Indus, in a bungalow[28] of twelve oars, for Lahore. He beheld, not without emotion, the second mightiest stream of the East; sacred in the religious traditions of the regions through which it flows, and memorable from its connexion with the most striking events in the history of the world; whose course became a guide to the spirit of fearless enterprise, and first opened to the conqueror of Asia a glimpse of those climes which have since been so intimately connected with the interests of Europe, which have so materially contributed to the wealth and luxury of modern states, and so obviously influenced the manners and habits of western nations. The scenery of the shores of the Indus changed its character with each succeeding day; its devious waters bathed, in their progress, the trackless deserts of Sivii, whose burning winds are never refreshed by the dews of happier regions; or fertilized the mango-groves of the Moultan;[29] or poured through the wild unprofitable jungle, glittering amidst its long and verdant tresses, which so often shelter the wary tiger, or give asylum to the wild boar, when pursued to its entangled grass by the spear of the Indian huntsman. Sometimes its expansive bosom reflected images of rural beauty, or warlike splendour; and Hindu villages, surrounded by luxuriant sugar-canes and rice-grounds, rich in plenteous harvest, and diversified by all the brilliant hues of a florid vegetation, were frequently succeeded by the lofty towers of a Mogul fortress, or the mouldering ramparts of a Rajah castle; by the minarets of a mosque, peering amidst the shades of the mourning cypress; or the cupolas of a pagoda, shining through the luxurious foliage of the maringo, or plantain-tree; while[a] the porpoise, tossing on the surface of the stream, basked in the setting sun-beam; or the hideous gurreal, voracious after prey, chased the affrighted fisherman, who, urging his canoe before the terrific monster, gave to a scene, wrapt in the solemn stillness of evening, an awful animation. Sometimes, when the innoxious shores awakened confidence, groups of simple Indians were seen, in the cool of those delicious evenings which succeed to burning days, offering their devotions on the banks of the stream, or plunging eagerly into its wave; the refreshing pleasure derived from the act, communicating itself to the soul and the frame, and both, in the belief of the enthusiast votarist, becoming purified by the immersion.

As the vessel glided down that branch of the Indus called the Ravii, every object, to the imagination of the Missionary, became consecrated to the memory of the enterprise of Alexander;[30] and, while the same scenes, the same forms, habits, dress, and manners, met his view, as had two thousand years before struck the minds of the Macedonians with amazement, his historic knowledge enabled him to trace, with accuracy, and his reflecting mind, with interest, those particular spots, where Alexander fought, where Alexander conquered!

Arrived at Lahore, he entered one of the most magnificent cities of the East, at a period when the unfortunate and royal Dara had sought it as an asylum, while he waited for the forces, led by his heroic son, Solyman, previously to the renewal of their exertions for the recovery of an empire, wrested from them by the successful genius of Aurengzebe.[*]

Lahore, at that period, formed the boundary of Christian enterprise in India; and the Jesuits had not only founded a convent there, but were permitted, by the tolerant Gentiles, publicly to perform their sacred functions, and to enjoy, with unrestrained freedom, the exercises of their religion.[†] The Missionary was received by the order, with the respect due to his sacred diploma and royal briefs; but neither his principles, nor the rigid discipline of his life, would permit him to reside with men, whose relaxed manners, and disorderly conduct, flung an odium on the purity of the religion, to which they were supposed to have devoted themselves. It was his ambition to make for himself a distinct and distinguished character; and, like the missionaries of old, or those pious sancassees[33] so highly venerated in India, he pitched his tent on the skirts of a neighbouring forest, and interested the attentions of the Indians, by the purity of a life, which shocked neither their ancient usages nor popular opinions; and which, from its self-denial and abstemious virtue, harmonized with their best and highest ideas of human excellence.[‡]

At Lahore he was determined to remain until he had made himself master of the dialects of Upper India, where the pure Hindu was deemed primeval; and his previous knowledge of the Hebrew and Arabic tongues, soon enabled him to conquer the difficulties of the task to which he devoted himself, with an ardour, proportioned to the enthusiasm of his genius and the zeal of his enterprise. He had placed himself under the tuition of a learned Pundit,[35] who was devoted to secular business, and had travelled into various countries of the East, as a secretary and interpreter. A follower of the Musnavi[36] sect, or 'worship of the

---

[*] Dara having advanced beyond the river Bea, took possession of Lahore; giving his army time to breathe; in that city, he employed himself in levying troops and in collecting the imperial revenue. – Dow's History of Hindostan,[31] vol. iii. p. 274.

[†] 'Autre fois les Jesuites avoient un établissement dans cette ville, et remplissoient leurs fonctions sacrés, et offroient aux yeux des Mahometans et des Gentiles, la pomp de leurs fêtes.' – BERNIER.[32]

[‡] Monsieur de Thevenot[34] speaks of a convent of religious Hindus, at Lahore: they have a general, provincial, and other superiors; they make vows of obedience, chastity, and poverty; they live on alms, and have lay brothers to beg for them; they eat but once a day; the chief tenet of their order is, to avoid doing to others, what they would not themselves wish to endure; they suffer injuries with patience, and do not return a blow; and they are forbidden even to *look* on women.

Invisible,' the religion of the philosophers of Hindostan, he yet gave his public sanction to doctrines which he secretly despised. To him, the wildest fictions and most rational tenets of the Brahminical theology appeared equally puerile; but the apprehension of 'loss of cast'[a][37] (an excommunication which involves every worldly evil) restrained the avowal of his sentiments, and secured his attention to forms and ceremonies, which were the objects of his secret derision. A Cashmirian by birth, he was endowed with all the acuteness of mind which peculiarly distinguishes his country; and equally indifferent to all religions, he was yet anxious to forward the Christian's views, whose doctrines he estimated, by the character of him who preached them.[b]

Although Cashmire was the principal object of Hilarion's mission, his zeal, no longer impeded by his ignorance of the language of those whom he was to address, already broke forth, accompanied by that brilliant enthusiasm, by that powerful eloquence, whose influence is invariable on popular feelings: he resorted to places of public meetings, to consecrated tanks, and to the courts of a pagoda. The tolerance of the followers of Brahma evinced itself, in the indulgence with which the innovating tenets of the Christian were received. They molested not a man, who thus daringly appeared among them, openly to dispute the doctrines of a faith, interwoven with the very existence of its professors: but a few of the lower casts only assembled around him, and even they listened to him with less conviction than curiosity,[*] and indolently rejected what they took not the trouble to examine or to dispute.

It was in vain, that the apostolic Nuncio sought an opportunity to converse with the learned and distinguished Brahmins of the province: his Pundit, whose confirmed deism set all hope of conversion at defiance, assured his pupil, that the highest class of that sacred order, who always adopt the sacerdotal stole, were seldom to be seen by Europeans, or by persons of any nation but their own. Acting as high-priests, devoted to religious discipline, in private families of distinction, or shut up in their colleges, when not engaged in the offices of their religion, they gave themselves up, exclusively, to the cultivation of literature, and to the study of logic and metaphysics, so prevalent in their schools, resembling, in the simplicity and virtue of their lives, the ascetics of the middle ages; except when they became elevated to some high dignity in their ancient and sacred hierarchy, and were then called upon, during certain seasons, to appear in the world, with all the imposing splendour and religious pomp, which peculiarly belongs to their distinguished rank and venerated profession.

---

[*] A Hindu considers all the distinctions and privileges of his cast, as belonging to him by an incommunicable right; and to convert, or be converted, are ideas equally repugnant to the principles, most deeply rooted in his mind; nor can either the Catholic or Protestant Missionaries in India, boast of having overcome those prejudices, except among a few of the lower casts, or of such as have lost their casts altogether. – Voyages aux Indes par M. SONNERAT,[38] tom i. p. 58.

While he spoke, the Pundit drew from his breast a gazette of the court of Delhi;* and read, from what might be deemed a literary curiosity, the following paragraph: 'The holy and celebrated Brahmin, Rah-Singh, the incarnation of Brahma upon earth, and the light of all knowledge, has been lately engaged in performing the Upaseyda[†] through the provinces of Agra and Delhi, from whence he returns by Lahore to Cashmire, the resemblance of paradise, by the attraction of the favour of Heaven. The Guru[40] is accompanied by the daughter of his daughter, who has adopted the sacerdotal stole, and has become a Brachmachira. The reputation of her holiness has spread itself over the earth, and her prophecies are rays of light from Heaven.'

The Pundit, then putting aside the gazette, said, 'This Guru, or bishop, who holds an high jurisdiction over all which relates to his cast, has long survived those powers of intellect, from which his brilliant reputation arose; and his influence must have wholly declined, had it not been supported by the merited celebrity of his grand-daughter: he has brought her up in the Vedanti sect, which he himself professes, the religion of mystic love: a creed finely adapted to the warm imagination, the tender feelings, and pure principles of an Indian woman; and which, sublime and abstracted, harmonizes with every idea of human loveliness and human grace.'[a]

'And what,' demanded the Missionary, 'are its leading tenets?'

'That matter has no essence, independent of mental perception; and that external sensation would vanish into nothing, if the divine energy for a moment subsided: that the soul differs in degree, but not in kind, from the creative spirit of which it is a particle, and into which it will be finally absorbed: that nothing has a pure and absolute existence, but spirit: and that a passionate and exclusive love of Heaven is that feeling only, which offers no illusion to the soul, and secures its eternal felicity.'

'This doctrine, so pure, and so sublime,' replied the Missionary, 'wants but the holy impress of revelation, to stamp it as divine.'

The Pundit answered: 'The religion of Brahma, under all its various sects and forms, is peculiarly distinguished by sublimity, and even the utmost extravagance of its apparent polytheism is resolvable into the unity of deity; while the mythological fables it offers to the credence of the multitude are splendid and poetical, like the forms and ceremonies of its religious duties. Of those you will be able to judge to-morrow, as the Guru of Cashmire enters Lahore, to perform the ceremony of the Upaseyda, in the Pagoda of Crishna;[41] where, after having distributed the holy waters, he will hear the learned men of the province dispute on theological subjects. As this is considered the grand field for acquiring dis-

---

* Gazettes de la cour de Delhi, des nouvelles publiques qui marquent, jour par jour, et non dans ce stile ampoullé qu'on reproche aux Orientaux, ce qui se passe d'importante à la cour et dans les provinces – ces sont de gazettes repandues dans toute l'empire. – ANQUETIL DU PERRON,[39] p. 47.

† A ceremony similar to that of confirmation in the Catholic church.

tinguished reputation among the Brahmins and literati of India, it is at this period, that you may seize on an opportunity of advancing your doctrines, as, by throwing off your European habit, and undergoing purification in the consecrated tanks of the temple, you become qualified to enter its vestibule.'[a]

To this proposal, the Missionary made no reply. He seemed lost in profound thought, but it was thought animated by some new and powerful excitement. His eye flashed fire, his countenance brightened, his whole frame betrayed the agitations of a mind roused to extraordinary exertion; the ambition of genius, and the enthusiasm of religious zeal, mingled in his look. The Pundit secretly observed the effects of his proposal, and withdrew. The Missionary, during the rest of the night, gave himself up to meditation and to prayer. Visions of a victorious zeal poured on his mind, and pious supplications offered to Heaven, for their accomplishment, breathed on his lips.

CHAPTER IV.

THE day on which the Guru of Cashmire made his entrance into Lahore, was a day of public festivity and joyous agitation to its inhabitants. The higher casts, the Brahmins and Chitterries, went out by the gate of Agra to meet him, some mounted on camels splendidly caparisoned; other reposing in palanquins, luxuriously adorned. At sunrise, the sacred procession appeared descending an eminence towards the town. The religious attendants of the Guru, mounted on Arabian horses, led the van; followed by the Ramganny, or dancing priestesses of the temple, who sung, as they proceeded, the histories of their gods, while incarnate upon earth. Their movements were slow, languid, and graceful; and their hymns, accompanied by the tamboora, the seringa, and other instruments, whose deep, soft, and solemn tones, seem consecrated to the purposes of a tender and fanciful religion, excited in the souls of their auditors, emotions which belonged not all to Heaven.

This group, which resembled, in form and movement, the personification of the first hours of Love and Youth, was succeeded by the Guru, mounted on an elephant, which moved with a majestic pace; his howdah,[42] of pure gold, sparkling to the radiance of the rising day. Disciples of the Brahmin surrounded his elephant, and were immediately followed by a palanquin, which from its simplicity formed a striking contrast to the splendid objects that had preceded it. Its drapery, composed of the snowy muslin of the country, shone like the fleecy vapour on which the sun's first light reposes: its delicate shafts were entwined with the caressing fibres of the camalata, the flower of the Indian heaven, dedicated to Camdeo,[43] the god of 'mystic love,' whose crimson blossoms breathed of odours which soothed, rather than intoxicated, the senses.

The acclamations which had rent the air on the appearance of the Guru, died softly away as the palanquin approached. An awe more profound, a feeling more pure, more sublimated, seemed to take possession of the multitude; for, indistinctly seen through the transparent veil of the palanquin, appeared the most sacred of vestals, the Prophetess and Brachmachira of Cashmire. Her perfect form, thus shrouded, caught, from the circumstance, a mysterious charm, and seemed, like one of the splendid illusions, with which the enthusiasm of religion brightens the holy dream of its votarist, like the spirit which descends amidst the shadows of night upon the slumbers of the blessed. Considered as the offspring of Brahma, as a ray of the divine excellence, the Indians of the most distinguished rank drew back as she approached, lest their very breath should pollute that region of purity her respiration consecrated; and the odour of the sacred flowers, by which she was adorned, was inhaled with an eager devotion, as if it purified the soul it almost seemed to penetrate.[a] The venerated palanquin was guarded by a number of pilgrim women, and the chief casts of the inhabitants of Lahore; while a band of the native troops closed the procession, which proceeded to the Pagoda of Crishna.

From the contemplation of a spectacle so new, so unexpected, the Missionary retired within his solitary tent, with that feeling of horror and disgust, which a profanation of the sentiment and purposes of religion might be supposed to excite, in a mind so pure, so zealous, so far above all the pomp and passions of life, and hitherto so ignorant of all the images connected with their representation. The music, the perfumes, the women, the luxury, and the splendour of the extraordinary procession, offended his piety, and almost disordered his imagination.[b] He thought, for a moment, of the perils of an enterprise, undertaken in a country where the very air was unfavourable to virtue, and where all breathed a character of enjoyment, even over the awful sanctity of religion; a species of enjoyment, to whose very existence he had been, hitherto, almost a stranger; but the genius of his zeal warmed in proportion to the obstacles he found he had to encounter, and he waited impatiently for the arrival of the Pundit, who was to lead him to the vestibule of the pagoda.

They proceeded, before mid-day, to the temple, which was approached through several avenues of lofty trees. On every side marble basins, filled with consecrated water, reflected from their brilliant surfaces, the domes and galleries of the pagoda. On every side the golden flowers of the assoca, the tree of religious rites, shed their rich and intoxicating odours.

In submission to those prejudices, which he could only hope finally to vanquish by previously respecting,[c] he suffered himself to be led to a consecrated tank, and, having bathed, he assumed the Indian jama.[44] As he passed the portals of the pagoda, he was struck by the grotesque figure of an idol, before whose shrine a crowd of deluded votarists lay prostrate: he turned away his eyes in horror, kissed the crucifix which was concealed within the folds of his dress, and proceeded to the vestibule of the temple. The ceremony of the day was concluded; the priestesses had performed their religious dances before Crishna, the Indian Apollo, and idol of the temple; the usual offerings of fruit and flowers, of gold and precious odours, had been made at his shrine; and the learned of the various sects of the Brahminical faith had assembled, at an awful distance round the Guru, to hold their religious disputation and controversial arguments.

In the centre of the vestibule, and on an elevated cushion, reposed the venerable form of the Brahmin. His beard of snow fell beneath his girdle; an air, still, calm, and motionless, diffused itself over his aged figure; a mild and holy abstraction involved his tranquil countenance; no trace of human passions furrowed his expansive brow; all was the repose of nature, the absence of mortality; and he presented to the fancy and the mind, a fine and noble image of that venerated God, an incarnation of whose excellence he believed himself to be. A railing of gold and ebony marked the hallowed boundary, which none were

23

permitted to pass, save the Prophetess of Cashmire. *She* sat near him, veiled only by that religious mystery of air and look, which involved her person, as though a cloud of evening mists threw its soft shadows round her. Forbidden the use of ornaments, by her profession, except that of consecrated flowers, the scarlet berries of the sweet sumbal, the flower of the Ganges, alone enwreathed her brow; a string of mogrees, whose odour exceeded the ottar of the rose, encircled her neck, with the dsandam, or three Brahminical threads, the distinguishing insignia of her distinguished cast.[*] Her downcast eyes were fixed upon the muntras,[45] the Indian rosary, which were twined round her wrist; and o'er whose beads she softly murmured the Gayatras,[46] or text of the Shaster.[47] And when, with a slight motion of the head, she threw back the dark shining tresses which shaded her brow, in the centre of her forehead appeared the small consecrated mark of the tallertum.[48] So finely was her form and attitude contrasted by the venerable figure of her aged grand-sire, that the spring of eternal youth seemed to diffuse its immortal bloom and freshness round her, and she looked like the tutelar intelligence of the Hindu mythology, newly descended on earth, from the radiant sphere assigned to her in the Indian zodiac.

At a little distance from the railing, stood the pilgrim-women who attended on the chief Priestess, fanning the air with peacock's feathers, and diffusing around an atmosphere of roses, from the musky tresses and fragrant flowers of the Brachmachira. On either side of the vestibule stood groups of the various sects of Brahma and of Bhudda,[49] while pilgrims and faquirs,[50] with the chief casts of Lahore, filled the bottom of the vast and mighty hall.[a]

The religious disputants spoke in orderly succession, without appearing to feel or to excite enthusiasm, contented to detail their own doctrines, rather than anxious to controvert the doctrines of others. A devotee of the Musnavi sect took the lead; he praised the mysteries of the Bhagavat,[51] and explained the profound allegory of the six Ragas,[†] who, wedded to immortal nymphs, and fathers of lovely genii,[52] presided in the Brahminical mythology over the seasons. A disciple of the Vedanti school spoke of the transports of mystic love, and maintained the existence of spirit only; while a follower of Bhudda[a] supported the doctrine of matter, as the only system void of all illusion. One spoke of the fifth element, or subtle spirit, which causes universal attraction, so that the most minute particle is impelled to some particular object; and another, of the great soul which attended the birth of all embodied creatures, connecting it with the divine essence which pervades the universe; while all, involved in mysteries beyond the comprehension of human reason, or lost in the intricacies of metaphysical theories, betrayed, in their respective doctrines, the wreck of that abstract learning, which, too little connected with the true happiness of society,

---

[*] From the time that they assume the dsandam, they are called the Brahmasaris, or children of Brahma.

[†] The 'Raga Mala,'[51] or Necklace of Melody, contains a highly poetical description of the Ragas and their attendant nymphs.

was anciently borrowed, even by the Greeks themselves, from the sages of India, and by the partial revival of which, even the philosophers of modern Europe once made a false, but distinguished reputation.[54]

It was during a pause which followed the declaration of the last-mentioned tenets, that the apostolic Nuncio suddenly appeared in the midst of the vestibule. His lofty and towering figure, the kindling lustre of his countenance, the high command which sat upon his brow, the bright enthusiasm which beamed within his eye, and[a] the dignified and religious meekness which distinguished his air and attitude, all formed a fine and striking contrast to the slight diminutive forms, the sallow hues, and timid sadness, of the Indians who surrounded him. Clad in a white robe, his fine-formed head and feet uncovered, he looked like the spirit of Truth descended from heaven, to spread on earth its pure and radiant light. The impression of his appearance was decisive: it sank at once to the soul; and he imposed conviction on the senses, ere he made his claim on the understanding.[b] He spoke, and the multitude pressed near him – he spoke of the religion of Brahma, of the Avaratas,[c] or incarnations of its founder, and of those symbolic images of the divine attributes, beneath whose mysterious veil a pure system of natural religion was visible, which, though inevitably dark, uncertain, and obscure, was not unworthy to receive upon its gloom the light of a divine revelation: then, raising his hands and eyes to heaven, and touching the earth with his bended knee, he invoked the protection of the God of Christians, even in the temple of Brahma, and, surrounded by idols and by idolaters, boldly unfolded the object of his mission, and preached that word, whose divinity he was ready to attest with his blood.

His eloquence resembled, in its progress, those great elementary conflicts, whose sounds of awe come rolling grandly, deeply on, breathing the mandate of Omnipotence, and evincing its force and power; till touched, rapt, inspired by his theme, the tears of holy zeal which filled his eyes, the glow of warm enthusiasm which illumined his countenance, the strong, but pure emotions, which shook his frame, kindled around him a correspondent ardour. Some *believed*, who sought not to *comprehend*; others were persuaded, who could not be convinced; and many admired, who had not been influenced; while all sought to conceal the effects his eloquence and his doctrine produced: for their hearts and their imaginations were still the victims of that dreadful fear, which *loss of cast* inspired; and the truths, so bright and new, now offered to their reason, were not sufficient in their effects to vanquish prejudices so dark and old, as those by which the Indian mind was held in thraldom. He ceased to speak, and all was still as death. His hands were folded on his bosom, to which his crucifix was pressed; his eyes were cast in meekness on the earth; but the fire of his zeal still played, like a ray from heaven, on his brow.

The Guru of Cashmire, who had listened to the wild mysteries of the Indian sophists, and the pure truths of the Christian Missionary, with equal composure, and, perhaps, with equal indifference, now arose to speak, and a new impulse was given to the attention of the multitude. Prejudice and habit resumed their influence, and all hung with veneration on the incoherent words pronounced by the tremulous and aged voice of a Brahmin, to whom his vota- rists almost paid divine honours, and who, with a motionless air and look, exclaimed: 'I set my heart on the foot of Brahma, gaining knowledge only of him: it is by devotion alone, that we are enabled to see the three worlds, celes- tial, terrestrial, and ethereal; let us, then, meditate eternally within our minds, and remember, that the natural duties of the children of Brahma are peace, self- restraint, patience, rectitude, and wisdom. Praise be unto Vishnu!'

He ceased: – the dome of the temple was rent with acclamations: the oracle of the north of India, his words were deemed rays of light. The rhapsody, which made no claim on the understanding, accorded with the indolence of the Indian mind: – the eloquence of the Missionary was no longer remembered; and the disciples of the Guru hastened to conduct him to the college prepared for his reception. The procession resumed its order. Incense was flung upon the air; the choral hymn was raised by the priestesses, and the imposing splendour of the most powerful of all human superstitions, resumed its influence over minds which sought not to resist its magic force.

The apostolic Nuncio remained alone in the temple. He inhaled the fra- grance of the atmosphere, he caught the languid strains of the religious women, and he beheld the splendid processions winding through the arches of the tem- ple, and disappearing among the trees which screened its approach. At his feet lay some flowers, which fell from the palanquin of the Prophetess, as she passed him. He stood, not confounded, but yet not unmoved. The rapid vicissitude of feeling, of emotion, which he had undergone, was so new to a mind so firm, to a soul so abstracted, that for a moment he felt as though his whole being had suf- fered a supernatural change. But this distraction was but momentary: the man of genius soon rallied those high unconquerable powers, which, for an instant, had bent to the impression of novel and extraordinary incidents, and had been diverted from their aspiring bias by circumstances of mere external influence. The man of God soon recovered that sacred calm, which a breast that reflected Heaven's own peace had, till now, never forfeited. He cast round his eyes, and beheld on every side disgustful images of the darkest idolatry: he shuddered, and hastened from the Pagoda. In one of its avenues he was met by the Pundit. The Cashmirian complimented him in all the hyperbole of Eastern phrase, on the power of his unrivalled eloquence, and the force of his unanswered argu- ments: he[a] said, 'that it rather resembled the inspiration of Heaven, than the ability of man;' and declared, 'that he believed its influence, though not general, was in some individual instances strong and decisive.' The Missionary turned his eyes on him with a religious solicitude of look. 'I allude,' replied the Pundit, 'to the Brachmachira, *the Priestess of Cashmire*, whose conversion, if once effected, might prove the redemption of her whole nation.'

A deep blush crimsoned the face of the Missionary, and he involuntarily drew his hand across his eyes, though unconscious that any look beamed there which Heaven should not meet. 'You are silent,' said the Pundit, 'and, doubtless, deem the task impracticable; and I confess it to be nearly so.[a] This may be the last pilgrimage the Priestess will undertake, and, consequently, the last time she will ever publicly show herself; for, except when engaged in the offices of their religion, as sacerdotal women, all the females of her cast, in India, are guarded in the retirement of their zenanas,[55] with a vigilance unknown in other countries. Habituated to this sacred privacy, the fairest Hindus sigh not after a world, of which they are wholly ignorant. Devoted to their husbands and their gods, religion and love make up the business of their lives. Such were they, when Alexander first invaded their country – such are they now. Pure and tender, faithful and pious, zealous alike in their fondness and their faith, they immolate themselves as martyrs to both, and expire on the pile which consumes the objects of their affection, to inherit the promise which religion holds out to their hopes; for the heaven of an Indian woman is the eternal society of him whom she loved on earth. In all the religions of the East, woman has held a decided influence, either as priestess or as victim; but the women of India seem particularly adapted to the offices and influence of their faith, and in the religion of Brahma they take a considerable part. The Ramgannies,[56] or officiating priestesses, are of an inferior rank and class, in every respect, and are much more distinguished for their zeal than for their purity; but the Brachmachira is of an order the most austere and most venerated, which can only be professed by a woman who is at once a widow[*] and vestal: a seeming paradox, but illustrated by the history of Luxima,[58] the Prophetess of Cashmire.

'Born in the most distinguished cast of India, she was betrothed, in childhood, to a young Brahmin of superior rank; but, from the morning she received the golden girdle of marriage, she beheld him no more. He had devoted himself to the Tupaseya,[59] or sacred pilgrimage, until the age of his bride should permit him to claim her. He went to the sacred Caves of Elora,[60] he visited the Temple of Jaggarnauth,[61] and died on his return to Cashmire, at Nurdwar, while engaged in performing penance near the source of the Ganges.[62] 'Tender, pious, and ambitious, Luxima would have ascended the funeral pile. The tears and infirmities of her grandsire prevailed. Childless but for her, she consented for his sake to live, and embraced the alternative held out to women in her situation of becoming a Brachmachira, being the only child of an only child. The riches of her opulent family, according to the laws of Menu,[63] centre in herself, and are expended in such acts of public and private beneficence as are calculated to increase the popular veneration, which her extraordinary zeal, and the austere purity of her life, have awakened. To make pilgrimages, frequently to repeat the worship of her sect, and to lead a life of vestal purity, are the peculiar duties of her order. To be endowed with the spirit of prophecy is its peculiar gift. Multitudes, from every part of India, come to consult her on future events; and her

---

[*] See 'Duties of a faithful Widow,' translated from the Shanscrit, by H. Colebrook, Esq.[57]

vague answers are looked upon as decisions, which, sometimes verified by chance, are seldom suffered by prepossession to be considered as false.

'There are few of this order now existing in India, and Luxima is the most celebrated. But it is not to her zeal only she owes her unrivalled distinction: she is, by birth, a sacerdotal woman and a Cashmirian; the ascendency of her beauty, therefore, is sometimes mistaken for the influence of the zeal which belongs to her profession; and perhaps the Priestess too often receives an homage which the woman only excites.* She is a disciple of the Vedanti school: the delicate ardour of her imagination finds a happy vehicle in the doctrines of her pure but fervid faith; and the sublime but impassioned tenets of religious love flow with peculiar grace from lips which seem equally consecrated to human tenderness. Every thing adds to the mystic charm which breathes o'er her character and person. Abstracted in her brilliant error, absorbed in the splendid illusion of her religious dreams, believing herself the purest incarnation of the purest spirit, her elevated soul dwells not on the sensible images by which she is surrounded, but is wholly fixed upon the heaven of her own creation; and her beauty, her enthusiasm, her graces, and her genius, alike capacitate her to propagate and support the errors of which she herself is the victim.[a]

'Such is the proselyte I propose to your zeal. Once converted, her example would operate like a spell on her compatriots, and the follower of Brahma would fly from the altar of his ancient gods, to worship in that temple in which she would become a votarist.'

The Pundit paused, and the Nuncio was still silent. At last he asked, 'if the Pundit had not observed, that an interview with an Indian woman of the Brahminical cast was next to impossible?'

'It is nearly so with all Indian women of distinction,' he replied; 'but a Brachmachira, from being more sacred than other women, excites more confidence in her friends.[†] To approach her would be deemed sacrilege in any cast but her own; but her obligation to perform worship to the morning and evening sun, on the banks of consecrated rivers, exposes her to the view of those who are withheld by no prejudices, or restrained by no law, from approaching her.'

They had now reached the Missionary's tent. The Pundit took his leave, and the Christian retired, to give himself up to the usual religious exercise of the evening.

---

* 'Certainly,' says De Bernier, 'if one may judge of the beauty of the sacred women by that of the common people, met with in the streets, they must be very beautiful.' p.96.

'The beauties of Cashmire, being born in a more northern climate, and in a purer air, retain their charms as long, at least, as any European women.' – GROSSE,[64] p. 239.

† The women are so sacred in India, that even the common soldiery leave them unmolested in the midst of slaughter and desolation. – Dow, History of Hindoostan, vol. iii. p.10.

CHAPTER V.

THE institutes of a religion which form a regular system of superstitious rites, sanctioned by all that can secure the devotion of the multitude, are rigidly observed by the followers of Brahma; and among the many splendid festivals held in honour of their gods, there is none so picturesque, and none so imposing, as that instituted in honour of Durga,[65] the goddess of nature, whose festival is ushered in by rural sounds and rural games. 'It is thus,' say the Puranas,[66] or holy text, 'she was awakened by Brahma, during the night of the gods.'

The dawn had yet but faintly silvered the plantain-trees which thatched the Christian's hut, when the distant strains of sylvan music stole on his ear, as he knelt engaged in the exercise of his morning devotions. The sounds approached: he arose, and observed a religious procession moving near his tent towards a pagoda, which lay embosomed in the dark shades of the forest. The band was led by faquirs and pilgrims. The idol was carried by women, underneath a canopy of flowers. A troop of officiating priestesses danced before its triumphal car: the splendour of their ornaments almost concealed their charms, and they moved with languid grace, to the strains of pastoral instruments, while small golden bells, fastened round their wrists and ancles, played with the motion of their feet, and kept time to the melody of their hymns. They were succeeded by the Guru of Cashmire, reposing on a palanquin, and the Brahmins of the temple followed. The Prophetess led the band of tributary votaries; *her* eyes, with a celestial meekness, threw their soft and dewy beams on the offerings which she carried in a small golden vase; and her cheek seemed rather to reflect the tint of the scarlet berries of the mullaca, which twined her dark hair, than to glow with the blush of a human emotion. The folds of her pure drapery, soft and fleecy as it was, but faintly defined the perfect forms of her perfect figure, of which an exquisite modesty, a mysterious reserve, were the distinguishing characteristics. Her thought seemed to belong to Heaven, and her glance to the offering she was about to make at its shrine. A train of religious women surrounded her, and the procession was filled up with votaries of every description, and of every class, from the princely Chittery to the humble Soodar,[67] all laden with their various offerings of rice and oil, of fruit and flowers, of precious stones and exquisite odours.

As they proceeded, they reached an altar erected to *Camdeo, the god of mystic love*. At the sight of this object, every eye turned with devotion on his consecrated Priestess. The procession stopped. The sibyl Priestess stood at the foot of the shrine of her tutelar deity, and the superstitious multitude fell prostrate at the feet of the Prophetess. They invoked her intercession with the god she served: mothers held up their infants to her view; fathers inquired from her the fate of their absent sons; and many addressed her on the future events of their lives; while she, not more deceiving than deceived, became the victim of her own imposition, and stood in the midst of her votarists, in all the imposing charm of holy illusion. Her enthusiasm once kindled, her imagination became disordered: believing herself inspired, she looked the immortality she fancied, and uttered rhapsodies in accents so impressive and so tender, and with emotions so wild, and yet so touching, that the mind no longer struggled against the imposition of the senses, and the spirit of fanatical zeal confirmed the influence of human loveliness.

Hitherto, curiosity had induced the Missionary to follow the procession; but he now turned back, horror-struck. Too long had the apostle of Christianity been the witness of those impious rites, offered by the idolaters to the idolatress; and the indignation he felt at all he had seen, at all he had heard, produced an irritability of feeling, new to a mind so tranquil, and but little consonant to a character so regulated, so subdued, so far above even the laudable weakness of human nature. He considered the false Prophetess as the most fatal opponent to his intentions, and he looked to her conversion as the most effectual means to accomplish the success of his enterprise. He shuddered to reflect on the weakness and frailty of man, who is so often led to truth by the allurements which belong to error; and he devoted the remainder of the day to the consideration of those pious plans, by which he hoped, one day, to shade the brow of the Heathen Priestess with the sacred veil of the Christian Nun.[a]

The complexional springs of passion in the character of the Missionary had been regulated and restrained by the habits of his temperate and solitary life; the natural impetuosity and ardour of his feelings had been tranquillized and subdued, by the principles of his pure and spiritual religion; and though his perceptions were quick and rapid in their exercise, yet he had so accustomed his mind to distrust its first impulse, that, all enthusiast as he was, he was yet less so from the vivacity of a first impression than from the mental operation which succeeded to it. The idea which was coolly admitted into his mind, gradually possessed itself of his imagination, and there gave birth to a series of impressions and emotions, which, in their combined force, finally mastered every thought and act of his life. Thus he became zealous in any pursuit, not because it had, in the first instance, struck him powerfully, nor that he had suffered himself to be borne away by its immediate impression, but because that, suspicious of himself, he had examined it, in all its points of view, considered it in all its references, and studied it in all its relations, till it exclusively occupied his reveries, received the glow of his powerful fancy, and engaged all the force of his intellectual being. It was thus that he frequently meditated himself into passion, and that the habits of his artificial character produced an effect on his conduct similar to that which the indulgence of his natural impulses would eventually have given birth to.

When the description of the Priestess of Cashmire first met his ear, it made no impression on his mind: when he beheld her receiving the homage of a deity, all lovely as she was, she awakened no other sentiment in his breast than a pious indignation, natural to his religious zeal, at beholding human reason so subdued by human imposition. When her story had been related to him, and her influence described, he then considered her as the powerful rival of his influence, and the most fatal obstacle to the success of the enterprise he had engaged in; but when the Pundit had awakened the hope of her conversion, and asserted the possibility of her influence becoming the instrument of divine grace to her nation, then the Indian gradually became the sole and incessant subject of his thoughts; and her idea was so mingled with his religious hopes, so blended with his sacred mission, so intimately connected with all his best, his brightest views and purest feelings,[a] that, even in prayer, she crossed his imagination; and when he sued from Heaven a blessing on his enterprise, the name of the idolatress of Cashmire was included in the orison.[b]

The Guru and his train had left Lahore, on the evening of the festival of the goddess Durga, for his native province; and, a few weeks after his departure, the Missionary commenced his pilgrimage towards Upper India. He was now equal to his undertaking; for he spoke the pure Hindu with the fluency of an educated native, and read the Shanscrit[68] with ease and even with facility. He had made himself master of the topography of the country – the valley of Cashmire, its villages, its capital, its pagodas, and the temple and Brahminical college, in which the Guru presided; and already furnished with the means of providing for the few contingencies of his pilgrimage, the most necessary luxury of which is afforded by the numerous tanks and springs, whose construction is considered a religious duty, the apostolic[c] Nuncio left Lahore, and commenced his journey towards Cashmire.

The black robe of his order flung over his lighter Indian vestment, his brow shaded by the monastic cowl, his hand grasping the pastoral crosier, wearing on his breast the sacred crucifix, and nourished only by the fruits and nutritious grains, with which a bounteous nature supplied him. His, resembled the saintly progress of the Apostles of old; a fine image of that pure, tender, and self-denying faith, whose divine doctrines he best illustrated by the example of his own sinless life; but he observed, with an acute feeling of disappointment, that the harvest bore no proportion to the exertions of the labourer. In whatever direction he turned his steps, the zeal of Hindu devotion met his view, while every where the religion of the Hindus gave him the strongest idea of the wild extravagance which superstition is capable of producing, or the acute sufferings which religious fortitude is equal to sustain. Every where he found new reason to observe, how perfectly the human mind could bend its plastic powers to those restraints, which the law of society, the prejudices of country, or the institutes of religion, imposed. He felt, how arbitrary was the law of human opinion; how little resorted to were the principles of human nature; how difficult to eradicate those principles impressed on the character without any operation of the reason, received in the first era of existence, expanding with the years, and associating with all the feelings, the passions, and the habits of life. But these reflections, equally applicable to human character in the West and in the East, were now first made under the new impressions formed by the observation of novel prejudices in others, not stronger, perhaps, but different from his own; and he whose life had been governed by a dream, was struck by the imbecility of those who submitted their reason to the tyranny of a baseless illusion.

Amidst the tissue of prejudices, however, which disfigure the faith of the Hindus, he sometimes perceived the force of their mild and benevolent natures bearing away the barriers of artificial distinctions; and though it is deemed infamous, and hazards loss of cast, for a follower of Brahma to partake of the same meal with the professor of any other faith, yet the Missionary found in India the true region of hospitality; choulteries,[69] or public asylums for travellers, frequently occurred in the course of his route; while the master of every simple hut was ready to spread the mat beneath the stranger's feet, and to weave the branches of his plantain-tree above the stranger's head; to present to the parched lip of the wanderer the milk of his cocoa-nut, and to his aching brow the shade of his humble roof. Happy are they who preserve, amidst the wreck of human reason, the dear and precious vestiges of human tenderness!

As the Missionary proceeded towards the north, he was still hailed with the pensive welcome of the Indian smile. Some few of the simple and patriarchal[70] people, who had heard of Europe, knew him by his complexion for a native of the West; but the greater number believed him to be a wandering Arab, from the lofty dignity of his stature, from the brilliant expression of his countenance; and then they would ask him to speak of the Genii of his religion, or to relate to them those splendid tales for which his nation is so celebrated: but when he sought to undeceive them, when he declared that he came, not to amuse by fiction, but to enlighten by truth; when he openly avowed to them the nature and object of his sacred mission, they fled him in fear, or heard him with incredulity.[a]

It was in vain that he invoked from Heaven some part of that miraculous power granted to those who had preceded him; that he might be able, with Francis Xavier, to cure the sick by a touch, or raise the dead by a look.* He could, indeed, watch with the saint, pray with the saint, and suffer with the saint, perhaps even far beyond those who had succeeded him: he could overwhelm by his eloquence, command by his dignity, attach by his address, and awe by his example; but he could not subvert a single law of nature, nor, by any miraculous

---

* 'The process of the saint's canonization,' says the biographer of Xavier,[71] 'makes mention of four dead persons, to whom God restored life at this time by the ministry of his servant.'

power, change the immutable decree of the First Will: – for, to him it was still denied to convert those from error, through the medium of astonishment, whom he could not subdue by the influence of truth.[a]

In less than a fortnight from his departure from Lahore, he reached the upper region, those dreadful and desolate plains, which stretch towards the base of the great and black rock of Bimbhar. Alone in the dreary waste, the Missionary felt all the value of an enterprise, marked by perils so terrific; but he felt it unsubdued. The dry and hot air[*] parched his lip; his feet trod in the channel of a torrent, dried up, whose bed seemed strewed with burning lava; a fever preyed upon the springs of being, and a parching thirst consumed his vitals; death, in the most dreadful form, met his view, but found him unappalled; and the tide of life was almost exhausted in his veins, when, worn out and feeble, he reached the foot of the rock of the pass of Bimbhar, denominated *The Mouth of the Vale of Cashmire*. High, sharp, and rude, it held a menacing aspect. Weak and enfeebled, the Missionary with difficulty ascended its savage acclivities. Nature seemed almost to have made her last effort when he reached its summit: his strength was wholly exhausted. Supported by his crosier, he paused, and cast one look behind him. He beheld the terrific wastes he had passed, and shuddered: he turned round, and flung his glance on the scene which opened at his feet; and the heaven which receives the soul of the blessed, met his view.[†]

Confined within the majestic girdle of the Indian Caucasus, Cashmire, the birth-place of Brahma, the scene of his avatars, came at once under his observation. The brilliant scene, the balmy atmosphere, renovated his spirits and his frame. He rapidly descended the rock, now no longer bleak, no longer rude, but embossed with odoriferous plants, and shaded by lofty shrubs. His vital powers, his mental faculties, seemed to dilate to the influence of the pure and subtil air, which circulated with a genial softness through his frame, and gave to his whole being a sense of vague but pure felicity, which made even life itself enjoyment. The cusa-grass,[74] which shrunk elastically beneath his steps, emitted a delicious odour; the golden fruit of the assoca-tree offered a luscious refreshment to his parched lip, and countless streams of liquid silver meeting, in natural basons, under the shade of the seringata,[75] whose beauty has given it a place in the lunar constellations, offered to his weary frame the most necessary luxury that he could now enjoy.

---

* 'Cet excès de chaleur vient de la situation de ces hautes montagnes qui se trouvent au nord de la route, arrêtent les vents frais, reflechissent les rayons du soleil sur les voyageurs, et laissent dans la campagne un ardeur brulante.'[72] – BERNIER.

† 'Il (Bernier) n'eut plutôt monté ce quil nomme l'affreuse muraille du monde (parcequil regard Cashmire un paradis terrestre), c'esta dire une haute montagne noir et pelée, qu'en descendant sur l'autre face il sentoit un air plus frais et plus temperé: mais rien ne se surprise tant, dans ces montagnes, que de se trouvir, tout d'un coup, transporté des Indes en Europe.' – Histoire Generale des Voyages,[73] livre ii. p. 301.

It was evening when he reached the vale of Cashmire.* Purple mists hung upon the lustre of its enchanting scenes, and gave them, in fairy forms, to the stranger's eye. The fluttering plumage of the peacocks and lories[77] fanned the air, as they sought repose among the luxuriant foliage of the trees: the silence of the delicious hour knew no interruption, but from the soothing murmurs of innumerable cascades. All breathed a tranquil but luxurious enjoyment; all invited to a repose which resembled a waking dream. The Missionary had no power to resist the soft and new emotions which possessed themselves of his whole being; it seemed as if sensation had survived all power of perception; and, throwing himself on the odorous moss, which was shaded by the magnificent branches of the pamelo, the oak of the East, he slept.

* According to Forster,[76] the utmost extent of this delicious vale from S.E. to N.W. is scarcely 90 miles; other travellers assert it to be but 40 miles from east to west, and 25 from north to south.

CHAPTER VI.

THE morning dawn, as it silvered the snows on the summits of the vast chain of the Indian Caucasus, and shed its light along the lower declivities of the hills of Cashmire, which swell at their base, awakened the Christian wanderer from a dream, pure and bright as a prophet's vision. In sleep he had believed himself to be in the abodes of the just, and he awaked in the regions of the blessed. Refreshed, invigorated, he arose, and offered the incense of the heart to Him, of whose power and beneficence his soul now received such new and splendid images.

Taking the broad stream of the Behat as his guide, he proceeded along its winding shores, towards the district of Sirinagar. Surrounded by those mighty mountains whose summits appear tranquil and luminous, above the regions of clouds which float on their brow, whose grotesque forms are brightened by innumerable rills, and dashed by foaming torrents, the valley of Cashmire presented to the wandering eye scenes of picturesque and glowing beauty, whose character varied with each succeeding hour. Sometimes the mango-groves, with their golden oblong fruit and gigantic leaves, were mingled with plantations of mulberry, which, rising in luxuriant foliage, give sustenance to myriads of industrious insects,[78] spinning from tree to tree their golden threads, which float like fairy banners, or brilliant particles of light, upon the fragrant gale; while, as emulous of their exertions, the Indian weaver seated at his loom beneath the shade of his plantain-tree, plied his slender fingers amidst the almost impalpable threads of his transparent web. Sometimes the ruins of a pagoda appeared through the boles of a distant forest, or the picturesque view of a Hindu village, formed of the slender bamboo, thatched with the brilliant leaves of the water-melon, appeared amidst the surrounding cotton-grounds, glowing with that tinted lustre of colouring, falsely deemed exclusively peculiar to the scenery of tropical climes; while herdsmen tending their snowy flocks on the brow of the surrounding hill, or youthful women carrying on their veiled heads vases of consecrated waters from the holy springs of the valley, recalled to the mind of the Missionary the venerable and touching simplicity of the patriarchal age.

Wherever the Christian wanderer appeared, he was beheld with curiosity and admiration. The dignity of his form commanded respect, and the meekness of his manner inspired confidence. They said, 'It is a sanaissee, or pilgrim, of some distant nation, performing tupesya[a] in a strange land;' and, with the same benevolent kindness with which they relieved the pilgrims of their own religion, did they administer to his comforts: but when, availing himself of the interest he excited, he endeavoured to unfold to them the nature and object of a mission, to accomplish which he had come from distant regions, they turned coldly from him, saying, 'God has appointed to each tribe its own faith, and to each sect its own religion: let each obey the appointment of God, and live in peace with his neighbour.'

This decided disappointment of all his holy views, grieved, without discouraging him. The perseverance of a genius not to be subdued, was the grand feature of his character; and a religious hope still hurried him towards that point, which was the object of his pious ambition. He deemed the conversion of the Prophetess a task reserved for him alone: the conversion of her nation a miracle which *she* only could accomplish.

He now proceeded to Sirinagar, and, within a few leagues of the capital,[*] he was struck by the appearance of a cave, in which he resolved to fix his abode. It was evening when the Missionary reached the base of a lofty mountain, which seemed a monument of the first day of creation. It was a solemn and sequestered spot, where an eternal spring seemed to reign, and which looked like the cradle of infant Nature, where she first awoke, in all her primeval bloom of beauty. It was a glen, skreened by a mighty mass of rocks, over whose bold fantastic forms and variegated hues dashed the silvery foam of the mountain torrent, flinging its dewy sprays around,[a] till, breaking into fairy rills, it stole into a branch of the Behat, whose overflowing, at some distant period, had worn its way into the heart of the rock, and produced a small sparry cavern which, from the splendour of the stalactites that hung like glittering icicles from its shining roof, had been named by the people of the country, *the grotto of congelations*. Wild and sequestered as was this romantic place, it yet, by its vicinity to the huts of some goalas, or Indian shepherds,[b] left not its inhabitant wholly destitute of such assistance as even his simple and frugal life might still require; while, on every side, the luscious milk of the cocoa-nut, the fruit of the bread-tree, the nutritious grains of the wild rice plant, the luxurious produce of innumerable fruit-trees, and the pure bath of the mountain spring, were luxuries, supplied by Nature, in these, her loveliest and favourite regions.

The Missionary employed himself, during the evening, in erecting at the most remote extremity of the grotto, a rude altar, on which he placed the golden crucifix he usually carried suspended from his girdle[c] and, having formed what might be even deemed a luxurious couch of mosses and dried leaves, a night of calm repose passed swiftly away. The dawn, as it shone through the crevices of his asylum grotto, was reflected by the golden crucifix suspended over his altar. The heart of the Christian throbbed with an holy rapture, as he observed the ray of consecrated light. He arose, and prostrated himself before the first shrine ever raised to his Redeemer, in the most distant and most idolatrous of the provinces

* So called by the Hindus and by the ancient annals of India; but Bernier and Forster denominate the capital and its district by the same name as the kingdom or province.

of Hindoostan: he then took his crosier, and issued forth, looking like the tutelar spirit of the magnificent region he was going to explore. A goala who was descending the rocks with his dogs,[a] gave him as he passed a look of homage, such as the mind instinctively sends to the eye when its glance rests upon a being whom Providence seemed to have formed in all the beneficence and prodigality of its creative power.

The Missionary, taking the path towards Sirinagar, emerged from the deep shade of his glen, into a scene of picturesque beauty, which burst, in all the radiance of the rising day, upon his view,[b] terminated by the cultivated hills of Sirinagar, and the snowy mountains of Thibet,[79] rising like a magnificent amphitheatre to the east; but a grove of mangoostin-trees,[80] still wrapt in the soft mists of dawn,[c] became an object peculiarly attractive, in proportion to the retiring mystery of its gloomy shade. The Missionary struck off from the high road, to pierce into its almost impenetrable recesses. He proceeded through a path, which, from the long cusa-grass netted over it, and the entangled creepers of the parasite plants, seemed to have been rarely, if ever, explored. The trees, thick and umbrageous, were wedded, in their towering branches, above his head, and knitted, in their spreading roots, beneath his feet. The sound of a cascade became his sole guide through the leafy labyrinth. He at last reached the pile of rocks whence the torrent flowed, pouring its tributary flood into a broad river, formed of the confluence of the Behat and a branch of the Indus: the spot, therefore, was sacred;[*] and a shrine, erected on the banks of the river, opposite to the rising sun, already reflected the first ray of the effulgent orb, as it rose in all its majesty from behind the snowy points of the mountains of Thibet. Before the altar, and near the consecrated shrine, appeared a human form, if human it might be called, which stood so bright and so ethereal in its look, that it seemed but a transient incorporation of the brilliant mists of morning; so light and so aspiring in its attitude, that it appeared already[d] ascending from the earth it scarcely touched, to mingle with its kindred air. The resplendent locks of the seeming sprite were enwreathed with beams, and[e] sparkled with the waters of the holy stream, whence it appeared recently to have emerged. A drapery of snow shone round a form perfect in grace and symmetry. One arm, decorated with a rosary, was pointed to the rising sun; the other, at intervals, was thrice applied to the brow, and the following incantation from the Brahminical scriptures was then lowly and solemnly pronounced: 'O pure waters! since you afford delight, grant me a rapturous view of heaven; and as he who plunges into thy wave is freed from all impurity, so may my soul live, free from all pollution.' Thrice again bowing to the sun, the suppliant thus continued: 'On that effulgent power, which is Brahma, do I meditate: governed by that mysterious light which exists internally within my breast, externally in the orb of the sun, being one

---

* The confluence of streams is sacred to the followers of Brahma.

and the same with that effulgent power, since I myself am an irradiated manifestation of the supreme Brahma.'*

This being of spiritual mystery seemed then given up to a silent and religious
rapture; and the Missionary, by a slight movement, changing his position,
beheld the rapt countenance of the votarist, who had so sublimely assimilated
herself to the orb she worshipped, and the God she served. It was Luxima! At the
rustling of his robe among the trees, she started, turned round, and her eyes fell
upon his figure, while her own was still fixed in the graceful attitude of devotion.[a] Silently gazing, in wonder, upon each other, they stood finely opposed, the
noblest specimens of the human species, as it appears in the most opposite
regions of the earth; she, like the East, lovely and luxuriant; he, like the West,
lofty and commanding: the one, radiant in all the lustre, attractive in all the
softness which distinguishes her native regions; the other, towering in all the
energy, imposing in all the vigour, which marks his ruder latitudes: she, looking
like a creature formed to feel and to submit; he, like a being created to resist and
to command: while both appeared as the ministers and representatives of the
two most powerful religions of the earth; the one no less enthusiastic in her brilliant errors, than the other confident in his immutable truth.

The Christian Saint and Heathen Priestess remained for some time motionless, in look as in attitude; till Luxima, from a sudden impulse, withdrawing her
eyes, the sensation of amazement depicted in her countenance, was rapidly succeeded by a bashful and timid emotion, which rosed her cheek with crimson
hues, and[b] threw round her an air of shrinking modesty, which softened the
inspired dignity of the offspring of Brahma. But when the Priestess disappeared, the woman stood too much confessed; and a feminine reserve, a lovely
timidity, so characteristic of her sex, overwhelmed the Missionary with confusion: he remained, leaning on his crosier, his eyes cast down upon his beads, his
lips motionless.

Luxima, who resembled as she stood, the flower which contracts and folds
upon itself, even to the influence of the evening air, was the first to interrupt
this unexpected and mysterious interview; with a sudden movement she glided
by the stranger, but with an air of chill reserve, of majestic distance, as though
she feared the unhallowed vestment of infidelity should pollute the consecrated
garb of vestal sanctity. He addressed her not, nor by a movement attempted to
oppose her intention. He saw her proceed up an avenue of asoca-trees, which
received the glittering form of the Priestess into their impervious shade. As she
disappeared amidst the deepening gloom, she seemed, to the eye of her sole
spectator, like the ray which darts its sunny lustre through the dark vapours
gathered, by evening, on the brow of night.[c] Still was his glance directed to the
path she had taken; still did the brilliant vision float on his imagination, till the

* 'L'Eternel, absorbé dans la contemplation de son essence, resolut dans la plenitude
des tems de former des êtres participants de son essence et de sa beatitude.'[81] – SHAS-
TAR, traduit en François.

sun, as it deepened the shadows of the trees around him, told how long a reverie, so new and singular in its object, had stolen him from himself. He started, and moved unconsciously towards the bank of the stream, where traces of her idolatrous rites were still visible. Some unctuous clay, mingled with the ottar[82] of the rose, strewed its perfume on the earth; and near it lay a wreath of the buchampaca, the flower of the dawn, whose vestal buds blow with the sun's first ray, and fade and die beneath his meridian beam, leaving only their odour to survive their transient blooms.

This wreath, so emblematic of the fragile loveliness of her who wore it, lay glistening in the sun. The Missionary took it up. A prejudice, or a pious delicacy, urged him to let it drop: he knew that it had made a part of an idolatrous ceremony; that it had been twined by idolatrous hands; but he could not forget, that those hands had looked so lovely and so pure, that they almost consecrated the act they had been engaged in: he wished also to believe, that those hands would yet adjust the monastic veil upon the Christian vestal's brow; he blamed, therefore, a fastidiousness, which almost resembled bigotry, and again took up the wreath. It breathed of the musky odours which had effused themselves from the tresses of the Indian as she passed him; and thus awakened to the recollection of their interview, he wandered back to his grotto, forgetful of his intention to visit Sirinagur, and occupied only in reflecting on the accident which had thus rendered him a resident in the neighbourhood of the Priestess of Cashmire.

CHAPTER VII.

THE day was bright and ardent, the grotto was cool and shady; and the Missionary felt no inclination to leave a retreat, so adapted to the season and his tone of mind. He engaged in the perusal of the Scriptures, an abridged translation of which he had made into the Hindu dialect, and in devotional exercises and pious meditations: yet, for the first time, he found his thoughts not always obedient to his will; but he perceived that they had not changed their character, but their object; and that, in reverting to the interview of the morning, they still took into the scale of their reflection, the subject of[a] his mission.

When he had finished the holy offices of the evening, he walked forth to enjoy its coolness and its beauty. He bent his steps involuntarily towards the altar erected at the confluence of the streams. The whole scene had changed its aspect with the sun's course: it was still and gloomy, and formed a strong relief to the luxuriancy of the avenue of asoca-trees, on whose summit the western sky poured its flood of crimson light. He wandered through its illuminated shades, till he suddenly found himself in a little valley, almost surrounded by hills, and opening, by a rocky defile, towards the mountains of Sirinagur, which formed a termination to the vista. In the centre of the valley, a stream, dividing into two branches, nearly surrounded a sloping mound, which swelled from their banks. The mound was covered with flowering shrubs, through whose entwining branches the shafts of a Verandah[83] were partially seen, while the Pavillion to which it belonged, was wholly concealed. The eye of the Missionary was fascinated by the romantic beauty of this fairy scene, softened in all its lovely features by the declining light, which was throwing its last red beams upon the face of the waters.[b] All breathed the mystery of a consecrated spot, and every tree seemed sacred to religious rites. The bilva, the shrub of the goddess Durga;[*] the high flowering murva, whose nectarous pores emit a scented beverage, and whose elastic fibres[c] form the sacrificial threads of the Brahmins; the bacula, the lovely tree of the Indian Eden; and the lofty cadamba, which, dedicated to the third incarnation,[84] is at once the most elegant and holy of Indian trees; all spoke, that the ground whereon he trod was consecrated; all gave a secret intimation to his heart, that his eyes then dwelt upon the secluded retreat of the vestal Priestess of Cashmire.

At the moment that he was struck by the conviction, a light and rustling noise seemed to proceed from the summit of the mound. He drew back, and casting

---

* The Goddess of Nature in the Indian mythology.

40

up his eyes,[a] perceived Luxima descending amidst the trees. She came darting lightly forward, like an evening iris; no less brilliant in hue, no less rapid in descent. She passed without observing the Missionary, and her dark and flowing tresses left an odour on the air, which penetrated his senses. He had not the power to follow, nor to address her: he crossed himself, and prayed. He, who in the temple of the idol had preached against idolatry to a superstitious multitude, bold and intrepid as a self-devoted martyr, now, in a lovely solitude, where all was calculated to sooth the feelings of his mind, and to harmonize with the tender mildness of his mission, trembled to address a young, a solitary, and timid woman. It seemed as if Heaven had withdrawn its favour; as if the spirit of his zeal had passed away. While he hesitated, Luxima had approached the stream, and the light of the setting sun fell warmly round her. Thrice she bowed to the earth the brow irradiated with his beams,[b] and then raising her hands to the west, while all the enthusiasm of a false, but ardent devotion, sparkled in her upturned eye, and diffused itself over her seraphic countenance, she repeated the vesper worship of her religion.[c]

It was then that a zeal no less enthusiastic, a devotion no less fervid, animated the Christian Priest. He darted forward, and seized an arm thus raised in impious homage. He discarded the usual mildness of his evangelic feelings; with vehemence he exclaimed, 'Mistaken being! know you what you do? that profanely you offer to the Created, that which belongs to the Creator only!'

The Indian, silent from amazement, stood trembling in his grasp; but she gazed for a moment on the Missionary, and, to an evident emotion of apprehension and astonishment, succeeded feelings still more profound.[d] A resentful blush crimsoned her cheek, and her dark brows knit angrily above the languid orbs they shaded.[e] The touch of the stranger was sacrilege. He had seized a hand, which the royal cast of her country would have trembled to have approached: he had equally shocked the national prejudice and natural delicacy of the woman, and violated the sacred character and holy office of the Priestess; she[f] withdrew, therefore, from his clasp, shuddering and indignant, and looking imperiously on him, exclaimed, 'Depart hence: – that, by an instant ablution in these consecrated waters, I may efface the pollution of thy touch; leave me, that I may expiate a crime, for which I must else innocently suffer.'

The Missionary, with an air of dignified meekness,[g] letting fall his arms, and casting down his eyes to the earth, replied: 'Daughter, in approaching thee, I obey a will higher than thy command; I obey a Power, which bids me tell thee, that the prejudice to which thy mind submits, is false alike to happiness and to reason; and that a religion which creates distinction between the species, cannot be the religion of truth; for He who alike made thee and me, knows no distinction: He who died to redeem my sins, died also for thy salvation. Children of different regions, we are yet children of the same Parent, created by the same Hand, and inheritors of the same immortality.'

He ceased. Luxima gazed timidly on him, and expressions strongly marked, and of a varying character, diffused themselves over her countenance. At last she exclaimed, 'Stranger, thou sayest we are of the same *cast*. Art thou, then, an irradiation of the Deity, and, like me, wilt thou finally be absorbed in his divine effulgence? Ah, no! thou wouldst deceive me, and cannot. Thou art *he*, the daring Infidel, who, in the temple at Lahore, denied all faith in the triple God, the holy Treemoortee;[85] Brahma, Vishna, and Shiven: thou art he, who boldly dared to imitate the sixth avatar, in which Brahma, as a priest, did come to destroy the religions of nations, and to diffuse his own: yes, thou art he, who would seem a god among us, and, by seducing our minds from the true faith, deprive us of our *cast* on earth, and plunge us, hereafter, into the dark Nerekah,[86] the abode of evil spirits. I knew thee well, and thy power is great and dreadful; for in the midst of the shrines of the Gods I worship, thy image only fixed my eye; and when Brahma spoke by the lips of his Guru, thy voice only left its accents on my ear. Ere thou didst speak, I took thee for the tenth avatar, which is yet to come; and when I listened to thee, I deemed thee one of the Genii of the Arab's faith, whose words are false though sweet. But they say thou art a Christian, and a sorcerer; and punishment, with a *black aspect* and a *red eye*, waits on the souls of them who listen to, and who believe thee.'

With these words, rapidly pronounced, blushing at her own temerity, in thus addressing a stranger of another sex, and involved in the confusion of her own new and powerful feelings, she would have glided away; but the Missionary following, caught the drapery of her robe, and said, with impressive dignity, 'I command thee, in the name of Him who sent me, to stay and hear.'

Luxima turned round. Her cheek was pale, she trembled, and raised her hands in the attitude of supplication. Shrinking back upon herself, fear, mingled with a sense of the profanation she endured, seemed to be the leading emotion of her soul. The Missionary, struck by the pleading softness of her air, and apprehensive of forfeiting all chance of another interview, by a perseverance in now detaining her, drew back a few paces, and crossing his hands on his bosom, and casting his eyes to earth, he sighed, and said, 'Go! thou art free; but take with thee the prayers and blessings of him, who, to procure thy eternal happiness, would joy to sacrifice his mortal life.' He spoke with enthusiasm and feeling: – Luxima heard him in amazement and emotion. Free to go, she yet lingered for a moment; then raising her eyes to heaven, as if she invoked the protection of some tutelary deity, she turned abruptly away, and gliding up the mount, disappeared amidst the ombrage of its trees.

The Missionary remained motionless. The result of this interview convinced him, that in the same light as the infidel appeared to him, in such had he appeared to her; alike beyond the pale of salvation, alike dark in error. Her prejudices, indeed, extended even beyond the abstract sentiment; for his words were not only deemed sacrilegious, but his very presence was considered as pollution: and her opinions seemed so animated by her enthusiasm, her religious faith so blended with her human ambition, that he believed he might well deem the conversion of her nation possible, could hers be once effected. But to those obstacles were opposed the success, which had even already crowned his progressive efforts: either by a fortunate chance, or by a divine providence, he had established himself near her residence; he was acquainted with the places of her morning and evening worship; he had addressed her, and she had replied to him. She had, indeed, confessed she feared his presence, and she had endeavoured to fly him; but had she not also avowed the deep impressions he had made on her mind? that she had mistaken him for an incarnation of her worshipped god; and, in the consecrated temple of her faith, where she stood, not more adoring than adored, that *his* image only rested on her imagination, *his* accents only dwelt upon her ear?

The Missionary moved rapidly away, as this conviction came home to his heart. He believed he felt it all, as a religious should only feel, through the medium of his mission, and not as a man through the agency of his feelings; and he returned thanks to Heaven, that the grace of conversion was already working in the pure, but erring, soul of the innocent infidel, slowly indeed, and under the influence of the senses; but the ear which had been charmed, the eye which had been fixed, were organs of intellect, the powerful sources of mind itself.

Another day rose on the cave of the apostolic Nuncio; but he extended not his wanderings beyond the huts of the neighbouring Goalas: when he approached them, he was hailed with smiles; but when he attempted to preach to them, they listened to him with indifference, or heard with incredulity. He sighed, and believing his hour was not yet come, looked forward, with religious patience, to the moment, when he should present, to the worshippers of Brahma, a Neophyte, whose conversion would be the sole miracle which graced his mission: but what miracle could better evince the divinity of the doctrine he advanced, than that a Priestess of Brahma, a Prophetess, a Brachmachira, should believe in, and receive it? He beheld, therefore, from the summit of his asylum, towns and villages, the palaces of Rajahs,[87] and the cottages of the Ryots;[88] but he approached them not. The charms of a solitude, so lovely and so profound, grew with an increasing and hourly influence on his heart and imagination. Pure light and pure air, the softest sounds and sweetest odours, skies for ever sunny, and shades for ever cool, the song of birds and murmur of cascades, all, in a residence so enchanting, rendered life itself an innocent enjoyment. The goalas called him 'The Hermit of the Grotto of Congelations;' and believing him to be an harmless fanatic, and a holy man of some unknown faith, they respected his solitude, and never intruded on it, but to furnish him with the simple necessaries his simple life required.*

For some time he forbore approaching the consecrated grove of the Priestess: he wished to awaken confidence, and feared to banish it by importunity. On the evening of the third day, he directed his steps towards the pavilion of Luxima, always concealing himself amidst the trees, lest he should be observed by any of

---

* 'Il ne faut à ces nations que des nourritures rafraichissantes, et mère la nature leur a prodigue des forêts de citroniers, d'oranges, de figuiers, de palmiers, de cocotiers, et des campagnes couvertes de riz.' – Essai sur les Mœurs et l'Esprit des Nations. VOLTAIRE.[89]

the few attendants who resided with her. At a little distance from the confluence of the streams, his ear was struck by a moan of suffering. He flew to the spot whence it proceeded, and beheld a young fawn in the fangs of a wolf; an animal rarely seen in the innoxious shades of Cashmire, but which is sometimes driven, by hunger, from the mountain wilds of Thibet into the valley. The animal, fierce in want, now suddenly dropt his bleeding prey, and turned on the man. The bright glare of his distended eyes, the discovery of his fang-teeth, his inclined head, the sure presages of destruction, all spoke the attack he meditated. The Missionary, firm and motionless, met his advance with the spear of his crosier; and though the wolf rushed upon its point, the slight wound it inflicted only served to whet his rage. He gained upon his opponent. The Missionary threw away the crosier. He had no alternative: he rushed upon the animal; he struggled with its strength: the contest was unequal; but it was but of a moment's duration: the animal lay strangled at his feet, and the Missionary returned his acknowledgments to that Power, which had thus nerved his arm, and preserved his life. He then turned to the fawn. It was but slightly wounded; and as it lay trembling on the grass, its preserver could not but admire its singular beauty. Its form was perfect, its velvet coat was smooth and polished, and its delicate neck was encircled by a silver collar, clasped with the mountain gem of Cashmire. Some Shanscrit characters were engraven on this collar, but the Missionary paused not to peruse them. The suppliant looks of the gentle and familiar fawn excited his pity: it seemed no stranger to human attentions, and caressed the hand of the Missionary, when he took it in his arms to bear it to his cave; for it was unable to move, and his benevolent nature would not permit him to leave it to perish. It was also evident, that it was the favourite of some person of distinction, to whom he would take pleasure in restoring it; for though he had conquered all human affections in himself, and had lived alone for Heaven, neither loving nor beloved on earth, yet sometimes he remotely guessed at the happiness such a feeling might bestow on others less anxious for perfection;[a] and a vague wish would sometimes escape his heart, that *he* too might love: but when that wish grew with indulgence, and extended itself to a higher object; when the possible existence of a dearer, warmer, feeling, filled his enthusiast soul, and vibrated through all his sensible being, then the blood flowed like a burning torrent in his veins, his heart quickened in its throb to a feverish pulsation – he trembled, he shuddered, he prayed, and was resigned.

When he had reached the grotto, he placed his helpless burden on some moss. He bathed its wound, and applying to it some sanative herbs, was about to bind it with the long fibres of the cusa-grass, when the light which flowed in upon his task was suddenly obscured. He was on his knees at the moment: he turned round his head, and perceived that the shadow fell from a form which hovered at the entrance of his grotto. The form was Luxima's: it was the Priestess of Brahma who presented herself at the entrance of the Christian's cave: it was the zealous Brachmachira, who stood within a few steps of the Christian's altar. The Missionary remained in the motionless attitude of surprise. He could not be deceived: it was no vision of ethereal mildness, such as descends upon the abodes of holy men; for, all pale, and spiritual, and heaven-born as it looked, it was still all woman: it was still the Idolatress. With eyes of languid softness, with looks so wild, so timid in their glance, as if she trembled at the shade her figure pictured on the sunny earth; before the Monk had power to rise,[a] she advanced into the centre of the grotto, and[b] kneeling opposite to him, and beside the fawn, she said,[c] 'Almora, my dear and faithful animal; thou whom I have fostered, as thy mother would have fostered thee; thou dost, then, still live! and the innocent spirit thy lovely form embodies, has not yet fled to some less pure receptacle.' At the sound of her caressing voice, the favourite raised her languid eyes, and fawned upon her hands. 'It lives!' she said joyfully; and turning her look upon the Missionary, added, in a softer voice, 'And thou hast saved its life?'

As she spoke, her eyes fell in bashful disorder, beneath the fixed look of the Missionary; and again gently raising their dewy light,[d] threw around the cavern, a glance of wonder and curiosity. The sun was setting radiantly opposite to its entrance, and the spars of its vaulted roof shone with the hue and lustre of vivid rubies: pure rays of refracted light fell from the golden crucifix on the surface of the marble altar; and the figure of the Monk, habited only in a white jama, finely harmonized with the scene, and gave to the grotto that air of enchantment, which the Indian fancy delights to dwell on. The mind of Luxima seemed rapt in the wondrous imagery by which she was surrounded. She again turned her eyes on the Monk, and suddenly starting from her position, the head of the fawn fell from her bosom.[e] 'Thou art wounded!' she exclaimed, with a voice of pity and of terror. The Monk perceived that the breast of his jama was stained with blood. 'Thou wilt bleed to death!' she continued, trembling, and approaching him: 'thou, who, unlike other infidels, art so tender towards a suffering animal, art thou to suffer unassisted?'

'My religion teaches me to assist and to relieve all who live and suffer,' said the Missionary; 'but here, who is there to assist me?' – Luxima changed colour; she flew out of the grotto, and in a moment returned. 'Here,' she said eagerly, 'here is a lotos-leaf filled with water; bathe thy wound: and here is an herb, sovereign in fresh wounds; apply it to thy bosom: and to-morrow an Arab physician from Sirinagur shall attend thee.' – 'The wound lies not in my bosom,' replied the Monk: 'it is my right arm which has been torn by the fangs of the wolf, and I cannot assist myself; yet I thank thee for thy charitable attentions.'

Luxima stood suspenseful and agitated. Natural benevolence, confirmed prejudice, the impulse of pity, and the restraint of religion, all were seen to struggle in the expression of a countenance, which faithfully indicated every movement of the soul. At last nature was victorious, and raising her eyes and hands to heaven, she exclaimed, 'Praise be to Vishnu! who still protects those who are pure in heart, even though their hands be polluted!' Then gently, timidly, approaching the Missionary, she knelt beside him, and raising the sleeve of his jama, she bathed the wound, which was slight, applied to it the sanative herbs, and, tearing off part of her veil, bound his arm with the consecrated fragment. Thus engaged, the colour frequently visited and retired from her cheek. When her hand met the Missionary's, she shuddered and shrank from the touch; and when his eye dwelt on hers, she suddenly averted their glance. They fell at last upon her own faded wreath of the buchamhaca,[90] which was suspended from a point of the rock: she blushed, and cast them down on the rosary of the Christian Hermit, which, at that moment, encircled her own arm. She perceived that his eyes also rested on them. 'I found them,' she said, replying to his look; 'for having missed a fawn, who had followed me to the stream of evening worship, I implored the assistance of Moodaivee, the Goddess of Misfortune, and she conducted me to a spot, where I perceived the shining hairs of my favourite, lying scattered around the body of a wolf, who lay, grim and terrific, even in death. I said, 'Who is he, powerful as the flaming column, in which Shiven did manifest his strength – who is he, bold and terrible, who thus destroys the destroyer?' Thy beads told the tale; and the red drops which fell from the wound of the fawn, tracked the path to this cave of wonders, where I have found thee, kind infidel, acting as an Hindu would have acted; who shudders as he moves, lest, beneath his incautious steps, some viewless insect bleeds. Receive, then, into thy care, this wounded animal; and when it can be removed, lead it, at sunrise, to the confluence of the streams; there I will receive it.'

As she spoke, she advanced to the entrance of the cave, and performing the salaam,[91] the graceful salutation of the East, disappeared. Had a celestial visitant irradiated with its brightness the gloom of his cavern, the Missionary would not have been more overwhelmed by emotions of surprise and admiration; but, in recovering from his confusion, he recollected, with a strong feeling of self-reproach, that he had suffered her to depart, without availing himself of so singular an opportunity of increasing her confidence, and extending their intercourse. He arose – and resuming his monkish robe, followed her with a rapid step. He perceived her, like a vapour which a sunbeam lights, floating amidst the dark shadows of the surrounding trees. The echo of his footsteps caught her ear: she turned round, and the flush of quick surprise mantled even to her brow; yet a smile of bashful[a] pleasure played round her lips. The Missionary turned away his eyes, and secretly wished she might not thus smile again; for the pearl, whose snowy lustre the chunam[92] had not yet dimmed, marked by contrast the ruby brightness of those lips, which, when they smiled, lost all their usual character of seraph meekness, and chased from the playful countenance of the woman, the dignified tranquillity which sat upon the holy look of the Priestess.[b]

The Missionary was now beside her. 'The dew of evening,' he said, 'falls heavy, the sun is about to withdraw its last beam from the horizon,[c] and the cause which drove a ferocious animal into these harmless shades may still exist, and send another from the heights of Thibet; therefore, daughter, have I followed thee!' The Indian looked not insensible, nor yet displeased by his attention; but when he called her *daughter*, she raised her eyes in wonder to the form of him, who thus assumed the sacred rights of paternity: but she read not there his claim, and repeated in a low voice – '*Daughter!*' – 'Yes,' he replied, as a vague sense of pleasure thrilled through his heart, when she repeated the word;[a] 'yes, I would look upon thee as a daughter, I would be unto thee as a father, I would guide the wanderings of thy mind, as now I guide thy steps, and I would protect thee from evil and from error, as I now protect thee from danger and from accident.'

The countenance of Luxima softened as he spoke. He now addressed himself, not to her prejudices, which were unvanquishable, but to her feelings, which were susceptible: he addressed her, not as the priest of a religion she feared, but as a man, whom it was impossible to listen to, or to behold, without interest; and the Missionary, observing the means most likely to fascinate her attention and to win her confidence, now dropt the language of his mission, and spoke to her with an eloquence, never before exerted but in the cause of religion. He spoke to her of the lovely wonders of her native region; of the impression which the venerable figure of her grandsire had made on his mind, in the temple of Lahore; and of her own story, which, he confessed, had deeply interested him: he spoke to her of the loss of affectionate parents, of the untimely fate of a youthful bridegroom, and of the nature of the austere life she herself led; of the tender ties she had relinquished, of the precious feelings she had sacrificed. In adverting thus to her life, he was governed by an acute consciousness of all the privations of his own; he spoke of the subjection of the passions, like one constituted to know their tyranny, and capable of opposing it; and he applauded the fortitude of virtue, like one who estimated the difficulty of resistance by the force of the external temptation and the internal impulse: he spoke a language not usually his own – the *language of sentiment:* but if it wanted something of the force, it wanted nothing of the pathos which distinguished the eloquence of his religion.

Luxima heard him with emotion. Her heart was eloquent, but the nature of her religion, and feminine reserve, alike sealed her lips. She replied to his observation by looks, and to his questions by monosyllables. He only understood, from her timid and brief answers, that her grandsire was then residing at his college at Sirinagur, and that she lived in religious retirement, in her pavilion, with only two female attendants, wholly devoted to the discipline and exercises of her profession. But though her words were few, reserved, and guarded; yet the warm blush of sudden emotion,[b] the playful smile of unrepressed pleasure, the low sigh of involuntary sadness, and all those simple and obvious expressions of strong and tender feelings, which, in an advanced state of society, are obscured by ceremony, or concealed by affectation, betrayed, to the Monk, a character, in which tenderness and enthusiasm, and genius and sensibility, mingled their attributes.

When she had reached the base of the mound, the Missionary sought not to proceed. 'Daughter,' he said, 'thou art now within the safe asylum of thy home. Peace be unto thee! and may He, who gave us equally hearts to feel his goodness, guard and protect thee!' As he spoke, he raised his illumined eyes to heaven, and clasped his hands in the suppliant attitude of prayer. The dovelike eyes and innocent hands of the Indian were raised in the same direction; for, gazing on the glories of the firmament, a feeling of rapturous devotion, awakened and exalted by the enthusiasm of the Missionary, filled her soul.[a]

In this sacred communion, the Christian Saint and Heathen Priestess felt in common and together; and their eyes were only withdrawn from heaven, to become fixed on each other. The beams of both were humid, and both secretly felt the sympathy by which they were united. Luxima withdrew in silence; and the Missionary, as he caught the last glimpse of her form, sighed, and said, 'How worthy she is to be saved! how obviously does a dawning grace shed its pure light over the dark prejudices of her wandering mind!' Then he recalled her looks, her blushes, her words: all alike breathed of a soul, formed for the highest purposes of devotion; a heart endowed with the most exquisite feelings of nature: and, in meditating on the character of his future proselyte, he remained wandering about the shades of her dwelling, until the rays of a midnight moon silvered their foliage; then a strain of soft and solemn music faintly stole on his ear, and powerfully awakened his attention. This mysterious sound proceeded from the summit of the mound; and led by strains which harmonized with the hour, the place, and with the peculiar tone of his feelings and his mind, he ascended the acclivity; but it was with slow and doubtful steps, as if he were impelled to act by some secret impulse, which he did not approve, and could not resist. As he reached the summit of the mound, he perceived, by the peculiar odours which breathed around him, that it was planted with the rarest and richest shrubs. A spring, gushing from its brow, shed a light dew on every side, which bestowed an eternal freshness on the balmy air, and on those fragrant flowers, which opened now their choicest sweets.

A pavilion, surrounded by a light and elegant verandah, rose, like a fairy structure, from the midst of the surrounding shades; and, from one of the lattices, proceeded those aërial sounds, which,

'Sweet as from blest voices uttering joy,'[93]

had first allured his attention. It seemed to inclose a particular apartment. Its lattices were composed of the aromatic verani, whose property it is, to allay a feverish heat; and which, by being dashed by the waters of an artificial fountain, bestowed a fragrant coolness on the air.[b] A light gleamed through one of the lattices, and the Missionary found no difficulty in penetrating, with his eye, into the interior of the room. He perceived that the light[c] proceeded from a lamp, suspended from the centre of the ceiling, which was painted with figures taken from the Indian mythology. Beneath the lamp stood a small altar, whose ivory steps were strewed with flowers and with odours.

The idol, to whom the offerings were made, wore the form and air of a child: by his cany[94] bow, his arrows tipt with Indian blossoms, the Missionary recognised him as the lovely twin of the Grecian Cupid; while, before her tutelar deity, knelt Luxima, playing on the Indian lyre, which she accompanied with a hymn to Camdeo. The sounds, wild and tender, died upon her lips, and she seemed to

> 'Feed on thoughts,
> Which voluntary mov'd harmonious numbers.'[95]

She then arose, and poured incense into a small vase, in which the leaves of the sacred sami-tree burnt with a blue phosphoric light: then bowing to the altar, she said, 'Glory be to Camdeo; him by whom Brahma and Vishnu are filled with rapturous delight; for the true object of glory is an union with our beloved: that object really exists; but, without it, both heart and soul would have no existence.'

As she pronounced this impassioned invocation, a tender and ardent enthusiasm diffused itself over her countenance: her eyelids gently closed, and soft and delightful visions seemed to absorb her soul and feelings.[a]

The Missionary hastened away, and rapidly descended the mound. He had seen, he had heard, too much: even the very air he breathed communicated its fatal softness to his imagination, and[b] tended to enervate his mind. A short time back, and the Indian had shared with him a feeling as pure and as devotional as it was sublime and awful: he found her now involved in idolatrous worship. Hitherto a chaste and vestal reserve had consecrated her look, and guarded her words; now a tender and impassioned[c] languor was distinguished in both: and the virgin priestess, the widowed bride, who had hitherto appeared exclusively consecrated to the service of that Heaven she imaged upon earth, seemed now only alive to the existence of feelings in which Heaven could have no share.

For whose sake was this tender invocation made? lived there an object worthy to steal between the vestal Prophetess and her paradise of Indra? He recalled her look and air, and thought that as he had last beheld her in all the grace and blandishment of beauty and emotion, she resembled less the future foundress of a religious order, than one of the lovely Rajini, or female Passions,[96] which, in the poetical mythology of her religion, were supposed to preside over the harmony of the spheres, and to steal their power over the hearts of men by sounds which breathed of heaven. But he discarded the seducing image, as little consonant to the tone of his mind, while he involuntarily repeated, 'The true object of soul and mind is the glory of a union with our beloved;' until, suddenly recollecting the doctrines of mystic love, and that, even in his own pure faith, there were sects who addressed their homage to Heaven in terms of human passion,[*] Luxima stood redeemed in his mind: for, whatever glow of imagination warms the worship of colder regions, he was aware that, in India, the ardent gratitude of created spirits was wont to ascend to the Creator in expressions of the most fervid devotion; that the tender eloquence of mystic piety too frequently assumed the character of human feelings; and that the faint line, which

---

[*] It is unnecessary to mention the well-known doctrine of quietism, embraced by the Archbishop of Cambray.[97]

sometimes separated the language of love from that of religion, was too delicate to be perceptible but to the pure in spirit and devout in mind. He was himself of a rigid principle and a stoical order, and the language of his piety, like its sentiment, was lofty and sublime. Yet he was not intolerant towards the soft and pious weaknesses of others; and he now believed that the ardent enthusiasm of the lovely[a] Heathen was a sure presage of the zeal and faith of the future Christian.

The little hills which encircled the vale where chance had fixed the residence of the Nuncio, seemed now to him as a magic boundary, whose line it was impossible to pass; and during the day which succeeded to that of Luxima's visit, he wandered near the path which led to her pavilion, or returned to his grotto, to caress the fawn she had committed to his care; but always with a feeling of doubt and anxiety, as if expectation and disappointment divided his mind; for he thought it probable, that the humanity of Luxima might lead her, now her first prejudices were vanquished, again to visit him, to inquire into the state of his own slight wound, or to see her convalescent favourite. Once he believed he heard her voice: he flew to the mouth of the grotto, but it was only the sweet soft whistle of the packimar, the Indian bird-catcher, as he hung, almost suspended, from the projection of a neighbouring rock, pointing his long and slender lines tipped with lime to the gaudy plumage of the pungola, who builds her nest in the recesses of the highest cliffs; or lured to his nets, with imitative note, the lovely and social magana, the red-breast of the East. Again he heard a light and feathery foot-fall: he thought it must be Luxima's, but he only perceived at a distance, a slender youth bending his rapid way, assisted by a slight and brilliant spear; and by his jama of snowy white, and crimson sash and turban, he recognised the useful and swift Hircarah, the faithful courier of some Indian rajah or Mogul omrah.

The sun, as it faded from the horizon, withdrew with it, hopes scarcely understood by him who indulged them. Hitherto his mind had received every impression, and combined every idea, through a religious influence; and even the Indian, in all the splendour of her beauty, her youth, and her enthusiasm, had stolen on his imagination solely through the medium of his zeal. Until this moment, woman was to him a thing unguessed at and unthought of. In Europe and in India, the few who had met his eye were of that class in society to whom delicacy of form was so seldom given, by whom the graces of the mind were so seldom possessed. Hitherto he had only stood between them and Heaven: they had approached him penitent and contrite, faded by time, or chilled by remorse; and he had felt towards them as saints are supposed to feel, who see the errors from which they are themselves exempt. His experience, therefore, afforded him no parallel for the character and form of the Priestess. A rapturous vision had, indeed, given him such forms of heaven to gaze on; but on earth he had seen nothing to which he could assimilate, or by which compare her.

Yet, in reflecting on her charms, he only considered them as rendering her more worthy to be converted, and more capable of converting. He remembered that the pure light of Christianity owed its first diffusion to the influence of woman; and that the blood of martyred vestals had flowed to attest their zeal and faith, with no inadequate effect. This consideration, therefore, sanctified the solicitude which Luxima awakened in his mind; and anxiously to expect her presence, and profoundly to feel her absence, were, he believed, sentiments which emanated from his religious zeal, and not emotions belonging to his selfish feeling.[a]

On the evening of the following day, he repaired to the altar at the confluence of the streams, accompanied by the fawn, which was now sufficiently recovered to be restored to its mistress. His heart throbbed with a violence new to its sober pulse, when he perceived Luxima standing beneath the shadowy branches of a cannella-alba, or cinnamon-tree, looking like the deity of the stream, in whose lucid wave her elegant and picturesque form was reflected. The bright buds of the water-loving lotos were twined round her arms and bosom: she seemed fresh from her morning worship;[b] and the enthusiasm of devotion still threw its light upon her features; but when the Missionary stood before her, this devotional expression was lost in the splendour of her illuminated countenance. The pure blood mantling to her cheek gradually suffused her whole face with radiant blushes: a tender shyness hung upon her downcast eyes; and a smiling softness, a bashful pleasure, finely blended with a religious dignity, involved her whole person. There was so much of the lustre of beauty, the freshness of youth, the charm of sentiment, the mystery of devotion, and the spell of grace, in her look, her air, her attitude, that the Missionary stood rapt in silent contemplation of her person, and wondering that one so fit for heaven should yet remain on earth.[c]

The fawn, which had burst from the string of twisted grass by which the Missionary led it, now sprung to the feet of her mistress, who lavished on her favourite the most infantile caresses; and this little scene of re-union gave time to the Missionary to recover the reserved dignity of the apostolic Nuncio, which the abruptly awakened feelings of the man had put to flight. 'Daughter,' he said, 'health and peace to thee and thine! May the light of the true religion effuse its lustre o'er thy soul, as the light of the sun now irradiates thy form!'

As he spoke a language so similar to that in which the devotions of the heathen were wont to flow, he touched, by a natural association of ideas, on the chord of her enthusiasm; and thrice bowing to the sun, she replied, 'I adore that effulgent power, in whose lustre I now shine, and of which I am myself an irradiated manifestation.'

The Missionary started; his blood ran cold as he thus found himself so intimately associated in the worship of an infidel; while, as if suddenly inspired, he raised his hands and eyes to heaven, and, prostrate on the earth, prayed aloud, and with the eloquence of angels, for her conversion.

Luxima, gazing and listening, stood rapt in wonder and amazement, in awe and admiration.[d] She heard her name tenderly pronounced, and inseparably connected with supplication to Heaven in her behalf: she beheld tears, and listened to sighs, of which she alone was the object, and which were made as offerings to the suppliant's God, that she might embrace a mode of belief, to whose existence, until now, she was almost a stranger. Professing, herself, a religion which unites the most boundless toleration to the most obstinate faith; the most perfect indifference to proselytism, to the most unvanquishable conviction of its own supreme excellence;[a] she could not, even remotely, comprehend the pious solicitude for her conversion, which the words and emotion of the Christian betrayed; but from his prayer, and the exhortations he addressed to her, she understood, that she had been the principal object of his visiting Cashmire, and that her happiness, temporal and eternal, was the subject of his ardent hopes and eloquent supplications.

This conviction sunk deep into her sensible and grateful heart, which was formed for the exercise of all those feelings which raise and purify humanity; and it softened, without conquering, the profound and firm-rooted prejudices of her mind; and when the Monk arose, she seated herself on a shelving bank, and motioned to him to place himself beside her. He obeyed, and a short pause ensued, which the eloquent and fixed looks of the Indian alone filled up; at last, she said, in accent of emotion, 'Christian, thou hast named me an idolatress; what means that term, which must sure be evil, since, when thou speakest it, methinks thou dost almost seem to shudder.'

'I call thee idolatress,' he returned, 'because, even now, thou didst offer to the sun that worship, which belongs alone to Him who said, "Let there be light; and there was light."' – 'I adore the sun,' said Luxima, with enthusiasm, 'as the great visible luminary; the emblem of that incomparably greater Light, which can alone illumine our souls.' – 'Ah!' he replied, 'at least encourage this first principle of true faith, this pure idea of an essential Cause, this sentiment of the existence of a God, which is the sole idea innate to the mind of man.' – 'I would adore Him in his works,' replied the Priestess; 'but when I would contemplate him in his essence, I am dazzled; I am overwhelmed; my soul shrinks back, affrighted at its own presumption. I feel only the mighty interval which separates us from the Deity; overpowered, I sink to the earth, abashed and humbled in my conscious insignificance.'

'Such,' said the Missionary, 'are the timid feelings of a soul, struggling with error, and lost in darkness. It is by the operation of divine grace only, that we are enabled to contemplate the Creator in himself; it is by becoming a Christian that that divine grace only can be obtained!'

Luxima shuddered as he spoke. 'No,' she said; 'the feeling which would prompt me to meet the presence of my Creator; to image his nature to my mind; to form a distinct idea of his being, power, and attributes, would overpower me with fear and with confusion.'

As she spoke, a religious awe seemed to take possession of her soul. She trembled; her countenance was agitated; and she repeated rapidly the creed of the faith she professed, prostrating herself on the earth, in sign of the profound submission and humility of her heart. The Missionary was touched by a devotion so pure and so ardent; and, when she had ceased to pray, he would have raised her from the earth; but, warm in all the revived feelings of her religion, her prejudices rekindled with her zeal; she shrunk from an assistance she would have now deemed it sacrilegious to accept, and, with a crimson blush,[a] she haughtily exclaimed, 'As the shadow of the pariah[98] defiles the bosom of the stream over which it hangs its gloom, so is the descendant of Brahma profaned by the touch of one who is neither of the same cast nor of the same sex.'

The Missionary stood confused and overwhelmed by sentiments so incongruous, and by principles so discordant, as those which seemed to blend and to unite themselves in the character and mind of this extraordinary enthusiast. At one moment, the purest adoration of the Supreme Being, and the most sublime conceptions of his attributes, betrayed themselves in her eloquent words; in the next, she appeared wholly involved in the wildest superstitions of her idolatrous nation. Now she hung upon his words with an obvious delight, which seemed mingled with conviction; and now she shrunk from his approach, as if he belonged to some species condemned of Heaven. To argue with her was impossible; for there was an incoherence in her ideas, which was not to be reconciled, or replied to. To listen to her was dangerous; for the eloquence of genius and feeling, and the peculiar tenets of her sect, gave a force to her errors, and a charm to her look, which weakened even the zeal of conversion in the priest, in proportion as it excited the admiration of the man.[b] Determined, therefore, no longer to confide in himself, nor to trust to human influence on a soul so bewildered, so deep in error, the Missionary drew from his bosom the scriptural volume, translated into the dialect of the country, and, presenting it to her, said, 'Daughter, thou seest before thee a man, who has subdued the passions incidental to his nature; a man, who has trampled beneath his feet the joys of youth, of rank, of wealth; who has abandoned his country and his friends, his ease and his pleasure, and crossed perilous seas, and visited distant regions, and endured pain, and vanquished obstacles, that others might share with him that bright futurity, reserved for those who believe, and follow the divine precepts which this sacred volume contains. Judge, then, of its purity and influence, by the sacrifices it enables man to make. Take it; and may Heaven pour into thy heart its celestial grace, that, as thou readest, thou mayst edify and believe!'

Luxima took the book, gazing silently on him who presented it. His countenance, the tone of his voice, seemed no less to affect her senses, than the solemnity of his address to impress and touch her mind. The Missionary moved slowly away; he had restored his mind to its wonted holy calm; he wished not again to encounter the eyes, or listen to the accents of the Indian. If she were not influenced by the inspired writings he had put into her hand, 'neither would she by one who should descend from heaven.'

He proceeded on, nor glanced one look behind him; and, though he heard a light foot-fall near him, yet his eyes were still fixed upon his rosary. At last a sweet and low voice pronounced the name of 'Father!' The tender epithet sunk to his heart: he paused, and Luxima stood beside him. He turned his eyes on her for a moment, but suddenly withdrawing them, he fastened their glances on the earth.[a] 'Daughter,' he said, 'what wouldst thou?' – 'Thy forgiveness!' she replied timidly: 'I shrunk from thy approach, and therefore I fear to have offended thee; for haply the women of thy nation offend not their gods, when men of other casts approach them, and they forbid it not.'

'The God whom they adore,' he said, 'judges not by the act alone, but by the motive. The pure in heart commit no evil deeds; and, perhaps, there are women, even of thy nation, daughter, who would deem the presence of a Christian minister no profanation to their purity.'

'But I,' she returned, with majesty, 'I am a sacerdotal woman! a consecrated vestal, and a guarded Priestess! And know, Christian, that the life of a vestal should resemble the snow-buds of the ipomea, when, hid in their virgin calix, the sun's ray has never kissed their leaves. Yet, lest thou part from me in anger, accept this sacrifice.'

As she spoke, she averted her eyes. A deep blush coloured her cheek; and, trembling between an habitual prejudice and a natural feeling, she extended to the Missionary hands of a pure and exquisite beauty, which never before had known a human pressure. The Missionary took them in silence. He believed that the rapid pulsation of his heart arose from the triumphant feeling excited by the conquest of a fatal prejudice; but when he recollected also, that this was the first time the hands of a woman were ever folded in his own, he started, and suddenly dropt them; while Luxima, animated by a devotional fervour, clasped them on her bosom, and said, in a low and tender voice, 'Father, thou who art thyself pure, and holy as a Brahmin's thought, pray for me to thy gods; I will pray for thee to mine!' Then turning her eyes for a moment on him, she pronounced the Indian salaam, and, with a soft sigh and pensive look, moved slowly away.

The Missionary pursued her with his glance, until the thickening shade of a group of mangoostan-trees concealed her from his view. Her sigh seemed still to breathe on his ear, with a deathless echo: at last, he[b] abruptly started, and walked rapidly away, as if, in leaving a spot where all breathed of her, he should leave the idea of her beauty and her softness behind him. He endeavoured to form an abstract idea of her character, independent of her person;[99] to consider the mind distinct from the woman;[c] to remember only the prejudice he had vanquished, and not the hands he had touched; but still he felt them in his own, soft and trembling; and still he sought[d] to lose, in the subject of his mission, the object of his imagination. He endeavoured to banish her look and her sigh from his memory; and to recall the last short, but extraordinary conversation he had held with her.[e] He perceived that a pure system of natural religion was innate in her sublime and contemplative mind; but the images which personified the attributes of Deity, in her national faith, had powerfully fastened on her ardent imagination, and blended their influence with all the habits, the feelings, and the expressions of her life. The splendid mythology of the Brahminical religion was eminently calculated to seduce a fancy so warm; and the tenets of her sect, to harmonize with the tenderness of a heart so sensible. But a life so innocent as that she led, and a mind so pure as that she possessed, rendered her equally capable to feel and to cherish that abstract and awful sense of a First Cause, without which all religion must be cold and baseless.

This consciousness of a predisposition to truth on her part, with the daily conquest of those prejudices which might prevent its promulgation on his, gave new vigour to his hopes, and, in the anticipation of so illustrious a convert, he already found the sacrifices and labours of his enterprise repaid.[a]

THE END OF VOL. I.

THE

MISSIONARY:

AN

INDIAN TALE.

_____

BY

MISS OWENSON.

_____

WITH A PORTRAIT OF THE AUTHOR.

=====

IN THREE VOLUMES.

=====

VOL. II.

================

LONDON:
PRINTED FOR J. J. STOCKDALE,
NO. 41, PALL MALL.
1811.

The Missionary.
Volume 2.

CHAPTER VIII.

IT was the season of visitation of the Guru of Cashmire to his granddaughter. The Missionary beheld him with his train approach her abode of peace, and felt the necessity of absenting himself from the consecrated grove, where he might risk a discovery of his intentions unfavourable to their success. He knew that the conversion of the Brachmachira was only to be effected by the frequent habit of seeing and conversing with her, and that a discovery of their interviews would be equally fatal to both. Yet he submitted to the necessity which separated them, with an impatience, new to a mind, whose firm tenour was, hitherto, equal to stand the shock of the severest disappointment. Still did his steps involuntarily bend to the skirts of the grove, and still did he return sad, without any immediate cause of sorrow, and disappointed, without any previous expectation. To contemplate the frailty, to witness the errors of the species to which we belong, is to mortify that self-love, which is inherent in our natures; yet to be dissatisfied with others, is to be convinced of our own superiority. It is to triumph, while we condemn – it is to pity, while we sympathize. But, when we become dissatisfied with ourselves; when a proud consciousness of former strength unites itself with a sense of existing weakness; when the heart has no feeling to turn to for solace; when the mind has no principle to resort to for support; when suffering is unalleviated by self-esteem, and no feeling of internal approbation soothes the irritation of the discontented spirit; then all is hopeless, cold, and gloomy, and misery becomes aggravated by the necessity which our pride dictates, of concealing it almost from ourselves.[a] Days listlessly passed, duties neglected, energies subdued, zeal weakened; these were circumstances in the life of the apostolic Nuncio, whose effects he rather felt than understood. He was stunned by the revolution which had taken place in his mind and feeling, by the novelty of the images which occupied his fancy, by the association of ideas which linked themselves in his mind.[b] He would not submit to the analysis of his feelings, and he was determined to conquer, without understanding their nature or tendency. Entombed and chained within the most remote depths of his heart, he was deaf to their murmurs, and resisted their pleadings, with all the despotism of a great and lofty mind, created equally to command others and itself.[a] With the dawn, therefore, of the morning, he issued from his cave, intending to proceed to Sirinagur, determined no longer to confine his views to the conversion of the solitary infidel;[b] but to change, at once, the scene and object, which had lately engrossed all the powers of his being, and to bestow upon a multitude, those sacred exertions, which he had, of late, wholly confined to an individual.

His route to Sirinagur lay near the dwelling of the Priestess. He perceived, at a considerable distance, the train of the Guru returning to his college; Luxima, therefore, was again mistress of her own delicious solitude. The impulse of the man was to return to the grotto, but the decision of the Priest was to proceed, to effect his original intention. As he advanced, the glittering shafts of Luxima's verandahs met his eye, and he abruptly found himself under the cannella-alba tree, beneath whose shade he had last beheld her. He paused, as he believed, to contemplate its luxuriancy and its beauty, which had before escaped his observation. He admired its majestic height, crowned by branches, which drooped with their own abundance, and hung in fantastic wreaths of green and brilliant foliage, mingling with their verdure, blossoms of purple and scarlet, and berries bright and richly clustered.[c] But an admiration so coldly directed, was succeeded by a feeling of amazement and delight, when he observed the date of the day of his last interview with Luxima carved on its bark; when he observed, hanging near it, a wreath of the may-hya, whose snowy blossoms breathe no fragrance, and to which an oly-leaf was attached, bearing the following inscription from the Persian of Saddi:[1] 'The rose withers, when she no longer hears the song of the nightingale.'

The lovely elegance of mind, which thus so delicately conveyed its secret feeling, received a tribute, which the votarist trembled as he presented; and pure and holy lips, which had hitherto only pressed the saintly shrine, or consecrated relic, now sealed a kiss, no longer cold, upon an object devotion had not sanctified. But the chill hand of religion checked the human feeling as it rose; and the blood ran coldly back to the heart, from which, a moment before, it had been impelled, with a force and violence he shuddered to recollect.

Suddenly assuming a look of severity, as if even to awe, or to deceive himself, he[d] hurried on, nor once turned his eye towards the sunny heights which Luxima's pavilion crowned. He now proceeded through the rocky defile, which formed the mouth of the valley, and advanced into an avenue, which extended for a league, and led to various towns, and different pagodas. This avenue, grand and extensive as it was, was yet composed of a single tree; but it was the banyan-tree,[2] the mighty monarch of Eastern forests; at once the most stupendous and most beautiful production of the vegetable world. The symbol of eternity, from its perpetual verdure and perpetual spring, independent of revolving seasons, and defying the decay of time, it stands alone and bold, reproducing its own existence, and multiplying its own form, fresh and unfaded amidst the endless generation it propagates; while every branch, as emulous of the parent great-ness, throws out its fibrous roots, and, fastening in the earth, becomes independent, without being disunited from the ancient and original stem. Thus, in various directions, proceeds the living arcade, whose great and splendid order the Architect of the universe himself designed; while above the leafy canopy descend festoons of sprays and fibres, which, progressively maturing, branch off in lighter arches, extending the growing fabric from season to season, and sup-plying, at once, shade, fruit, and odour, sometimes to mighty legions, encamped beneath its arms; sometimes to pilgrim troops, who make its shade the temple of their worship, and celebrate, beneath its gigantic foliage, their holy festivals and mystic rites. This tree, which belongs alone to those mighty regions, where God created man, and man beheld his Creator, excited a powerful emotion in the bosom of the Missionary as he gazed on it.

It was through the arcades of the wondrous banyan, that a scene finely appro-priate struck his view – an Eastern armament in motion; descending the brow of one of the majestic mountains of Sirinagur: the arms of the troops glittering to the sun-beam, flashed like lightning through the dark shade of the intervening woods, while, in their approach, were more visibly seen, elephants surmounted with towers; camels, bearing on their arched necks the gaudy trappings of war; the crescent of Mahomet beaming on the standard of the Mogul legions; and bright spears, and feathery arrows, distinguishing the corps of Hindu native troops; the van breaking from the line to guard the passes, and detachments hanging back in the rear to protect the equipage; while the main body, as if by an electric impulse,[a] halted, as it gradually reached the valley where it was to encamp. This spectacle, so grand, so new, and so imposing, struck on the gov-erning faculty of the Missionary's character – his strong and powerful imagination.[b] He approached with rapid steps the spot where the troops had halted; he observed the commander-in-chief descend from a Tartar horse; he was distinguished by the imperial turban of the Mogul princes, but still more by the youthful majesty of his look, and by the velocity of his movements. Darting from rank to rank, he appeared like a flashing beam of light, while his deep voice, as it pronounced the word of command, was re-echoed from hill to hill with endless vibration. Already a camp arose, as if by magic, among the luxuri-ant shrubs of the glen. The white flags of the royal pavilion waved over a cascade of living water, and tents of snowy whiteness, in various lines, intersected each other amidst the rich shades of the mango and cocoa-tree; the thirsty elephants, divested of their ponderous loads, steeped their trunks in the fountains; and the weary camel reposed his limbs on banks of odorous grasses. All now breathed shade, refreshment, and repose, after heat, fatigue, and action. Faquirs, and pil-grims, and jugglers, and dancers, were seen mingling among the disarmed troops; and the roll of drums, the tinkling of bells, the hum of men, and noise of cattle, with the deep tone of the Tublea,[3] and the shrill blast of the war-horn, bestowed appropriate sounds upon the magic scene. As the Missionary gazed on the animated spectacle, a straggler from the camp approached to gather fruit from the tree under which he stood, and the Missionary inquired if the troops he beheld were those of Aurengzebe? 'No,' replied the soldier; 'we do not fight under the banners of an usurper, and a fratricide; we are the troops of his eldest brother, and rightful sovereign, Daara, whom we are going to join at Lahore, led on by his gallant son, the 'lion of war,' Solyman Sheko. Harassed by fatigue, and worn out by want and heat, after crossing the wild and savage mountains of Sirinagur, Solyman has obtained the protection of the Rajah of Cashmire, who permits him to encamp his troops in yonder glen, until he receives intelligence from the Emperor, his father, whose fate is at present doubtful.'*

The soldier, having then filled his turban with fruit, returned to his camp.

He who truly loves, will still seek, or find, a reference, in every object, to the state and nature of his own feelings; and that the fate of a mighty empire should be connected with the secret emotions of a solitary heart, and that 'the pomp and circumstance of war'[5] should associate itself with the hopes and fears, with the happiness and misery of a religious recluse living in remote wilds, devoted to the service of Heaven, and lost to all the passions of the world, was an event at once incredible – and true!

A new sense of suffering, a new feeling of anxiety, had seized the Missionary, when he understood the gallant son of Daara, the idol of the empire, had come to fix himself in the vicinage of the consecrated groves of the Cashmirian Priest-ess. He knew that, in India, the person of a woman was deemed so sacred, that, even in all the tumult of warfare, the sex was equally respected by the conqueror and the conquered; but he also knew[a] in what extraordinary estimation the beauty of the Cashmirian women was held by the Mogul princes; and though Luxima was guarded equally by her sacred character and holy vows, yet Soly-man was a hero and a prince! and the fame of her charms might meet his ear, and the lonely solitude of her residence lure his steps. This idea grew so power-fully on his imagination, that he already believed some rude straggler from the camp might have violated, by his presence, the consecrated groves of her devo-tion, and, unable to dismiss the thought, he hurried back, forgetful of his intention to visit Sirinagur, and believing that his presence only could afford safeguard and protection to her, who, but a short time back, shrunk in horror from his approach. So slow and thoughtful had been his movements, and so long had he suffered himself to be attracted by a spectacle so novel as the one he had lately contemplated, that, notwithstanding[b] the rapidity of his return, it was evening when he reached the sacred grove; he advanced within view of the verandah, he darted like lightning through every alley or deep-entangled glen; but no unhallowed footstep disturbed the silence, which was only animated by the sweet, wild chirp of the mayana; no human form, save his own, peopled the lovely solitude; all breathed of peace, and of repose.[c] In the clear blue vault of

---

* The new Emperor Aurengzebe[4] had scarcely mounted his throne near Delhi, when he was alarmed with intelligence of the march of Solyman Sheko, by the skirts of the northern mountains, to join his father, Daara, at Lahore. – DOW, 286.

heaven the moon had risen with a bright and radiant lustre, known only in those pure regions, where clouds are deemed phenomena. The Missionary paused for a moment to gaze on Luxima's verandah, and thought that, haply, even then, with that strange mixture of natural faith and idolatrous superstition, which distinguished the character of her devotion, she was worshipping, at the shrine of Camdeo, in the almost inspired language of religious sublimity. This thought disturbed him much; and he asked himself what sacrifice he would not make, to behold that pure but wandering soul, imbued with the spirit of Christian truth; but what sacrifice on earth was reserved for him to make, who had no earthly enjoyment to relinquish? 'Yes,' he exclaimed, 'there is yet one: to relinquish, for ever, all communion with Luxima!' As this thought escaped his mind, he shuddered: had she then become so necessary to his existence,[a] that to relinquish her society, would be deemed a sacrifice? He dismissed the terrific idea, and hurried from a place where all breathed of[b] her, whom he endeavoured to banish from his recollection. As he approached his cave, he was struck by the singular spectacle it exhibited: a fracture in the central part of the roof admitted the light of the moon, which rose immediately above it; and its cloudless rays, concentrated as to a focus, within the narrow limits of the grotto, shone with a dazzling lustre, which was increased and reflected by the pendent spars, and surrounding congelations; while a fine relief was afforded by the more remote cavities of the grotto, and the deep shadow of the œcynum, whose dusky flowers and mourning leaves drooped round its entrance. But it was on the altar, from its peculiar position, that the beams fell with brightest lustre; and the Missionary, as he approached, thought that he beheld on its rude steps, a vision brighter than his holiest trance had e'er been blessed with; for nothing human ever looked so fair, so motionless, or so seraphic. His eye was dazzled; his imagination was bewildered; he[c] invoked his patron saint, and crossed himself; he approached, and gazed, and yet he doubted; but it was no spirit of an higher sphere; no bright creation of religious ecstacy: – it was Luxima! it was the pagan! seated on the steps of the Christian altar; her brow shaded by her veil; her hands clasped upon the Bible which lay open on her knee, and a faint glory playing round her head, reflected from the golden crucifix suspended above it. She slept; but yet so young was her repose, so much it seemed the stealing dawn of doubtful slumber, that her humid eyes still glistened beneath the deep shadow of her scarce-closed lashes: the hue of light which fell upon her features, was blue and faint; and the air diffused around her figure, harmonized with the soft and solemn character of the moonlight cave. The Monk stood gazing, every sense bound up in one; his soul was in his glance, and his look was such as beams in the eye when it snatches its last look from the object dearest to the doting heart, till an involuntary sigh, as it burst from his lips, chased by its echo, the soft and stealing sleep of Luxima. She started, and looked round her, as if almost doubtful of her identity. She beheld the Missionary standing near her, and arose in confusion, yet with a confusion tinctured by[d] pleasurable surprise.

'Luxima!' he exclaimed, in a voice full of softness, and for the first time addressing her by her name. 'Father!' she timidly returned, casting down her eyes; then, after a short but touching[a] pause, she added, 'Thou wonderest much to see me here, at such an hour as this!'

'Much,' he returned: 'but, dearest daughter, seeing thee as I have seen thee, I rejoice much more.'

'Many days,' she said, in a low voice, 'many days have fled since I beheld thee; and I prophesied, from the vision of my last night's dream, that thy wound would gangrene, were it not speedily touched by the three sacrificial threads of a Brahmin; therefore came I hither to seek thee, and brought with me thy Christian Shaster, but I found thee not; thinking thou wast performing poojah,[6] near some sacred tank, I sat me down upon thy altar steps, to wait thy coming, and to read thy Shaster; till weariness, the darkness, and the silence of the place, stole upon my senses, the doubtful slumber in which thou didst find me wrapt.'

'And dost thou regret,' said the Missionary, with a pensive smile, 'that the spirit of thy prophecy is false? Or dost thou rejoice, that my wound, which awakened thy anxiety, is healed?' Luxima made no reply – the feeling of the woman, and the pride of the Prophetess, seemed to struggle in her bosom; yet a smile from lips, which on *her* had never smiled before, seemed to excite some emotion in her countenance. And[b] after a short pause, she arose, and presenting him the Scriptures, said, 'Christian, take back thy Shaster, for it should belong to thee alone. 'Tis a wondrous book! and full of holy love; worthy to be ranked with the sacred *Veidam*,[7] which the great Spirit presented to Brahma to promote the happiness and wisdom of his creatures.' The Missionary had not yet recovered from the confusion into which the unexpected appearance of Luxima, in his groto, had thrown him; he was, therefore, but ill prepared to address her on a subject so awfully interesting, as that to which her simple, but sacrilegious commentary, led. He stood, for a moment, confounded; but, observing that Luxima was about to depart, he said, 'Thou camest hither to seek and to do me a kindness, and yet my presence banishes thee: at least, suffer me to give thee my protection on thy return.' As he spoke, they left the grotto together; and, after a long silence, during which, both seemed engaged with their own thoughts, the Missionary said, 'Thou hast observed truly, that the inspired work I have put into thy hands is full of holy love; for the Christian doctrine is the doctrine of the heart, and, true to all its purest feelings, is full of that tender-loving mercy, which blends and unites the various selfish interests of mankind, in one great sentiment of brotherly affection and religious love!'

'Such,' said Luxima, with enthusiasm, 'is that doctrine of mystic love, by which our true religion unites its followers to each other, and to the Source of all good; for we cannot cling to the hope of infinite felicity, without rejoicing in the first daughter of love to God, which is charity towards man. Even here,' she continued, raising her eyes in transport, 'in a dark forlorn state of separation from our beloved, we live solely in him, in contemplating the moment when we shall be reunited to him in endless beatitude!'

'Luxima! Luxima!' exclaimed the Missionary, with emotion, 'this rhapsody, glowing and tender as it is, is not the language of religion, but the eloquence of an ardent enthusiasm; it bears not the pure and sacred stamp of holy truth, but the gloss and colouring of human feeling. O my daughter! true religion, pure and simple as it is, is yet awful and sublime – to be approached with fear and trembling, and to be cultivated, not in fanciful and tender intimacy, but in spirit and in truth; by sacrifices of the earthly passions, and the human feeling;[a] by tears which sue for mercy, and by sufferings which obtain it.' As he spoke, his voice rose; his agitation increased. Luxima looked timidly in his eyes, and sighed profoundly: the severity of his manner awed her gentle nature; the rigid doctrines he preached, subdued her enthusiasm. She was silent: and the Monk, touched by her softness and trembling, lest, in scaring her imagination or wounding her feelings, he might counteract the effects he had already, and with such difficulty, produced; or, by personally estranging her from himself, loosen those fragile ties which were slowly drawing her to Heaven; he addressed her in a softened and a tender voice: 'Luxima, forgive me! if to thy gentle nature, the manners of a man, unused to any intercourse with thy sex, and wholly devoted to the cause for which he sacrifices every selfish feeling; if, my daughter, I say, they appear cold, rigid, and severe; judge not of the *motive*, by the *manner*; nor think that aught, but the most powerful interest in thy temporal and eternal welfare, could move him to a zeal so ardent, as he has now betrayed. Forgive him, then, who, to recall thy wandering mind to truth, would risk a thousand lives. Forgive him, whose thoughts, and hopes, and views, are now, all, all engrossed by thee; who makes no prayer to Heaven, which calls not blessing on thy head; whose life is scarcely more than one long thought of Luxima!' The Missionary stopt, abruptly: never had his zeal for conversion led him before to such excess of enthusiasm, as that he now betrayed; while Luxima, touched and animated by a display of tender and ardent feeling, so sympathetic to her own, exclaimed, with softness and with energy,[b] 'O father, thus I also feel towards thee; and yet, to see thee prostrate at the shrine of Brahma, *I* would not see thee changed from what thou art – for thou belongest to thy sublime and pure religion; and thy religion to thee, who art thyself so noble and so true, that, much as I do stand in awe of thee, yet more do I delight to hear, and to behold thee, than any earthly good beside!'

The Missionary pressed his hand to his forehead as she spoke, and drew his cowl over his face. He returned no answer, to a speech, every word of which had reached his inmost heart. Thoughts of a various nature crossed each other in his mind; and those he endeavoured to suppress, were still more dominant than those he sought to encourage. At last a glimmering light fell from the summit of the mound which was crowned by Luxima's pavilion; and denoted that the moment of separation was near. To conceal from Luxima, that Solyman and his army were encamped in her neighbourhood – and yet to warn her of the danger of wandering alone in the consecrated shades of her dwelling; were points, in his opinion, necessary, but difficult, to reconcile. He, therefore, slightly observed, that, as the scattered troops of Daara were proceeding through Cashmire to Lahore, he would, in future, become the guardian of her wanderings, and hover round her path, at sunset, until the absence of the intruders should banish all apprehension of intrusion. Luxima replied to him only by a sigh half suppressed, and by a look, timid, tender, and doubtful; in which a lingering prejudice, mingled with a growing confidence, and feeling, and opinion, fading into each other, still seemed faintly opposed.[a] She half-extended to him a hand which instinctively recoiled from the touch of his; and when he *almost* pressed it, trembled, and hastily withdrew.

Hilarion, as he wandered back, alone, to his grotto, recalled his last conversation with Luxima; and gave himself up to a train of reflection, new as the feelings by which it was inspired. Hitherto he had considered pleasure and sin as inseparably connected, since, to suffer and to resist, was the natural destiny of man: but the Indian Priestess, so pure, though mistaken in her piety; so innocent, and yet so pleasurable in her life; so wholly devoted to Heaven, yet so enjoying upon earth, convinced[b] him that his doctrine was too exclusive; and that there were, in this world, sources of blameless pleasure, which it were, perhaps, more culpable to neglect than to embrace.[c]

'It is impious,' he said, 'to suppose that God created man to taste bitterness only; it is also folly; since, formed as we are, the existence of evil presupposes that of good: for the suffering we endure is but the loss of happiness we have enjoyed, or the privation of that we sigh for: and, though the pride of human virtue may resist the conviction, yet the energy of intellect, the fortitude of virtue, or the zeal of faith, can have no value in our eyes, but as they lead to the happiness of others, or to our own. The object, even of religion itself, points out to us, a good to be attained, and an evil to be avoided; it prescribes to us as the end of our actions, eternal felicity; nor can a rational being be supposed to act voluntarily, but with a view to his own immediate or distant happiness. That good can indeed alone be termed happiness, which is the most lasting, the most pure; and is not that "the good which faith preferreth?"' At this conclusion he sighed profoundly, and added, 'Providence has indeed also placed within our reach, many lesser intermediate enjoyments, and endowed us with strong and almost indestructible propensities to obtain them; but are they intended as objects of our pursuit and acquirement, or as tests by which our imperfect and frail natures are to be tried, purified, and strengthened? Alas! it is instinct to desire; it is reason to *resist!* The struggle is sometimes too much for the imperfection of humanity. Man, to be greatly good, must be supremely miserable; man, to secure his future happiness, must sustain his existing evil; and, to enjoy the felicity of the world to come, he must trample beneath his feet the pleasures of that which is.' It was thus that his new mode of feeling was still opposed by his ancient habit of thinking; and that a mind, struggling between a natural bias and a religious principle of resistance, between a passionate sentiment and an habitual self-command, became a scene of conflict and agitation. His restless days passed slowly away, in endless cogitations, equally unproductive of any

influence upon his feelings or his life. But when evening came, in all the mildness of her softened glories, peace and joy came with her; for then the form of
his Neophyte rose upon his view: her smile of languid pleasure met his eye, her
accent of tender softness sighed upon his ear: sometimes moving beside him,
sometimes seated at his feet – he spoke, and she listened – he looked on her, and
she believed: while he trembled from a twofold cause – to observe, that her mind
seemed more engaged with the object who spoke, than with the subject dis-
cussed; and that she too frequently appeared to attend to the doctrine, for the
sake of him only who preached it. But if in one hour her pure soul expanded to
the reception of truth; in the next, it gave up its faculties to a superstition the
most idolatrous: if now she pressed to her vestal lips the consecrated beads of
the Christian rosary – again she knelt at the shrine of her tutelar idol: when her
spiritual guide, affecting a severity foreign to his feelings, reproved the incon-
sistency of her principles, exposed the folly and incongruity of a faith so
vacillating, and urged her openly to embrace, and publicly to profess the Christian doctrine, she fell at his feet – she trembled – she wept.[a] The feelings of the
woman, and the prejudices of the idolatress, equally at variance in her tender
and erring mind; fearing equally to banish from her sight the preacher, or to
embrace the tenets he proposed to her belief; she said, 'It were better to die, than
to live under the curse of my nation; it were better to suffer the tortures of
Narekah,[*] than on earth to *lose cast*, and become a wretched Chancalas!'[b8] As she
pronounced these words, so dreadful to an Indian ear, her whole frame became
convulsed and agitated. And the Missionary, endeavouring to sooth the emotions he had excited, sought only to recall that mild and melting loveliness of
look and air, his admonitions had chased away, or his severity discomposed;
while, frequently, to vary the tone of their intercourse, and to give it a home-felt
attraction in the eyes of his Neophyte, he led her to speak of the domestic circumstances of her life, of the poetical mysteries of her religion, and the singular
usages and manners of her nation. It was in such moments as these, that the
native genius of her ardent character betrayed itself; and that she poured on his
listening ear, that tender strain of feeling, or impassioned eloquence, which,
brightened with all the sublimity of Eastern style, was characterized by all that
fluent softness, and spirited delicacy, which belongs to woman, in whatever
region she exist, when animated by the desire of pleasing *him*, the object of her
preference. 'And while looks intervened, or smiles,'[9] the pleasure which these
interesting conversations conferred on a mind so new to such enjoyments, was
secretly and[c] unconsciously cherished by the Missionary, and obviously
betrayed, by the soft tranquillity and increasing languor of his manner; by the
long and ardent gaze of his fixed eyes; by the low-drawn sigh, which so often lingered on the top of his breath; and by all those traits of pleasurable sensation,
which spoke a man, in whose strong mind, rigid principles, and tranquil heart,
human feeling, even under the pure and sacred veil of religion, was making an

* The Brahminical hell.

67

unconscious and insidious inroad. Confirmed[a] by the opinion of others, and by his own experience, into a belief of his infallibility, he dared not even to *suspect* himself: yet there were moments when a look of ineffable tenderness, a ringlet wafted by the wind over his cheek, or eyes drawn in sudden confusion from his face, awakened him from his illusionary dream – and then he flew to prayers and penance, for the indulgence of feelings, which had not yet stained his spotless life, by any thought or deed of evil; and, though the sudden consciousness sometimes struck him, that temptation only was the test of virtue, and that nature could not be said to be subdued, till she had been tried – yet he seldom suffered himself to analyze feelings, which perhaps would have ceased to exist, had they been perfectly understood. It was thus, the innate purity of the mind betrayed the unconscious sensibility of the heart, while the passions became so intimately incorporated with the spirit, as to leave their influence and agency almost equal.[b] Frequently seeking, in the sophistry of the heart, an excuse for its weakness, he said, 'It is Heaven which has implanted in our nature the seeds of all affection, and the love we bear to an individual is but a modification of that sentiment we are commanded to cherish for the species; and surely that love must be pure, which we cherish, without the wish or hope of gathering any fruit from its existence, but that of the pleasure of loving: the disinterestedness of a Christian may go thus far, but can go no further; the purest of all canonized spirits[*] has said, "The wicked are miserable, because they are incapable of loving. Love, therefore, is solely referable to virtue; it is by the corruption of passion that it ceases to be love. May we then continue to love, that we may continue to be guiltless!"'[11]

---

* Saint Catherine de Genes.[10]

CHAPTER IX.

Peace had fled the breast of the man of God! It had deserted him in wilds, which the tumults of society had not reached; it had abandoned him in shades, where the ravages of passion were unknown; and left him exposed to affliction and remorse, in scenes, whose tranquil loveliness resembled that heaven his faith had promised to his hope. He had brought with him into deserts, the virtues and the prejudices which belong to social life, in a certain stage of its progress; and in deserts, Nature, reclaiming her rights, unopposed by the immediate influence of the world, now taught him to feel her power, through the medium of the most omnipotent of her passions. Hitherto, forming his principles and regulating his feelings, by an artificial standard of excellence, which admitted of no application to the actual relations of life; governed by doctrines, whose fundamental tenets militated against the intentions of Providence, by doctrines, which created a fatal distinction between the species, substituted a passive submission for an active exercise of reason, and replaced a positive, with an ideal virtue – he resembled the enthusiast of experimental philosophy,[12] who shuts out the light and breath of heaven, to inhale an artificial atmosphere, and to enjoy an ideal existence.

But Nature had now breathed upon his feelings her vivifying spirit: and as some pleasurable and local sensation, which, at first, quivers in the lip, and mantles on the cheek, gradually diffuses itself through the frame, and communicates a vibratory emotion to every nerve and fibre; so the sentiment, which had, at first, imperceptibly stolen on his heart, now mastered and absorbed his life. He now lived in a world of newly connected and newly modified ideas; every sense and every feeling was increased in its power and acuteness – thoughts passed more rapidly through his mind, and he felt himself hurried away by new and powerful emotions, which he sought not to oppose, and yet trembled to indulge. He had not, indeed, relinquished a single principle of his moral feeling – he had not yet vanquished a single prejudice of his monastic education; to feel, was still with him to be weak – to love, a crime – and to resist, perfection; but the doctrines which religion inculcated and habit cherished, the vows which bigotry exacted, and prejudice observed; while they scrupulously guarded the inviolable conduct of the priest, had lost their influence over the passions of the man. And the painful vibration, between the natural feeling and conscientious principle, left him a prey to those internal and harassing conflicts, which rose and increased, in proportion to the respective exercise and action of a passionate impulse, and a rigid sense of duty.

Thus, among the privations of a week, peculiarly holy in his church, and exclusively devoted to religious exercises, he imposed on himself the most difficult of all restraints, that of abstaining from the society of his dangerous Neophyte; but the restless impatience with which he submitted to the severe and voluntary penance, enhanced every pleasure, and exaggerated every enjoyment, he had relinquished. It more sweetly melodized the voice he languished again to hear. It heightened the lustre of those eyes he sighed again to meet; it endeared those innocent attentions which habit had made so necessary to his happiness;[a] and, by rendering the Indian more dangerous to his imagination than to his senses, invested her with that splendid, that touching ideal charm, which love, operating upon genius, in the absence of its object, can alone bestow.

Dearer to his heart, as she became more powerful to his imagination, her idea grew upon his mind with a terrific influence, disputing with Heaven his nightly vigil and daily meditation. It was in vain that he imposed on himself the law not to behold, or to commune with her for six tedious days: his steps, involuntarily faithful to his feelings, still led him against his better reason to those places, in whose fragrant shades she appeared to him a celestial visitant: sometimes he beheld her at a distance at the confluence of the streams, engaged in the idolatrous, but graceful rites of her half-resigned religion – and then he believed himself commanded by duty to fly to her redemption, and to rescue her from the ancient errors into which his absence again had plunged her; till, suddenly distrusting the impulse which led him towards her presence, he fled from the sight of the dangerous Heathen, and almost wished, that infidelity could assume an appearance more appropriate to its own deformity. Sometimes, when the ardour of the meridian sun obliged her to seek the impervious shades of her consecrated grove, he beheld her reclined on flowers, engaged in the perusal of the religious fables of her poetic faith; and then a recollection of a genius which shone bright and luminous even through the errors which clouded its lustre, mingled itself with the actual impression of her beauty; and he believed a communion with a mind so pure, would counteract the influence, while it added to the charm, of a form so lovely.[b]

But when, from the summit of his rocks, when the moonlight silvered their abrupt points, he beheld her, gliding like a pure and disembodied spirit, through the shades of her native paradise, and, with a timid and uncertain step, moving near the woody path which led to his grotto; her countenance and person characterized by the solicitude of anxious tenderness, and the sadness of disappointed hope; then she appeared to him a creature loving as beloved; then he admitted the blessed conviction, that he had inspired another with that feeling, which had given to him a new sense of being; then he was tempted to throw himself at her feet, and to avow the existence of that passion which he now believed, with a mingled emotion of rapture and remorse, was shared and returned by her who had inspired it. Yet still, habits of religious restraint, even more, perhaps, than religion itself, checked the dangerous impulse; and that ardent sentiment which resisted the force of his reason and the influence of his faith, submitted to the dictates of what might be deemed rather his prejudice than his principle. Shuddering and trembling, he fled from her view, and sought, in the recollection of the infidelity of the Brahminical Priestess, a resource against the tenderness and the charms of the lovely woman. But when, at last, this insupportable absence finally and irresistibly 'urged a sweet return;'[13] when the stated exercises of devotion no longer opposed the more active duties of conversion; then love, consecrated by the offices of religion, pursued the object of its secret desire; and, the[a] week of self-denial past, the evening of the seventh day became, to him, the sabbath of the heart. He left the cave of his solitude and his penance, and, with a rapid but unequal step, proceeded towards the fatal stream, on whose flowery shores the Priestess of Brahma still offered up her vesper homage to the luminary, whose fading beam was reflected in the up-turned eyes of its votarist.

As he approached the Priestess and the shrine, his heart throbbed with a feverish wildness unknown to its former sober pulse. Pleasure, enhanced by its recent privation; love, warming as it passed through the medium of an ardent imagination; a consciousness of weakness, cherished by self-distrust; and an apprehension of frailty proportioned to the exaggerated force of the temptation – all mingled a sensation of suffering with the sentiment of pleasure; and the visitation of happiness, to a heart which had of late studiously avoided its enjoyment, resembled that rapid return of health, which is so frequently attended with pain to the exhausted organs; while conscience, awakened by the excess of emotion, dictated a reserve and coldness to the studied manners, to which the ardour of unpractised and impetuous feelings with difficulty submitted. At last, through the branches of a spreading palm-tree, he beheld, at a distance, the object who had thus agitated and disturbed the calmest mind which Heaven's grace had ever visited. She was leaning on the ruins of a Brahminical altar, habited in her sacerdotal vestments, which were rich but fantastic. Her brow was crowned with consecrated flowers; her long dark hair floated on the wind; and she appeared a splendid image of the religion she professed – bright, wild, and illusory; captivating to the senses, fatal to the reason, and powerful and tyrannic to both.[b]

The Missionary paused and gazed – and advanced, and paused again; till, on a nearer approach, he observed that her eager look seemed to pursue some receding object; that her cheek was flushed, and that her veil, which had fallen over her bosom, heaved to its rapid palpitation. Never before had he observed such disorder in her air, such emotion in her countenance, while the abstraction of her mind was so profound, that she perceived not his approach, till he stood before her: then she started as from the involvement of some embarrassing dream; a soft and unrepressed transport beamed in her eyes, which at once expressed joy, surprise, and apprehension;[c] and the changeful hues of her complexion resembled the dissolving tints of an iris, as they melt and mingle into each other, blending their pale and ruby rays till the vivid lustre fades slowly away upon the colourless air.[a] Pale and smiling as one who was at the same time sad and pleased, she extended her hand to the Missionary, and said, in a voice replete with tenderness and emotion, 'My father, thou art then come at last!' While, suddenly starting at the faint rustling of the trees as the wind crept among their leaves, she cast round an anxious and inquiring glance. The Missionary let fall her hand, and, folding his own, he remained silent, and fixed on her a look equally penetrating and melancholy; for the rapture of a re-union so wished for, was now disturbed by doubts, whose object was vague, and embittered by suspicions, whose existence was agony.[b] Luxima, timid and pensive, cast her eyes to the earth, as if unable to support the piercing severity of his gaze; a transient blush mantled on her cheek, and again left it colourless.

'Luxima,' said the Missionary, in emotion, 'we meet not now, as we were wont to meet, hailing each other with the smile of peace.' With eyes which spoke the heart in every glance, and all the precious confidence of innocence and truth,[c] 'I would say,' he continued, looking earnestly on her, 'that, since we parted, something of thy mind's angelic calmness was forfeited, or lost; something of thy bosom's sunshine was shadowed, or o'ercast.'

'But thou art here,' she returned, eagerly, 'and all again is peace and brightness.' The Missionary withdrew his eyes from her blushing and eloquent countenance, and cast them on the earth. Her looks made too dangerous a comment on the words her lips had uttered, which he felt were too delightful, and feared were too evasive; which his heart led him to believe, and his reason to distrust;[d] and, seating himself beside her on the bank where she now reposed, after a silent pause, which the half-breathed sighs of the Indian only interrupted, he said, 'Well! be it so, my daughter; be still the guardian of thy bosom's secret; pure it must be, being thine. I have no right to wrench it from thee. If it be a human feeling, belonging only to mortality, to hopes which this world bounds, or thoughts which this life limits, I, who am not thy temporal, but thy spiritual friend, can have no claim upon thy confidence. Oh, no! believe me, Luxima, that, between thee and me, nothing can now, or ever will, exist, but the sacred cause which first led me to thee.'

This he said with a vehemence but little corresponding to the character he had assumed, and with an air so cold and so severe, that Luxima, timid and afflicted, had no force to reply, and no power to restrain her emotions. Drooping her head on her bosom, she wept. Touched by her unresisting softness, moved by a sadness, his severity had caused, and gazing with secret admiration on the grace and loveliness of her looks and attitude, as she chased away the tears which fell on her bosom, with her long hair, 'Luxima,' he said, in a tone which struggled between his secret emotion, and assumed coldness, 'Luxima, why do you weep? I am not used to see a woman's tears, save when they fall from hearts which penitence, or grief, has touched; but yours, Luxima – they fall in such tender softness: dearest daughter, have I offended you?'

''Tis true,' said Luxima, cheered by the increasing tenderness of his manner, 'thou art so grandly good, so awful in thy excellence, that, little used to wisdom or to virtue so severe, I fear thee most, even when most I—' She paused abruptly, and blushed; then raising her eyes to his, a soft confidence seemed to grow upon their gaze, and, with that fatal smile that so changed the character of her countenance, from the sedate tranquillity of the Priestess to the bashful fondness of the woman, she said, [a] 'Father, with us the divine wisdom is not personified, as cold, severe, and rigid; but as the infant twin of love, floating in gay simplicity in the perfumed dews which fill the crimson buds of young camala-flowers.'*

'Luxima,' he returned, seduced into softness by her tender air,[b] 'if I am in look and word severe, such are my habits; but my heart, dear daughter, at least I fear to thee, is too, too weak; and, when I see thee sad, and am denied thy confidence – ' He paused; and the rainbow-look of Luxima changing as she spoke, she replied: 'I am, indeed,[c] not quite so happy as I have been. Once my lip knew no mystery, my heart no care, my brow no cloud; but, of late, I strive to hide my thoughts even from myself. I oft am sad, and oft regret the glorious death they robbed me of; for, oh! had I expired upon my husband's pyre, in celestial happiness with him I should have enjoyed the bliss of Heaven while fourteen Indras reign.'

The Missionary started as she pronounced this rhapsody; a new pang seized his heart, and made him feel as if the deadly drop, which lurks beneath[d] the adders' fang, had been distilled into a vital artery: for Luxima had loved, since Luxima lamented even that dreadful death itself, which, in her own belief, would have united her eternally to the object for whom her passion still seemed to survive.

'Luxima,' he said coldly, 'till now I never knew you loved; but though you had, a woe so idle and so causeless, as that you cherish for a long-lost object, is sanctioned neither by sentiment nor duty, by reason nor religion.'

'Had he lived,' said Luxima, with simplicity, 'it would then have been no sin to love.'

'Bound to a vestal life,' returned the Missionary, changing colour, 'like me devoted to eternal celibacy, can *you* lament an object who would have loved you with a *human passion*; with such a love as should not even be dreamed of in a vestal's thoughts?'[e]

'He was my husband,' said Luxima, turning away her eyes, and sighing.

'Not by religion's holy law,' replied the Missionary, in a hurried tone of voice; 'for forms idolatrous and wild but mock the sacred name; not by the law of sentiment, for no endearing intercourse of heart and soul blended your affections in one indissoluble union, for ye were almost strangers to each other; he saw thee but in childhood, and not, as now, a woman! – and so lovely!' He paused, and a deep scarlet suffused even his brow.

'He was at least,' said Luxima, with mild firmness, '*my husband* according to the law and the religion of my country.'

* It is thus Brahma is represented in his avatar of divine wisdom.

'But if you have abandoned that religion,' returned the Missionary, 'the ties it formed are broken, and with them should their memory decay.'

'Abandoned it!' repeated Luxima, shuddering, and raising her eyes to heaven. 'O Brahma!!'

'Luxima,' said the Missionary, sternly, 'there is no medium; either thou art a Pagan or a Christian; either I give thee up to thy idols, and behold thee no more, or thou wilt believe and follow me.'

'Then I will believe and follow thee,' she replied quickly, yet trembling as she spoke.

'O Luxima! would I could confide in that promise! for, through thee alone, I count upon the redemption of thy nation.'

'Father,' she returned, 'a miracle like *that*, can only be performed by thee. Look as I have seen thee look – speak[a] as I have heard thee speak; – give to others that new sense of truth, which thou hast given to me: – and then – '

'Luxima,' interrupted the Missionary, in great emotion, 'you are misled, my daughter; misled by the ardour of your gratitude, by an exaggerated sense of powers which belong not to man, but to Heaven, whose agent he is. The power of conversion rests not exclusively with me; in you it might effect more miracles than I have ever manifested.'

Luxima waved her head incredulously. 'Never,' said she, 'shall I become the partner of thy pious labours! and should I even appear as thy proselyte, if I were not looked on with horror, I should at least be considered with indifference.'

'With indifference!' he repeated, throwing his eyes over the perfect loveliness of her form and countenance:[b] 'Luxima, is there on earth a being so divested of all human feeling, as to behold, to hear thee with indifference?'

'Art thou not such a one?' demanded Luxima, with a timid and trembling anxiety of look and voice.

'I, Luxima! – I—' he faltered, and changed colour; then, after a momentary pause, casting down his eyes, he resumed, 'To be divested of all faculty of sense, were it possible, would be a state of organization so fatal and so imperfect, as to leave the being thus formed equally without the wish and without the power of becoming virtuous; for virtue, the purest, the most severe, and, O Luxima! by much the most difficult to attain, is that virtue which consists in the conquest over the impulses of a frail and perverse nature, by religion and by reason. Thinkest thou then, dearest daughter, that it belongs to *my* nature, being man, to live divested of all human feeling, of all human passion; to behold, with perfect insensibility, forms created to delight; to listen with perfect indifference to sounds breathed to enchant; and that when, upon thy cheek, the crimson hues of modesty and pleasure mantle and mix their soft suffusion; when in thy eyes, rays of languid light –[c] Luxima! Luxima!' he continued vehemently, and in confusion, 'I repeat to thee, that there can be no virtue where there is no temptation; no merit, but in resistance; but in an entire subjection, through religion, of those feelings which, by a sweet but dread compulsion, drag us towards perdition. And, oh! if trial be indeed the test of virtue, I at least may hope to find some favour in the sight of Heaven, for my trials have not been few.' As he spoke, his whole frame trembled with uncontrollable emotion, and the paleness of death overspread his face.

Luxima, moved by an agitation in one, who had hitherto appeared to her eyes superior to human feeling, and to human weakness, was touched by an emotion so accordant to the tender softness and ardent sensibility of her own character; and timidly taking his hand, and[a] looking with an half-repressed fondness in his eyes, she said, 'Art thou then also human? Art thou not all-perfect by thy nature? I thought thee one absorbed in views of heaven, resembling the pure spirit of some holy Saneasse, when, having passed the troubled ocean of mortal existence, it reaches the Paradise of Kylausum,[14] and reposes in eternal beatitude, at the foot of *Him* who is clothed with the *fourteen worlds*.'*

The Missionary withdrew his hand, and reposing on it his head,[b] remained for some time lost in thought; at last he said, 'Luxima, have you then among your people such men as you have now described; who, by a perfect abstraction of mind, live divested of all human feeling, and who, walking through life in a state of rigid self-denial, renounce all its enjoyments, from a conviction of their vanity? Can a religion so false as theirs produce an effect so perfect? And can the most powerful sensations, the most tyrannic passions incident to the very constitution of our natures, making an inseparable part of our structure, connected and interwoven with all the powers of existence – can they submit and bend to the influence of *opinion*; to an idea of excellence originating in, and governed by, a fatal and fanatic superstition; but worthy, from its purity and elevation, to be the offspring of that *grace*, which comes alone from Heaven?'

Luxima replied, 'It is written in the Vaides and Shastries,[16] whose light illuminates the earth, that '*the resignation of all pleasure is better than its enjoyment*;' and that he who resists the passions of his nature shall be planted in the world of *daivers*,[17] or pure spirits; there to enjoy eternal bliss. And *one such* person I once knew; who, having abandoned all earthly attachments, and broken all earthly ties, lived remote from man, absorbed in the contemplation of the *Divine Essence:* never had his lip imbibed the refreshing beverage of the delicious *caulor*, or the juice of newly-gathered fruits; never had he inhaled the odour of morning blossoms, nor bathed in the cool wave which smiles to the light of the night-flower-loving god; never had he pillowed his sacred brow with the downy leaves of the *mashucca*,[18] nor pressed the hand of affection, nor listened to the voice of fondness; and his eye, fixed on earth or raised to heaven, still met no objects but such as tended to chasten his thoughts, or to elevate his soul; – till one day a *holy woman*, devoted to the service of her religion, ascended the high hill, where the hermit dwelt in peace. She came, with others, in faith and sanctity, to ask his mediation with Heaven, according to the custom of her nation. The woman departed edified from his presence, for she had communed with him on the subject of the nine great luminaries,[19] which influence all human

---

* Paraubahzah Vushtoo, or First Cause.[15]

events; – but the soul of the hermit pursued her in secret; *he* whose infant hand grasps the lightning's flash,* the god of the flowery bow, had touched the cold, pure thought of the recluse with a beam of his celestial fire: – *he loved*! – but he loved a *vestal priestess*, and therefore was forbidden all hope. The Faquir pined in sadness, and sought to wash away his secret fault in the holiest wave which purifies the erring soul from sin; and the *goddess* of the *eight virgins* received him in her consecrated bosom.† Doubtless he is now one of the *diavers*, the saints, who, by the voluntary sacrifice of mortal life, obtain instant admittance to the heavenly regions.' Luxima sighed as she concluded her little tale.

The Missionary echoed her sigh, and raising a look of sadness to her pensive countenance, he demanded, 'And knew the vestal priestess the secret of the hermit's love?'

'Not until he had passed into the world of spirits; and then a wandering yogi,[20] who had received his last words ere he plunged into the Ganges, brought her, at his desire, a wreath of faded flowers:‡ the red rose of passion was twined with the ocynum, the flower of despondency; and the fragile mayhya, the emblem of mortality, drooped on the camalata, the blossom of heaven. The faded wreath thus told the love and fate of him who wove it.'

'And this fatal priestess, Luxima?' said the Missionary, with an increased emotion, showing there was a nerve in his heart, which vibrated in sympathy to the tale she told. Luxima made no reply to the doubtful interrogatory; and the Missionary, raising his eyes to her face, perceived it crimsoned with blushes, while her tearful eyes were fixed on the earth. He started – grew pale; and, covering his face with his hands, after a long silence, he said, 'Luxima! thy Hermit was a virtuous though a most misguided man; his temptation to error was powerful; the virtue of resistance was his, and the crime of self-destruction was the crime of his dark and inhuman superstition – terrific and fatal superstition! in all its views injurious to society, and pernicious to the moral nature of man, which thus offers a soothing but impious alternative to the human suffering, and the human woe; which thus, between infamy and an almost impossible resistance to a clear and fatal temptation, offers a final resource beyond all which reason can bestow, or time effect; beyond all; save that which religion proffereth; and thus alluring the worn, the weary, and long-enduring life to its own wished-for *immolation*, crowns and conceals the fatal act beneath a host of bright illusions, and offers to the suicide rewards, which should belong to him alone who dares to *live* and *suffer*, who feels and who resists; and who, though impelled by passion, or seduced by sentiment, still restrains the wish, corrects the impulse, and rules and breaks the stubborn feeling nature breathed into his

---

* The Indian Cupid is frequently represented armed with a flash of lightning.

† Gungee, the presiding deity of the Ganges: she has eight vestal attendants, which personify the eight principal rivers in Hindoostan.

‡ Flowers have always been the tasteful medium for the eloquence of Eastern love; like the Peruvian quipas, a wreath, in India, is frequently the record of a life.

soul when it was first quickened, that, by this daily death, he might ensure that life which is eternal. If, Luxima, there lived such a man, thus enduring and thus resisting, would you not give him your applause?'

'I would give him my pity,' said Luxima, raising her hands and eyes in great emotion.

The Missionary replied with a deep sigh, 'You would do well, my daughter; it is pity only he deserves.' Then, after a long pause, he said firmly, 'Luxima, I came hither this evening to commune with thee upon that great subject, which should alone unite us; but the mysterious emotion in which I found thee wrapt, distracted thoughts, which are not yet, I fear, all Heaven's; nor did thy little story, dearest daughter, serve to tranquillize or sooth them; for, in the mirror of another's faults, man, weak and erring, may still expect to see the sad reflection of his own. But now the dews of evening fall heavily, the light declines, and it is time we part; and, O Luxima! so long as we continue thus to meet, thus may we ever part, in the perfect confidence of each other's virtue, and each other's truth.' He arose as he spoke.

Luxima also arose; she moved a few paces, and then paused, and raised her timid eyes to his, with the look of one who languishes to repose some confidence, yet who stands awed by the severity of the elected confidant.

The Missionary, who now studiously avoided those eloquent looks of timid fondness, whose modesty and sensibility so sweetly blended their lovely expressions, withdrew his eyes, and fixed them on the rosary he had taken from his breast, with the abstracted air of one wrapt in holy meditation. Thus they walked on in silence, until they had reached the vicinage of Luxima's habitation. There, as was his custom, the Missionary paused, and Luxima turning to him said, 'Father, wilt thou not bless me, ere we part?' The Missionary extended his pastoral hands above her seraph head; the blessing was registered in his eyes, but he spoke not, for his heart was full. Luxima withdrew, and he stood pursuing, with admiring eyes, her perfect form, as she slowly ascended to her pavilion: then turning away as she disappeared, he sighed convulsively, as one who gives breath to emotion after a long and painful struggle to suppress or to conceal it. His thoughts, unshackled by the presence of her to whom they pointed, now flowed with rapidity and in confusion; sometimes resting on the mysterious emotion he had observed in the countenance and air of the ingenuous Indian; sometimes on the suicide Hermit; and sometimes on himself, on his past life, his former vows, and existing feelings; but these recollections, conjured up to sooth and to confirm, served but to disquiet and to agitate;[a] and thus involved in cogitation, slow and lingering in his step, he involuntarily paused as he reached the bank, whose elastic moss still bore the impression of Luxima's light form. He paused and gazed on the altar of her worship; it was to him as some sad memorial, whose view touches on the spring of painful recollection; and the pang which had shot through his heart, when for a moment he had believed her false as the religion at whose mouldering shrine she stood, again revived its painful sensation, like the memory of some terrific vision, which long leaves its shade of horror upon the awakened mind, when the dream which gave it has long passed away from the imagination. There is no love where there is no cause for solicitude; and the first moment when hope and fear slumber in the perfect consciousness of exclusive and unalienable possession, is perhaps the first moment when the calm of indifference dawns upon the declining ardour of passion. To the eye of philosophy it would have been a curious analysis of the human heart, to have observed the workings of a strong and solitary feeling, in a character unsophisticated and unpractised; to have observed a passion, neither cherished nor opposed by any external object, feeding on its own vitals, and seeking instinctively to maintain its own vivacity, by fancying doubts for which it had no cause, and forming suspicions for which it had no subject. Still in search of some hidden reason for the restless conflicts of his unhappy mind, the Missionary stood musing and gazing on the spot where the mysterious emotion of Luxima had excited that painful, suspicious, and indefinite sentiment, of whose nature and tendency he was himself ignorant. He could fear no rival in that consecrated solitude, which his presence alone violated; but he was afflicted to believe that Luxima could muse, when he was not the subject of her reverie; that Luxima could weep, when he caused not her tears to flow; that Luxima could be moved, touched, agitated, and he not be the sole, the powerful cause of her emotion. It is this exacting, tyrannic, and exclusive principle which forms the generic character of a true and unmixed passion: it is this feeling by which we seek and expect to master and possess the whole existence of the object beloved, which distinguishes a strong, ardent, and overwhelming sentiment, from those faint modifications of the vital feeling, which serve rather to amuse than to occupy life; to interest rather than absorb existence. It is thus that love, operating upon genius, is assisted by the imagination, which creates a thousand collateral causes of hope and fear, of transport and despair; which, in moderate characters, find no existence, and which, at once fatal and delightful, are the unalienable inheritance of natural and exquisite sensibility, of a peculiar delicacy of organization, and of those refined habits of thought and feeling to which it gives birth.[a]

While thus occupied, creating for himself ideal sources of pain and pleasure, the twilight of evening was slowly illumined by the silver rising of a cloudless moon; which threw upon the shining earth the shadow of his lofty figure; it tinged with living light the crystal bosom of the consecrated waters; it scattered its rays upon the motionless foliage of the night-loving sephalica, and found a bright reflection in some object which lay glittering amidst the fragments of the ruined altar. When the heart is deeply involved, every sense allies itself to its feelings, and the eye beholds no object, and the ear receives no sound, which, in their first impression, awakens not the master pulse of emotion. The Missionary saw, in the beaming fragment, some ornament of the sacerdotal vestments of the Brahminical Priestess. Considering it as more consecrated by her touch than by the purposes to which it had been devoted, he stooped, and blushed as he did it, to rescue and preserve it; – but it was no gem sacred to religious ornament; it made no part of the insignia worn by the children of Brahma; it was the *silver crescent* of Islamism; it was the device of the disciples of Mahomet; the ornament worn in the centre of the turban of the Mogul officers; and deeply impressed on its silvery surface, obvious even to a passing glance, and engraven in Arabic characters, was the name of the heroic and imperial Prince Solyman Sheko.[a]

The Missionary saw this, and saw no more; a tension in his brow, a sense of suffocation, as though life were about to submit to annihilation; a pulse feeble and almost still, limbs trembling, and eyes which no longer received the light,[b] left him no other voluntary power than to throw himself on the earth; while the strong previous excitement produced, for a few seconds, a general diminution of the vital action;[c] and he lay as though death had given peace to those feelings which nothing in life could at the moment sooth or assuage. From this temporary suspension of existence he was roused by the sound of horses' feet: he startled; he arose, and sprung forward in that direction whence the sound proceeded: he perceived (himself unseen, amidst the trees) a person on horseback, who, standing in his stirrup, and shading his eyes from the lustre of the moonlight, cast round an anxious and inquiring glance, then approached within the hallowed circle of the Brahminical altar.

The Missionary rushed from his concealment – the paleness of his countenance rendered more livid by the moonlight which fell on it, and by the dark relief of his black cowl and flowing robe. He stood, amidst the ruins of the heathen shrine, resembling the spirit of some departed minister of its idolatrous rites, the terrific guardian of the awful site of ancient superstition. Whatever was the impression of his abrupt and wild appearance, the effect was instantaneous: ere he had uttered a sound, the stranger suddenly disappeared, as if borne on the wings of the wind. The Missionary in vain pursued his flight. After having followed the sounds of the horse's feet, till a deathlike silence hung upon their faded echo, the sole result of his observation was, that the mysterious intruder had fled towards the Mogul camp, which still lay in the plains of Sirinagur; and the sole inference to be drawn from the singular adventure was, that Luxima was beloved by the son of the imperial Daara – that Luxima was false – and that he was most deceived! This conviction fell on him like a thunderbolt. Thoughts of a new and gloomy aspect now rushed on each other, as if they had been accelerated by the bursting of some barrier of the mind, which, till that moment, had retained them in their natural course. He could not comprehend the nature of those frightful sensations which quivered through his frame – that deadly sickness of the soul with which the most dreadful of all human passions first seizes on its victim. His mind's fever infected his whole frame – his head raged – his heart beat strongly; and all the vital motions seemed hurried on, as if their harmony had been suddenly destroyed by some fearful visitation of divine wrath.[d] He threw himself on the dewy earth, and felt something like a horrible enjoyment, in giving himself up, without reservation, to pangs of love betrayed, of faith violated, of a jealousy, whose fury rose in proportion to the loveliness of its object, and to the force and ardour of the character on which it operated.[e] His memory, faithful only to the events which aimed at his peace, gave back to his imagination Luxima in all her bewitching tenderness, in all the seduction of her seeming innocence: he felt the touch of her hand, he met the fondness of her look; his heart kindled at her blush of love, and melted at her voice of passion. He beheld her, bright and fresh, as the rising sun – tender and languid at its setting;[a] but by him these delights of a first and true love were now only remembered to be resigned – these joys,[b] which he had almost purchased with the loss of heaven, could now no longer live for him. Another would gaze upon her look, and meet her caress, and answer to her tenderness; another would send his hopes forth, with the rising and the setting sun: but for him there was no longer a morning, there was no longer an evening! all was the sad gloom of endless night. In a mind, however, such as his, to doubt one moment, was to decide the next – his sole, his solitary,[c] his tyrannic passion, becoming its own retribution, would, he believed, accompany him to the grave; its object he determined to resign for ever. To strengthen him in his intention, he opposed the holy calm, the sacred peace, the heavenly hopes and solemn joys of his past and sinless life, to the sufferings, the conflicts, the conscious self-debasement of his late and present existence. He remembered that he was the minister of Heaven;[d] devoted, by vows the most awful and the most binding, to its cause alone; and that he had come into perilous and distant regions, to preach its truths, not by precept only, but by example, and to substitute, in the land of idolatry, the religion of the Spirit, for that of the senses. He sought pertinaciously to deceive himself, and to mistake the feelings which rose from the pangs of jealousy, for the visitation of conscience, suddenly awakened from its long and deathlike slumber, by the fatal consequences of that intoxicating evil, which had so long entranced and 'steeped it in forgetfulness.'[21] He sought to believe that his guardian angel had not yet abandoned him, and that Heaven itself, by miraculous interposition, had snatched him from an abyss of crime, towards which, an ardent and unguarded zeal for its sacred cause had insensibly seduced him. Struck by the conviction, he prayed fervently, and vowed solemnly; but his prayers and his vows alike partook of the vehemence of those contending passions by which he was moved and[e] agitated. He wept upon the cross he pressed to his lips – but his tears were not all the holy dew of pious contrition; religion became debtor to the passions she opposed, and the ardour of his devotion borrowed its warmth and energy from the overflowing of those human feelings it sought to combat and to destroy. At last his emotions, worn out by their own force and activity, subsided into the torpor of extreme exhaustion. Throwing himself upon the earth, encompassed by those deep shades of darkness which precede the twilight dawn of day, he[f] slept; but his slumber was broken and transient, and the dreams it brought to his disordered imagination were harassing to his spirits as the painful vigil which had preceded them; for the affliction which is deep rooted in the heart, which presses upon the vital spring of self-love, and disturbs the calm of conscientious principle, blasting hope, rousing remorse, and annihilating happiness, sets at defiance the soothing oblivion of sleep.[a] Nature, thus opposed to herself, in vain presents the balmy antidote to the suffering she has inflicted – and the repose she offers, flies from the lids her unregulated feelings have sullied with a tear.

CHAPTER X.

The day arose brightly upon the valley of Cashmire. It came in all the splendid majesty of light, bathing in hues of gold the summits of the Indian Caucasus: it came in all the renovating influence of warmth, raising the blossom the night-breeze had laid low; it shed the dews of heaven upon the towering head of the mighty banyan, and steeped in liquid silver the flowers of the vesanti creeper; pervading, with a genial and delicious power, the most remote recess, the most minute production of nature, and pouring upon the face of the earth, the benef-icent influence of that Being from whose word it proceeded. But the day brought no solace in its dawn, no joy in its course, to him, who, in the scale of creation, came nearest in his nature to the Creator; –[a] it brightened not his thoughts; it revived not his hopes; and, for him, its beams shone, its dews fell, in vain.

The minister of the religion of peace arose from his harassing slumber with an heart heavy and troubled, with a frame chilled and unrefreshed. He arose, agitated by that vague consciousness of misery, which disturbs, without being understood, when the mind, suddenly awakened from the transient suspension of its powers, has not yet regained its full vigour of perception, nor the memory collected and arranged the freshly traced records of some stranger woe, and when the faculty of suffering, alone remains to us in all its original force and activity. Agitated by the tumults of passion, distracted by the suspicions of jeal-ousy, torn by the anguish of remorse, and humbled by the consciousness of weakness, the Missionary now felt the full extent of his progressive and obsti-nate illusion, in the consequences it had already produced; he felt that the heart which once opens itself to the admission of a strong passion, is closed against every other impression, and that objects obtain or lose their influence, only in proportion as they are connected with, or remote from, its interest. Love was now to him what his religion had once been, and the strongest feeling that rules the human heart stood opposed to the most powerful opinion which governs the human mind: – the conflict was terrific, and proportioned in obstinacy and vig-our to the strength of the character in which it was sustained. Knowing no solace in his misery but what arose from the belief that the secret of his weakness was known only to Heaven and to himself, he resolved not to trust its preservation to the issue of chance; but, ere the dreadful passions which shook his soul could realize their fatal influence in crime; ere the fluctuating emotions which degraded his mind could resolve themselves into iniquity; ere he debased the life which sin had not yet polluted, or broke the vows which were revered, even while they were endangered, he determined to fly the scenes of his temptation, and to cling to the cross for his redemption and support. Yet still, with an heart vibrating from the recent convulsion of its most powerful feelings, he remained irresolute even in his resolution.[a] Convinced of the imperious necessity which urged him to leave, for ever, the object of a passion which opposed itself equally to his temporal and to his eternal welfare; to leave for ever, those scenes which had cherished and witnessed its progress; he still doubted whether he should again, and for the last time, behold her, whose falsehood it was his interest to believe, and his misery to suspect. Now governed by conscience and by jealousy; now by tenderness and passion – the alternate victim of feeling and religion, of love and of opinion; he continued (wretched in his indecision) to wander amidst the voluptuous shades of his perilous seclusion; hoping that chance might betray him into the presence of his dangerous and faithless disciple, and vowing premeditatedly to avoid her, or to behold her only to upbraid, to admonish, and to leave her for ever.[b] The day, as it passed on, vainly told to his unheeding senses its rapid flight in all the sweet gradations of light and odour, in beams less ardent, and in gales more balmy; till the Missionary, unconsciously descending a path worn away through a gigantic mass of pine-covered rocks, found himself, at the setting of the sun, near the too well remembered stream of evening worship. He started and shuddered, and involuntarily recoiled; and that fatal moment when he had first seized the up-raised arm of the idolatrous Priestess, rushed to his recollection: the hour – the place – the stream which had since so often reflected in its course the pastor and the proselyte – the tree which had so often shaded their fervid brows when the glow which suffused them was not all the influence of season – the sun, whose descending beam had so often been the herald of their felicity – all looked, all was now, as it had been then, unaltered and unchanged. The Missionary gazed around him, and sighed pro-foundly: 'All here,' he said, 'still breathes of peace, as when, myself at peace with all the world, I first beheld this scene of tranquil loveliness. All here remains the same. O man! it is then thy dreadful prerogative alone, to sustain that change of all thy powers which leaves thee a stranger to thyself, lost in the wild vicissitude of feelings, to which thy past experience can prove no guide, thy reason lend no light: one fixed immutable law of harmony and order, regulates and governs the whole system of unintelligent creatures; but thou, in thy fatal pre-eminence, makest no part in the splendid mechanism of nature: exclusive and distinct among the works of thy Creator, to thee alone is granted a self-existing principle of intellectual pain; a solitary privilege of moral suffering. Vicegerent of Heaven! thou rulest all that breathes, save only thyself: and boasting a ray of the divine intelligence, thou art the slave of instinct, thy principle of action a selfish impulse, and thy restraint an inscrutable necessity.' – He paused for a moment, and raising his eyes to the sun, which was descending in all the magnificence of retiring light, still apostrophizing the species to which he belonged, and whose imperfections he felt he epitomized in himself, he continued: 'That orb, which rises brightly on thy budding hopes, sets with a changeless lustre on their bloom's destruction; but, in the brief interval of time in which it performs its wonted course, in uninterrupted order, what are the sad transitions by which the mind of man is subject! what are the countless shades of hope and fear, of shame and triumph, of rapture and despair, by which he may be depressed or elevated, ennobled or debased!' He sighed profoundly, as he concluded a picture of which he was himself the unfortunate original; and, withdrawing his eyes from the receding sun, he threw them, with the looks of one who fears an intrusion upon his solitary misery, in that line where a gentle rustling in the leaves had called his attention. The branches, thick and interlaced, slowly unclasped their folds, and thrown lightly back on either side, by a small and delicate hand, the Priestess of Brahma issued from their dusky shade; her form lighted up by the crimson rays of that life-giving power, to which she was at this hour wont to offer her vesper homage.[a] She had that day officiated in the Pagoda, where she served, and she was habited in sacerdotal vestments, but there was in her look more of the tender solicitude of an expecting heart, than the tranquil devotion of a soul which religion only occupied. Advancing with a rapid, yet doubtful step, she cast round her eyes with a look timid, tender, and apprehensive, as if she wished and feared, and hoped and dreaded the presence of some expected object – then pausing, she drew aside her veil, lest the almost impalpable web should intercept the fancied sound which expectation hung on. Thus, as she stood animated by suspenseful love, glowing with the hues of heaven, her upheld veil floating, like a sun-tinged vapour, round her; she looked like the tender vision which descends upon Passion's dream, like the splendid image, to whose creation Genius entrusts its own immortality.

O woman! Nature, which made you fair, made you fairest in the expression of this her best feeling; and the most perfect loveliness of a cold insensibility becomes revolting and deformed, compared to that intelligence of beauty which rushes upon the countenance from the heart that is filled with a pure and ardent affection: then thought breathes upon the lip, independent of sound; and the eye images in a glance, all that the soul could feel in an age![b]

Unseen, though haply not unexpected, the[c] Missionary stood lost in gazing, and finely illustrated the doctrine which gave birth to his recent soliloquy; for in a moment, thought was changed into emotion, and musing into passion;[d] resolves were shaken, vows were cancelled, sufferings were forgotten; on earth he saw only her, whom a moment before he had hoped never to behold again; and from the world of feelings which had torn his heart, one only now throbbed in its rapid[e] pulse – it was the consciousness of being loved! He saw it in the look, intently fixed upon the path he was wont to take: he saw it on the cheek which lost or caught its colouring from sounds scarce audible; he saw it in the air, the attitude; he saw it in the very respiration, which gave a tremulous and unequal undulation to the consecrated vestment which shaded, with religious mystery, the vestal's hallowed bosom. Sight became to him the governing sense of his existence; and the image which fascinated his eye, absorbed and ruled every faculty of his mind.[f] A moment would decide his destiny – the least movement, and he was discovered to Luxima: a look turned, or a smile directed towards him, and the virtues of his life would avail him nothing. – He trembled, he shuddered! – Love was not only opposed to religion, to reason – in his belief, it was at that moment opposed to his eternal salvation! Suddenly struck by the horrible conviction, he turned his eyes away, and implored the assistance of that Heaven he had abandoned.[a] The voice of Luxima came between him and his God. His prayer died, unfinished, on his lips. He paused, he listened; but that voice, sweet and plaintive as it was, addressed not him – its murmuring sounds, broken and soft, seemed only intended for another; for one who had sprung from behind a clump of trees, and had fallen at her feet – It was the Prince Solyman Sheko!! The Missionary stood transfixed, as though a blast from Heaven had withered up his being!

Luxima, apparently agitated by amazement and terror, seemed to expostulate; but in a voice so tremulous and low, that it scarcely could have reached the ear it was intended for.

'Hear me,' said the Prince, abruptly interrupting her, and holding the drapery of her robe, as if he feared she would escape him; 'hear me! I who have lived only to command, now stoop to solicit; yet it is no ordinary suitor who pleads timidly at thy feet, desponding while he supplicates – it is[b] one resolved to know the *best* or *worst* – to conquer thee, or to subdue himself. Amidst the dreams of glory, amidst[c] the tumults of a warrior's life, the fame of thy unrivalled beauty reached my ear. I saw thee in the temple of thy gods, and offered to thee that homage thou dost reserve for them. From that moment my soul was thine. Thy loveliness hung upon me like a spell; and still I loitered 'midst the scenes thy presence consecrates, while duty and ambition, my fame and glory, vainly called me hence. Thy absence from the temple where thou dost preside, not more adoring than adored; thy holy seclusion, which all lament, and none dare violate, which even a Mussulman respects, blasted my hopes and crossed my dearest views: till yesterday a mandate from my father left to my heart no time for cool deliberation. With the shades of evening I sought the consecrated grove forbidden to the foot of man; and for the first time presented myself to eyes whose first glance fixed my destiny. Amazed and trembling, thou didst seem to hear me in pity and disdain; then thou didst supplicate my absence – yet still I lingered; but thou didst weep, and I obeyed the omnipotence of those sacred tears – yet, ere I reached the camp, I cursed my weakness, and, listening only to my imperious passion, returned to seek and sue, perhaps, to conquer and be blessed! But in thy stead, I saw, or fancied that I saw, some prying Brahmin, some jealous guardian of the vestal Priestess, placed in these shades to guard and to preserve her from the unhallowed homage of human adoration, as if none but the God she served was worthy to possess her. For thy sake, not for mine, I fled: but now, while all thy brethren are engaged, performing in their temples their solemn evening worship, I come to offer mine to thee. The sun has *their* vows – thou hast mine. They offer to its benignant influence, prayers of gratitude. Oh! let mine cease to be prayers of supplication; for I, like them, am zealous in my idolatry; and thus, like them, devote what yet remains of my existence to my idol's service.' He ceased, and gazed, and sighed.

Luxima had heard him in silence, which was only interrupted by broken exclamations of impatience and apprehension; for her attitude imaged the very act of flight. The averted head, the advanced step, the strained eye, the timid disorder of her countenance, all intimated the agitation of a mind, which seemed labouring under the expectation of some approaching evil. A pause of a moment ensued; and the Prince, construing her silence and emotion as his wishes directed, would have taken her hand. The indignant glance of Luxima met his. There[a] were, in his eyes, more terrors than his words conveyed. She would have fled. The arms of the unhallowed infidel were extended to inclose in their fold the sacred form of the vestal priestess; but an arm, stronger than his, defeated the sacrilegious effort, and seizing him in its mighty grasp, flung him to a considerable distance. The Mussulman was stunned: amazement, consternation, and rage, mingled in his darkened countenance. He drew a dagger from his girdle, and flew at the intruder – who suddenly darted forward to ward off the death-blow which threatened him; and, seizing the up-raised arm of the infuriate Prince, he struggled with his strength, and wrenching the weapon from the hand that brandished it, flung it in the air. Then, with a look dignified and calm, he said, 'Young stranger, thou wouldest have dishonoured thyself, and destroyed me. I have saved thee from the double crime; give Heaven thanks: return whence thou camest; and respect, in future, the sacred asylum of innocence, which thy presence and thy professions alike violate.'

The Prince, struck, but not daunted, by a firmness so unexpected, replied, with indignation in his look, and rage storming on his brow,[b] 'And who art thou, insolent! who thus darest command? By thy garb and air, thou seemest some adventurer from the West, some wretched Christian, unconscious that, for the first time, thou art in the presence of a Prince.'

The large dark eye of the Missionary rolled over the form of the youth in haughtiness and pity. His lips trembled with a rage scarcely stifled, his countenance blazed with the indignant feelings which agitated his mind. He struggled religiously against himself; but the saintly effort was unequal to combat the human impulse – he paused to recover his wonted equanimity of manner, and then returned:

'Who am I, thou wouldest know? I am, like thee, young Prince, a man, alive to the dignity of his nature as man, resolved, as able, to defend it; with sinews no less braced than thine, a heart as bold, an arm as strongly nerved; descended, like thyself, from royal race, and born, perhaps like thee, for toil and warfare, for danger and for conquest: but views of higher aim than those which kings are slaves to, replaced a worldly, with a heavenly object; and he, whom thou hast dared to call a wretch, tramples beneath his feet the idle baubles for which thy kindred steep their hands in brothers' blood; great in the independence of a soul which God informs, and none but God can move!' The Missionary paused – the grandeur of his imperious air fading gradually away, like the declining glories of an evening sky, as all their lustre melts in the solemn tints of twilight. His eyes fell to the earth, and a cast of meekness subdued the fire of their glance, and smoothed the lowering furrow of his close-knit brow.

'Prince,' he added, 'thou didst ask me, who I am. – I am a Christian Missionary, lowly and poor who wandered from a distant land, to spread the truth my soul adores, to do what good I can, and still to live in peace and Christian love with thee and all mankind!' He ceased.

Wonder and amazement, shame and disappointment, mingled in the expressive countenance of the Mussulman: he remained silent, alternately directing his glance towards the Missionary, who stood awfully[22] meek and grandly humble before him, and to Luxima, who, faint and almost lifeless, leaned against the trunk of a tree, beaming amidst its dark foliage like a spirit of air, whom the power of enchantment had spell-bound in the dusky shade. The young and ardent Solyman had nothing to oppose to the speech of the Missionary, and offered no reply; but rushing by him, he fell at the feet of the Priestess. 'Fair creature,' he said, 'knowest thou this wondrous stranger, and has he any influence o'er thy mind? for though I hate him as an infidel, yet I would kneel to him, if he could but move thee in my favour.'

'And what wouldst thou of a Brahmin's daughter, and a consecrated vestal?' interrupted the Missionary, trembling with agitation; while Luxima hid her blushing face in her veil.

'I would possess her affections!' returned the impassioned Solyman.

'She has none to bestow,' said the Missionary, in a faltering voice; 'her soul is wedded to Heaven.'

'Perhaps thou lovest her thyself,' said the prince, rising from the feet of Luxima, and darting a searching glance at the Missionary; who replied, while a crimson glow suffused itself even to his brow, 'I love her in Christian charity, as I am bound to love all mankind.'

'And nothing more?' demanded the Prince, with a piercing look.

'Nothing more?' faintly demanded Luxima, turning on him eyes which melted with tenderness and apprehension, as if her soul hung upon his reply.[a]

'Nothing more!' said the Monk, faintly.

'Swear it then,' returned Solyman, while his eyes ran over the anxious countenance of the drooping Neophyte, who stood pale and sad, chasing away with her long hair[b] the tears which swelled to her eyes; 'swear it, Christian, by the God you serve.'

'And by what compulsion am I to obey thy orders,' said the Missionary vehemently, and in unsubdued emotion, 'and profane the name of the Most High, by taking it in vain, because a boy desires it?'

'Boy! boy!' reiterated the Prince, his lips quivering with rage; then, suddenly recovering himself, he waved his head, and smiled contemptuously; and turning his eyes on Luxima, whose loveliness became more attractive from the tender emotion of her varying countenance,[c] he said, 'Beautiful Hindu! it is now for thee to decide! Haply thou knowest this Christian; perhaps thou lovest him! as it is most certain that he loves thee. I also love thee: judge then between us. With me thou mayst one day reign upon the throne of India, and yet become the empress of thine own people; what he can proffer thee, besides his love, I know not.'

'Besides his love!' faintly repeated Luxima; and a sigh, which came from her heart, lingered long and trembling on her lips, while she turned her full eyes upon the Missionary.

'Ah! thou lovest him then?' demanded the Prince, in strong and unsubdued emotion.

'It is my religion now to do so,' replied the Indian, trembling and covered with blushes; and chasing away her timid tears,[a] she added faintly, 'Heaven has spoken through his lips to my soul.'

A long pause ensued; the eyes of each seemed studiously turned from the other; and all were alike engrossed by their own secret emotions. Solyman was the first to terminate a silence almost awful.

'Unfortunate Indian!' exclaimed the Prince, with a look of mingled anger and compassion; 'thou art then a Christian, and an apostate from thy religion, and must *forfeit cast.*'

At this denunciation, so dreadful, Luxima uttered a shriek, and fell at his feet, pale, trembling, and in disorder. 'Mercy!' she exclaimed, 'mercy! recall those dreadful words. Oh! I am not a Christian! not *all* a Christian! His God indeed is mine; but Brahma still receives my homage: I am still his Priestess, and bound by holy vows to serve him; then save me from my nation's dreadful curse. It is in thy power only to draw it on my head: for here, hidden from all human eyes, I listen to the precepts of this holy man, in innocence and truth.'

The Prince gazed on her for a moment, lovely as she lay at his feet, in softness and in tears; then concealing his face in his robe, he seemed for some time to struggle with himself; at last he exclaimed, 'Unhappy Indian, thou hast my pity! and if from others thou hast nought to hope, from me thou hast nought to fear.' Again he paused and sighed profoundly; and then, in a low voice, added, 'Farewell! Though I have but thrice beheld thy peerless beauty, I would have placed the universe at thy feet, had I been its master; but the son of the royal Daara cannot deign to struggle, in unequal rivalship, with an obscure and unknown Christian wanderer. Yet still remember, should the imprudence of thy Christian lover expose thee to the rage of Brahminical intolerance; or thy apostacy call down thy nation's wrath upon thy head; or should aught else endanger thee; seek me where thou mayest, I promise thee protection and defence.' Then, without directing a glance at the Missionary, he moved with dignity away; and mounting a Tartar horse, whose bridle was thrown over the trunk of a distant tree, he was in a moment out of sight.

The Missionary, overwhelmed, as if for the first time his secret were revealed even to himself, stood transfixed in the attitude in which the Prince's last speech had left him; his arms were folded in the dark drapery of his robe; his eyes cast to the earth; and in his countenance were mingled expressions of shame and triumph, of passion and remorse, of joy and apprehension. Luxima too remained in the suppliant attitude in which she had thrown herself at the Prince's feet; not daring to raise those eyes in which a thousand opposite expressions blended their rays.[a] Solyman had called the Missionary her *lover;* and this epithet, by a strange contrariety of feeling and of prejudice, at once human and divine, religious and tender, filled her ardent soul[b] with joy and with remorse. The affectionate, the impassioned woman triumphed; but the pure, the consecrated vestal shuddered; and though she still believed her own feelings resembled the pious tenderness of *mystic love,* yet she trembled to expose them even to herself, and remained buried in confusion and in shame. A long and awful pause ensued, and the silent softness of the twilight no longer echoed the faintest sound; all around resembled the still repose of nature, ere the eternal breath had warmed it into life and animation; but all within the souls of the solitary tenants of shades so tranquil was tumult and agitation. At last, Luxima, creeping towards the Missionary, in a faint and tender voice,[c] pronounced the dear and sacred epithet of 'Father!' He started at the sound, and, turning away his head, sighed profoundly.[d] 'Look on me,' said Luxima, timidly; 'it is thy child, thy proselyte, who kneels at thy feet; the wrath of Heaven is about to fall heavily on her head; the gods she has abandoned are armed against her; and the Heaven, to which thou hast lured the apostate, opens not to receive and to protect her.' She took the drapery of his robe as she spoke, and wept in its folds. She was struck to the soul by the cold resistance of his manner; and beholding not the passions which convulsed his countenance, she guessed not at those which agitated his mind. The instinctive tenderness and[e] delicacy of a woman, whose secret has escaped her, ere an equal confidence has sanctioned the avowal of her love, was deeply wounded; and not knowing that man, who has so little power over the mere impulse of passion, could subdue, confine, and[f] resist the expressions of his sentiments, she believed that the unguarded discovery of her own feelings had awakened the abhorrence of a soul so pure and so abstracted as the Christian's and, after a pause which sighs only interrupted, she added, 'And have I also sinned against thee, for whose sake I have dared the wrath of the gods of my fathers; and, in declaring the existence of that divine love, enchanting and sublime,[g] which thou hast taught me to feel, that mysterious pledge for the assurance of heavenly bliss, by which an object on earth, precious and united, yet distinct from our own soul, can—'

'Luxima! Luxima!' interrupted he, in wild and uncontrollable emotion, nor daring to meet the look which accompanied words so dangerous, 'cease, as you value my eternal happiness. You know not what you do, nor what you say. You are confounding ideas which should be eternally distinct and separate: you deceive yourself, and you destroy me! The innocence of your nature, your years, your sex, the purity of your feelings, and your soul,[h] must save you; but I! I! – Fatal creature! it must not be! Farewell, Luxima! – O Luxima! on earth at least we meet no more!' As he spoke, he disengaged his hand from the clasp of hers, and would have fled.

'Hear me,' she said, in a faltering voice, and clinging to his robe; 'hear me! and then let me die!'

The Missionary heard and shuddered: he knew that the idea of death was ever welcome to an Indian's mind; and, that the crime of suicide to which despair might urge its victim, was sanctioned by the religion of the country, by its customs and its laws.* He paused, he trembled, and turning slowly round, fearfully beheld almost lifeless at his feet, the young, the innocent, and lovely woman, who, for his sake, had refused a throne; who, for his sake, was ready to embrace death. 'Let you die, Luxima?' he repeated, in a softened voice; and seating himself on a bank beside her, he chased away with her veil, the tears which hung trembling on her faded cheek – 'Let you die?'

'And wherefore should I live?' she replied with a sigh. 'Thou hast torn from me the solace of my own religion; and, when I lose thee, when I no longer look upon or hear thee, who can promise that the faith, to which thou hast won me from the altars of my ancient gods, will remain to sooth my suffering soul? and, O father! though it should, must I worship alone and secretly, amidst my kindred and my friends; or, must I, by a public profession of apostacy, lose my cast, and wander wretched and an alien in distant wilds, my nation's curse and shame? Oh! no; 't were best, ere that, I died! for now I shall become a link between thy soul and a better, purer state of things; spotless and unpolluted, I shall reach the realms of peace, and a part of thyself will have gone before thee to the bosom of that great Spirit, of which we are alike emanations. O father!' she added, with a mixture of despair and passion in her look and voice, ''t were best that *now* I died, and that I died for *thee.*'

'For me, Luxima! for me!' repeated the Missionary, in a frenzied accent, and borne away by a variety of contending and powerful emotions – 'die for me! and yet it is denied *me* even to *live* for thee! – And live I not for thee? O woman! alike fatal and terrific to my senses and my soul, thou hast offered thy life as a purchase of my secret – and it is thine! Now then, behold prostrate at thy feet, one who, till this dreadful moment, never bent his knee to ought[a] but God alone; behold, thus grovelling on the earth, the destruction thou hast effected, the ruin thou hast made! behold the unfortunate, whose force has submitted to thy weakness; whom thou hast dragged from the proudest eminence of sanctity and virtue, to receive the law of his existence from thy look, the hope of his felicity from thy smile; for know, frail as thou mayst be, in all thy fatal fondness, he is frailer still; and that thou, who lovest with all a seraph's purity, art beloved with all the sinful tyranny of human passion, strengthened by restraint, and energized by being combated.[b] Now then, all consecrated as thou art to heaven; all pure and vestal by thy vows and life; save, if thou canst, the wretch whom thou hast made; for, lost alike to heaven and to himself, he looks alone *to thee* for his

* To quit life, before it quits them, is among the Hindus no uncommon act of heroism; and this fatal custom arises from their doctrine of metempsychosis, in which the faith of all the various casts is equally implicit.

redemption!' As he spoke, he fell prostrate and almost lifeless on the earth: for two days no food had passed his lips; for two nights no sleep had closed his eyes; passion and honour, religion and love, opposed their conflicts in his mind;[a] nature sunk beneath the struggle, and he lay lifeless at the feet of her who had for ever destroyed the tranquillity of his conscience,[b] and rendered valueless the sacrifices of his hitherto pure, sinless, and self-denying life.

Luxima, trembling and terrified, yet blessed in her sufferings, and energized by those strong affections which open an infinite resource to woman in the hour of her trial, gently raised his head from the earth and chafed his forehead with the drops which a neighbouring lotos-leaf had treasured from the dews of the morning. He loved her; he had told her so; and she again repeated in her felicity, as she had done in her despair, 'It were best that now I died!'

CHAPTER XI.

Slowly restored to a perfect consciousness of his situation; to a recollection of the fatal avowal, by which he had irretrievably committed himself, and of the singular event which had produced it; the Missionary still lay motionless and silent; still lay supported by the Neophyte which love alone had given him. He dreaded a recovery from the partial suspension of all his higher faculties; he shrank from the obtrusive admonitions of reason and religion,[a] and sought to perpetuate an apparent state of insensibility, which gave him up to the indulgence of a passive but gracious feeling, scarcely accompanied by any positive perception, and resembling, in its nature and[b] influence, some confused but delightful dream, which, while it leaves its pleasurable impression on the senses, defies the accuracy of memory to recall or to arrange it. His heart now throbbed lightly, for it was disburdened of its fatal secret; his mind reposed from its conflicts, for it had passed the crisis of its weakness in betraying it: he felt the tears of love on his brow; he felt an affectionate hand returning the pressure of his; and a sense of a sacred communion, which identified the soul of another with his own, possessed itself of his whole being; and passion was purified by an intelligence which seemed to belong alone to mind. Alive to feelings more acute, to a sensibility more exquisite, than he had hitherto known; all external objects faded from his view for the moment; life was to him a series of ideas and feelings, of affections and emotions: he sought to retain no consciousness, but that of loving and being loved; and if he was absorbed in illusion, it was an illusion which, though reason condemned, innocence still ennobled and consecrated.[c]

Luxima hung over him in silence, and her countenance was the reflection of all the various emotions which flitted over his. The repose which smoothed his brow, communicated to hers its mild and tranquil expression; her pulse quickened to the increasing throb of his temples; and the vital hues which revisited his cheek, rosed hers with the bright suffusion of love and hope. Fearing[d] almost for his life, she bowed her head to catch the low-drawn respiration, and returned every breath of renovating existence with a sigh of increasing joy.

'Luxima!' said a voice, which, though low and tremulous, reached her inmost soul.

'I am here, father!' she replied in emotion, and bashfully withdrawing her arm from beneath a head which no longer needed support.

The Missionary took the hand thus withdrawn, and pressed it, for the first time, to his lips. The modest eyes of the vestal Priestess sank beneath the look which accompanied the tender act: it was the first look of love acknowledged and returned; it penetrated and mingled itself with the very existence of her to whom it was directed; it resembled, in its absorbing and delicious influence, the ecstacy of enthusiasm, which, in the days of her religious illusion, descended on her spirit to kindle and to entrance it; which had once formed the inspiration of the Prophetess, and animated beyond the charms of human beauty the loveli- ness of the woman.[a] Turning away her glance in timid disorder, she sought for resource against herself in the objects which encompassed her: she threw up her eyes to that heaven, to whose exclusive love she had once devoted herself, and, from a sudden association of ideas, she turned them to the mouldering altar of the god whose service she had abandoned. The religion of her spirit and of her senses, of truth and error, alike returned with all their influence on her soul;[b] and she shuddered as she looked on the shrine where she had once worshipped with a pure, pious, and undivided feeling: the moonlight fell in broken rays upon its shining fragments, and formed a strong relief to their lustre in the mas- sive foliage of a dark tree which shaded it. The air was breathless, and the branches of this consecrated and gigantic tree alone were agitated; they waved with a slow but perceptible undulation; the fearful eyes of the apostate pursued their mysterious motion, which seemed influenced by no external cause: they bowed, they separated, and through their hitherto impervious darkness gleamed the vision of a human countenance! if human it might be called; which gave the perfect image of Brahma, as he is represented in the *Avatar* of 'the Destroyer.'[23] It vanished – the moon sank in clouds – the vision lasted but a moment; but that moment for ever decided the fate of the Priestess of Cashmire! Luxima saw no more – with a loud and piercing shriek she fell prostrate on the earth.

The Missionary started in horror and amazement; the form which now lay pale and lifeless at his feet, had, an instant before, by its animated beauty rivet- ted his eyes, absorbed his thoughts, and engrossed his exclusive attention, as half-averted, half-reposing in his arms, it had mingled in its expression and its attitude the tender confidence of innocence and love, the dignified reserve of modesty and virtue; still[c] seeing no object but herself, he remained ignorant of the cause of her emotion, and was overwhelmed by its effects. He trembled with a selfish fondness for a life on which his happiness, his very existence, now depended: he[d] raised her in his arms; he murmured on her ear words of peace and love.[e] He threw back her long dark tresses that the air might play freely on her face; and he only withdrew his anxious looks from the beauty of her pale and motionless countenance, to try if he could discover, in the surrounding scene, any cause for a transition of feeling so extraordinary; but nothing appeared which could change happiness into horror, which could tend to still the pulse of love in the throbbing heart, or bleach its crimson hue upon the glowing cheek. The moon had again risen in cloudless majesty, rendering the minutest blossom visible: the stillness of the air was so profound, that the faintest sigh was heard in dying echoes.[f] All was boundless solitude and soothing silence. The mystery, therefore, of Luxima's sudden distraction was unfathomable. She still lay motionless on the shoulder of the Missionary; but the convulsive starts, which at intervals shook her frame, the broken sighs which fluttered on her lips,[a] betrayed the return of life and consciousness. 'Luxima!' exclaimed the Missionary, pressing the cold hands he held; 'Luxima, what means this heart-rending, this fearful emotion? Look at me! Speak to me! Let me again meet thine eye, and hang upon thy voice – fatal eye and fatal voice – my destruction and my felicity! still I woo and fear the return of their magic influence. Luxima, if[b] Heaven forbids our communion in happiness, does it also deny us a sympathy in sorrow? Art thou to suffer alone? or rather, are my miseries to be doubled in my ignorance of thine? Oh! my beloved, if conscience speak in words of terror to thy soul, what has not mine to fear? It is I, I alone, who should be miserable in being weak. Created to feel, thou dost but fulfil thy destiny, and in thee nature contemns the false vow by which superstition bound thee to thy imaginary god. In thee it is no crime to love! in me, it is what I abhor no less than crime – it is sin, it is shame, it is weakness. It is I alone who should weep and tremble; it is I alone who have fallen, and whose misery and whose debasement demand pity and support. Speak to me then, my too well beloved disciple; solace me by words, for thy looks are terrific. O Luxima! give me back that soft sweet illusion, which thy voice of terror dissipated, or take from me its remembrance; give me up at once to reason and to remorse, or bid me, with one look of love, renounce both for ever at thy feet, and I will obey thee! I! – Redeemer of the World! hast thou then quite forsaken him whom thou didst die to save? Is the bearer of thy cross, is the minister of thy word, abandoned by his Saviour? Is he so steeped in misery and sin, that the spirit, which thy grace once enlightened, dares not lift itself to thee, and cry for mercy and salvation? Is the soul, which was tempted to error in its zeal for thy cause, to sink into the endless night prepared for the guilty? Woman! fiend! whatever thou art, who thus by the seeming ways of Heaven leadest me to perdition, leave me! fly me! loose thy fatal hold on my heart, while yet the guilty passions, which brood there, have made me criminal in thought alone.'[c]

Luxima shuddered; she raised her drooping head from the bosom which recoiled from supporting her, and she fixed on the agitated countenance of the Monk a look, tender, and reproachful, even through the expression of horror and remorse, which darkened its softness and its lustre. This look had all its full effect; but Luxima shrunk back from the arms which again involuntarily extended to receive and to support her;[d] and, in a solemn and expressive voice, she said, 'It is all over! – ere that orb shall have performed its nightly course we shall be *parted for ever!*'

The Missionary was silent, but horror and consternation were in his looks.

Luxima threw round her a wild and timid glance; then creeping toward him, she said, in a low whispering voice, 'Sawest thou nothing, some few minutes back, which froze thy blood, and harrowed up thy soul?'[e]

'Nothing,' he replied, watching, in strong emotion, the sad wild expression of her countenance.

'That is strange,' she returned, with a deep sigh, 'most strange!' Then, after a pause, she demanded, with a vacant look, 'Where are we, father?'

'Luxima! Luxima!' he exclaimed, gazing on her in fear and in amazement, 'what means this sudden, this terrific change? Merciful Heaven! does thy mind wander; or hast thou quite forgotten thine own consecrated shades, the *'confluence of the streams,'* where first the Christian Missionary addressed the Priestess of Brahma? Hast thou forgotten the altar of thy once worshipped god?'

At these words, emphatically pronounced, to steady her wavering recollection, lightning from heaven seemed to fall upon the head of the apostate Priestess; her limbs were convulsed, her complexion grew livid, she threw her eyes wildly round her, and murmuring, in a low quick voice, a Brahminical invocation, she sprung forward with rapid bound, and fell prostrate before the shrine of her former idol. There the Christian dared not follow her: he arose, and advanced a few steps, and paused, and gazed; then, wringing his hands in agony, he said, 'Happy in her illusion, she returns to her false gods for support and comfort, while I, debased and humbled, dare not raise my eyes and heart in supplications to the God of Truth.' As he spoke, he cast a look on the cross, which hung from his rosary; but it was still humid with tears, which love had shed, it still breathed the odours of the tresses the wind had wafted on its consecrated surface. He shuddered, and let it fall, and groaned, and covered his eyes with his robe, as if he sought to shut out the light of the Heaven he had offended. When again he raised his head, he perceived that Luxima was moving slowly towards him, not, as she had left him, in delirium, and in tears; but in all the dazzling lustre[a] of some newly-awakened enthusiasm; resembling in her motions and her look the brilliant, the blooming,[b] the inspired Prophetess, who had first disturbed his imagination and agitated his mind, in the groves of Lahore; extending her right hand to forbid his approach, she paused and leaned on the branch of a blasted tree, with all the awful majesty of one who believed herself fresh from a communion with a celestial being, and irradiated with the reflection of his glory. 'Christian!' she said, after a long pause, 'the crisis of human weakness is past, and the powers of the immortal spirit assert themselves: – Heaven has interposed to save its faithless servant, and she is prepared to obey its mandate: a divine hand has extended itself to snatch her from perdition, and she refuses not its aid. Christian! the hour of sacrifice is arrived – Farewell. Go! while yet thou mayest go, in innocence; while yet the arm of eternal destruction has not reached thee. O Christian! dangerous and fatal! while yet I have breath and power to bid thee depart, leave me! The light of the great Spirit has revisited my soul. Even now I am myself become a *part of the Divinity.'* As she spoke, her eyes were thrown up, and the whites only were visible; a slight convulsive smile gleamed across her features; and she passed her right hand from her bosom to her forehead with a slow movement. This mysterious act seemed to bestow upon her a new sense of existence.* Her religious ecstacy slowly subsided – her eyes fell – the colour revisited her cheek – she sighed profoundly, and after a silent pause, she said,

'Christian, thou hast witnessed my re-union to the source of my spiritual being. Oppose not thyself to the Heaven, which opens to receive me: depart from me; leave me now – and for ever.'

'Luxima,' interrupted the Missionary, in the low wild accent of terror and amazement; and perceiving that some delirium of religious fanaticism had seized her imagination – 'Luxima, what means this wondrous resolution, this sudden change? Are all our powers alike reversed? Hast thou risen above humanity, or have I fallen below it? And art thou, the sole cause of all my weakness and my shame, to rise upon the ruin thou hast made, to triumph upon the destruction thou hast effected? Part with me now! abandon me in a moment such as this! O Luxima,' he added, with tenderness and passion, and in a voice soft and imploring, 'am I deceived, or do you love me?'

Luxima replied not, but her whole countenance and form changed their expression: she no longer looked like an inspired sibyl, borne away by the illusions of her own disordered imagination, but like a tender and devoted woman.[a] She advanced; she fell at his feet, and kissed with humility and passion the hem of his robe;[b] but when he would have raised her in his arms, she recoiled from his support, and seating herself on a bank, at a little distance from him, she wept. He approached, and stood near[c] her: he saw in the rapid transitions of her manner, and her conduct, the violent struggles of feeling and opinion, the ceaseless conflicts of love and superstition; he saw imaged in her emotions the contending passions which shook him to dissolution. He sighed heavily, and mentally exclaimed,

'Alas! her virtue derives more strength even from error, than mine from truth: she obeys her ideas of right as a Brahmin; I, as a Christian, violate and forsake mine.' He turned his eyes on Luxima, and perceived that she was now gazing with a look of exquisite fondness on him,[d] tempered with something of melancholy and sadness.

'It is hard,' said she, 'to look on thee, and yet to part with thee! but who will dare to disobey the mandate of a *God*, who comes in his *own presence to save and to redeem us?*'

'What mean you, Luxima?' interrupted the Missionary, in emotion, and throwing himself beside her.

'Hear me,' she returned; '*believe*, and *obey*. – From the moment I first beheld thee, first listened to thee, I have ceased to be myself; thy looks, thy words, encompassed me on every side; it seemed as if my soul had anticipated its future fate, and already fled to accomplish it in thee. I felt that, in ceasing to be near thee, I should cease to exist: therefore I concealed from thee the danger which

---

* This mystery is called the *Matricha-machom*. The Brahmins believe that the soul is thus conducted to the brain, and that the spirit is re-united to the Supreme Being.

hung upon our interviews, and all that might lead thee, for thine own sake or for mine, to withdraw from me the heaven of thy presence – but the dream is over! the God whom thou didst teach me to abandon, has this night appeared on earth to reclaim his apostate.'

'Luxima! Luxima!'

'Hear me, father! If I live, this night the vision of Brahma, the God whom I forsook, appeared to me amidst the ruins of his own neglected altar!'

'Impossible! impossible!' exclaimed the Missionary vehemently.

'Then,' she returned, in a voice which resembled the heart-piercing accent of melancholy madness, 'then there lives some human testimony of our interview, and thou art lost! thou, my soul's own idol! Oh! then, fly – for ever fly: let me feel death and shame but once, and not a thousand, thousand times through thy destruction. But, no,' she added in a calmer tone; 'it was no human form I saw; I have oft before met that awful vision in my dream of inspiration! haply it came to warn me of thy danger, and to save *my* life through *thine* – then go, leave me while yet I have power to say – *leave me!*'

The Missionary heard her in uncontrolled emotion; but without any faith in a fancied event, which he deemed but the vision of her own disordered imagination, influenced by the agitation of her feelings, by the hour, the scene, and by the fanaticism and superstitious horrors which still governed her vacillating mind:[a] but he saw that there was evidently, at that moment, an obstinacy in her illusion, a bigotry in her faith, it would be vain to attempt to dissipate or to vanquish, until a calmer mood of thought and feeling should succeed to their present tumultuous and unsettled state. Less surprised at the nature of her vision, than at the peculiar result of its influence,[b] he could not comprehend the miracle by which she submitted to an eternal separation, at a moment when his mind, broken and enervated, sunk under the tyranny of a passion which had just reached its acme. But he knew love only as a man, and could not comprehend its nature in the heart of a woman: – with him the existing moment was every thing, but her affection took eternity itself into its compass; and though she could have more easily parted with her life than with her lover, yet she did not hesitate to sacrifice her felicity to his safety, to his glory, and to the hope of that eternal reunion which might await two souls, which crime had not yet degraded, for her tolerant, but zealous, religion, shut not the gates of Heaven against all who sought it by a different path; and consecrating a human feeling, in ascribing to it an immortal duration, love itself enabled her to make the sacrifice religion demanded. The Missionary sought not to subdue the influence of that wild and fervid imagination, which now, he believed, held the ascendant; but he sought to combat the resolution it had given birth to – and gazing on a countenance, where the enthusiasm of religion still mingled with the expressions of tenderness and passion, he said,[c]

'Wondrous and powerful being! equally fatal in thy weakness and thy force, in thy seducing softness, and resisting virtue: wilt thou now, thus suddenly, thus unprepared, abandon me? – now, that thou hast trampled on my religion and my vows; now that thou hast conquered my habits of feeling, my principles of thinking, subdued every faculty of my being to thy influence, and bereft me of all, save that long latent power of loving passionately – that tyrannic and dreadful capability of an exclusive devotion to a creature frail and perishable as myself, by which thou hast effected my ruin, and changed the very constitution of my nature?'

'Oh, no!' returned Luxima, endeavouring to conceal her tenderness and her tears; 'oh, no! Part we cannot. Go where thou mayest, my life must still hang upon thine! my thoughts will pursue thee.[a] Indissolubly united, there is now but one soul between us. But, O father! to preserve that soul pure and untainted – the human intercourse, that dear and fatal symbol of our eternal union, ought, and can, no longer exist; the voice of God and the law of man, alike oppose it: let us not further provoke the wrath of both, let us remember our respective vows, and immolate ourselves to their performance.' She arose as she spoke. The tears stood trembling in her inflamed eyes, and that deadly sickness of the soul which ushers in the moment of separation from all the heart holds dearest, spread its livid hues over her cheek, its agony of expression over her countenance.[b]

'Woman! woman!' exclaimed the Missionary, wildly, and seizing her trembling hands, 'give me back my peace, or remain to solace me for its loss; give me back to the Heaven from which you have torn me, or stay, stay, and teach me to forget the virtue by which I earned its protection. While yet a dreadful remembrance of my former self remains, you dare not leave me to horror and remorse! You dare not, cold, or cruel, or faithless, as you may be, you dare not say, "This moment is our last." O Luxima! Luxima!' – Overcome by a sense of his weakness, he drooped his head upon her hands, and wept. Had not the salvation of his life been the purchase of her firmness and her resistance, Luxima would have granted to the tears of love, what its ardour or its eloquence could now have obtained: but she knew the danger of remaining longer, or of again meeting him in a place, where they had either been discovered by the jealous guardians of her rigid order, or from which they had been warned by a divine intimation. Mingling her tears with his, after an affecting pause, she said, in a low voice, and scarcely articulate from contending emotions,[c]

'To-morrow, then, we shall again meet, when the sun sets behind the mountains: but not here – not here! Oh, no! These shades have become fearful and full of danger to my imagination.[d] But if thou wilt repair to the western arcades of the great banyan-tree, then – – ' The words died away on her trembling lips, and she cast round a wild and timid look, as if some minister of Heaven's mercy was near to forbid an appointment, which might be, perhaps, pregnant with destruction to both.

'*And then*,' repeated the Missionary, with vehemence and with firmness, 'we meet to part *for ever! – or – to part no more!*'

Luxima, at these words, turned her eyes on him, with a look of love, passionate and despairing – then, folding her hands upon her bosom, she raised those eloquent eyes to Heaven, with a glance of sweet and holy resignation to its will.[e]

This seraph look of suffering and piety operated like a spell upon the frantic feelings of her lover.[a] The arms, extended to detain her, fell back nerveless on his breast. He saw her move slowly away, resembling the pensive spirit of some innocent sufferer, whom sorrow had released from the bondage of painful existence. He saw[b] her light and perfect form, faintly tinged with the moon-ray, slowly fading into distance, till it seemed to mingle with the fleecy vapours of the night: then he felt as if she had disappeared from his eyes for ever, and, turning to her image in his heart, he gave himself up to suffering and to thought, to the alternate influence of passion and remorse.

CHAPTER XII.

THE habit of suffering brings not always with it the power of endurance; the nerves, too frequently acted on, become morbid and less capable of sustaining the pressure of a reiterated sensation; and the mind,[a] no longer able to support or to resist a protracted conflict, sinks under its oppression, or by some natural impulse abandons the object of its painful cogitation, and finds relief in the effort of seeking change.

The Missionary had reached the crisis of passion, the feverish paroxysm of long-combatted emotions. He had reached the utmost limits of human temptation and human resistance, and shuddered at the risk he had run and the peril he had escaped. He resembled a wanderer in an unknown land, who reaches a towering and fearful eminence; who beholds at a single glance the dangers he has passed, and those he has still to encounter; and who endeavours to regulate his future course by the inferences of his past experience. That wild delirium of the senses which left him an unpractised victim to their tyranny, subsided in some degree with the absence of that tender and enchanting object who distanced all that his fancy had ever dared to picture of woman's loveliness or woman's love; and his mind, comparatively enabled to think and to decide, with something of its former tone and vigour, gave itself up to a meditation which had for its subject the consequences of that fatal avowal by which he had so irretrievably committed his character and his profession. The mysterious veil which the cold pure hand of religion had flung over his feelings, was now for ever withdrawn, and the frailties of a being once deemed infallible, the passions and weaknesses incidental to his nature as being human, were not only exposed to himself, but were betrayed to others; and to the followers of Brahma and Mahomet, the apostle of Christianity appeared alike frail, alike subdued by passion and open to temptation, as he on whom the light of revealed truth has never beamed. He felt that he had dishonoured the religion he professed, by making no application of its principles to his conduct in the only instance in which his virtue had been put to a severe test; and that the doctrine of opinion had failed practically in its influence upon the interests and feelings of self-love. He could no longer conceal from his awakened conscience, that the proselyte his zeal had sought for Heaven, had become the object of a human passion; of a passion, imprudent in the eye of reason, criminal in the eye of religion; and which, in its nature and consequences, was scarcely referable to any order, or to any state of society; for, by the doctrines of their respective religions, by the laws and customs of their respective countries, they could never be united by those venerated

100

and holy ties, which regulate and cement the finest bonds of humanity, and which obtain from mankind, in all regions of the earth, respect and sanction, as being founded in one of the great moral laws of nature's own eternal code. No Brahmin priest could consecrate an union, sacrilegious according to his habits of thinking and believing. No Christian minister could bless an alliance formed upon the violation of vows solemnly pledged before the altar of the Christian's God. If, therefore, human opinion was of moment to one, whose secret ambition to obtain its favour had rendered even *religion* subservient to its purpose; if the habits, the principles, and the faith of a whole life, held any power over conduct and action in a particular instance; if self-estimation were necessary to the self-love of a proud and lofty character, between the Christian Priest and Heathen Priestess was placed an insuperable bar, which if once removed, risked their exposure to infamy and to shame in this world, and offered, according to their respective creeds, eternal suffering in the next. But the alternative was scarce less dreadful. In the first instance it was deemed impossible, for it was immediate and eternal separation! Reason dictated, religion commanded, even love itself, influenced by pity, admitted the terrific necessity. Yet still passion and nature struggled, and resisted, with an energy and an eloquence, to which the heart, the imagination, and the senses, devotedly listened. Oh! it is long, very long, before the strongest mind, in obedience to the dictates of prudence and of pride, can dismiss from its thoughts the object of an habitual meditation, before it can strike out some new line of existence, foreign to its most cherished sentiments and dearest views. It is long, very long, before we can look calmly into the deserted heart, and behold unmoved a dreary void, where late some image erected by our hopes, filled from the source of pleasure, every artery with the tide of gladness. It is difficult for human reason to argue away passion, by cold and abstract principles, and to substitute the torpor of indifference for the pang of disappointment; but it is still more difficult for human fortitude, though actuated by the highest human virtue, to tear asunder the ties of love, in all their force and vigour, ere habit may have softened their strength, or satiety relaxed their tension. To effect this sudden breaking up of the affections, ere they have been suffered gently to moulder away in the mild and sure decay of consuming time, the silent, certain progress of mortal oblivion, some power more than human is requisite.[a]

On the luxurious shores of the confluence of the streams, with the light of heaven dying softly round them, the air breathing enjoyment, and the earth affording it, the stoicism of the man would not perhaps have continued proof against the charms of the woman. But in darkness, in solitude, and in silence, in a cavern cold and gloomy, religion borrowed a superadded influence from the impression of the senses; and at the foot of the cross, raised by his own hands in the land of the unbelieving, and faintly illuminated by the chill pure rays of an approaching dawn, that season of the day so solemn and so impressive, when passion slumbers, and visions of fear and gloom steal upon the soul, did the

Christian Missionary vow to resign for ever, the object of the only human weakness which had disgraced his sinless life. The vow had passed his lips; it was registered in heaven; and nature almost sunk beneath the sacrifice which religion had exacted.

The great immolation resolved on, all that now remained to be effected, was to fly from a spot which he had found so fatal to his pious views, and to pursue the holy cause of the Mission in regions more favourable to its success; but the energy of zeal was subdued or blunted, and a complexional enthusiasm, once solely directed to the interests of Christianity, had now found another medium for its ardour and activity. Scarcely knowing whither to direct his steps, he mechanically inquired from a Goala, whom kindness that morning brought to his grotto with some fruit, the road, which at that season, the caravan passing through Cashmire from Thibet, usually took. The information he received tended to facilitate his departure from Cashmire, for the caravan had halted in the district of Sirinagur.

To behold Luxima for the last time was now all that remained! But the feelings of tenderness and despair, with which this trying interview was contemplated, plunged him in all the pangs of irresolution; vibrating between desire and fear, between the horror of leaving her, unprepared and unexpecting their eternal separation, or of beholding her in love and in affliction, expressing in her beautiful and eloquent countenance, the agony of that tender and suffering heart which, but for him, had still been the asylum of peace and happiness.[a]

At last, a day of conflict and of misery, alternately devoted to an heavenly and to an earthly object, now passed in tenderness and grief, and now in supplication and in prayer, hastened to its conclusion! The sun had set – a few golden rays still lingered in the horizon, and found a bright reflection on the snows which covered the mountains of Thibet. It was the hour of *the appointed interview!* The Christian prostrated himself for the last time before the altar, and invoked the protection of Heaven to support him through the most trying effort of his life; to subdue the hidden 'man of the heart,'[24] and, upon the ruins of a frail and earthly passion, to raise a sentiment of hope and faith, which should point alone to that eternal recompense reserved for those who suffer and who sustain, who are tempted and who resist. He arose, sublimed and[b] tranquillized, from the foot of the altar. Religion encompassed him with her shield, and poured her spirit on his soul.[c] He took from the altar the Scriptural volume, and placed it on his bosom; and grasping in his right hand the pastoral crosier, he paused for a moment, and gazed around him; then proceeding with a rapid step, he passed, for the last time, the rude threshold of a place which had afforded him so sweet and so fatal an asylum, which had so often re-echoed to his sighs of passion, and resounded to his groans of penitence. Yet once again he paused, and cast back his eyes upon this beloved grotto: but the faded wreath of the Indian Priestess, suspended from one of its projections, caught his glance. He shuddered. This simple object was fatal to his resolutions – it brought to his heart the recollection of love's delicious dawn; the various eras of its successive and blissful emotions. But he wished to meet *her*, on whose brow this frail memento had once exhausted its odours and its bloom, as he had first met her, with eyes so cold, and thoughts so pure and so free from human taint, that even Religion's self might say, 'A communion such as this belongs to Heaven!' Yet he[a] withdrew his eyes with a long and lingering look, and sighed profoundly as he retreated. He reached the arcade of the banyans, as the sunbeam reflected from the mountains threw its last light on a dark bower of branches, beneath whose shade he beheld the Indian Neophyte. She was kneeling on the earth, pale, and much changed in her appearance, and seemingly invoking the assistance of Heaven with fervid devotion. No consecrated flower bloomed amidst the dark redundancy of her neglected tresses. No transparent drapery shadowed, with folds of snow, the outlines of her perfect form: her hair, loose and dishevelled hung in disorder round her; and she was habited in the dress of a Chancalas, or *outcast* – a habit coarse and rude, and calculated[b] to resist the vicissitude of climate to which such unhappy wanderers are exposed. A linen veil partly shaded her head: her muntras were fastened round her arm with an idol figure of Camdeo: from the dsandam which encircled her neck, was suspended a small cross, given to her by the Missionary; and those symbols of faith and of idolatry expressed the undecided state of her mind and feelings, which *truth* taught by *love*, and *error* confirmed by *habit*, still divided – equally resembling in her look, her dress, and air, a Christian Magdalene, or a penitent Priestess of Brahma.

In this object, so sad and so touching, nothing appeared to change the resolutions of the Missionary, but much to confirm them. It was a fine image of the conquest of virtue over passion – and the most tender of women seemed to set a bright example to the firmest of men. Yet, when Luxima beheld him, a faint colour suffused her cheek, her whole frame thrilled with obvious emotion. She arose, and extended her trembling hand – but he took it not; for her appearance awakened sensations of love and melancholy, which, when they mingle, are of all others the most profound; and casting down his eyes, he said,

'I am come, my daughter, in obedience to thy commands, to behold thee for the last time, and to give thee up exclusively to Him, whose grace may operate upon thy soul, without the wretched aid of one so frail and weak as I have proved. Thou wearest on thy breast, the badge of that pure truth which already dawns upon thy soul. Take also this book – it is all I have to bestow; but it is all-sufficient for thy eternal happiness.' He paused, and the emotion of his countenance but ill accorded with the coldness of his words.

Luxima took the book in silence: something she would have said, but the words died away on her trembling lips; and she raised her eyes to his face, with a look so tender, and yet so despairing, that the Missionary felt how fatal to every resolution he had formed, another such look might prove.

Averting his eyes, therefore, and extending his hands over her head, he would have spoken – he would have blessed her – he would have said, 'Farewell for ever!' but the power of articulation had deserted him. Again he tried to speak, and failed; his lips trembled, his eyes grew dim, his heart sickened, and the agonies of death seemed to convulse his frame. Luxima still clung to his arm. Had the life-blood flowed from her bosom, beneath the sacrificial knife, her countenance could not have expressed more acute anguish. He sought, by a feeble effort, to release himself from her grasp: but he had not power to move; and the mutual glance which mingled their souls at the moment they were about to part for ever, operated with a force they had no longer power to resist. Faint and pale, Luxima sunk on his bosom. At that moment, sounds came confusedly on the winds, and growing louder on the ear, seemed to pierce the heart of the Indian. She started, she trembled, she listened wildly; and then, with a shriek, exclaimed,

'So soon, so soon, does death overtake me. Now then, now, farewell for ever! Leave me to die, and save thyself!' As she spoke, she would have fallen to the earth, but that the Missionary caught her in his arms. All the powers of life seemed to rush upon him; a vague idea of some dreadful danger which threatened the object of his pity and his love, roused and energized his mind and nerved his frame. He no longer reasoned, he no longer resisted. Obedient only to the impulse of the immediate feeling, he bore away his lifeless charge in his arms, and plunging into the deepest shades of the banyan, endeavoured to reach a dark pile of towering rocks, whose sharp high points still caught a hue of light from the west, and among whose cavities he hoped to find refuge and concealment. The mists of evening had hid from his view a mighty excavation, which he now entered, and perceived that it was the vestibule of an ancient Pagoda: its roof, glittering with pendent stalactites, was supported by columns, forming a magnificent colonnade, disposed with all the grand irregularity which Nature displays in her greatest works, and reflecting the images of surrounding objects, tinged with the rich and purple shade of evening colouring. This splendid portico opened into a gloomy and terrific cavern, whose half-illuminated recess formed a striking contrast to the exterior lustre. Pillars of immense magnitude hewn out of the massive rocks, and forming an imperishable part of the whole mighty mass, sustained the ponderous and vaulted ceiling: receding in the perspective, they lost their magnitude in distance, till their lessening forms terminated in dim obscurity, and finely characterized the awful mystery of the impervious gloom. Idols of gigantic stature, colossal forms, hideous and grotesque images, and shrines emblazoned with offerings, and dimly glittering with a dusky lustre, were rudely scattered on every side. For the Missionary had borne the Priestess of Brahma to the temple in which she herself presided: the most ancient and celebrated in India, after that of Elephanta.[25] This sanctuary of the most awful superstition, worthy of the wildest rites of a dark idolatry, was now wrapt in a gloom, rendered more obvious by the faint blue light which issued from the earth, in a remote part of the cavern, and which seemed to proceed from a subterraneous fire,* which burst at intervals into flame, throwing a frightful glare upon objects in themselves terrific.

The Christian shuddered as he gazed around him: but every thought, every feeling of the lover and the man, was soon concentrated to the object still supported in his arms, and who he believed and hoped, in this sad and lonely retreat, had nothing to apprehend from immediate danger. Life again reanimated her frame, but she was weak and faint, and an expression of terror was still marked on her features. He placed her near a pillar, which supported her drooping form, and flew to procure some water from a spring, whose gushing fall echoed among the rocks; when the sound of solemn music, deep, sad, and sonorous, came upon the wind, which at intervals rushed through the long surrounding aisles of the cavern, disturbing with their hollow murmurs the death-like silence of the place. The Missionary listened: the sounds grew louder; they were no longer prolonged by the wind; they came distinctly on the ear; they were accompanied by the echo of many footsteps; and hues of light thrown on the darkness of the rocks, marked the shadows of an approaching multitude. The Missionary rushed back to his charge: she had raised her head from the earth, and listened with the air of a maniac to the increasing sounds.

'Unfortunate as innocent,' he said, encircling her with his extended arms, 'there is now, I fear, no refuge left thee but this. O Luxima! thy danger has reunited us, and I am alike prepared to die for or with thee.' As he spoke, a blue phosphoric light glanced on the idols near the entrance of the Pagoda: it proceeded from a large silver censer, borne by a venerable Brahmin, who was followed by a procession of the same order, each Brahmin holding in his hand a branch of the gloomy and sacred ocynum, the symbol of the dreadful ceremony of *Brahminical excommunication*. The procession, which passed near the pillar, by whose deep shadow the unfortunate victims who thus had rushed upon destruction, stood concealed, was closed by the venerable Guru of Cashmire; he was carried in a black palanquin, and his aged countenance was stamped with the impress of despair. The Brahmins circled round the subterraneous fire, each in his turn flinging on its flame the leaves of the sandal-tree and oils of precious odour. The kindling flames discovered on every side, thrones, columns, altars, and images; while the priests, dividing into two bands, stood on each side of the fire, and the Guru took his place in the centre of his disciples.

All now was the silence of death, and the subterraneous fire spread around its ghastly hues: the chief of the Brahmins, then prostrating himself before the shrine of Vishnu, drew from his breast the volume of the sacred laws of MENU, and read the following decree, in a deep and impressive voice: 'Glory be to

---

* The vapour of naphtha which issues through the crevices of the earth, is supposed to be the cause of the flame which is sometimes observed in India. At Chittagong is a fountain which bursts into flame, and which has its tutelar deities and presiding priests. When it is purposely extinguished, it rekindles spontaneously.

Vishnu! who thus speaks by the mouth of his Prophet Menu.* He who talks to the wife or the widow of a Brahmin, at a place of pilgrimage, in a consecrated grove, or at the confluence of rivers, incurs the punishment of guilt; the seduction of a guarded Priestess is to be repaid with life: but if she be not only guarded, but eminent for good qualities, he is to be burnt with the fires of divine wrath!' At these words the solemn roll of the tublea, or drum of condemnation, resounded through the temple; and when the awful sound had died away in melancholy murmurs, two Brahmins coming forward, made their depositions of the guilt of the chief Priestess of the temple. They deposed, that, passing near the sacred grove which led to the pavilion of the Priestess, they observed issuing from its shades the Mogul Prince Solyman – that, induced by their zeal for the purity of their sacred order, they repaired at the same hour on the following evening to the place of her evening worship, where they had discovered the Brachmachira, not indeed as they had expected, with the worshipper of Mahomet, but with a Frangui or Impure, who had already endeavoured to seduce some of the children of Brahma to abandon the God of their fathers; that they found her supporting the infidel in her arms – a circumstance sufficient to confirm every suspicion of her guilt, and to call for her excommunication, or forfeiture of cast. The sanctity, the age and reputation of the Brahmins, gave to their testimony a weight which none dared dispute. It was now only reserved for the Guru to pronounce sentence on his granddaughter. He was supported by two Yogis. A ghastly and livid hue diffused itself over his countenance; and in his despairing look were mingled with the distracted feelings of the doting parent, the superstitious horrors of the zealous Priest. Thrice he essayed to pronounce that name, hitherto never uttered but with triumph; and to heap curses upon that beloved head, on which blessings and tears of joy had so often fallen together. At last, in a low, trembling, and hollow voice, he said,

'Luxima, the Brachmachira of Cashmire, Chief Priestess of the Pagoda of Sirinagur, and a consecrated vestal of Brahma, having justly forfeited cast, is doomed by the word of Brahma, and the law of Menu, to become a Chancalas, a wanderer, and an outcast upon earth! – with none to pray with her, none to sacrifice with her, none to read with her, and none to speak to her; none to be allied by friendship or by marriage to her, none to eat, none to drink, and none to pray with her. Abject let her live, excluded from all social duties; let her wander over the earth, deserted by all, trusted by none, by none received with affection, by none treated with confidence – an apostate from her religion, and an alien to her country, branded with the stamp of infamy and of shame, the curse of Heaven and the hatred of all good men.'†

The last words died on the lips of him who pronounced them; and the unfortunate grandsire fell lifeless in the arms of his attendants. The conch, or religious shell, was then blown with a blast so shrill and loud, that it resembled

---

* See translation of the Laws of Menu,[26] by Sir William Jones.
† Such is the form of the Indian excommunication.

the sound of the last trump; the tublea rolled, and was echoed by endless rever-
berations; hideous shouts of superstitious frenzy mingling their discordant jar,
ran along the mighty concave like pealing thunderbolts, until gradually these
sounds of terror fainted away in sobbing echoes; and the awful procession
departed from the temple to the same solemn strains, in the same order in
which it had entered it. All was again silent, awful, and gloomy; like the night
which preceded creation, or that which is to follow its destruction. The subterraneous fires still faintly emitted their flame above the surface of the earth, and
threw their mystic light on the brow of the excommunicated Priestess. She lay
lifeless on the earth, where she had fallen during the conclusion of the ceremony
of her excommunication, with a shriek so loud and piercing, that the horrid
crash of sounds, which at that moment filled the Pagoda, could alone have
drowned her shrill and plaintive voice, or prevented the discovery of her situation to the ministers of the temple. The Missionary knelt beside her, watching,
in breathless agony, the slow departure and fading sounds of the procession.
When all was still, he turned his eyes on the Outcast; he saw her lying without
life or motion, cold and disfigured, and, save by him alone, abandoned and
abhorred by all. Thus lost, thus fallen, he beheld her in a place where she had
once received the homage of a deity: he saw her an innocent and unoffending
victim, offered by himself, by his mistaken zeal and imprudent passion, on the
altar of a rigid and cruel superstition: his brain maddened as he gazed upon her,
for he almost believed her tender heart had broken its life-chords, under the
pressure of feelings and sufferings beyond the power of human endurance; and,
in this dreadful apprehension, all capability of thought or action alike deserted
him. Alike bereaved of reflection or resource, alike destitute of effort or energy,
he remained mute, agonized, and gazing on the object of his tenderness and his
despair. At last a sigh, soft, yet convulsive, breathed from the lips of Luxima,
and seemed to operate on his frame like electricity: it was a human sound, and it
dispelled the dead-like silence of all around him; it was the accent of love and
sorrow, and his heart vibrated to its respiration. He raised the sufferer in his
arms; he addressed to her soothing murmurs of love and pity, of hope and consolation. At the sound of his voice she raised her eyes, and gazed, with a look of
fear and terror, round her, as if she expected to meet the forms, or to hear the
voices, of the awful ministers of her malediction; but the moment which succeeded was cheaply purchased, even by its preceding horrors. She turned back
her languid eyes in despair, believing herself abandoned alike by Heaven and
earth, but she fixed them in transport on him who was now her universe; her
whole being received a new impulse from the look which answered to her own.

'Thou art safe! thou art near me!' she exclaimed, in a sobbing accent; and,
falling on his shoulder, she wept. Some moments of unbroken silence passed
away, devoted to emotions too exquisite and too profound to be imaged by
words. Where a true and perfect love exists, there is a melancholy bliss in the
sacrifices made for its object; and the tender Indian was now soothed, under her
affliction, by the consideration of him for whose sake she had incurred it: for to

suffer, or to die, for him she loved, was more precious to her feelings, than even to have enjoyed security and life, independent of his idea, his influence, or his presence. But equal[a] to sustain her own miseries, she was overpowered by the fate which remotely threatened him; and in a moment when her affection rose in proportion to the peril he risked for her sake, she resolved on the last and greatest sacrifice the heart of woman could make to effect his safety, by again urging his flight, and resigning him for ever. Gazing on him, therefore, with a melancholy smile, which love and agony disputed, she said, 'My father and my friend! a creature avoided and abhorred by all, labouring under the curse of her nation and the wrath of Heaven, has no alternative but to submit to a fate, which she can neither avert nor avoid: but for thee, who hast incurred the penalty of a crime, of which thou art innocent, and which thy pure soul abhors, a life of safety and of glory is yet reserved. A law, which seems dictated by cruelty, is always reluctantly executed by the gentle and benevolent Hindus; and they shudder to take the life which they yet forbear not to render miserable. Provoke not then their wrath by thy presence, but fly, and live for those most happy and most blessed, who shall meet thy looks and hang upon thy words.[b] For me, my days are numbered – sad and few, they will wear away in some trackless desert; where, lost to my cast, my country, and my fame, death, welcome and wished for, shall yet find my soul wedded to one deathless bliss, the bliss of knowing I was beloved by thee.' As she spoke, her head drooped on the trembling hands which were clasped in hers; her tears bathed them. A long and an affecting pause ensued.

A thousand feelings, opposite in their nature and powerful in their influence, seemed to struggle in the bosom of the Missionary: a thousand ideas, each at variance with the other, seemed to rush on and to agitate his mind.[c] At last, withdrawing the hand which trembled in hers, and with the look and voice of one whose soul, after a long tumultuous conflict, is wound up to unalterable resolution, he said, 'Luxima, I am a Christian, and a priest, and I am bound by certain vows to Heaven, from the observance of which no human power can absolve me; but I am also a man; as such, led by feeling, impelled by humanity, and bound by duty, to aid the weak and to succour the unfortunate: – but when I am myself the cause of sorrow to the innocent! of affliction to the unoffending! – O Luxima!' he passionately added, 'lost to thee for ever, as lover or as husband, thinkest thou that I can also abandon thee as pastor and as friend? Hast thou then, my daughter, the courage to leave for ever the temples of thy God, and the land of thy forefathers? Art thou so assured of thyself and of me, as to follow me through distant regions, to follow me as my *disciple only;* to take up the cross of Christianity, and to devote what remains of thy young and blooming life exclusively to Heaven? Luxima, wilt thou follow me to Goa?'

'Follow *thee?*' wildly and tenderly repeated the Indian. An hysteric laugh burst from her lips, a crimson blush rushed over her face, and again deserting it, left it colourless.[d] 'Follow thee! O Heaven! *through life to death!*'

The Missionary arose: he averted his eyes from the fatal eloquence of hers: he paced the temple with an unequal but rapid step; he seemed wrapt in thoughts wild and conflicting. At last, turning to Luxima, he fixed his eyes on her face, and said, with a voice firm, solemn, and impressive, 'Daughter, it is well! from this moment I am thy guide on earth to heaven – no more!'

'No more!' faintly repeated Luxima, casting down her looks and sighing profoundly. Then, after a short pause, the Missionary extended his hand to raise her; but suddenly relinquishing the trembling form he supported, he moved away. Luxima, with a slow and feeble step, followed him to the entrance of the temple; but, as they reached together the extremity of the cavern, the blue light of the subterraneous fire flashed on an image of Camdeo, her tutelar deity. She started, involuntarily paused before the idol, and bowed her head to the earth.

The Missionary threw on her a glance of severe reproof, and, taking her hand, would have led her on; but this little image had touched on the chord of her most profound feelings, and awakened the most intimately associated ideas of her mind.[a]

'Father,' she said, in a timid supplication of look and voice, 'forgive me; but here, in this spot, no less an idol than that at whose shrine I bow – my nation's pride and sex's glory – here did I devote myself to Heaven; and becoming the Priestess of mystic love, here did I renounce, by many a sacred vow, all human passion and all human ties.'

'Luxima,' he replied, still leading her on, 'such as were thy vows, such *are* mine; let us alike keep them in our recollection, and renew them in our hearts. O my daughter! let us more than tacitly renew them in our hearts; let us together kneel, and—'

'*But not here, father!*' tremulously interrupted Luxima, looking fearfully round her – 'not here!'

'No,' he replied, and shuddered as he spoke, 'not here!'

In silence, and with rapid steps, they passed beneath the frowning and gigantic arch, which hung its ponderous vault above the threshold of the Pagan temple; to its impervious gloom, its mysterious obscurity, succeeded the sudden brightness of the moonlight glen, in whose lovely solitudes the awful pile reared its massive heights, to intercept the rising, or catch the parting beam of day. Here the proscribed wanderers paused; they listened breathlessly, and gazed on every side; for danger, perhaps death, surrounded them: but not a sound disturbed the mystic silence, save the low murmurs of a gushing spring, which fell with more than mortal music from a mossy cliff,[b] sparkling among the matted roots of overhanging trees, and gliding, like liquid silver, beneath the network of the parasite plants. The flowers of the Mangoosten gave to the fresh air a balmy fragrance. The mighty rocks of the Pagoda, which rose behind in endless perspective, scaling the heavens, which seemed to repose upon their summits, lent the strong relief of their deep shadows to the softened twilight of the foreground.

'All is still,' said the Missionary, pausing near the edge of the falling stream, and relinquishing the hand he had till now clasped; 'all is still, and spirits of peace seem to walk abroad, to calm the tumult of human cares,[a] to whisper hope, and to inspire confidence. My daughter, eternity is in these moments. The brief and frail authority of man, reduced to its own insignificance, holds no jurisdiction now, and the spirit ascends free and fearless to the throne of its Creator.' The Missionary stood gazing on the firmament as he spoke, his soul mingling with the magnificent and sublime objects he contemplated; then, turning his eyes on Luxima, he was struck with the peculiar character of her air and person. She looked, as she stood at a little distance, half hid in the mists of shade, like some impalpable form, which imaged on the air the spirit of suffering innocence, in the first moment of its ascent to heaven. Her head was thrown back, and a broken moonbeam, falling through the trees, encompassed it with a faint glory: the tears of human suffering had not yet dried upon her cheek of snow; but it was the only trace of human feeling visible: her soul seemed to commune with him of whom it was an emanation.

'Luxima,' said the Missionary, approaching her, 'the[b] moment of thy perfect conversion is surely arrived: in spirit thou belongest to Him who died to save thee; be then his also by those rites, which, in a place like this, he thought it not beneath him to receive, from the hands of one by whom he was preceded, as the star of the morning ushers in the radiance of the rising sun. O my daughter! ere together we commence our perilous and trying pilgrimage, we have need of all the favour which Heaven's mercy can afford us, for we have much to dread, from others and ourselves; let then no tie be wanting which can bind us faster to virtue and religion. Luxima, innocent and afflicted as thou now art, pure and sublime as thou now lookest, feelest thou thyself not worthy to become a Christian in form as in faith?'

'If *thou* thinkest me not unworthy,' she replied, in a low voice, 'that which thou art, I am willing to be.'

The Missionary led her forward, in silence, to the edge of the spring, and blessing the living waters as they flowed, he raised his consecrated hands, and shed the dew of salvation upon the head of the proselyte, pronouncing, in a voice of inspiration, the *solemn sacrament of baptism*. All around harmonized with the holy act; Nature stood sole sponsor; the incense which filled the air, arose from the bosom of the earth; and the light which illuminated the ceremony, was light from heaven.

A long and solemn pause ensued; then the Missionary, clasping and holding up the hands of Luxima in his, said, 'Father, receive into thy service this spotless being; for to thy service do I consecrate her.'

A beam of religious triumph shone in the up-turned eyes of the Missionary. The conversion of the Priestess of Brahma was perfected, and human passion was subdued. 'Daughter of heaven!' he said, 'thou hast now nothing to fear; and I, on this side eternity, have nothing to hope.' As he spoke the last words, an involuntary sigh burst from his lips, and he turned his eyes on the Christian vestal; but hers were fixed upon the Pagoda, the temple of her ancient devotion. Her look was sad and wild; she seemed absorbed and overwhelmed by the rapidity of emotions which had lately assailed her. 'Let us proceed,' he said, in a softened voice, 'if thou be able; let us leave for ever the monument of the dark idolatry which thou hast abjured.' As he spoke, he took her arm to lead her on; but he started, and suddenly let it fall, for he found it was encircled with the muntra, or Brahminical rosary, from which the image of Camdeo was suspended. 'Luxima,' he said, 'these are not the ornaments of a Christian vestal.'

Luxima clasped her hands in agony; the tears dropped fast upon her bosom; and she fell at his feet, exclaiming, in a voice of tenderness and despair, 'Oh! thou wilt not deprive me of these also? I have nothing left now *but these!* nothing to remind me, in the land of strangers, of my country and my people, save only these: it makes a part of the religion I have abandoned, to respect the sacred ties of nature; does my new faith command me to break them? This rosary was fastened on my arm by a parent's tender hand, and bathed in Nature's holiest dew – a parent's tender tears:[a] hold not the Christians relics, such as these, precious and sacred? Thou hast called thy religion the religion of the heart; will it not then respect the heart's best feelings?' A deep convulsive sob interrupted her words; all the ties she had broken pressed upon her bosom, and the affections of habit, those close-knit and imperishable affections, interwoven, by time and circumstance, with the very life-nerves of the heart, bore down for the moment, every other passion. The Outcast, with her eyes fixed upon the religious ornaments of her youth, wept, as she gazed, her country, parents, friends – 'and would not be comforted.'

The Missionary sighed and was silent: he sighed to observe the strong influence of a religion, which so intimately connected itself with all the most powerful emotions of nature and earliest habits of life; and which, taking root in the heart, with its first feelings, could only be perfectly eradicated by the slow operation of expanding reason, by the strengthening efforts of moral perception, or by the miraculous effects of divine grace, and he was silent; because, the appeal which the tender and eloquent Indian made to his feelings, found an advocate in his breast it was impossible to resist.[b] Instead, therefore, of reproving her emotion, he suffered himself to be infected by its softness, and mingled his tears with hers.

The grief of Luxima subsided in the blessed consciousness of a sympathy so precious, so unexpected; and love's warm glow dried up the tear, which the grief of natural affection shed on the cheek of the Outcast. 'Thou weepest for me,' she said, chasing away the trembling drops which hung in her up-turned eyes; 'and in the indulgence of a selfish feeling, I hazard thy safety and thy life! That cruel, that accusing Brahmin, who has watched my steps to my destruction, whom I mistook last night for the vision of that God he too zealously serves – may he not even now lurk in these shades; or may he not, when we are vainly sought for in our respective asylums, seek us here? – O my father! forgive these tears. But it was the tenderness of him who lately cursed me; it was my aged grandsire, whom I have dragged to death and covered with shame (for something of my infamy must light on all my kindred); it was he who, with the morning's dawn, sent me the tidings of my approaching fate, and bade me fly and shun it: he would not see, he would not hear me; nor dare he breathe my name, but to heap curses on my head. But for this timely tender warning I should have else been hunted, like some noxious reptile, to wilds and wastes, there to die and be forgotten. All day I lay concealed amidst the shades of the impervious banyan, to wait thy coming with the evening sun, to bid thee a last farewell, and urge thee to save thyself by an immediate flight; but by a miracle, wrought doubtlessly by thy God for thee, that which seemed to lead us to destruction, became the wondrous mean[a] of preservation; and we found safety where we could only hope for death.'

'Luxima,' said the Missionary, 'let us believe that He, who alone could save us, still extends around us the shelter of his wing.[b] Let us, while yet thou hast strength, fly these fatal shades. Behind those pine-covered rocks, which the moon now silvers, there lies, I know, a deep and entangled glen, which, I have heard, is held in superstitious horror, and never approached by pious Hindus. This glen leads to Bembar, by many a solitary path, made to facilitate the march of the caravan from Thibet to Tatta, at this season of the year.[*] It was but yesterday, some straggling troops, belonging to the caravan, passed through the valley, and halted at no great distance hence, to traffic with the Cashmirian merchants: these, as they often halt, we may overtake in some lone way, out of the view of thy intolerant country-men.' While he spoke, they had proceeded on, and reached the entrance to a ravine in the rocks, which, dark and tremendous, seemed like a closing chasm above their heads, threatening destruction; but, when they had reached its extremity, they found themselves in a delicious glen, through whose trees were discernible the crescent banners of the Mogul camp; and the sky-lamps, which marked the outposts of the midnight guards. At this sight, the prophetic warning and generous offers of the gallant Solyman rushed with equal force to the minds of the wanderers; but both remained silent – Luxima, from an instinctive delicacy, which mocked the refinement of acquired sentiment; the Missionary, from a feeling less laudable and less disinterested. Both involuntarily turned their eyes on each other, and suddenly withdrawing them, changed colour; for, in spite of the awful vows since made, and the virtuous resolutions since formed, the hearts of each throbbed responsively to the dangerous recollection of that fatal scene, to which the unexpected presence of the Mogul Prince had given birth.

Ere the mild and balmy night had passed its noon, the weary proselyte, exhausted equally from fatigue of mind and body, felt that she would be unable to proceed, if she snatched not the invigorating refreshment of a short repose. The Missionary, with tender watchfulness, was the first to observe her faltering

---

[*] 'Selon les témoignages de tous les Katchmeriens, on voyoit partir chaque année de leur pays plusieurs caravans.'[27] – *Voyages de* BERNIER.

steps, and sought out for her a mossy bank, cradled by the luxuriant branches of a mango-tree; and, withdrawing to a little distance, he at once guarded her slumber and gave himself up to meditate on some precise plan for their future pilgrimage; which, if they could overtake the caravan, whose track they had already discovered, would be attended with but few difficulties. Yet he dared no longer seek 'the highways and public places,' to promulgate his doctrines, and to evince his zeal. Withheld less by a principle of self-preservation than by his fears for the safety and even life of his innocent proselyte; he also felt his enthusiasm in the cause weakened, by the apparent impossibility of its success; for he perceived that the religious prejudices of Hindostan were too intimately connected with the temporal prosperity of its inhabitants, with the established opinions, with the laws, and even with the climate of the country, to be universally subverted, but by a train of moral and political events which should equally emancipate their minds from antiquated error, in which they were absorbed, and which should destroy the fundamental principles of their loose and ill-digested government. He almost looked upon the Mission, in which he had engaged, as hopeless; and he felt that the miracle of that conversion, by which he expected to evince the sacred truth of the cause in which he had embarked, could produce no other effect than a general abhorrence of him who laboured to effect it, and of her who had already paid the forfeit of all most precious to the human breast, for that partial proselytism, to which her affections, rather than her reason, had induced her. Yet, when he reflected that he should return to Goa, the scenes of his former triumphs, followed only by one solitary disciple, and that disciple a young and lovely woman, his mind became confused, and he trembled to dwell on an idea fraught with a thousand mortifying and cruel recollections. The dawn had already beamed upon his harassing vigils, when Luxima stood before him, resembling the star of the morning, bright in her softness, the mists of a tender sadness hanging on the lustre of her looks. The Missionary was revived by her presence; but the sweet and subtle transport, which circulated through his veins, as he gazed on the being who now considered him as her sole providence, he endeavoured to conceal beneath a tranquil coldness of manner, which the secret ardour of his feelings, the delicacy of his situation, and the pure and virtuous resolutions of his mind, alike rendered necessary and laudable.

As they proceeded, he spoke to her of the plans he had devised, and of his intention of placing her in a religious house when they arrived at Goa. He spoke to her of the false religion she had abandoned, and of the pure faith she had embraced.

Luxima answered only by gentle sighs, and by looks, which seemed to say, 'Whatever may be my future destiny, I am at least *now* near you.'

The Missionary sought to avoid these looks, which, when they met his eye, sunk to his heart, and disturbed his best resolutions; for never had his Neophyte looked more lovely. Supported by a white wand, which he had formed for her, of a bamboo, she moved lightly and timidly by his side, like the genius of the sweet

and solitary shades, in which they wandered. The course of the rivers, the varia-
tion of the soil, and the beacons held out to them by the surrounding mountains,
with whose forms they were well acquainted, were their guides; while the milk
of the young and luscious cocoa-nut, the cheering nectar extracted from the
pulp of the bilva-fruit, and the rice, and delicious fruits, which on every side
presented themselves, afforded at once nutrition and refreshment.* Sometimes
catching, sometimes losing, the faint track of the caravan, the conviction of
increasing safety, and the certainty of overtaking it at Bembar, left them
scarcely a fear, and scarcely a hope, on the subject. For to wander through the
lovely and magnificent valley of Cashmire, was but to loiter amidst the
enjoyments of Eden; and to proceed by each other's side – to catch the half-
averted eyebeam, which penetrated the soul – to observe the sudden glow which
mantled on the cheek – to participate in the same blissful feeling, and yet to
heighten, by submitting it to the same pure sense of virtue, was a state of being
too exquisite not to obliterate, in its transient enjoyment, the memory of the
past and the apprehension of the future. Restrained and reserved even in the
intimacy of their intercourse, they sought to forget the existence of a passion it
was now so dangerous to cherish. The Missionary was regulated by religion and
by honour; the Indian, by sentiment and by instinctive delicacy. Solicitude
tempered by reserve, tenderness blended with respect, distinguished the
manner of the Priest. Modesty, which shrunk from the appearance of intrusion;
and bashfulness, trembling to betray the feelings it guarded, marked the
conduct of the Neophyte. Silent, except on subjects of religious sublimity, a look
suddenly caught and as suddenly withdrawn, alone betrayed their dangerous
secret. They were frequently parted during the ardours of the day, which
prevented their continuing their journey; and sometimes, when the night-dews
fell heavily, the guardian Priest sought out for his weary charge a grassy couch,
where the madhucca had spread its downy leaves; or where a luxurious and
perfumed shade was afforded by the sephalica, whose flowers unfold only their
bloom and odour to the sighs of night, and droop and wither beneath the first
ray the sun darts o'er their fragile loveliness: while *he*, not daring, even by a
look, to violate the pure and seraph slumber of confiding innocence, waked only
to guard her repose; or slept, to woo to his fancy the dream, which too often, in
illusive visions, gave to his heart her whom waking he trembled to approach.
When they arose, the twilight of the dawn conducted them to the respective
bath, which innumerable springs afforded; and, when again they met, they
offered together the incense of the heart to Heaven, and proceeded on their
pilgrimage.ᵃ The path they had taken was so sequestered, that they seldom
risked discovery, but when, amidst the haze of distance, they observed a human
form, or caught a human sound, they plunged into the umbrage of the
surrounding shades, until the absence of the intruder again gave them up to

* 'Il faut surtout considérer que l'abstinence de la chair des animaux est une suite de
la nature du climat.' – *Essai sur les Mœurs des Nations, &c. &c. &c.*[28]

solitude and silence. It was in moments such as these only, that the high mind of the Missionary felt that it had forfeited its claim to the independence which belongs to unblemished rectitude, and that the Indian remembered she was an alien and an Outcast.[a]

THE END OF VOL. II.

THE

MISSIONARY:

AN

INDIAN TALE.

———————

BY

MISS OWENSON.

———————

WITH A PORTRAIT OF THE AUTHOR.

=====

IN THREE VOLUMES.

=====

VOL. III.

================

LONDON:
PRINTED FOR J. J. STOCKDALE,
NO. 41, PALL MALL.
1811.

The Missionary
Volume 3

CHAPTER XIII.

ON the second day of their wandering, the deep shade of the forest scenery, in which they had hitherto been involved, softened into a less impervious gloom, the heights of the black rock of Bembhar rose on their view, and the lovely and enchanting glen which reposes at its northern base,[a] and which is called the Valley of Floating Islands burst upon their glance. These phenomena, which appear on the bosom of the Behat, are formed by the masses of rock, by the trees and shrubs which the whirlwind tears from the summits of the surrounding mountains, and which are thus borne away by the fury of the torrents, and plunged into the tranquil waters beneath; these rude fragments, collected by time and chance, cemented by the river Slime, and intermixed by creeping plants, and parasite grasses, become small but lovely islets, covered with flowers, sowed by the vagrant winds, and skirted by the leaves and blossoms of the crimson lotos, the water-loving flower of Indian groves. This scene, so luxuriant and yet so animating, where all was light, and harmony, and odour, gave a new sensation to the nerves, and a new tone to the feelings[b] of the wanderers, and their spirits were fed with balmier airs, and their eyes greeted with lovelier objects, than hope or fancy had ever imagined to their minds. –[c] Sometimes they stood together on the edge of the silvery flood, watching the motion of the arbours which floated on its bosom, or pursuing the twinings of the harmless green serpent, which, shining amidst masses of kindred hues, raised gracefully his brilliant crest above the edges of the river bank. Sometimes from beneath the shade of umbrageous trees, they beheld the sacred animal of India[1] breaking the stubborn flood with his broad white breast, and gaining the fragrant islet, where he reposed his heated limbs; his mild countenance shaded by his crooked horns, crowned by the foliage in which he had entangled them; thus reposing in tranquil majesty, he looked like some river-deity of antient fable.

Flights of many-coloured perroquets, of lorys,[2] and of peacocks, reflected on the bosom of the river the bright and various tints of their splendid plumage; while the cozel, the nightingale of Hindoo bards, poured its song of love from the summit of the loftiest *mergosa*, the eastern lilac. It was here they found the *Jama,* or rose apple-tree, bearing ambrosial fruit – it was here that the sweet sumbal, the spikenard of the antients, spread its tresses of dusky gold over the clumps of granite, which sparkled like coloured gems amidst the saphire of the mossy soil – it was here that, at the decline of a lovely day, the wanderers reached the shade of a natural arbour, formed by the union of a tamarind-tree with the branches of a *covidara*, whose purple and rose-coloured blossoms mingled with the golden fruit which, to the Indian palate, affords so delicious a refreshment.

It was Luxima who discovered this retreat so luxurious, and yet so simple. The purity of the atmosphere, the brilliancy of the scene, had given to her spirits a higher tone than usually distinguished their languid character. Looking pure and light as the air she breathed, she had bounded on before her companion, who, buried in profound reverie, seemed at once more thoughtful and more tender than he had yet appeared in look or manner. When he reached the arbour, he found Luxima seated beneath its shade – her brow crowned with Indian feathers, and her delicate fingers engaged in forming a wreath of odoriferous berries; looking like the emblem of that lovely region, whose mild and delicious climate had contributed to form the beauty of her person, the softness of her character, and the ardour of her imagination. No thought of future care contracted her brow, and the smile of peace and innocence sat on her lips. Not so the Missionary: the morbid habit of watching his own sensations had produced in him an hypochondriasm of conscience, which embittered the most blameless moments of his life; his diseased mind discovered a lurking crime in the most innocent enjoyments; and the fear of offending Heaven, fastened his attention to objects which were only dangerous, by not being immediately dismissed from his thoughts. The moral economy of his nature suffered from the very means he took to preserve it; and his danger arose less from his temptation, than from the sensibility with which he watched its progress, and the efforts he made to combat and to resist its influence. He now beheld Luxima more lovely than he had ever seen her; she was gracefully occupied, and there was something picturesque, something almost *fantastic*, in her appearance, which gave the poignant charm of novelty to her air and person. She was murmuring an Indian song, as he approached her. The Missionary stood gazing on her for some moments in silence, then suddenly averting[a] his eyes, and seating himself near her, he said – 'And to what purpose, my dearest daughter, dost thou so industriously weave those fragrant wreaths?'

'To hang upon the bower of thy repose,' she replied, 'as a spell against evil; – for dost thou not, on every side, perceive the *bacula* plant, so injurious to the nerves, and whose baneful influence the odour of these berries can alone dispel?'*

* The odour of this flower produces violent head-aches.

'Alas!' he exclaimed, 'in scenes so lovely and remote as those in which we now wander, who could suspect that latent evil lurked? But the evil which always exists, and that against which it is most difficult to guard, exists within ourselves, Luxima.'

'Thou sayest it,' returned Luxima, 'and therefore must it be true; and yet, methinks, in us at least no evil can exist – look around thee, Father; behold those hills which encompass us on every side, and which, seeming to shut out the universe, exclude all the evil passions by which it is agitated and disordered; and since absent from all human intercourse, our feelings relate only to each other, surely in us at least no evil *can* exist.'

'Let us hope, let us trust there does not, Luxima,' said the Missionary, in strong emotion; 'and oh! my daughter, let us watch and pray that there *may not*.'

'And here,' said Luxima with simplicity, and suspending her work, 'where all breathes of peace and innocence, against what are we to pray?'

'Even against *those thoughts* which involuntarily start into the mind, and which, though confined, and perhaps referring exclusively to each other, may yet become fatal and seductive, may yet plunge us into error beyond the mercy of Heaven to forgive!'

'But if one *sole* thought occupies the existence!' said Luxima, tenderly and with energy, 'and if it is sanctified by the perfection of its object!'

'But to what earthly object does perfection belong, Luxima?'

'To thee;' replied the Neophyte, blushing.

'It is the ardour of thy gratitude only,' said the Missionary with vehemence, 'which bestows on me, an epithet belonging alone to Heaven. And lovely as is this purest of human sentiments, yet, *being human*, it is liable to corruption, and may be carried to an excess fatal to us both; for, oh! Luxima, were I to avail myself of this excess of gratitude, this pure but unguarded tenderness, and in wilds solitary and luxuriant as these, where happiness and security might mingle, where, forgetting the world, and its opinions, abandoning alike *heaven* and its *cause!*' – he paused abruptly – he trembled, and a deep groan burst from a heart, agitated by all the conflicting emotions of a sensitive conscience, and an imperious passion.

Luxima, moved by his agitation – tender, timid, yet always happy and tranquilly blessed in the presence of him, the idol of her secret thoughts, and fearing only those incidents which might impede the innocent felicity of being near him – endeavoured to soothe his perturbation, and, taking his hand in hers, and bending her head towards him, she looked on his eyes with innocent fondness, and her sighs, sweet as the incense of the evening, breathed on his burning cheek! Then the sacred fillet of religion fell from his eyes; he threw himself at her feet, and pressing her hands to his heart, he said passionately – 'Luxima, tell me, dost thou not belong exclusively to Heaven? Recall to my wandering mind that sacred vow, by which I solemnly devoted thee to its service, at the baptismal font! Oh! my daughter, thou wouldst not destroy me? thou wouldst not arm Heaven against me, Luxima?'

'I!' returned Luxima tenderly, 'I destroy thee, who art dear to me as heaven itself!'

'Oh! Luxima,' he exclaimed in emotion, 'look not thus on me! tell me not that I am dear to thee, or ... .' At that moment his rosary fell to the earth, and lay at the feet of the Indian.

An incident so natural and so simple struck on the conscience of the Missionary, as though the Minister of Divine wrath had blasted his gaze with his accusing presence; – he grew pale and shuddered, his arms fell back upon his breast; – overpowered by shame, and by self-abhorrence, rushing from the bower, he plunged into the thickest shade of the grove; there he threw himself on the earth; and that mind, once so high and lofty in its own conscious triumph, was now again sunk and agonized by the conviction of its own debasement. From this state of unsupportable humiliation, he was awakened by the sound of horses' feet; he raised his eyes, and beheld approaching an Indian, who led a small Arabian horse, laden with empty panniers: the Missionary hastily arose – and the stranger, moved by the dignity of his form, and the disorder of his pale and haggard countenance, gave him the *Salaam*; and invited him, with the hospitable courtesy of his country, to repair to his cottage, which lay at a little distance, – 'Or perhaps,' he said, 'you wish to overtake the caravan, and—'

'To *overtake* it!' interrupted the Missionary; 'has it then long passed?'

'It halts now,' returned the peasant; 'on the other side of *Bembhar*, I have been disposing of some *touz*★ to a merchant of Tatta; if you have no other mode of proceeding, you will scarcely overtake it on foot.'

A new cause of suffering now occupied his mind. – Luxima, hitherto cheered and supported by the lovely and enlivening scenes through which she passed, by the smoothness of her path and the temperature of her native climes, was yet wearied and exhausted by a journey performed in a manner to which the delicacy of her frame was little adequate – but it was now impossible she could proceed as she had hitherto done; in a few hours the Eden which had cheated fatigue of its influence, would disappear from their eyes; and, should the caravan have proceeded much in advance, it was impossible that the delicate Indian could encounter the horrors of the desert which lay on the southern side of Bembhar.

It was then that, believing Providence had sent the Indian in his path, a new hope revived in his heart, a new resource was opened in his mind: – he offered a part of what remained of the purse of rupees he had brought with him from Lahore, for the Arabian horse. It was more than its value, and the Indian gladly accepted his proposal, and, pointing out to him the shortest way to *Bembhar*, and offering his good wishes for the safety of his journey, he pursued his way to his cottage. As soon as he had disappeared, Hilarion led the animal to the bower, where Luxima still remained, involved in reveries so soft, and yet so pro-

★ Une laine, ou plutôt un poil, qu'on nomme *touz*, se prend sur les poitrines des chèvres sauvages des montagnes de Cashmire.[3] – *Bernier*.

found, that she observed not the approach of him who was their sole and exclusive object.

'Luxima!' he said in a low and tremulous voice – Luxima started, and, covered with blushes, she raised her languid eyes to his, and faintly answered – 'Father!'[a]

'My daughter,' he said, 'that Heaven, of whose favour I at least am so unworthy, has mercifully extended its providential care to us. A stranger, whom I met in the forest, has informed me, that the caravan has passed the rock of Bembhar; but I have purchased from him this animal, by which thou wilt be able to proceed!'

Luxima arose, and, drawing her veil over a face in which the lovely confusion of a sensitive modesty and ardent tenderness still lingered, she suffered the Missionary[b] to place her on the gentle Arabian – and he moving with long and rapid steps by her side, they again renewed their pilgrimage.

Already the bloom and verdure of Cashmire appeared fading into the approaching heights of the sterile Bembhar, and the travellers, silent and thoughtful, ascended those acclivities, which seemed but to reflect the smiling lustre of the scenes they left; no sound, even of nature, disturbed the profound silence of scenes – so still and solemn, that they resembled the primæval world, ere human existence had given animation to its pathless wilds, or human passions had disturbed the calm of its mild tranquillity![c] No sound was heard, save the jackall's dismal yell, which so often disturbs the impressive and serene beauty of Indian scenery.

But this death-like calm failed to communicate a correspondent influence to the bosom of the solitary wanderers: – again together, in a boundless solitude, they were yet silent, as though they feared a human accent would destroy the impassioned mystery which existed between them; while religion and penitence, and delicacy and self-distrust, enforced the necessity of a reserve, to which both alike submitted with difficulty but with fortitude. Solitude, with the object of a suppressed tenderness, is always too dangerous! and that great passion which seeks a desart, finds the proper region of its own empire.[d] Thus, those helpless and tender friends, in whom love and grace struggled with equal sway, now eagerly looked forward to their restoration to society, which would afford them that protection against themselves, which nature, in her loveliest regions, had hitherto seemed to refuse them.

The travellers at last reached the summit of the *rock of Bembhar*; and, ere they descended the wild and burning plains of Upper Lahore, the Indian turned round to take a last view of her native Eden. The sun was setting in all his majesty of light upon the valley; and villages, and pagodas, and groves, and rivers, were brilliantly tinted with his crimson rays. Luxima cast one look in that direction where lay the district of Sirinagur – another towards Heaven – and then fixed her tearful eyes on the Missionary, with an expression so eloquent and so ardent, that they seemed to say, 'Heaven and earth have I resigned for thee!' – The Missionary met and returned her look, but dared not trust his lips to speak;

and, in the sympathy and intelligence of that silent glance, the Indian found country, kindred, friends; or ceased for a moment to remember she had lost them all.

Sad, silent, and gloomy, resembling the first pair, when they had reached the boundary of their native paradise, they now descended the southern declivities of Bembhar: the dews of Cashmire no longer embalmed the evening air, and the heated vapours which arose from the plains below, rendered the atmosphere insupportably intense.

As they reached the plains of Upper Lahore, a few dark shrubs and blasted trees alone presented themselves in the hot and sandy soil; and when a stalk of rosemary and lavender, or the scarlet tulip of the desert, tempted the hand of the Missionary, for her to whom flowers were always precious, they mouldered into dust at his touch!

Luxima endeavoured to stifle a sigh, as she beheld nature in this her most awful and destructive aspect – and the Missionary, with a sad smile, sought to cheer her drooping spirit, by pointing out to her the track of the caravan, or the snowy summit of *Mount Alideck*, which arose like a land-mark before them. Having paused for a short time, while the Missionary ascended a rock, to perceive if the caravan was in view – which if it had been, the light of a brilliant moon would have discovered, – they proceeded during the night, in sadness and in gloom, while the intense thirst produced by the ardour of the air had already exhausted the juicy fruits with which the Missionary had supplied himself for Luxima's refreshment; at last the faint glimmering of the stars was lost in the brighter lustre of the morning-planet; the resplendent herald of day, riding in serene lustre through the heavens, ushered in the vigorous sun, whose potent rays rapidly pervaded the whole horizon. –[a] The fugitives found themselves near a large and solitary edifice; it was a *Choultry*, built for the shelter of travellers, and, as an inscription indicated, 'built by *Luxima*, the *Prophetess and Bramachira of Cashmire!*' – At the sight of this object, the Indian turned pale – all the glory and happiness of her past life rushed on the recollection of the excommunicated Chancalas; and her guide, feeling in all their force the sacrifices which she had made for him, silently and tenderly chased away her tears, with her veil. As it was impossible to proceed during the meridional ardours of the day, the wearied and exhausted Indian[b] sought shelter and repose beneath that roof which her own charity had raised; and a cocoa-tree, planted on the edge of a tank which she had excavated, afforded to her that refreshment, which she had benevolently provided for others. Here, it was evident, the caravan had lately halted; for the remains of some provisions, usually left by Indian travellers for those who may succeed them, were visible, and the track of wheels, of horses, and of camels' feet, was every where apparent. Revived and invigorated by an hour's undisturbed repose, they again re-commenced their route; still pursuing the track of the caravan, while, in forms rendered indistinct by distance, they still fancied they beheld the object of their pursuit. Scenes more varied than those through which they had already journeyed, now presented themselves to their view.

Sometimes they passed through a ruined village, which the flame of war had desolated; sometimes beneath the remains of a Mogul fortress, whose moulder-ing arches presented the most picturesque specimens of eastern military architecture; while from the marshy fosse, which surrounded the majestic ruins, arose a bright blue flame, and moving with velocity amidst its mouldering bas-tions, floating like waves, or falling like sparks of fire, became suddenly extinct – Luxima gazed upon this spectacle with fear and amazement, and, governed by the superstition of her early education, saw, in a natural phenomenon, the effects of a supernatural agency; trembling, she clung to her pastor and her guide, and said, 'It is the spirit of one who fell in the battle, or who died in the defence of these ruins, and who, for some crime unredeemed, is thus destined to wander till the time of expiation is accomplished, and he return into some form on earth.'

The Missionary sought to release her mind from the bondage of imaginary terrors, and at once to amuse her fancy, to enlighten her ideas, and to elevate her soul; he explained to her, with ingenious simplicity, the various and wonderful modes by which the Divine Spirit disposes of the different powers of nature, still teaching her to feel 'God in all, and all in God.'[4]

Luxima gazed on him with wonder while he spoke, and hung in silent admi-ration on words she deemed inspired; yet when, as it sometimes occurred, she beheld the rude altars raised, even in the most unfrequented places to *Boom-Daivee*, the goddess of the earth;[*] or to the Daivadergoel,[16] the tutelar guardians of wilds and forests, her senses acknowledged these images of her antient super-stition in spite of her reason, and she involuntarily bowed before the objects of her habitual devotion. Then the Missionary reproved her severely for the per-petual vacillation of her undecided faith; but, disarming his severity by looks and words of tenderness, she would fondly reply – 'Oh! my Father! it is not all devotion which bows my head and bends my knee before these well remembered shrines of my antient faith! Alas! it is not all a pious impulse, but a natural sym-pathy: for the genii to whom these altars are raised, were once, as I was, happy and glorified; but they incurred the wrath of *Shiven*,[†] by abandoning his laws; and, banished from their native heaven, were doomed to wander in solitary wastes to expiate their error: – but here, that sympathy ceases; for *they* found not, like me, a compensation for the paradise they forfeited; they found not on earth, something which partook of heaven, and they knew not that perfect com-munion, which images to the soul, in its transient probation through time, the bliss which awaits it in eternity.'

It was by words like these, timidly and tenderly pronounced, that the feelings of the spiritual guide were put to the most severe test; it was words like these, which chilled his manner, while they warmed his heart; which increased the

---

* See Kindersley's History of the *Hindu* Mythology.[5]

† 'C'est dans le *Shasta* que l'on trouve l'histoire de la Chute des Anges.'[7] – Essai sur les Mœurs des Nations. *P. 2, T. 2.*

hidden sentiment, and restrained the external emotion, and[a] which cherished and fed his passion, while they awakened his self-distrust: but Luxima, at once his peril and his salvation, counteracted by her innocence the effects of her tenderness, and alternately awakened, excited or subdued, by that feminine display of feeling and sentiment, which blended purity with ardour, and elevation of soul with tenderness of heart.[b] More sensitive than reflecting, she was guided rather by an instinctive delicacy, than a prudent reserve; in *her*, sentiment supplied the place of reason, and she was the most virtuous, because she was the most affectionate of women.

The evening again arose upon their wanderings, and they paused ere they proceeded to encounter the pathless way through the gloom of night;[c] they paused near the edge of a spring, which afforded a delicious refreshment; and, under the shadow of a lofty tamarind-tree, which, blooming in solitary beauty, supplied at once both fruit and shade, and seemed dropt in the midst of a lonesome waste, as a beacon to hope, as an assurance of the providential care of *him*, who reared its head in the desert for the relief of his creatures. Here the Missionary left Luxima to take repose; and, having fastened the *Arabian* to a neighbouring rock, embossed with patches of vegetation, he proceeded across some stoney acclivities which were covered by the caprice of nature with massy clumps of the *bamboo tree*. When he had reached the opposite side, he looked back to catch, as he was wont, a glimpse of Luxima; but, for the first time since the commencement of their pilgrimage,[d] she was hidden from his view by the intervening foliage of the plantation, trembling at the fancied dangers which might assail her in his absence: he proceeded with a rapid step towards an eminence, in the hope of ascertaining, from its summit, the path of the caravan, or of discovering some human habitation, though but the hut of a *pariah*, whose owner might guide their now uncertain steps.[e] Turning his eyes towards the still glowing West, he perceived a forest whose immense trees marked their waving outline on saffron clouds, which hung radiantly upon their gloom, tinging their dark branches with the yellow lustre of declining light; he perceived also, that this awful and magnificent forest was skirted by an illimitable jungle, through whose long-entangled grass a broad path-way seemed to have been recently formed, and, vision growing strong by exercise, the first confusion of objects which had distracted his gaze, gradually subsiding into distinct images, he perceived the blue smoke curling from a distant hut, which he knew, from its desolate situation, to be the miserable residence of some *Indian outcast*; he soon more distinctly observed some great body in motion: at first it appeared compact and massive; by degrees broken and irregular; and at last the form and usual pace of a troop of camels were obvious to his far-stretched sight, by a deep red light which suddenly illumined the whole firmament, and, throwing its extended beams into the distant fore-ground, fell, with bright tints, upon every object, and confirmed the Missionary in hopes, he almost trembled to encourage, that the caravan at that moment moved before his eyes! But the joy was yet imperfect; unshared by *her*, who was now identified with all his hopes and all his fears; and descending[a] the hill with the rapidity of lightning, he suddenly perceived his steps impeded by a phenomenon which at first seemed some sudden vision of the fancy, to which the senses unresistingly submitted; for a brilliant circle of fire gradually extending, forbid his advance, and had illuminated, by its kindling light, the surrounding atmosphere! Recovering from the first emotion of horror and consternation, his knowledge of the natural history of the country soon informed him of the cause of the apparent miracle,[*] without reconciling him to its effects; he perceived that the *bamboos*, violently agitated by a strong and sultry wind, which suddenly arose from the South, and crept among their branches, had produced a violent friction in their dry stalks, which emitted sparks of fire, and which, when communicated to their leaves, produced on their summits one extended blaze, which was now gradually descending to their trunks. Though this extraordinary spectacle fulfilled, rather than violated, a law of nature, the Missionary's heart, struck by the obstacle it opposed to his wishes and his views, and the terrors it held out to his imagination, felt as if, by some interposition of Divine wrath, he had been separated, for ever, from her who had thus armed Heaven against him. Given up to a distraction which knew no bounds from reason or religion, he accused the Eternal Judge, who, in making the object of his error the cause of his retribution, had not proportioned his punishment to his crime, and who had implicated in the vengeance which bowed *him* to the earth, a creature free and innocent of voluntary error. – Yet, considering less his own sufferings, than the probable and impending destruction of Luxima, thus exposed, alone, in solitary deserts, to want! to the inclemency of treacherous elements! to the fury of savage beasts! perhaps to men, scarce less savage! who might refuse her that protection, their very presence rendered necessary – his mind and feelings were roused, even to frenzy, by the frightful images conjured up by a heart distracted for the safety of its sole object; and the instinct of self-preservation, that strong and almost indestructible instinct, submitted to the paramount influence of a *sentiment*; but that sentiment before which nature stood checked, blended the united passions of *love* and *pity*, the best and dearest which fill the human breast – and, resolved to risk his life for the salvation of hers, dearer to him still than life, – he threw around him a rapid glance, in the faint hope of discerning some object which might assist him in the perilous enterprise he meditated, and enable him to encounter the rage of those flames which opposed his return to the goal of his solicitude and anxiety.[b] It was then he perceived that the surrounding rocks were covered with the entangled web of the *mountain flax*, the inconsumable *amianthus* of India.[†]

---

* This singular spectacle frequently presents itself to the eye of the traveller in the hilly parts of the Carnatic, as well as in Upper India, particularly about the *Ghauts*, which are covered with the bamboo tree.

† One of the varieties of the *asbestos*, which when long exposed to air, dissolves into a downy matter, unassailable by common fire.

At this sight, the providential care of the Divinity, who every where presents an *antidote* to that evil which may eventually become the bane of human preservation, smote his heart – and, raising his soul and eyes in thankfulness to Heaven, he wrapped round his uncovered head, the fibres of this singular and indestructible fossile,[8] and, folding his robe closely round his body, he plunged daringly forward, throwing aside the branches of the burning trees, which flamed above his head, with the iron point of his crosier, as he flew over the arid path, and looking as he moved like the mighty *spirit* of that *element* to which the popular superstition of the region he inhabited would have offered its homage.* The fire had nearly exhausted itself in the direction in which he moved, and soon left nothing but its smoking embers to impede his course. Scorched, spent, and almost deprived of respiration, he reached the opposite side of the plantation, and, with the recovery of breath and strength, he flew towards the spot where he had left his charge, whom every new peril, by adding anxiety to love, bound more closely to his heart. He found her wrapt in profound slumber; the moonlight, chequered by the branches of the tree through which it fell, played on her face and bosom; but her figure was in deep shade, from its position; and a disciple of her own faith would have worshipped her, had he passed, and said, ''Tis the messenger of Heaven,† who bears to earth the mandate of *Vishnoo;*[9] for it is thus the Indian *Iris* is sometimes mystically represented – nothing visible of its beauty, but the countenance of a youthful seraph. Close to the brow of the innocent slumberer lay, in many a mazy fold, a serpent of immense size: his head, crested and high, rose erect; his scales of verdant gold glittered to the moon-light, and his eyes bright and fierce were fixed on the victim, whose first motion might prove the signal of her death. These two objects, so singular in their association, were alone conspicuous in the scene, which was elsewhere hid in the massive shadows of the projecting branches. At the sight of this image, so beautiful and so terrific, so awfully fine, so grandly dreadful, where loveliness and death, and peace and destruction, were so closely blended, the distracted and solitary spectator stood aghast! – A chill of horror running through his veins, his joints relaxed; his limbs, transfixed and faint, cold and powerless, fearing lest his very respiration might accelerate the dreadful fate which thus hung over the sole object and tie of his existence, – breathless, motionless, – he wore the perfect semblance of that horrible suspense, which fills the awful interval between impending death, and lingering life![a] Twice he raised his crosier to hurl it at the serpent's head; and twice his arm fell nerveless back, while his shuddering heart doubted the certain aim of his trembling hand, – and whether, in attempting to strike at the vigilant reptile, he might not reach the bosom of his destined victim, and urge him to her immediate destruction! – But, feelings so acute were not long to be endured: cold drops fell from his brow, his inflamed eye had gazed itself into dimness, increasing agony became madness, – and,

---

* *Augne-Baugauvin*, the God of Fire, and one of the eight keepers of the world.
† Saindovoer.

unable to resist the frenzy of his thronging emotions, he raised the pastoral spear, and had nearly hurled it at the destroyer, when his arm was checked by a sound which seemed to come from Heaven, breathing hope and life upon his soul; for it operated with an immediate and magic influence on the organs of the reptile, who suddenly drooped his crested head, and, extending wide his circling folds, wound his mazy course, in many an indented wave, towards that point, where some seeming impulse of the 'vocal aid'[10] lured his nature from its prey.

Luxima slowly awakening from her sweet repose, to sounds too well remembered, for it was the vesper hymn of the Indian huntsmen, raised her head upon her arm, and threw wildly round her the look of one wrapt in the visionary trance – now resting her eye upon the Missionary, who stood before her motionless, suspended between joy and horror, between fear and transport – now upon the flaming circles which hung upon the burning *bamboos* – and now on the receding serpent, whose tortuous train, veering as he moved, still glistened brightly on the earth, till slowly following the fainting sounds, his voluble and lengthening folds were lost in the deep shade of a sombre thicket; – then the Indian raised her hands and eyes to heaven in thankfulness to that Power who had mercifully saved her from a dreadful death. The music ceased; nature had reached the crisis of emotion in the breast of the Missionary: without power to articulate or to move, he bent one knee to the earth; he raised his folded hands to Heaven; but his eyes were turned on the object of its protection: he sighed out her name, and Luxima was in a moment at his side.

CHAPTER XIV.

THE left arm of the Missionary had suffered from the flames; Luxima was the first to perceive it: she applied to it the only remedy which nature afforded them in a spot so desolate; and the ingenuity of love, and of necessity, supplied the place of skill. She gathered from the neighbouring spring, the oily *naptha*, whose volatile and subtil fluid so frequently floats on the surface of Indian wells, and, steeping in it the fragment of her veil, she bound it round the arm of her patient. Thus engaged, the thoughts of the wanderers, by a natural association, mutually reverted to their first interview in the grotto of Congelations; when the rigid distinctions of prejudice first gave way to an impulse of humanity, and the Priestess of Brahma, no less in fear than pity, bound up the wound of him whom she then deemed it a sacrilege to approach! The sympathy of the recollection was visible in the disorder of[a] their looks, which were studiously averted from each other; and the Neophyte, endeavouring to turn the thoughts of her spiritual guide from a subject she trembled to revert to, spoke of the danger which he had recently incurred for her sake, and spoke of it with all the fervour which characterized her eloquence.

The Missionary replied with the circumspect reserve of one who feared to trust his feelings: he said, 'That which I have done *for thee*, I would have done for another, for it is the spirit of the religion I profess, to sacrifice the selfish instinct of our nature to the preservation of a fellow-creature whose danger claims our interference, or whose happiness needs our protection.'

'Oh! Father,' she returned in emotion, 'refer not to thy faith alone, a sentiment inherent in thyself; let us be more just *to him* who made us, and believe, that there is in nature, a feeling of benevolence which betrays the original intention of the Deity, to promote the happiness of his creatures. If thou art prone to pity the wretched, and aid the weak, it is because thou wast thyself created of those particles which, at an infinite distance, constitute the Divine essence.'

The Missionary interrupted her by a look of reprehension; he knew such was the doctrine, and such the phrase of the Brahmins, with respect to those of their holy men who led a religious and sinless life: but he felt, at the moment, how little claim he had to make any application of it to himself.

'Thy religion, at least,' continued Luxima, with softness and timidity, 'forbids not the expression of *gratitude*. It is said in the Shaster, that the first thought of Brahma, when created by the great Spirit, was a sentiment of gratitude; he offered up thanks to the Author of his existence, for the gift of life, and a reasonable soul: is then the Christian doctrine less amiable than that I have

130

abandoned? and, if through thee, my life has been preserved, and my soul enlightened, must I stifle in my heart, the gratitude thou hast awakened there?'

'Luxima,' exclaimed the Missionary, with vehemence, '*all* sentiments merely of the heart are dangerous, and to be distrusted; whatever soothes the passions, tends to cherish them, – whatever affords pleasure, endangers virtue, – and even the love we bear to Heaven, we should try, were it possible, to separate from the happiness which that love confers. Oh! Luxima, it is a dangerous habit, – the habit of enjoying any earthly good, and until now—' he broke off suddenly, and sighed, then added, 'Thou talkest much of gratitude, Luxima; but wherefore? It was for Heaven I sought thee – it is for Heaven I saved thee! It was not for *thy* sake, nor for mine, that I lured thee from the land of the unbelieving, or that I would risk a thousand lives to save thine, – it is for *his* sake, whose servant I am. But, if *thou* talkest of gratitude, to whom is it due? *Art thou not here?* in dreary deserts, encompassed round by danger and by death: to follow me, thou art here, – thou, the native of an earthly paradise, – the idol of a nation's homage. Oh! I should have left thy pure soul, all innocent as it was of voluntary error, to return to its Creator, untried by the dangers, unassailed by the tempting evils of passion and of life, virtuous in thy illusions, pure from the errors and misfortunes of humanity, an inmate fit for the Heaven which awaited thee.'

'Be that Heaven my witness,' returned Luxima, with devotion and solemnity, 'that I would not for the happiness I have abandoned, and the glory I have lost, resign that desert, whose perilous solitudes I share with thee. Oh! my father, and my friend, thou alone hast taught me to know, that the paradise of woman is the creation of her heart; that it is not the light or air of Heaven, though beaming brightness, and breathing fragrance, nor all that is loveliest in nature's scenes, which form the *sphere* of *her* existence and enjoyment! – it is alone the presence of *him she loves*: it is that mysterious sentiment of the heart, which diffuses a finer sense of life through the whole being; and which resembles, in its singleness and simplicity, the *primordial idea*, which, in the religion of my fathers, is supposed to have preceded *time* and *worlds*, and from which all created good has emanated.'

The Missionary arose, in disorder; he turned, for a moment, his eyes on Luxima: the glow which mantled to her brow, the bashful confusion of her look, the modesty with which she drew her veil over her downcast eyes, spoke the involuntary error of one, whose ardent feelings had for a moment over-ruled the circumspect reserve of a rigid virtue. He sighed profoundly, and withdrew his glance. Luxima[a] now also arose; and they were both proceeding on in silence, when a rustling in the thicket was distinctly heard, and the next moment a large but meagre dog sprang forward, followed by an Indian, on whose dark and melancholy countenance the light of the moon fell brightly; a scanty garment, woven of the fibres of trees, partially concealed his slender and worn form; an Indian pipe was suspended from his girdle; and he leaned, as he paused, to gaze on the wanderers, upon a huntsman's *spear*. But, scarcely had he fixed his haggard eyes on the brow of Luxima, which still bore the consecrated *mark of the* *tellertum,*[*] than he fell prostrate on the earth, in token of reverential homage. Luxima shrieked, and hiding her head in the bosom of the Missionary, exclaimed[a] 'Let us fly, or we are lost! it is a *pariah!*'

The *unfortunate*, rising from the earth, and withdrawing a few paces, said, in a timid and respectful accent: – 'I am indeed of that wretched cast, who live under the curse of Heaven – an outcast! an alien! I claim no country, I *own no kindred;*[b] but still I am human, and can pity in others the suffering I myself endure: I ask not the daughter of Heaven, who sprang from the head of Brahma, to repose beneath the roof of a pariah; but I will conduct her to a spot less perilous than this, and I will lay at her feet the pulp of the young cocoa-nut, which grows by the side of my hut; and when the morning star dawns above yonder forest, I will guide her steps to a path of safety, and teach her how to shun the abode of the wild beast, and to avoid the nest of the serpent.'

To these humane offers, Luxima replied only by tears: an *outcast* herself, the unconquerable prejudice and religious pride of the cast she had forfeited, still operated with unabated influence on her mind, and she shuddered when she beheld the Missionary stretch out his hands and press in their grateful clasp those of the unfortunate and benevolent *pariah*: he had been the saviour of the life of her she loved; for it was the music of his sylvan reed, which had seduced the serpent from his prey, and the point of his spear was still red with the blood of the reptile he had destroyed.[†]

But for the first time, neither the example nor the persuasions of the Missionary had any effect upon the mind of his neophyte. Suddenly awakened to all the tyranny of habitual prejudice and superstitious fear, she rejected the repose and safety to be found beneath the shadow of a pariah's *hut*, she rejected the fruit planted by a pariah's hand; and the pride of a Brahmin's daughter, and the bigotry of a Brahmin priestess, still governed the conduct of the excommunicated *chancalas*, still over-ruled the reason of the Christian neophyte: accepting, therefore, only the advice of the unhappy pariah, who directed them to a woody path, by which they might soonest gain the caravan road, and who taught them how to avoid whatever was most dangerous in these unfrequented wilds, they again re-commenced their wanderings. The Missionary, with difficulty[c] guiding the Arabian through the intricacies of the forest-path, remained silent and thoughtful; while Luxima, fearing that she had displeased him by an unconquerable obstinacy, which had its foundation in the earliest habits and feelings of her life, sought to cheer his mind and amuse his attention by the repetition of some of those mythological romances, which had formed a part of her professional

---

[*] The *tellertum* is a mark which is at once an ornament and an indication of cast and religious profession.

[†] According to the *Abbé* Guyon, there is in India a species of serpent, which even in the pursuit of its prey is to be lulled into a profound slumber by the sounds of *musical instruments*. The Indian serpent-hunters frequently make use of this artifice, that they may destroy them with greater facility.

acquirements. But the Missionary, alive to dangers which in his society *she* felt not, and borne down by the recent disappointment of his flattering hopes, of which *she* was ignorant, gave not to her brilliant and eloquent details, the wonted look of half-repressed transport, the wonted reserved smile of tenderness and admiration; his whole thoughts rested in a faint expectation of overtaking the caravan, which moved slowly, and[a] which had taken a more circuitous road than that to which the pariah had directed him.

In the unfrequented wilds through which they now passed, no trace of human life appeared, save that once, and at an immense distance,[b] they beheld the arms of some Indian troops glittering brightly to the moon-beams;[c] but the welcome spectacle passed away like a midnight phantom; and, that again they observed a circle of glimmering fires, before which the remote[d] shadows of an elephant's form seemed to pass. Luxima, acquainted with the customs of her country, believed this spectacle to belong to a hunting match of elephants; a diversion in India truly royal. At last, having recovered the traces of the caravan, which were deeply impressed on the soil, they found themselves on a wild and marshy waste, skirted by the impenetrable forest, from whose gloom they now emerged; – the earth trembled beneath their sinking feet, and particles of light arising from putrescent substances, rose like meteors before them; while frequently the high jungle grass, almost surmounting the lofty figure of the Missionary, stubbornly resisted the efforts which he made with his extended arms to clear a passage for the animal on which Luxima was mounted; – the moon,[e] suddenly absorbed in clouds, left them with '*danger and with darkness compassed round;*'[11] – while the low and sullen murmurs of the elements foretold a rising storm. Exhausted by heat and by fatigue, no longer able to perceive the track of the caravan, the unfortunate wanderers sought only to avoid the dreadful inclemency of the moment: sounds of horror mingled in the wild expanse; the hiss of serpents, and the yell of ferocious animals which instinctively sought shelter amidst the profound depths of the forest, (whose mighty trees, bending their summits to the sweeping blast, rolled like billows in deep and dying murmurs) all around bowed as in awful reverence to the omnipotent voice of nature, thus pouring her accents of terror in the deep roll of endless thunder; the crash of shattered rocks, the groans of torn-up trees, and all those images of terror which mark the *land-tempests* in those mighty regions, where even destruction wears an aspect of magnificence and sublimity, all struck upon the soul of the fainting Indian, and left there an impression never to be effaced. It was then that the religion which she had abandoned, less from *conviction* than from *love*, and the superstitious errors which were still latent in her mind, resumed at this moment (to her, of dreadful retribution) all their former influence; and she felt the wrath of Heaven in every flash of lightning which darted round her head: for the mind long devoted to an illusion interwoven with all its ideas, however it may abandon its influence in the repose of safety, or the blessings of enjoyment, still clings to it, as to a resource, in suffering and in danger; and, contrite for the transient apostacy, adds the energy of repentance to the zeal of returning faith.

The Missionary, who beheld remorse in the bosom of his proselyte strength-ening under the dangers which had awakened it,[a] in vain endeavoured to soothe and to support her; she shrank from his arms, and, prostrate on the earth, invoked those deities whom she still believed to have been the tutelar guardians of the days of her innocence and her felicity; while he, still feeling only through her, stood near to shield and to protect her: awed, but not subdued, he presented a fine image of the majesty of man; – his brow fearlessly raised to meet the light-ning's flash, a blasted tree in ruins at his feet, and while all lay desolate and in destruction round him, looking like one whose spirit, unsubdued by the mighty wreck of matter, defied that threatened annihilation, which could not reach the immortality it was created to inherit![b]

The storm ceased in a tremendous crash of the elements, with all the abrupt grandeur with which it had arisen; and a breathless calm, scarcely less awful, succeeded to its violence; the clouds dispersed from the face of the Heavens, and the moon, full and cloudless, rose in the firmament: every thing urged the departure of the wanderers, for danger, in various forms, surrounded them. – Luxima, alive to every existing impression, was cheered even by the solemn calm, but nearly exhausted and overcome by suffering and fatigue, the Mission-ary was obliged[c] to support her on the horse; and though she tried to smile, yet her silent tears, and uncomplaining sufferings, relaxed the firmness of his mind; he felt, that, were even her conversion perfected, which he hourly discovered it was far from being, she would have purchased the sacred truths of Christianity at the dearest price, and that Heaven alone could compensate the unhappy and apostate Indian, who thus sought it at the expence of every earthly good and human happiness.

At length the trees of the forest, on whose remotest skirts they wandered,[d] gradually disappeared; and, still following the track of the caravan, which in the course of the night they had again recovered as well as the moon's declining light would permit,[e] they crossed a hill, where it seemed by its impressions on the soil recently to have passed: they then descended into a boundless plain, dis-mal, wild, and waste. Ere the sun had risen in all its fiercest glories above the horizon, they found themselves surrounded by a desert: the[f] guiding track indeed still remained; but, in the illimitable waste, far as the eye could stretch its view, no object which could cheer their hearts, or dispel their fears, presented itself: – sky and earth alone appeared, alike awful, and alike unvaried; the heav-ens, shrouded with a deep red gloom, spread a boundless canopy to the view, like the concave roof of some earth-embosomed mine, whose golden veins shine duskily in gloomy splendour;[g] and the sandy and burning soil, unvaried by a single tree or shrub, reflected back the scorching ardour of the skies, and min-gled its brilliant surface with the distant horizon; both alike were terrific to the fancy, and boundless to the eye; both alike struck horror on the mind, and chased hope from the heart; alike denying all resource, withholding all relief;[h] while the disconsolate wanderers, as they trod the burning waste, now turned their looks on the bleak perspective, now tenderly and despairingly on each other. Convinced that to return or to advance threatened alike destruction, thus they continued to wander in the lonesome and desolate wild, enduring the intense heat of the ardent day, the noxious blast of the chilly night, with no shelter from the horrors of the clime but what a clump of naked rocks at intervals afforded them; and when this rude asylum presented itself, the Missionary spread his robe on the earth for Luxima – endeavouring to soothe her to repose, only leaving her side to seek some spring, always vainly sought, or to look for those hardy shrubs which even the desert sometimes produces, and which frequently treasure in their flowers the lingering dews of moister seasons; if he found them, it was mouldering amidst the dry red sand of the soil. At[a] last the delicate animal, which had hitherto afforded them so much relief and aid, sunk beneath the intemperature of the clime, and expired at their feet. Luxima was now borne hopelessly along by the associate and the cause of her sufferings; and they proceeded slowly and despairingly, their parched and burning lips, their wearied and exhausted frames, scarcely permitting them to speak without effort, or to move without pain. But it was for Luxima only the Missionary suffered – he saw her whom he had found in the possession of every enjoyment, now almost expiring beneath his eyes; her lips of roses, scorched by the noxious blasts, and gust after gust of burning vapour, drying up the vital springs of life; while she, confounding in her mind her afflictions, and what she believed to be their cause, offered up faint invocations to appease those powers, whom love had induced her thus to provoke and to abandon.[b]

It was in moments such as these, that the unfortunate Hilarion beheld that hope frustrated, which had hitherto solaced him in all the sufferings he had caused, and those he sustained; it was then that he felt it was the heart of the woman he had seduced, and not the mind of the heathen he had converted. At last, wholly overcome by the intense heat and immoderate fatigue, by insupportable thirst and a long privation of sustenance and sleep, Luxima was unable to proceed.[c] The Missionary bore her in his feeble clasp to the base of a rock, which afforded them some shelter from the rays of the sun. He would have spoken to her of the Heaven to which her soul seemed already taking its flight; he would have assured her that his spirit would soon mingle with hers, and that an eternal union awaited them: but, in a moment, when love was strengthened by mutual suffering, and despair gave force to passion, and when each at once only lived and died for the other, words were poor vehicles to feelings so acute; and sighs, long and deep drawn, were the only sounds which emotions so profound, so tender, and so agonizing, would admit of: all was the silence of love unspeakable, and the awful stillness of dissolution. But[d] when over the beautiful countenance which lay on his bosom, the Missionary beheld the sudden convulsion of pain throw its dread distortion, – madness seized the brain of the frantic lover, and he threw round a look wild and inquiring, but looked in vain; all was still, hopeless, and desolate. At last, something like a vapour appeared moving at a distance. He sprung forward, and, ascending the point of a rock, discovered at a distance a form which resembled that of a camel: faint as was the hope now awakened, it spread new life through his whole being; he snatched the dying Indian to his bosom; strength and velocity seemed a supernatural gift communicated to his frame; he flew over the burning sand, he approached the object of his wishes; hope with every step realizes the blessed vision; human forms grew distinct on his eye, human sounds vibrate on his ear – 'She lives, she[a] is saved!' he exclaims with a frantic shriek, and falls lifeless beneath his precious burthen in the midst of the multitude which forms the rear of the caravan. The caravan had stopped in this place near a spring, accidentally discovered, and the motley crowd which composed it, were all verging towards one point, eagerly contending for a draught of muddy water; but the sudden and extraordinary appearance of the now almost lifeless strangers, excited an emotion in all who beheld them. The few Hindus who belonged to the caravan shrank in horror from the unfortunate *Chancalas*, thus so closely associated with a *frangui*, or impure; but those in whom religious bigotry had not deadened the feelings of nature, beheld them with equal pity and admiration.[b] Every assistance which humanity could devise was administered; and cordials, diluted with water, moistened lips parched with a long consuming thirst, and recalled to frames nearly exhausted, the fading powers of life. The Missionary, more overcome by his anxiety for Luxima, and the sudden transition of his feelings from despair to hope, than even by weakness, or personal suffering, was the first to recover consciousness and strength, and love instinctively claimed the first thought of reviving existence. In the transport of the moment he forgot the crowd that was its witness; he flew to Luxima, and shed tears of love and joy on the hands extended to him. He beheld the vital hues revisiting that cheek which he had lately pressed in hopeless agony, and saw the light of life beaming in those eyes whose lustre he had so lately seen darkened by the shades of death. Again, too, the voice of Luxima addresses him by the endearing epithet of 'Father:' and though the venerated title found no sanction in their looks or years, yet many who beheld the scene of their re-union were touched by its affecting tenderness; and a general interest was excited for persons so noble, and so distinguished in their appearance, so interesting by their sufferings and misfortunes, which were registered in their looks, and attested by the singularity of their situations.

CHAPTER XV.

LUXIMA, restored to life, was still feeble and exhausted: but though faded, she was still lovely; and, being immediately recognized as a *Hindu*, that peculiar circumstance awakened curiosity and surmise. Those of her own nation and religion still shrank from her in horror, and declared her to be a *Chancalas*, or outcast; the Moslems who beheld her, sought not to conceal their rude admiration, and recognized her at once for a *Cashmirian* by her complexion and her beauty; but the persons who seemed to observe her with most scrutiny, were *two Europeans*, whose features were concealed by hoods, worn apparently to shade off the ardour of the sun. Luxima was permitted to share the *mohaffah* or litter of a female seik[12] who was going with her husband, a dealer in gems, to Tatta. The Missionary was suffered to ascend the back of a camel, whose proprietor had expired the day before in the desert. Having declared himself a Portuguese of distinction, a Christian missionary, and shewed the briefs which testified his rank, he found no difficulty in procuring such necessaries as were requisite for the rest of their journey, until his arrival at Tatta should enable him to defray the debt of obligation which he of necessity incurred.

But though he had declared the nature of the relation in which he stood to his Neophyte to those immediately about him, yet he fancied, that the fact was, received by some with suspicion, and by others with incredulity. He was evidently considered the seducer of the fugitive Indian; and neither his innocence nor his dignity could save him from a profound mortification, new and insupportable to his proud and lofty nature: yet, trembling to observe the admiration which Luxima[a] inspired, he still hovered near her in ceaseless disquietude and anxiety. The caravan was composed of five hundred persons of various nations and religions; – Mogul pilgrims, going from India to visit the tomb of their prophet at Mecca; merchants from Thibet and China, carrying the produce of their native climes, the Western coasts of Hindostan; Seiks, the Swiss of the East, going to join the forces of rebelling Rajahs; and faquirs and dervises, who rendered religion profitable by carrying for sale in their girdles, spices, gold-dust, and musk. Luxima, obviously abhorred by those of her own religion, closely observed by some, and suspected by all, felt her situation equally through her sex and her prejudices, and shrunk from the notice she unavoidably attracted in shame and in confusion: it was now that her forfeiture of cast for the first time appeared to the Missionary[b] in all its horrors, and he no longer wondered that so long as the prejudice existed, with which it is connected, it should hold so tyrannic an influence over the Indian mind. His tenderness increasing with his pity, and his jealousy of those who attempted to approach, or to address her, giving a new force and character to his passion, he seldom left the side of her *litter:* yet he endeavoured to moderate the warmth of feelings it was now more than ever necessary to conceal. That[a] passion, dangerous in every situation, was now no longer solitary as the wilds in which it sprang, but connected with society, and exposed to its observation; and the reserve with which he sought to temper its ardour, restored to it all that mysterious delicacy, which constitutes, perhaps, its first, and perhaps its best charm.

The caravan proceeded on its route, and, having passed the Desert, crossed the *Setlege,* and entered the *Moultan,*[13] it halted at one of its usual stations, and the tents of the travellers were pitched on the shores of the Indus: the perils of the past were no longer remembered, and the safety of the present was ardently enjoyed; while the views and interests of the motley multitude, no longer subdued by personal danger, or impeded by personal suffering, again operated with their original force and activity. The merchants bartered with the traders, who came from the surrounding towns for the purpose; and the professors of the various religions and sects preached their respective doctrines to those whom they wished to convert, or to those who already believed, all but the Christian Missionary! Occupied by feelings of a doubtful and conflicting nature, sometimes hovering round the tent which Luxima shared with the family of the Seik, sometimes buried in profound thought, and wandering amidst the depths of a neighbouring forest, where he sought to avoid the idle bustle of those among whom he was adventitiously thrown; anxious, unquiet, and distrustful even of himself, he was now lost to that evangelic peace of mind, to that sober tranquillity of feeling, so indispensable to the exercise of his mission. Though buried in a reserve which awed, while it distanced, there was a majesty in his air, and a dignified softness in his manner, which daily increased that popular interest in his favour, which his first appearance had awakened: to this he was not insensible; for, still ambitious of distinction as saint or as man, he beheld his influence with a triumph natural to one, who, emulous of unrivalled superiority, feels that he owes it not to extraneous circumstance, but to that proud and indefeasible right of supreme eminence, with which nature has endowed him. But he could not but particularly observe, that he was an object of singular attention to the two European travellers, who, wrapped in mystery, seemed to shun all intercourse, and avoid all observation; and, though they crossed him in his solitary walks, pursued him to the entrance of Luxima's tent, and hung upon his every word and action, yet so subtilely had they eluded his notice, that he had not yet obtained an opportunity of either distinctly seeing their features, or of addressing them; all he could learn was, that they had joined the caravan from *Lahore,* with two other persons of the same dress and description as themselves, who had proceeded with the advanced troop of the caravan, and that they were known to be Europeans and Christians. It was not till the caravan had entered the province of *Sindy,*[14] that one of them, who rode near the camel of the Missionary, seemed inclined to address him; after some observations he said, 'It is understood that you are a Christian Missionary! but, while in this mighty multitude the professor of each false religion appears anxious to advance his doctrine, and to promulgate his creed, how is it that the *apostle of Christianity* is alone silent and indifferent on the subject of that pure faith, to the promulgation of which he has devoted himself?' –

The Missionary threw a haughty look over the figure of the person who thus interrogated him; but, with a sudden recollection, he endeavoured to recall the humility of his religious character, and replied: 'The question is natural – and the silence to which you allude is not the effect of weakened zeal, nor the result of abated enthusiasm, in the sacred cause to which I have devoted myself – it is a silence which arises from a consciousness that though I spoke with the tongues of angels, it *would be here but as the sound of tinkling brass;*[15] for *truth*, which always prevails over unbiassed ignorance, has ever failed in its effect upon bigoted error – and the dogma most difficult to vanquish, is that which is guarded by self-interest.'

'You allude to the obstinate paganism of the Brahmins?'

'I allude to the power of the most powerful of all human superstitions; a superstition which equally presides over the heavenly hope, and directs the temporal concern; and which so intimately blends itself with all the relations of human life, as equally to dictate a doctrinal tenet, or a sumptuary law, to regulate alike the salvation of the soul, and fix the habits of existence.'

'It is the peculiar character of the zeal of Christianity to rise in proportion to the obstacles it encounters!'

'The zeal of Christianity should never forsake the mild spirit of its fundamental principles; in the excess of its warmest enthusiasm, it should be tempered by charity, guided by reason, and regulated by possibility; forsaken by these, it ceases to be the zeal of religion, and becomes the spirit of fanaticism, tending only to sever man from man, and to multiply the artificial sources of aversion by which human society is divided, and human happiness destroyed!'

'This temperance in doctrine, argues a freedom in opinion, and a languor in zeal, which rather belongs to the character of the heathen philosophy, than to the enthusiasm of Christian faith; had its disciples been always thus moderate, thus languid, thus philosophically tolerant, never would the cross have been raised upon the remotest shores of the Eastern and Western oceans!'

'Too often has it been raised under the influence of a sentiment diametrically opposite to the spirit of the doctrine of him who *suffered on it*, and who came not to *destroy*, but to *save* mankind. Too often has it been raised by those whose minds were guided by an evil and interested policy, fatal to the effects which it sought to accomplish, and who lifted to Heaven, hands stained with the blood of those, to whom they had been sent to preach the religion of peace, of love, and of salvation; for even the zeal of religion, when animated by human passions, may become fatal in its excess, and that daring fanaticism, which gives force and activity to the courage of the man, may render merciless and atrocious, the zeal of the bigot.'

'You disapprove then of that energy of conversion which either by art or force secures or redeems the soul from the sin of idolatry?'

'*Force* and *art* may indeed effect profession, but cannot induce the conviction of faith; for the individual perception of truth is not to be effected by the belief of others, and an act of faith must be either an act of private judgment, or of free will, which no human artifice, no human authority can alter or controul.'

'You disapprove then of the zealous exertions of the Jesuits in the cause of Christianity, and despair of their success?'

'I disapprove not of the zeal, but of the mediums by which it manifests itself: I believe that the coercion and the artifice to which they resort, frequently impel the Hindus to a resistance, which they perhaps too often expiate by the loss of life and property, but seldom urge them to the abjuration of a religion, the loss of whose privileges deprives the wretched apostate of every human good! It is by a previous cultivation of their moral powers, we may hope to influence their religious belief; it is by teaching them to love us, that we can lead them to listen to us; it is by inspiring them with respect for our virtues, that we can give them a confidence in our doctrine: but this has not always been the system adopted by European reformers, and the religion we proffer them is seldom illustrated by its influence on our own lives. We bring them a spiritual creed, which commands them to forget the world, and we take from them temporal possessions, which prove how much *we live for it.*'

'With such mildness in opinion, and such tolerance towards the prejudices of others, you have doubtless succeeded in your mission, where a zeal not more pure, but more ardent, would have failed?'

The Missionary changed colour at the observation, and replied – 'The zeal of the members of the congregation of the Mission can never be doubted, since they voluntarily devote themselves to the cause of Christianity;[a] yet to effect a change in the religion of sixty millions of people, whose[*] doctrines claim their authority from the records of the most ancient[b] nations, – whose faith is guarded by the pride of rank, the interest of priesthood, by its own abstract nature, by local habits, and confirmed[c] prejudices; a faith which resisted the sword of Mahmoud and the arms of Timur, – requires a power seldom vested in man, and which time, a new order of things in India, and the Divine will, can alone, I believe, accomplish.'

'You return then to the centre of your mission without any converts to your exertion and your eloquence?'

'No fruit has been indeed gathered equal to the labour or the hope; for I have made but one proselyte, who purchases the truths of Christianity by the forfeiture of every earthly good!'[d]

---

[*] 'Notwithstanding the labours of the Missionaries for upwards of two hundred years, out of perhaps one hundred millions of *Hindus*, there are not twelve thousand *Christians*, and those are almost all entirely *chancalas*, or *outcasts*.' – *Sketches of the History of the Religion, Learning, and Manners of the Hindus*,[16] p.48.

'A *Brahmin* perhaps?'

'A Brahmin's daughter! the chief priestess of the pagoda of Sirinagar, in Cashmire, a prophetess, and *Brachmachira*; whose conversion may indeed be deemed a miracle!'

'Your neophyte is then that young and beautiful person we first beheld lifeless *in your arms*, in the desert?'

'The same,' said the Missionary, again changing colour: 'She has already received the rites of baptism, and I am conveying her to *Goa*, there her profession of some holy order may produce, by its example, a salutary effect, which her conversion never could have done in Cashmire; a place where the Brahminical bigotry has reached its zenith, and where her forfeiture of cast would have rendered her an object of opprobrium and aversion!' – As the Missionary spoke, he raised his eyes to the face of the person he addressed; but it was still shaded by the hood of his cloak, yet he met an eye so keen, so malignant in its glance, that, could he have shrunk from any mortal look, he would have shrunk from this. Struck by its singular expression, and by the certainty of having before met it, he remained for many minutes endeavouring to collect his thoughts, and, believing himself justified by the freedom of the stranger's inquiries, to question him as to his country and profession, he turned round to address him: but the strangers had now both moved away, and the Missionary then first observed, that he who had been silent during this short dialogue, and whom he still held in view, was employed in writing on a tablet, as though he noted down the heads of the conversation. This circumstance appeared too strange not to excite some curiosity, and much amazement. The person who addressed him spoke in the Hindu dialect, as it was spoken at *Lahore*; but he believed it possible, that he might have been some emissary from the Jesuits convent there, on his way to the Inquisitorial college at Goa: this for a moment disquieted him; for his mind, long divided by conflicting passions, had lost its wonted self possession and lofty independence: he had been recently accustomed to suspect himself; and he now feared that his zeal, relaxed by passion, had weakened that severity of principle which once admitted of no innovation, and thought it not impossible that he might have expressed his sentiments with a freedom which bigotry could easily torture into an evidence of heresy itself. He again sought the two strangers, but in vain; for they had joined the advanced troop of the caravan; while a feeling, stronger than any they had excited, still fixed him in the rear, near the mohaffah of Luxima.

The caravan now pursued its toilsome route through the rich and varying district of *Scindi*; and the fresh and scented gales, which blew from the Indian sea, revived the languid spirits of the drooping Neophyte; and gave to her eye and cheek, the beam and glow of health and loveliness.[a] Not so the Missionary: – as he advanced towards the haunts of civilized society, the ties by which he was bound to it, and its influence and power over his opinions and conduct, which a fatal passion, cherished in wilds and deserts, had banished from his mind, now rushed to his recollection with an overwhelming force – he gloomily anticipated the disappointment which awaited his return to Goa; the triumph of his enemies, and the discomfiture of his friends; the inferences which might be drawn from the sex and beauty of his solitary Neophyte; and, above all, the eternal separation from the sole object, that alone had taught him the supreme bliss, which the most profound and precious feeling of nature can bestow, – a separation, imperiously demanded by religion, by honour, and by the respect still due to his character and holy profession. It was his intention to place her in a house of Franciscan Sisters, an order whose purity and mildness was suited to her gentle nature. But, when he remembered the youth and loveliness he was about to entomb, the feelings and affections he was about to sacrifice – the warm, the tender, the impassioned heart he should devote to a cold and gloomy association, with rigid and uncongenial spirits – when he beheld her in fancy ascending the altar steps, resigning, by vows she scarcely understood, the brilliant illusions of her own imposing and fanciful faith, and embracing doctrines to which her mind was not yet familiarized, and against which her strong rooted prejudices and ardent feelings still revolted, – when he beheld her despoiled of those lovely and luxuriant tresses which had so often received the homage of his silent admiration, and almost felt his own hands tremble, as he placed on her brow the veil which concealed her from him for ever, – when he caught the parting sigh, – when his glance died under the expression of those dove-like eyes, which, withdrawing their looks from the cross, would still throw their lingering and languid light upon his receding form! – then, worked up to a frenzy of love and of affection,[a] by the image which his fancy and his feelings had pictured to his heart, he eagerly sought her presence as though the moment was already arrived, when he should lose her love for ever; and he hung, in such despairing fondness round her, that Luxima, touched by the expression of his countenance, sought to know the cause of his agitation, and to soothe his spirits. The Missionary leaned over the vehicle, in which she reposed, to catch the murmurings of her low and tender voice.

'Thou art sad,' she said, 'and melancholy hangs upon thy brow, now that danger is over, and suffering almost forgotten. Is it only in the midst of perils, which strike death upon weaker souls, that *thine* rejoices? for amidst the conflicts of varying elements, thou wast firm; in the burning desert, thou wast unsubdued – Oh! how often has my fancy likened thee to the great *vesanti* plant, which, when it meets not the mighty stem round which it is its nature to twine and flourish, droops not, though forsaken, but assuming the form and structure of a towering tree, betrays its aspiring origin, and points its lofty branches towards the heavens, whose storms it dares – and thus doth thou seem greatest, when most exposed – and firmest, when least supported. Oh! father,' she added, with an ardour she had long suppressed, 'didst thou feel as I feel, one look of love would chase all sorrow from thy heart, and sadness from thy brow.'

'But Luxima,' returned the Missionary, infected by her impassioned tenderness, as if that were almost love's last look, 'if, when every tie was drawn so closely round the heart, that both must break together – if the fatal consciousness of being loved, have become so necessary to existence, that life seems without it, a cold and dreary waste – if under the influence of feelings such as these, the moment of an eternal separation dawns in all its hopeless and insupportable misery on the soul, then every look which love bestows, mingles sadness with affection, and despair with bliss.' Luxima turned pale; and she raised her tearful eyes to his face, not daring to inquire, but by look, how far that dreadful moment was yet distant. The Missionary pointed out to her a distant view of Tatta, whence they were to sail for Goa; and, stifling the emotions of the lover, and the feelings of the man, he endeavoured to rally back his fading zeal; he spoke to her only in the language of the Missionary and the Priest; he spoke of resigning her to God[a] alone; of that perfect conversion which his absence even *more* than his presence would effect! – he described to her the nature and object of the life she was about to embrace, – its peace – its sanctity – its exemptions from human trials, and human passions – and above all, the eternal beatitude to which it led;[b] – he spoke to her of their separation, as inevitable, – and, concealing the struggles which existed in his own mind, he sought only to soothe, to strengthen, and to tranquillize hers. Luxima heard him in silence: she made neither objections nor reply. He was struck by the sudden change which took place in her countenance, when she learned how soon they were to part, and how inevitable was their separation; it was a look resolute and despairing, – as if she defied the destiny, cruel as it was, which seemed to threaten her. At[c] some distance from Tatta, the ardours of a vertical sun obliged the caravan to halt, and seek a temporary shade amidst the umbrageous foliage of a luxuriant grove, refreshed by innumerable streams, flowing into the Indus.

Luxima left her mohaffah, and, supported by the Missionary, sought those shades, which so strongly recalled to her remembrance, the lovely groves of Cashmire, – and the recollections so sad, and yet so precious, which rushed on her mind, were opposed by those feelings which swelled in her bosom, when a distant view of Tatta recalled to her memory the approach of that hour which was so soon to lead her to Goa, to the destined altar of her immolation! – She reflected on the past – she anticipated the future; – and, for the first time, the powerful emotions of which she was capable, betrayed themselves with a violence almost irreconcilable with her gentle and tender nature. – Convulsed with long-stifled feelings, to which she now gave vent, she bathed the earth whereon she had thrown herself, with tears; and, with an eloquence dictated by love and by despair, she denied the existence of an affection which could voluntarily resign its object; – she upbraided equally her lover and herself; and, amidst expressions of reproach and remorse, was still less penitent than tender, – still less lamented her errors, than the approaching loss of him, for whom she had committed them.

'Thou sayest that I am dear to thee,' she said; 'and yet I am sacrificed; and by him for whom I have abandoned all, I am now myself abandoned. – Oh! give me back to my country, my peace, my fame; or suffer me still to remain near thee, and I will rejoice in the loss of all. – Thou sayest it is the law of thy religion that thou obeyest, when thou shalt send me from thee: – but, if it is a virtue in thy religion to stifle the best and purest feelings of the heart, that nature implants, how shall I believe in, or adopt, its tenets? – I, whose nature, whose faith itself, was love – how from thee shall I learn to subdue my feelings, who first taught me to substitute a human, for a heavenly passion? – Alas! I have but changed the object, the *devotion* is still the same; and thou art loved by the *outcast*, as the Priestess once loved Heaven only.'

'Luxima,' returned the Missionary, distracted equally by his own feelings and by hers, 'let us from the sufferings we now endure, learn the extent of the weakness and the errors which we thus, be it hoped, so painfully expiate; for, it is by despair, such as now distracts us, that Heaven punishes the unfortunate, who suffers a passionate and exclusive sentiment to take possession of the heart, for a creature frail and dependant as ourselves. Oh! my daughter, had we but listened to the voice of religion, or of reason, as we have hearkened to our own passions, the most insupportable of human afflictions could not now have befallen us; and that pang by which we are agonized, at the brink of eternal separation, would have been spared to those souls, which a divine and imperishable object would then have solely occupied and involved.'

'I, at least,' said Luxima, firmly, yet with wildness, 'I shall not long endure that pang: – Thinkest thou that I shall long survive *his* loss for whom I have sacrificed all? Oh! no; it was *thou* I followed, and not thy doctrines; for, pure and sublime as they may be, they yet came darkly and confusedly to my soul: but the sentiments thy presence awakened in my heart, were not opposed by any previous thought or feelings of my life; they were true to all its natural impulses, and, if not understood, they were *felt* and *answered*; they mingled with my whole being, and now, even now, form an imperishable part of my existence. – Shudder not thus, but pity, and forgive me! nor think that, weak as I am, I will deprive thee of thy triumph: – yes, thou shalt lead to the Christian Temple, the descendant of Brahma! thou shalt offer up, a sacrifice on the Christian altar, the first apostate, drawn from the most illustrious of the Indian casts, – a Prophetess! who for thee abandoned the homage of a Divinity, – a woman, who for thee resisted the splendours of an empire. – And this I will tell to the Christians in the midst of their temple, and their congregation – that they may know the single solitary convert thy powers have made, is more than all the proselytes thy brethren e'er brought to kiss the Cross: – this I shall do *less in faith* than *love*; not for *my* sake, but for *thine*. – Yet, oh! be thou near me at the altar of sacrifice; let me cling to thee to the last – for, stern and awful as thy religion is, its severity will not refuse me that: yet, if it punish thee, even for pitying—'

'And, thinkest thou,' interrupted the Missionary wildly, 'that it is *punishment* I fear, or that if the enjoyment of thy love, fatal and dear as thou art,[a] could be purchased by suffering, that I would shrink from its endurance? No! it is not torture the most acute I shun – it is *crime that I abhor* – and, equal to sustain all sufferings but those of conscience, I now live only in dread of myself! For oh! Luxima, even yet I might spare myself and thee a life so cold, so sad and dreary, that conscious virtue and true religion only can support us through it, – even yet, escaping from every eye, save Heaven's, we might together fly to the pathless wilds of these delicious regions, and live in sinful bliss, the commoners of nature: – But, Luxima, the soul of him who loves, and who resists thee, is formed of such a temper, that it can taste no perfect joy in weakness or in crime. Pity then, and yet respect, him who, loving thee and virtue equally, can ne'er know happiness without nor with thee, – who, thus condemned to suffer, without ceasing, submits not to his fate, but is overpowered by its tyranny, and who, alike helpless and unresigned, opposes while he suffers, and repines while he endures; knowing only the remorse of guilt without its enjoyments, and expecting its retribution, without daring to deprecate its weight.' – Exhausted and overpowered, he fell prostrate on the earth; cold damps hung on his brow, and burning tears fell from his inflamed eyes. – Luxima,[a] terrified by his emotion, faint and trembling, crept timidly and tenderly towards him; and, pressing his hands, she murmured soothingly, yet with firmness, 'Since then we can both only live to suffer or to err, to be miserable or to be guilty, wherefore should we not die?'

The Missionary raised his eyes to her face, and its expression of loveliness and love, though darkened by despair, rendered her more enchanting in his eyes, than she had ever yet appeared: he felt her tears on his hands, which she pressed alternately to her eyes and to her lips; and this eloquent though silent expression of an affection so pure, which he believed was to be the last proof of love he might ever receive, overwhelmed him.

Silent[b] and motionless, he withdrew not his hands from the clasp of hers; he gazed on her with unrestrained feelings of love and pity, his whole soul seeming to diffuse itself through his eyes, over her countenance and figure. It[c] was in this transient moment of high-wrought emotions, that they were suddenly surrounded by a group of persons who sprang from behind a rock. Luxima was torn from the arms, which but now protectingly encircled her; and the Missionary was seized with a violence, that, in the first moment of amazement and horror, deprived him of all presence of mind. But the feeble plaints of Luxima, who was borne away in the arms of one of the assailants, recalled to his bewildered mind a consciousness of their mutual sufferings, and situations: – he[d] struggled with all the strength of frenzy, in the strong grasp of the two persons who held him; – he shook them from him as creatures of inferior force and nature;[e] and looked so powerful, in his uncurbed rage, that a third, who stood armed before him, attempted not to arrest his flight, as he sprang forward to the rescue of Luxima, who lay lifeless in the arms of the person who was carrying her away; but in the next moment his own encircled her: the person from whom he had torn her, seemed no less bold, no less resolved than he; drawing a pistol from beneath his robe, he pointed it to the Missionary's breast; and exclaimed, 'To resist, is but to increase your crimes, and to endanger your life.' The Missionary gently disengaged himself from Luxima, who sunk to the earth and, springing like a lion on his opponent, he seized his arm; – closely entwined in bonds of mutual destruction, they wrestled for life and death, with a strength almost supernatural, – at last, Hilarion wresting the pistol from the hand of his adversary, flung him against a rock, at whose base he lay apparently without life. – His three associates now came to the scene of action – armed, and with looks that threatened to avenge the fate of their companion; but the Missionary stood firm and unappalled, his eye lowring defiance, and raising Luxima in one arm, while with the other he pointed the pistol towards them, he said boldly, 'Whoe'er you be, and whatever may have tempted you to this desperate outrage, I shall not spare the life of him who dares approach one single step.'

The persons looked in consternation on each other; but one of them, whose face was till now concealed, threw back his hood and robe, and discovered on his breast, the Badge which distinguishes *the officers of the Inquisition!** It was then, that the Missionary recognized in the European traveller the Coadjutor whom he had disgraced and dismissed from his appointment, during their voyage to India. Amazed, confounded,[a] but not subdued, he met, with an undaunted look, the keen, malignant, and avengeful glance, which was now directed at him: 'Knowest thou me?' demanded the Inquisitor scoffingly, 'who, now high in power in the highest of all human tribunals was once covered with shame and opprobrium, by thy superior excellence! Where now are all the mighty virtues of the *man without a fault?* where now are the wonders which his zeal and genius promised? what are the fruits of his unrivalled Mission? Behold him! supporting on his bosom, the victim of his seductive arts! – his sacrilegious hand, pointing an instrument of death at those who are engaged in the duties of that holy office, whose censure he has incurred by dreadful heresies, by breach of solemn vows, and by his heretical defamation of a sacred Order!' – While the Inquisitor yet spoke, several persons from the Caravan had arrived on the spot, to witness a scene so singular and so unexpected: Luxima too, who had recovered her senses, still trembling and horror-struck, clung to the bosom, which now so wildly heaved to the emotions of rage and indignation.

Silent for many minutes, the Missionary stood gazing with a look of proud defiance and ineffable contempt upon his avengeful enemy: 'And know *you* not me?' he at last exclaimed, with a lofty scorn – 'you knew me once, supreme, where *you* dared not *soar!* – Such as *I* then *was*, such *I* now *am*; in every thing unchanged – and still, in every thing, *your* superior! – Grovelling and miserable *as you are* even in your unmerited elevation – this you *still* feel; – speak, then; what are your orders! – tremble not, but declare them! – It is the Count of Acugna, it is the Apostolic *Nuncio* of *India*, who commands you!' – Pale with stifled rage, the Inquisitor drew from his bosom the brief, by which he was empowered to call those before the Inquisitorial Court, whose conduct and whose opinions should fall under the suspicions of those emissaries, which it

---

* 'They all wear (the Familiares[17] de Santo Officio), as a mark of creditable distinction, a gold medal, upon which are engraven the Arms of the Inquisition.' *Stockdale's History of the Inquisitions.*[18]

had deputed to visit the Christian establishments in the interior of India. – The Missionary glanced his eye over the awful instrument, and bowed low to the Red Cross imprinted at its head: the Inquisitor then said, 'Hilarion, of the Order of St. Francis, and member of the Congregation of the Mission; – I arrest you in the name of the Holy Office, and in presence of these its ministers, that you may answer to such charges as I shall bring against you, before *the tribunal* of the Inquisition.' At these words, the Missionary turned pale! – nature stood checked by religion! – passion submitted to opinion, and prejudice governed those *feelings*, over which *reason* had lost all sway. He let fall the instrument of death, which he had held in his hand till now; the voice of the Church had addressed him, and all the powerful force of his religious habits returned upon his soul: he, who till now had felt only as a *man*, remembered he was a *religious*; he who had long, who had so recently, acknowledged the precious influence of human feeling, now recalled to mind that he had vowed the sacrifice of *all* human feeling to Heaven! – and he who had resisted oppression, and avenged insult, now recollected that by the religion he professed, he was bound when one *cheek was smitten, to turn the other*.[19]

The rage which had blazed in the eyes of the indignant, the blood which had boiled in the veins of the brave, no longer flashed in the glance, or crimsoned the cheek of the Christian Missionary; yet still it was –

'Awe from above, that quelled his heart, nought else dismayed.'[20]

The officers of the Inquisition now approached, to bind his arms, and to lead him away; but Luxima, with a shriek of horror, threw herself between them, ignorant of the nature of the danger which assailed her lover and her friend, and believing it nothing less than death itself: her wild and frenzied supplications, her beauty and affection, touched the hearts of those who surrounded them. The Missionary had already excited a powerful interest in his favour: the popular feeling is always on the side of resistance against oppression – for men, however vicious individually, are generally virtuous in the mass: his fellow-travellers, therefore, boldly advanced, to rescue one, whose air and manner had captivated their imaginations. The passions of a multitude know no precise limit; the partisans of the Missionary only waited for the orders of him whom they were about to avenge: they said, 'Shall we throw those men under the camels feet? or shall we bind them to those rocks, and leave them to their fate?'

The Europeans shuddered, and turned pale!

The Missionary cast on them a glance of contempt and pity, and, looking round him with an air at once dignified and grateful, he said, 'My friends, my heart is deeply touched by your generous sympathy; good and brave men ever unite, of whatever region, or whatever faith they may be: but I belong to a religion whose spirit it is to save and not to destroy; suffer then, these men to live; they are but the agents of a higher power, whose scrutiny they challenge me to meet. – I go to appear before that tribunal of that church, whose voice is my law, and from which a Christian minister can make no appeal, – I trust I go to contend *best* with the *best*; prepared rather to suffer death myself, than to cause the death of others.'

Then turning to the Inquisitor he said, pointing to Luxima, whom he again supported in his arms, 'Remember, that by a word I could have had you mingled with the dust I tread on; but, as you prize that life I have preserved, guard and protect this sacred, this consecrated vestal! – *look at her!* – otherwise than pure and innocent, you dare not believe her: know then, also, she is a Christian Neophyte, who has received the Baptismal rites, and who is destined to set a bright example to her idolatrous nation, and to become the future spouse of God.'[a]

Subdued and mortified, the officers of the Inquisition made no reply. He whom the Missionary had wounded, now crawled towards the others – they[b] surrounded their unresisting prisoner, who bore along the feeble form of the Indian: silent, and weeping, she was consigned to the mohaffah she had before occupied; and, the Missionary having ascended the back of his camel, the caravan was again in motion – two of the Inquisitors remained with their prisoner – the other two had rode on before the caravan to *Tatta*.

CHAPTER XVI.

IT was night when the travellers reached the suburbs of the ancient city of Tatta; the caravan had been lessened of its numbers during its progress; those who remained, now dispersed in various directions: the Inquisitors, instead of proceeding with their charge to a *Caravansera*,[21] carried him and the Neophyte to a small fortress which belonged to a Spanish garrison; a guard of soldiers, headed by the two Inquisitors, who had preceded the caravan, received them at its portals.

The Missionary guessed his fate, – dreadful as it was, he met it not unprepared: he saw himself surrounded by an armed force; he knew that, were he inclined to offer it, all resistance would be vain; and he submitted, with all the grandeur of human dignity, with all the firmness of religious fortitude, to a destiny now inevitable.

But Luxima still clung to him: the gloomy air of all around her, the fierce looks of the soldiers, their arms glittering to the dusky light of a solitary lamp, which hung suspended in the centre of a vast and desolate guard-room; the black cowls and scowling countenances of the Inquisitors, all struck terror on the timid soul of the Indian. She cast round a fearful and terrified glance, and would then have sunk upon the bosom of her sole protector and friend on earth, but, exposed as they were to the observation of their persecutors, the Missionary, for her sake even more than for his own, rejected the impulse of his feelings, and, turning away his head to conceal the agony of his countenance, he held her from him. – It was then that the heart of Luxima, sinking within her bosom, seemed to have received its death wound; – she fixed her closing eyes on him, who thus almost seemed to resign her to misery and to suffering, unsupported and unpitied – but she wept not, and one of the Inquisitors bore her away, unresisting, and almost lifeless, in his arms. An exclamation of horror burst from the lips of the Missionary; and, with an involuntary motion, he advanced a few steps to follow her; betraying, in his wild and haggard looks, the feelings by which his soul was torn. But the guards interposed – he could not even himself desire, that she might remain with him; and the Inquisitor, fixing his eyes on his agitated countenance, with a look of scoffing malignancy, said: 'Fear not for your concubine, she shall be taken care of.' – At these words, a deep scarlet suffused the cheek of the Missionary; fire flashed from his dark rolling eye, and he cast a look on his insulting oppressor, so blasting in its glance, that he seemed to wither beneath its terrific influence. – 'Observe!' he said, with a voice of thunder, 'I repeat it to you, it is a Christian Neophyte, pure, spotless, and unsullied, which you have now taken under your protection; look therefore that you consider her as such, as you shall answer it to that God, to whom she is about to consecrate her sinless life; as you shall answer it to that Church, whose ministers you are. – Be this remembered by you as priests; as *men*, forget not *she is a woman!*' Then, turning to his guards, he said with haughtiness, 'Lead on;' – as though he still commanded, even in obeying; and he was immediately led to a tower in a remote part of the fortress.

The members of the Inquisitorial Court, into whose power a singular coincidence of circumstances had thrown the Missionary, were returning from visiting the Christian institution at Lahore, of whose abuses and disorders the grand Inquisitor had received secret intelligence, when the chief of the party, who had been raised to his present dignity by the low arts of cunning and duplicity, discovered in the supposed lover of a fugitive Indian, that once infallible man, of whose rigid virtue, and severe unbending justice, he had been the victim; conscious, that in detecting and exposing the frailty of one who had 'bought golden opinions, from all sorts of persons,'[22] he should, while he gratified his own private vengeance, present a grateful victim to the Jesuits and Dominicans, who equally hated the Franciscan, for his order, his popularity, and his unrivalled genius, – he soon sought and found sufficient grounds of accusation, to lay the basis of his future ruin. With an artifice truly jesuitical, he drew the Missionary into a conversation, which he obliged one of his brethren to listen to, and note down; and, from the freedom of those religious opinions he had induced the Missionary to discuss, and from the tender nature of the ties which seemed to exist between him and his lovely associate, – Heresy, and the seduction of a Neophyte, were the crimes to be alleged against a man, whose disgrace was destined to be commensurate to the splendour of his triumphs.

On the day following their arrival at Tatta, the Missionary was conveyed on board a Spanish vessel, which lay in the Indus, and was bound for Goa. On his way he passed the *litter* which Luxima, he believed, occupied; but it was closely covered. He shuddered, and for a moment the heroism of virtue deserted him – he doubted not that she would be conveyed in the same vessel with him to Goa; and, as he knew that supplication would be fruitless, and that in humbling himself to intreaty he would not effect the purpose for which he stooped, he made no effort to obtain an interview with her: he believed too that the insatiable desire of the[a] Jesuits for conversion would render her safety and preservation an object to them; and that she would owe to the bigotry of their zeal, that mercy which she could not expect from the suggestions of their humanity – but that he should never again behold her, the object of his only love, the companion of his wandering, and the partner of his sufferings,[b] was an idea dictated by despair, from which religion withdrew her light, and hope her solace. Placed in a close and unwholesome confinement, it was in vain he sought to catch the sound of Luxima's voice; it was in vain he hazarded an inquiry relative to her situation: silence and mystery still surrounded him; no beam shone upon the darkness of his days; no answer was returned to his inquiries; no pity was given to his sufferings; all was dreary hopeless gloom! all was the loss of fame, the loss of love! of all that the high ambition of piety had promised! of all that the exquisite feelings of nature had bestowed! – Still pursued 'by thoughts of lost happiness and lasting shame,'[23] and joined only in *equal ruin* with her for whom he had encountered misery and affliction, and on whose innocent head he had heaped it, – he now saw that the sufferings of man resulted less from the constitution of his nature, than from the obstinacy with which he abandons the dictates of Providence, and devotes himself to[a] those illusions which the law of human reason, and the impulse of human affection, equally oppose. He remembered the feelings with which the Brahmin Priestess and the Christian Missionary had first mutually met; he contrasted their first interview with their present situations, alike as they now were *the victims of mistaken* zeal; and he accused that misconstruction of the laws of Providence, those false distinctions, which superstition has erected between the species, as the source of the severest sufferings to which mankind was condemned. For himself, he had no hope: he knew the character of his judges, the sentiments they bore in general to his order, and in particular to him; he knew the influence of the tribunal at which they presided, he knew that those whom they intended to destroy, no human power could preserve. But while he accused himself of relaxation in his zeal, of negligence in his mission, of suffering a guilty passion to subdue the force of his mind, and the influence of his religion, he believed his enemies to be but the blind agents of that Heaven, whose wrath he had justly provoked; for, still bringing his new-born feelings to the test of his ancient opinions, he continued to oppose religion to nature, and deemed himself sunk in guilt, because he had not risen above humanity.

It was on a day bright and sunny as that on which the Apostolic Nuncio left *Goa* in all the triumph of superior and unrivalled excellence,[b] that he returned to it a *prisoner* and in *chains*. His enemies had determined that his disgrace should be as striking and as public as his triumph; that the idol of the people should be dashed before their eyes from the shrine erected to his glory; and that envy and bigotry, under the guise of religion and justice, should gratify the insatiate spirit of persecution and vengeance. Before the illustrious criminal was permitted to land, the intelligence of his return under circumstances so different from those his departure had promised, and dark inuendos of the nature and extent of his fault, were artfully circulated through *Goa*, till the public mind, soured by the disappointments of its hopes and its confidence, was prepared to receive the Nuncio with a contempt equal to the admiration it formerly bestowed on him. At last a guard of Spanish soldiers, accompanied by the officers of the Holy Office, were sent to conduct him to the prison of the Inquisition. A multitude of persons had assembled to see him pass; but they no longer beheld the same creature whom they had last so loudly greeted with acclamations of reverential homage, and on whose mild and majestic brow passion had impressed no trace, whose commanding eye was brightened by holy joy, and whose life of sinless purity was marked in the seraphic character of his inspired countenance! His person was now almost as changed as his fate: it was worn away by suffering, by fatigue, by internal conflicts, and faded by its exposure to the varying clime; the experience of human frailty in himself, and of human turpitude in others, marked his brow with traces of distrust and disappointment; – his enthusiasm was fled! his zeal subdued by the fatal consequences of its unsuccessful efforts! and love, and affliction,[a] and shame, and indignation, the opprobrium he endured, and the innocence he could not establish; the injustice under which he laboured, and the malignity he despised – all mingled their conflicts in his soul, all shed over his air and look[b] the sullen grandeur of a proud despair, superior to complaint, and inaccessible to hope; yet 'not all *lost* in *loss* itself,'[24] gleams of his mind's untarnished glory still brightened at intervals his look of gloom – and, still appearing little less than 'archangel ruined,'[25] he proceeded, manacled, but lofty and towering above the guards who surrounded him. An awful silence reigned on every side; and even those who deemed him culpable, saw him so mighty in *his fall*, that while they accused him of guilt, they believed him superior to weakness; respecting while they condemned, and admiring while they pitied him.[c] As a member of the noble house of *Acugna*, whatever were the charges brought against him, he could not fail to excite interest in Goa, where the Portuguese were coalesced by a common feeling of suffering under the oppression of the Spanish government: but the terrors which surrounded the most dreadful of all human tribunals; a tribunal which was seconded, in the hierarchy of Goa, by all the influence of civil authority; its being invested with the power of life and death, and superstitiously believed even with that of salvation itself, awed the boldest heart, and alike silenced the feelings of patriotism, and stilled the impulse of humanity! Not even a murmur of resistance was heard; the accused and his guards passed silently on to the prison of the Holy Office; they reached its gloomy court; the portals closed upon the victim, and the light of hope was shut out for ever!

No breath transpired of the dark mysterious deeds which passed within the mansion of horror and superstition; and its awful investigations were conducted with a secrecy which baffled all inquiry:* the impenetrable cloud which hung over the fate of the Missionary, could only be cleared up when that dreaded day arrived, upon which the dungeons of the Inquisition were to yield up their tenants to punishment, to liberty, or – to death!

At this period a sullen gloom hung over the city of Goa, resembling the brooding of a distant storm: – it was rumoured, that the power of the Spanish government in Portugal and its colonies was on the point of extinction, and it

---

* The people also dare not speak of this Inquisition, but with the utmost respect and reverence; and if by accident the slightest word should escape one, which concerned it ever so little, it would be necessary immediately to accuse and inform against one's self. People are frequently confined to the prison for one, two, or three years, without knowing the reason, and are visited only by officers of the Inquisition, and never suffered to behold any other person. – *History of the Inquisition by Stockdale*, p. 213.

was known by many fatal symptoms, that the Indians were ripe for insurrection. The arts used by the Dominicans and the Jesuits for the conversion of the followers of Brahma, the evil consequences which had arisen by forfeiture of cast, (for many families had shared the ignominy heaped on the devoted head of the individual apostate) with the coercive tyranny of the Spanish government, had excited in the breasts of the mild, patient, and long-enduring Hindus, a principle of resistance, which waited only for some strong and sudden impulse to call it into action;* and it was observed that this disposition had particularly betrayed itself on a recent and singular occasion.

A woman who bore on her forehead the mark of a descendant of Bramah (the sacred *tellertum*), and round her neck the sacrificial threads or *dsandam* of their tutelar god, was seen to enter a convent of Dominican nuns led by an officer of the Inquisition, and surrounded by Dominican and *Jesuit priests!* The faded beauty of her perfect form, her noble and distinguished air, the agony of her countenance, and the silent tears which fell from her eyes when she turned them on those of her own cast and country, who stood near the litter from which she alighted, awakened a strong and powerful emotion in their feelings; and it was not decreased, when a Cashmirian, who was present, declared that the said apostate was Luxima, the Brahmachira and prophetess of Cashmire. The person who industriously circulated this intelligence, was the *pundit* of Lahore, the preceptor of the Missionary. His restless and unsettled spirit had led him to Goa: some imprudent and severe observations which he had let fall against the Inquisitorial power, had nearly proved his destruction, but his talents had extricated him; he had engaged as secretary and interpreter to the Spanish Viceroy, and obtained his favour and protection by those arts of conciliation, of which he was so perfectly the master. His hatred of the Inquisition, and his love of intrigue and of commotion, which gave play to the finesse of his genius, and the activity of his mind, led him to seize every opportunity of exciting his compatriots to resist the European power in Goa; and it was about this period that the arrival of Luxima furnished him with an event favourable to his views. He had in vain sought to attract her attention on her way to the Convent of the Dominicans; nor until her arrival at its portal had he succeeded in catching her eye; he then effected it by dropping his muntras at her feet. Absorbed as she appeared to be, this little incident did not escape her attention: she raised her tear-swollen eyes to his, with a look of sudden recognition, for she had known him in the days of her glory; but the Cashmirian, with an almost imperceptible motion of his finger across his lips, implying silence, carelessly picked up his beads and passed on, as the doors of the Christian sanctuary shut out from the eyes of the multitude the priestess of Brahma.

* An insurrection of a fatal consequence took place in *Vellore* so late as 1806, and a mutiny at Nundydrag and Benglore, occurred about the same period: both were supposed to have originated in the religious bigotry of the natives, suddenly kindled by the supposed threatened violation of their faith from the Christian settlers.

It was on the eve of St. Jago de Compostello,[26] that the usually tranquil abode of the Dominican sisters exhibited a scene of general consternation: the *Indian Catechuman*,[27] committed to their pious care, had mysteriously disappeared a few days after her reception into their Order. Her conduct had not prepared them for an event so extraordinary from her: either unable or unwilling to speak their language, they had not once heard the sound of her voice, save that at sunset she sung a few low wild notes, through the bars of the casement of her cell, which the younger nuns delighted to catch in the garden beneath, believing that the day was not distant, when a voice so angelic would blend its melody with the holy strains of the Christian choir; but she appeared in every other respect docile, unresisting, and timid almost to wildness. She had suffered them to exchange her Indian dress for the habit of a novice of St. Dominick; she had unreluctantly accompanied them to their church, and assisted at their devotions: her looks were indeed wandering and wild, and seemingly always sent in search of some particular object; but she made no inquiry, she uttered no complaint, and the secret disorder of her mind was only visible in her countenance; which wore the general expression of confirmed melancholy, the sadness of unutterable affliction. A meekness so saintly, a gentleness so seraphic, excited hopes in the breast of the abbess and the sisterhood, which were suddenly destroyed by the miraculous disappearance of the Catechuman. The convent grounds, the gardens of the Viceroy, which were only divided from them by a low wall, were vainly searched; and no circumstance attending her flight could be ascertained, but that she had escaped by the casement of her cell; one of the bars of which had been removed from the brick-work. The *Provincial* of the Order having been made acquainted with the event, which was placed to the account of *pagan sorcery*, an order was issued from the Holy Office, offering a reward to whoever should give up the *relapsed infidel*, and threatening death to those who should conceal her; but week after week elapsed, and no one came forward to claim the recompense, or to avert the punishment. The pagan sorceress was no where to be heard of.[*]

---

[*] The Pagans and Moors of Goa are not subject to the Inquisition till they have been baptized. A disgusting and absurd cruelty is displayed in its treatment of those unfortunate Indians who are accused of magic and sorcery, and, as guilty of such offences, are committed to the flames. – See *Hist. of the Inquisition*, p. 243.

CHAPTER XVII.

HOWEVER a propensity to evil may be inherent in human nature, it is impossible to conceive an idea of abstract wickedness, uninfluenced by some powerful passion, and existing without any decided reference to some object we wish to attain, or some obstacle we desire to vanquish.

The Pundit of Lahore had seen the Christian Missionary dragged in chains to the dungeon of the Inquisition, and the Priestess of Cashmire delivered up to the tyranny of a fanaticism no less dreadful in the exercise of its power than that from which she had escaped. He considered himself as the remote cause of their mutual sufferings: equally incredulous as to the truth or influence of their respective doctrines, when opposed to the feelings of nature, he had felt a kind of triumph in putting their boasted infallibility to the test, which deserted him the moment he discovered the fatal consequences which arose from the success of his design. Unprincipled and corrupt to a certain degree, when a dereliction from right favoured the views of his interests, or established the justness of his opinions, (for the human mind, whether it credulously bends to imposition, or boldly resists in scepticism, can never wholly relinquish the intolerance of self-love,) he was yet naturally humane and benevolent; and the moment he discovered the fate which awaited the Missionary and his proselyte, he determined to use every exertion to avert it.

Free at all times of admittance to the Viceroy's gardens, he continued to wander incessantly beneath the wall which divided them from the grounds of the convent. He had caught a few notes of Luxima's vesper song, and recognized the air of an Indian hymn, sung upon certain festivals by the priestesses of *Brahma*; he ventured therefore to scale the wall, veiled by the obscurity of a dark night; and by means of a ladder of ropes, he finally effected the escape of the Neophyte: he conveyed her to his own lodging in a retired part of the city, and gave her up to the care of a Jewess,[28] who lived with him, and who, though outwardly professing Christianity from fear and policy, hated equally the Christians and the Pagans; love, however, secured her fealty to her protector, to whom she was ardently devoted; and pity secured her fidelity to the trust he had committed to her care; for the unfortunate Indian was now alike condemned by the religion of truth and the superstition of error – driven with shame and obloquy from the altar of Brahma, her life had become forfeit by the laws of the Inquisition as a relapsed Christian.* It was from the order issued from the Holy Office that the

---

* The Inquisition, which punishes with death relapsed Christians, never inflicts any capital punishment on those who have not received the rites of baptism. – *History of the Inquisition*, p. 244.

Pundit learned the latter circumstances. It was from the lips of the apostate that he learned she had forfeited cast, according to all the awful rites of Braminical excommunication. It was therefore impossible to restore her to her own cast, and difficult to preserve her from the power of her new religion; and he found with regret and dismay, that the efforts he had made to save her, might but ultimately tend to her destruction; – he now considered that his life was involved in hers, and that his own preservation depended upon her concealment. His first thought was to remove her from Goa: but the disorder of her mind had fallen upon her constitution, and she was seized with the *mordechi** – that disease so melancholy, and so dangerous, in those burning climes, where exercise, the sole preventive, is impossible. The ill success of his endeavours hitherto, the impossibility of gaining admittance into the interior of the Santa Casa, destroyed the hopes and checked the intentions of the Pundit, which pointed to the liberation of the Missionary; and the mystery which hung over the fate of a man for whom all Goa was interested, no human power could fathom. But the festival upon which the next *auto da fè*[29] was to be celebrated was fast approaching; and the result of those trials, the accused had sustained at the *messa di santo officio*,[30] could at that period only be ascertained.

The day had already passed, upon which the ministers of the Inquisition, preceded by their banners, marched from the palace of the Holy Office to the *Campo Santo*, or place of execution, and there by sound of trumpet proclaimed the day and hour on which the *solemn act* of faith was to be celebrated.

That awful day at length arrived – its dawn, that beamed so fearfully to many, was ushered in by the deep toll of the great bell of the Cathedral; a multitude of persons, of every age and sex, Christians, Pagans, Jews, and Mussulmen, filled the streets, and occupied the roofs, the balconies and windows of the houses, to see the procession pass through the principal parts of the city. The awful ceremony at length commenced – the procession was led by the Dominicans, bearing before them a white cross; the scarlet standard of the Inquisition, on which the image of the founder was represented armed with a sword, preceded a band of the *familiars of the Holy Office*, dressed in black robes, the last of whom bore a green cross, covered with black crape; six penitents of the *San Benito*[31] who had escaped death, and were to be sent to the galleys, each conducted by a familiar, bearing the standard of St. Andrew, succeeded, and were followed by the penitents of the *Fuego Revolto*,[32] habited in grey scapulars, painted with reversed flames; then followed some persons bearing the effigies of those who had died in prison, and whose bones were also borne in coffins; the victims condemned to death appeared the last of the awful train; they were preceded by the

---

* A species of delirious fever.

Alcaid[33] of the Inquisition, each accompanied on either side by two officers of the Holy Office, and followed by an officiating priest: a corps of *Halberdeens*,[34] or guards of the Inquisition, closed the procession. In this order it reached the church of St. Dominick, destined for the celebration of *the act of faith*. On either side of the great altar, which was covered with black cloth, were erected two thrones; that on the right was occupied by the Grand Inquisitor; that on the left by the Viceroy and his court: each person having assumed the place destined for him, two Dominicans ascended a pulpit, and read aloud, alternately, the sentences of the guilty, the nature of their crimes, and the species of punishment to which they were condemned. While this awful ceremony took place, each unfortunate, as his sentence was pronounced, was led to the foot of the altar by the Alcaid, where he knelt to receive it. Last of this melancholy band, appeared the *Apostolic Nuncio of India*. Hitherto no torture had forced from him a confession of crimes of which he was guiltless; but the power of his enemies had prevailed, and his innocence was not proof against the testimony of his interested accusers. Summoned to approach the altar, he advanced with the dignity of a self-devoted martyr to receive his sentence; firm alike in look and motion, as though created thing 'nought valued he or shunned,'[35] he knew his doom to be irrevocable, and met it unappalled.

Man was now to him an atom, and earth a speck! the collective force of his mind was directed to *one sole* object, but that object was – *eternity!* The struggle between the mortal and immortal being was over; passion no longer gave to his imagination the vision of its disappointed desires, nor love the seductive images of its frail enjoyment: the ambition of religious zeal, and the blandishments of tender emotion, no longer influenced a soul which was, in so short a space of time, to be summoned before the tribunal of its God.

Less awed than aweful, he stood at the foot of the judgment seat of his earthly umpire, and heard unshrinking and unmoved his accusation publicly pronounced; but when to the sin of heresy, and breach of monastic vow, was added the *seduction of a Neophyte*, then *nature* for a moment asserted her rights, and claimed the revival of her almost extinguished power – his spirit again descended to earth, his heart with a resistless impulsion opened to the influence of human feeling! to the recollection of human ties! and Luxima, even at the altar's feet, rushed to his memory in all her loveliness, and all her affliction; innocent and persecuted, abandoned and despairing: then, the firmness of his look and mind alike deserted him – his countenance became convulsed – his frame shook – an agonizing solicitude for the hapless cause of his death disputed with Heaven the last thoughts of his life – and his head dropped upon the missal on which his hand was spread according to the form of the ceremony: – but when closely following the enumeration of his crimes, he heard pronounced the aweful sentence of a dreadful and *an immediate death*, then the inspired fortitude of the martyr re-called the wandering feelings of the man, steadied the vibration of nerves, which love, for the last time, had taught to thrill, strengthened the weakness of the fainting heart, and restored to the troubled spirit the soothing peace of holy resignation and religious hope.

The fate of those condemned to the flames was at last announced – the officers of the secular tribunal came forward to seize the victims of a cruel and inexorable bigotry; and the procession increased by the Vice-roy, and the Grand Inquisitor, with their respective courts, proceeded to the place of execution. – It was a square, one side of which opened to the sea; the three others were composed of the houses of the Spanish grandees, before which a covered platform was erected, for the *Grand Inquisitor* and the Viceroy; in the centre of the square, three piles of faggots were erected, at a certain distance from each other, one of which was already slowly kindling; the air was still, and breathed the balmy softness of an eastern evening; the sun, something shorn of his beams, was setting in mild glory, and threw a saffron hue on the luxuriant woods which skirt the beautiful bay of Goa – not a ripple disturbed the bosom of the deep; every thing in the natural scene declared the beneficent intentions of the Deity, every thing in the human spectacle declared the perversion of man from the decrees of his Creator. It was on such an evening as this, that the Indian Priestess witnessed the dreadful act of her excommunication; the heavens smiled then, as now; and man, the minister of error, was then, as now, cruel and unjust, – substituting malevolence for mercy, and the horrors of a fanatical superstition for the blessed peace and loving kindness of true religion.

The secular judges had already taken their seats on the platform; the Grand Inquisitor and the Viceroy had placed themselves beneath their respective canopies; the persons who composed the procession were ranged according to their office and orders, – all but the three unhappy persons condemned to death; they alone were led into the centre of the square, each accompanied by a familiar of the Inquisition, and a confessor. The condemned consisted of two relapsed Indians, and *the Apostolic Nuncio* of *India*. The pile designed for him, was distinguished by a standard[*] on which, as was the custom in such cases, an inscription was written, intimating, 'that he was to be burnt as a *convicted Heretic who refused to confess his crime!*'

The timid Indians, who, in the zeal and enthusiasm of their own religion, might have joyously and voluntarily sought the death, they now met with horror, hung back, shuddering and weeping in agony and despair, endeavouring to defer their inevitable sufferings by uttering incoherent prayers and useless supplications to the priests who attended them. The Christian Missionary, who it was intended should suffer first, alone walked firmly up to the pile, and while the martyr light flashed on his countenance, he read unmoved the inscription imprinted on the standard of death; which was so soon to wave over his ashes – then, withdrawing a little on one side, he knelt at the feet of his confessor; the last appeal from earth to heaven was now made; he arose with a serene look; the officers of the bow-string[36] advanced to lead him towards the pile: the silence

---

[*] 'Morreo queimado por hereje convitto-negativo.'

which belongs to death, reigned on every side; thousands of persons were present; yet the melancholy breeze that swept, at intervals, over the ocean, and died away in sighs, was distinctly heard. Nature was touched on the master-spring of emotion, and betrayed in the looks of the multitude, feelings of horror, of pity, and of admiration, which the bigoted vigilance of an inhuman zeal would in vain have sought to suppress.[a]

In this aweful interval, while the presiding officers of death were preparing to bind their victim to the stake, a form scarcely human, darting with the velocity of lightning through the multitude, reached the foot of the pile, and stood before it, in a grand and aspiring attitude; the deep red flame of the slowly kindling fire shone through a transparent drapery which flowed in loose folds from the bosom of the seeming vision, and tinged with golden hues, those long dishev-elled tresses, which streamed like the rays of a meteor on the air; – thus bright and aerial as it stood, it looked like a spirit sent from Heaven in the aweful moment of dissolution to cheer and to convey to the regions of the blessed, the soul which would soon arise, pure from the ordeal of earthly suffering.

The sudden appearance of the singular phantom struck the imagination of the credulous and awed multitude with superstitious wonder. – Even the minis-ters of death stood for a moment, suspended in the execution of their dreadful office. The Christians fixed their eyes upon the *cross*, which glittered on a bosom whose beauty scarcely seemed of mortal mould, and deemed themselves the wit-nesses of a miracle, wrought for the salvation of a persecuted martyr, whose innocence was asserted by the firmness and fortitude with which he met[b] a dreadful death.

The Hindoos gazed upon the sacred impress of *Brahma*, marked on the brow of his consecrated offspring; and beheld the fancied *herald* of the tenth *Avater*,[37] announcing vengeance to the enemies of their religion. The condemned victim, still confined in the grasp of the officers of the bow-string, with eyes starting from their sockets, saw only the *unfortunate* he had made – the creature he adored – his disciple! – his mistress! – the Pagan priestess – the Christian Neo-phyte – his still lovely, though much changed Luxima. A cry of despair escaped from his bursting heart; and in the madness of the moment, he uttered aloud her name. Luxima, whose eyes and hands had been hitherto raised to Heaven, while she murmured the *Gayatra*,[38] pronounced by the Indian women before their vol-untary immolation, now looked wildly round her, and, catching a glimpse of the Missionary's figure, through the waving of the flames, behind which he strug-gled in the hands of his guards, she shrieked, and in a voice scarcely human, exclaimed, 'My beloved, I come! – *Brahma*[c] receive and eternally unite our spir-its!' – She sprang upon the pile: the fire, which had only kindled in that point where she stood, caught the light drapery of her robe – a dreadful death assailed her – the multitude shouted in horrid frenzy – the Missionary rushed forward – no force opposed to it, could resist the energy of madness, which nerved his powerful arm – he snatched the victim from a fate he sought not himself to avoid – he held her to his heart – the flames of her robe were extinguished in his

159

close embrace; – he looked round him with a dignified and[a] triumphant air – the officers of the Inquisition, called on by their superiors, who now descended from the platforms, sprang forward to seize him: – for a moment, the timid multitude were *still* as the pause of a brooding storm. – Luxima clung round the neck of her deliverer – the Missionary, with a supernatural strength, warded off the efforts of those who would have torn her from him – the hand of fanaticism, impatient for its victim, aimed a dagger at his heart; its point was received in the bosom of the Indian; – she shrieked, – and called upon 'Brahma!' – Brahma! Brahma! was re-echoed on every side. A sudden impulse was given to feelings long suppressed: – the timid spirits of the Hindoos rallied to an event which touched their hearts, and roused them from their lethargy of despair; – the sufferings, the oppression they had so long endured, seemed now epitomized before their eyes, in the person of their celebrated and distinguished Prophetess – they believed it was their god who addressed them from her lips – they rushed forward with a hideous cry, to rescue his priestess – and to avenge the long slighted cause of their religion, and their freedom; – they fell with fury on the Christians, they rushed upon the cowardly guards of the Inquisition, who let fall their arms, and fled in dismay.

Their religious enthusiasm kindling their human[b] passions, their rage became at once inflamed and sanctified by their superstitious zeal. Some seized the prostrate arms of the fugitives, others dealt round a rapid destruction by fire; they scattered the blazing faggots, and, snatching the burning brands from the pile, they set on fire the light materials of which the balconies, the verandahs, and platforms were composed, till all appeared one horrid and entire conflagration. The Spanish soldiers now came rushing down from the garrison upon the insurgents, – the native troops, almost in the same moment, joined their compatriots – the engagement became fierce and general – a promiscuous carnage ensued – the Spaniards fought as mercenaries, with skill and coolness; the Indians as enthusiasts, for their religion and their liberty,[c] with an uncurbed impetuosity; the conflict was long and unequal; the Hindoos were defeated; but the Christians purchased the victory of the day by losses which almost rendered their conquest a defeat.

CONCLUSION.

IN the multitude who witnessed the aweful ceremony of the *auto da fè*, in the church of St. Dominick, stood the Pundit of Lahore; and he heard with horror the sentence of death pronounced against the Christian Missionary. Considering himself as the remote cause of his destruction, he was overwhelmed by compassion and remorse – aware of the ripeness of the Indians to a revolt, he determined on exciting them to a rescue of their compatriots at the place of execution; he knew them prompt to receive every impression which came through the medium of their senses, and connected with the popular prejudices of their religion; when he beheld them following, with sullen looks, the slow march of the procession, to witness the execution of their countrymen, whom they conceived by their obstinate abjuration of the Christian religion to have been seduced from their ancient faith, his hopes strengthened, he moved rapidly among them, exciting the pity of some, the horror of others, and a principle of resistance in all: but it was to an unforeseen accident that he owed the success of his hazardous efforts.

Of the disorder by which Luxima had been attacked, a slight delirium only remained; her health was restored, but her mind was wandering and unsettled; the most affecting species of mental derangement had seized her imagination – the melancholy insanity of sorrow:[a] she wept no tears, she heaved no sighs – she sat still and motionless, sometimes murmuring a Braminical hymn, sometimes a Christian prayer – sometimes talking of her grandsire, sometimes of her lover – alternately gazing on the muntras she had received from one, and the cross that had been given her by the other.

On the day of the *auto da fè*, she sat, as was her custom since her recovery, behind the gauze blind of the casement of the little apartment in which she was confined; she beheld the procession moving beneath it with a fixed and vacant eye, until a form presented itself before her, which struck like light from heaven on her darkened mind; she beheld the friend of her soul; love and reason returned together; intelligence revived to the influence of affection – she felt, and thought, and acted – whatever were his fate, she resolved to share it: – she was alone, her door was not fastened, she passed it unobserved, she darted through the little vestibule which opened to the street; the procession had turned into another, but the street was still crowded – so much so, that even her singular appearance was unobserved; terrified and bewildered, she flew down an avenue that led to the sea, either because it was empty and silent, or that her reason was again lost, and she was unconscious whither she went, till chance

161

brought her into the 'square of execution!' – she saw the smoke of the piles rising above the heads of the multitude – in every thing she beheld, she saw a spectacle similar to that which the self-immolation of the Brahmin women presents: – the images thus presented to her disordered mind, produced a natural illusion – she believed the hour of her sacrifice and her triumph was arrived, that she was on the point of being united in heaven to him whom she had alone loved on earth; and when she heard her name pronounced by his well-known voice, she rushed to the pile in all the enthusiasm of love and of devotion. The effect produced by this singular event was such as, under the existing feelings of the multitude, might have been expected. During the whole of the tumult, the Pundit did not for a moment lose sight of the Missionary, who, still clasping Luxima in his arms, was struggling with her through the ranks of destruction; the Pundit approaching him, seized his arm, and, while all was uproar and confusion, dragged him towards the shore, near to which a boat, driven in by the tide, lay undulating; assisting him to enter, and to place Luxima within it, he put the only oar it contained into his hands; driving it from the shore, he himself returned to the scene of action.

The Missionary,[a] wounded in his right arm, with difficulty managed the little bark; yet he instinctively plied the oar, and put out from the land, without any particular object in the effort – his thoughts were wild, his feelings were tumultuous – he was stunned, he was bewildered by the nature and rapidity of the events which had occurred. He saw the receding shore covered with smoke; he saw the flames ascending to Heaven, which were to have consumed him; he heard the discharge of firearms, and the shouts of horror and destruction: but the ocean was calm; the horizon was bathed in hues of living light, and the horrors he had escaped, gradually faded into distance, and sunk into silence. He steered the boat towards the rocky peninsula which is crowned by the fortress of Alguarda; he saw the crimson flag of the Inquisition hoisted from its ramparts – he saw a party of soldiers descending the rocks to gain a watchtower, placed at the extremity of the peninsula, which guards the mouth of the bay: – here, remote as was the place, there was for him no asylum, no safety; he changed his course, and put out again to sea – twilight was deepening the shadows of evening; his little bark was no longer discernible from the land; he threw down the oar, he raised Luxima in his arms – her eye met his – she smiled languidly[b] on him – he held her to his heart, and life and death were alike forgotten – but Luxima returned not the pressure of his embrace, she had swooned; and as he threw back her tresses, to permit the air to visit her face more freely, he perceived that they were *steeped in blood!* He now first discovered that the poignard he had escaped, had been received in the bosom of the Indian: distracted, he endeavoured to bind the wound with the scapular which had made a part of his death dress; but though he thus stopped for the time the effusion of blood, he could not recall her senses. He looked round him wildly, but there was no prospect of relief; he seized her in his arms and turned his eyes on the deep, resolved to seek with her eternal repose in its bosom – he approached the edge of the boat

–[a] 'To what purpose,' he said, 'do I struggle to protract, for a few hours, a miserable existence? Death we cannot escape, whatever way we turn – its horrors we may – O God! am I then obliged to add to the sum of my frailties and my sins the crimes of suicide and murder?' He gazed passionately on Luxima, and added, 'Destroy thee, my beloved! while yet I feel the vital throb of that heart which has so long beaten only for me – oh, no! The Providence which has hitherto miraculously preserved us, may still make us the object of its care.' – He laid Luxima gently down in the boat, and, looking round him, perceived that the moon, which was now rising, threw its light on a peninsula of rocks, which projected from the main land to a considerable distance into the sea – it was the light of heaven that guided him – he seized the oar, and plying it with all the strength he could yet collect, he soon reached the rocks, and perceived a cavern that seemed to open to receive and shelter them.

*　*　*　*　*　*　*　*　*　*　*　*

The Pundit of Lahore was among the few who escaped from the destruction he had himself excited. Pursued by a Spanish soldier, he had fled towards the shore, and, acquainted with all the windings of the rocks, their deep recesses and defiles, he had eluded the vigilance of the Spaniard, and reached a cavern, which held out a prospect of temporary safety, till his strength should be sufficiently recruited to permit him to continue his flight towards a port, where some Bengal vessels were stationed, which might afford him concealment, and convey him to a distant part of India: as he approached the cavern, he looked round it cautiously, and by the light of the moon, with which it was illuminated, he perceived that it was already occupied – for kneeling on the earth, the *Apostolic Nuncio* of India, supported on his bosom the dying *Priestess of Cashmire*. The Pundit rushed forward; 'Fear not,' he said, 'be cheered, be comforted, all may yet go well: here we are safe for the present, and when we are able to proceed, some Bengalese merchantmen who lie at a little port at a short distance from hence, will give us conveyance to a settlement, where the power of Spain or of the Inquisition cannot reach us.'

The presence, the words of the Pundit were balm to the harassed spirits of the Missionary;[b] a faint hope beamed on his sinking heart, and he urged him to procure some fresh water among the rocks, the only refreshment for the suffering Indian, which the desolate and savage place afforded. The Pundit, having sought for a large shell to contain the water, flew in search of it; and the Missionary remained gazing upon Luxima, who lay motionless in his arms. The presence of the Pundit suddenly recalled to his memory the first scene of his mission; and he again beheld in fancy the youthful priestess of mystic love, borne triumphantly along amidst an idolizing multitude; he cast his eyes upon the object that lay faint and speechless in his arms; and the brilliant vision of his memory faded away, nor left upon his imagination one trace of its former lustre or its beauty; for the image which succeeded, was such as the *genius* of Despair could only pourtray in its darkest mood of gloomy creation.

In a rude and lonesome cavern, faintly lighted up by the rays of the moon, and echoing to the moaning murmurs of the ocean's tide, lay *that Luxima*, who once, like the delicious shade of her native region, seemed created only for bliss, and formed only for delight; those eyes, in whose glance the spirit of devotion, and the enthusiasm of tenderness, mingled their brilliancy and their softness, were now dim and beamless; and that bosom, where love lay enthroned beneath the vestal's veil, was stained with the life-blood which issued from its almost exhausted veins. Motionless, and breathing with difficulty, and with pain, she lay in his arms, with no faculty but that of suffering, with no sensibility but that of pain: – he had found her like a remote and brilliant planet, shining in lone and distant glory, illuminating, by her rays, a sphere of harmony and peace; but she had for him deserted her *orbit*, and her light was now nearly extinguished for ever.

When the Pundit returned, he moistened her lips with water, and chafed her temples and her hands with the pungent herbs the surrounding rocks supplied; and when the vital hues of life again faintly revisited her cheek, the Missionary,[a] as he gazed on the symptoms of returning existence, gave himself up to feelings of suspense and anxiety, to which despondency was almost preferable, and pressing those lips in death, which in life he would have deemed it the risk of salvation to touch, his soul almost mingled with that pure spirit, which seemed ready to escape with every low-drawn sigh; and his heart offered up its silent prayer to Heaven, that thus they might unite, and thus seek together mercy and forgiveness at its throne. *Luxima* revived, raised her eyes to those which were bent in agony and fondness over her, and on her look of suffering, and smile of sadness, beamed the ardour of a soul whose warm, tender, and imperishable feelings were still triumphant over even pain and death.

'Luxima!' exclaimed the Missionary, in a melancholy transport, and pressing her to a heart which a feeble hope cheered and re-animated, '*Luxima*, my beloved! wilt thou not struggle with death? wilt thou not save me from the horror of knowing, that it is *for me thou* diest? and that what remains of my wretched existence, has been purchased at the expence of thine? Oh! if *love*, which has led thee to death, can recall or attach thee to life, still live, even though thou livest *for my destruction*.' A faint glow flushed the face of the Indian, her smile brightened, and she clung still closer to the bosom, whose throb now replied to the palpitation of her own.

'Yes,' exclaimed the Missionary, answering the eloquence of her languid and tender looks, 'yes, dearest, and most unfortunate, our destinies are now inseparably united! Together we have loved, together we have resisted, together we have erred, and together we have suffered; lost alike to the glory and the fame, which our virtues, and the conquest of our passions, once obtained for us; alike condemned by our religions and our countries, there now remains nothing on *earth* for us, but each other! – Already have we met the horrors of death, without its repose; and the life for which thou hast offered the precious purchase of thine own, must *now belong alone to thee*.'

Luxima raised herself in his arms, and grasping his hands, and fixing on him her languid eyes, she articulated in a deep and tremulous voice, *'Father!'* but, faint from bodily exhaustion and mental emotion, she again sunk in silence on his bosom! At the plaintive sound of this touching and well-remembered epithet, the Missionary shuddered, and the blood froze round his sinking heart; again he heard the voice of the proselyte, as in the shades of Cashmire he had once heard it, when pure, and free from the taint of human frailty, he had addressed her only in the spiritual language of an holy mission, and she had heard him with a soul ignorant of human passion, and opening to receive that sacred truth, to whose cause he had proved so faithless: the religion he had offended, the zeal he had abandoned, the principles, the habits of feeling, and of thinking, he had relinquished, all rushed in this awful moment on his mind, and tore his conscience with penitence, and with remorse; he saw before his eyes the retribution of his error in the sufferings of its innocent cause; he sought to redeem what was yet redeemable of his fault, to recall to his wandering soul the duties of the minister of Heaven, and to put from his guilty thoughts the feelings of the impassioned man! He sought to withdraw his attention from the perishable woman, and to direct his efforts to the salvation of the immortal spirit; but when again he turned his eyes on the Indian, he perceived that hers were ardently fixed on the rosary of her idolatrous creed, to which she pressed with devotion her cold and quivering lips, while the crucifix which lay on her bosom was steeped in the blood she had shed to preserve him.

This affecting combination of images so opposite and so eloquent in their singular but natural association, struck on his heart with a force which his reason and his zeal had no power to resist: – and the words which religion awakened to its duty, sent to his lips, died away in sounds inarticulate, from the mingled emotions of horror and compassion, of gratitude and love – and, wringing his hands, while cold drops hung upon his brow, he exclaimed in a tone of deep and passionate affliction, 'Luxima, Luxima! are we then to be *eternally disunited?*'

Luxima replied only by a look of love, whose fond expression was the next moment lost in the convulsive distortions of pain. Much enfeebled by the sudden pang, a faintness, which resembled the sad torpor of death, hung upon her frame and features; yet her eyes were still fixed with a gaze so motionless and ardent, on the sole object of her dying thought, that her look seemed the last look of life and love, when both inseparably united dissolve and expire together. 'Luxima,' exclaimed the Missionary wildly, 'Luxima, thou wilt not die! Thou wilt not leave me alone on earth to bear thy innocent blood upon my head, and thy insupportable loss for ever in my heart! – to wear out life in shame and desolation – my hope entombed with thee – my sorrows lonely and unparticipated – my misery keen and eternal! – Oh! no, fatal creature! sole cause of all I have ever known of bliss or suffering, of happiness or of despair, thou hast bound me to thee by dreadful ties; by bonds, sealed with thy blood, indissoluble and everlasting! And if thy hour is come, mine also is arrived, for triumphing over the fate which would divide us; we shall *die*, as we dared *not live* – together!'

Exhausted by the force and vehemence of an emotion which had now reached its crisis – enervated by tenderness, subdued by grief, and equally vanquished by bodily anguish, and by the still surviving conflicts of feeling and opinion – he sunk overpowered on the earth; and Luxima, held up by the sympathizing Pundit, seemed to acquire force from the weakness of her unfortunate friend, and to return from the grasp of death, that she might restore him to life. Endeavouring to support his head in her feeble arms, and pressing her cold cheek to his, she sought to raise and cheer his subdued spirit, by words of hope and consolation. At the sound of her plaintive voice, at the pressure of her soft cheek, the creeping blood quickened its circulation in his veins, and a faint sensation of pleasure thrilled on his exhausted nerves; he raised his head, and fixed his eyes on her face with one of those looks of passionate fondness, tempered by fear, and darkened by remorse, with which he had so frequently, in happier days contemplated that exquisite loveliness which had first stolen between him and Heaven. Luxima still too well understood that look, which had so often given birth to emotions, which even approaching death had not quite annihilated; and with renovated strength (the illusory herald of dissolution) she exclaimed – 'Soul of my life! the God whom thou adorest, did doubtless save thee from a dreadful death, that thou mightest live for others, and still he commands thee to bear the painful burthen of existence: yet, oh! if for others thou *wilt not live*, live at least for *Luxima*! and be thy beneficence to her nation, the redemption of those faults of which for thy sake she has been guilty! – Thy brethren will not dare to take a life, which God himself has miraculously preserved – and when *I* am no more, thou shalt preach, not to the Brahmins only, but to the Christians, that the sword of destruction, which has been this day raised between the followers of thy faith and of mine, may be for ever sheathed! Thou wilt appear among them as a spirit of peace, teaching mercy, and inspiring love; thou wilt soothe away, by acts of tenderness, and words of kindness, the stubborn prejudice which separates the mild and patient Hindu from his species; and thou wilt check the Christian's zeal, and bid him follow the sacred lesson of the God he serves, who, for years beyond the Christian era, has extended his merciful indulgence to the errors of the Hindu's mind, and bounteously lavished on his native soil those wondrous blessings which first tempted the Christians to seek our happier regions. But should thy eloquence and thy example fail, tell them my story! tell them how I have suffered, and how even thou hast failed: – thou, for whom I forfeited my cast, my country, and my life; for 'tis too true, that still *more loving* than enlightened, my ancient habits of belief clung to my mind, thou to my *heart*: still I lived thy seeming proselyte, that I might *still live thine*; and now *I die* as Brahmin women *die*, a *Hindu* in my feelings and my faith – dying for him I loved, and believing as my fathers have believed.'

Exhausted and faint, she drooped her head on her bosom – and the Missionary, stiffened with horror, his human and religious feelings alike torn and wounded, hung over her, motionless and silent. The Pundit, dropping tears of compassion on the chilling hands he chafed, now administered some water to the parched lips of the dying Indian, on whose brow, the light of the moon shone resplendently. Somewhat revived by the refreshment, she turned on him her languid but grateful eyes, and slowly recognizing his person, a faint blush, like the first doubtful colouring of the dawn, suffused the paleness of her cheek; she continued to gaze earnestly on him for some moments, and a few tears, the last she ever shed, fell from her closing eyes, – and though the springs of life were nearly exhausted, yet her fading spirits rallied to the recollection of *home*! of *friends*! of *kindred*! and of *country*! which the presence of a sympathizing compatriot thus painfully and tenderly awakened – then, after a convulsive struggle between life and death, whose shadows were gathering on her countenance, she said in a voice scarcely audible, and in great emotion – 'I owe thee much, let me owe thee more – thou seest before thee Luxima! the Prophetess and Brachmachira of Cashmire! – and thou wast haply sent by the interposition of Providence to receive her last words, and to be the testimony to her people of her innocence; and when thou shalt return to the blessed paradise of her nativity, thou wilt say – "that having gathered *a dark spotted flower in the garden of love*, she expiates her error by the loss of her life; that her disobedience to the forms of her religion and the laws of her country, was punished by days of suffering, and by an untimely death; yet that her *soul* was pure from sin, as, when clothed in transcendent brightness, she outshone, in faith, in *virtue*, all women of her nation!"'

This remembrance of her former glory, deepened the hues of her complexion, and illumined a transient ray of triumph in her almost beamless eyes: then pausing for a moment, she fixed her glance[a] on the image of her tutelar god, which she still held in her hand – the idol, wearing the form of infant beauty, was symbolic of that religious mystic love, to which she had *once* devoted herself! she held it for a moment to her lips, and to her heart – then, presenting it to the Cashmirian, she added, 'Take it, and bear it back to him, from whom I received it, on the day of my consecration, in the *temple* of *Serinagur*! to him! the aged grandsire whom I abandoned! – dear and venerable! – should he still survive the loss and shame of her, his child and his disciple! should he still deign to acknowledge as *his* offspring the outcast whom he cursed – the Chancalas whom—' the words died away upon her quivering lips, 'Brahma!' she faintly exclaimed, 'Brahma!' and, grasping the hands of the Missionary, alternately directed her looks to him and to Heaven; but he replied not to the last glance of life and love. He had sunk beneath the acuteness of his feelings; and the Indian, believing that his spirit had fled before her own to the realms of eternal peace, and there awaited to receive her, bowed her head, and expired in the blissful illusion, with a smile of love and a ray of religious joy shedding their mingled lustre on her slowly closing eyes.

    ★   ★   ★   ★   ★   ★   ★   ★   ★   ★   ★   ★

   ★   ★   ★   ★   ★   ★   ★   ★   ★   ★   ★   ★

The guards, who by order of the Inquisition were sent in pursuit of the fugitives, reached the cavern of their retreat three days after that of the insurrection; but here they found only a pile partly consumed, and the ashes of such aromatic plants as the interstices of the surrounding rocks afforded, which the Hindus usually burn with the bodies of their deceased friends, at the funeral pyre; they continued therefore their search farther along the shore; it was long, persevering and fruitless. The Apostolic Nuncio of India was *never heard of more.*

Time rolled on, and the majestic order of nature, uninterrupted in its harmonious course, finely contrasted the rapid vicissitudes of human events, and the countless changes in human institutions! In the short space of *twenty* years, the mighty had fallen, and the lowly were elevated; the lash of oppression had passed alternately from the grasp of the persecutor to the hand of the persecuted; the slave had seized the sceptre, and the tyrant had submitted to the chain. Portugal, resuming her independence, carried the standard of her triumph even to the remote shores of the Indian ocean, and, knowing no ally but that of *compatriot unanimity*, resisted by her single and unassisted force, the combined powers of a mighty state, the intrigues of a wily cabinet, and the arms of a successful potentate.* While *Freedom* thus unfurled her spotless banner in a remote corner of the West, she lay mangled and in chains, at the foot of victorious tyranny in the East. *Aurengzebe* had waded through carnage and destruction to the throne of India – he had seized a sceptre stained with a brother's blood, and wore the diadem, torn from a parent's brow! worthy to represent the most powerful and despotic dynasty of the earth, his genius and his fortunes resembled the regions he governed, mingling sublimity with destruction; splendour with peril; – and combining, in their mighty scale, the great extremes of good and evil. Led by a love of pleasure, or allured by a natural curiosity, he resolved on visiting the most remote and most delicious province of his empire, where his ancestors had so often sought repose from the toils of war, and fatigue of government; and where, *twenty years* before, his own heroic and unfortunate nephew, Solymon Sheko, had sought asylum and resource against his growing power and fatal influence. He left *Delhi* for Cashmire, during an interval of general prosperity and peace, and performed his expedition with all the pomp of eastern magnificence.†

In the immense and motley multitude which composed his suite, there was an European *Philosopher*,[41] who, highly distinguished by the countenance and protection of the emperor, had been led, by philosophical curiosity and tasteful research, to visit a country, which, more celebrated than known, had not yet attracted the observation of genius, or the inquiry of science. He found the natu-

---

* Revolution of Portugal[39]

† Historical.[40]

ral beauty of the vale of *Cashmire*, far exceeding the description of its scenes which lived in the songs of the Indian bards, and its mineral and botanic productions curious, and worthy of the admiration and notice of the naturalist; and in a spot which might be deemed the region of natural phenomena, he discovered more than *one* object to which a moral interest was attached. Yet to *one object only* did the *interest of sentiment* peculiarly belong; it was a sparry cavern, among the hills of Serinagur, called, by the *natives* of the valley, the '*Grotto of congelations!*'* They pointed it out to strangers as a place constructed by magic, which for many years had been the residence of a recluse! a stranger, who had appeared suddenly among them, who had been rarely seen, and more rarely addressed, who led a lonely and an innocent life, equally avoided and avoiding, who lived unmolested, awakening no interest, and exciting no persecution – 'he was,' they said, 'a wild and melancholy man! whose religion was unknown, but who prayed at the confluence of rivers, at the rising and the setting of the sun; living on the produce of the soil, he needed no assistance, nor sought any intercourse; and his life, thus slowly wearing away, gradually faded into death.'

A *goalo*, or Indian shepherd, who missed him for several mornings at his wonted place of matinal devotion, was led by curiosity or by compassion to visit his grotto. He found him dead, at the foot of an altar which he had himself raised to the deity of his secret worship, and fixed in the attitude of one who died in the act of prayer. Beside him lay a small urn, formed of the sparry congelations of the grotto – on opening it, it was only found to contain some ashes, a cross stained with blood, and the dsandum of an Indian Brahmin. On the lucid surface of the *urn* were carved some characters which formed the name of '*Luxima!*' – It was the name of an *outcast*, and had long been condemned to oblivion by the crime of its owner. The Indians shuddered when they pronounced it! and it was believed that the *Recluse* who lived so long and so unknown among them, was the same, who once, and in days long passed, had seduced, from the altar of the god she served, the most celebrated of their religious women, when he had visited their remote and lovely valley in the character of

A Christian Missionary.[a]

THE END.

---

* Monsieur de Bernier laments, in his interesting account of his journey to Cashmire which he performed in the suite of Aurengzebe, that circumstances prevented him visiting the grotto of congelations, of which so many strange tales were related by the natives of the valley.

EXPLANATORY NOTES

Volume I

1 Spain achieved control of Portugal with military victory at Alcántara in 1581; after several revolts, the Portuguese re-established an independent monarchy in 1640; the novel's action precedes that event.

2 The Jesuits, or Society of Jesus, is a religious order founded by Ignatius Loyola (1491–1556) in 1540, emphasising self-discipline, dedicated to achieving spiriual perfection for themselves and all humanity, and devoted in its early period to strengthening Catholicism in the face of the protestant reformation. In 1773 the growing power of the Jesuits and long-standing friction with other orders led to its suppression by the church; the order was reinstated in 1814.

3 The Franciscans were founded in the early thirteenth century by St Francis of Assisi as a mendicant order devoted to serving the poor and the sick and to preaching; they were the most numerous of the religious orders, and had several divisions.

4 Innocent X was pope from 1644 to 1655; he favoured Spanish over French interests and refused to recognise the independence of Portugal.

5 A reference to the Punic wars, a struggle for dominance of the ancient Mediterranean world during the third and second centuries BC, in which the general Hannibal for a time gave Carthage the advantage, ended by the victory of the Roman general Scipio Africanus at Zama in 202 BC. The reference places both the history of Portugal and the situation of early nineteenth-century Europe and its empires in world-historical terms.

6 St Hilarion was born near Gaza, Palestine, around AD 291 and, inspired by St Antony, lived as a hermit and became famous for his asceticism, miracles, and conversion of pagans by his example; he later attracted many disciples, inspired the building of monastic communities, and drew so many visitors that he had to go into hiding; he died in Cyprus around 371.

7 Criticism of asceticism and monasticism was common in Gothic novels of Owenson's day, especially since M. G. Lewis's *the Monk* (1796), and in Enlightenment, Revolutionary and liberal discourse generally.

8 Shakespeare, *Macbeth*, I.iii.149–50, from Macbeth's soliloquy reflecting on the witches' prophecies of his future greatness.

9 Paul was the first great missionary of Christianity, travelling around the Mediterranean world; his instructions to the early Christian communities helped form the Christian church and his letters constitute a large part of the New Testament of the Bible; arrested at Jerusalem for causing disorder by his activities, he was sent to Rome for trial and convicted and executed there around AD 67.

10 'Romance' here means 'fanciful', 'visionary', pertaining to the idealism and impracticality of early medieval and renaissance chivalric romances, satirised by Cervantes in *Don Quixote*.

11 Miguel de Vasconcellos de Brito was the minister of Margaret of Savoy, Duchess of Mantua, to whom the Spanish monarchy had delegated rule of Portugal.

12 The Spanish and Portuguese word for 'messenger'; here, the offical representative of the Papacy at a foreign court.

13 Goa was the first Portuguese colony in Asia, conquered in 1510; at the time of the novel's story, it was at its height as capital of the Portuguese Asian empire; Franciscan missionaries arrived there in 1517 and proselytised so successfully that Goa became the centre of Catholicism in India. It was occupied by India in 1961.

14 St Francis Xavier (1506–52), a co-founder of the Jesuits (Society of Jesus), arrived at Goa in 1542, took charge of training native missionaries, proselytised through Asia, died in China, and was buried at Goa. In his letters, later published, he criticised Portuguese oppression of the Indians and the bad example set by the European colonists' vicious living.

15 Equator.

16 From Arachosia, the ancient Greek name for the area now known as Baluchistan, in present-day Pakistan.

17 Tamerlane, or Timur, (d. 1405), a muslim Tartar from near Samarkand who conquered vast areas of central Asia and the Middle East, plundering and massacring wherever he went; in his sixties he conquered northern India; after his death, his empire fell apart. In European literature he was a figure for relentless but ultimately futile military ambition, and thus in Owenson's day easy to compare with Napoleon.

18 Mohamed, founder of Islam, called an impostor by Europeans, especially during the Enlightenment, when he was represented as more a cunning trickster than true religious prophet; he established Mecca in Arabia as the centre of Islam and his followers conquered and converted much of northern Africa, the middle east, northern India, and southern Asia.

19 The term 'pagoda' for the house of a religious image was first used by the Portuguese in sixteenth-century India, from a mispronunciation and misapprehension of a Persian or Sanscrit word, perhaps but-kadah; the term was later applied to any Asian temple, and especially a tower-like building of several storeys in Japan and China. In the Hindu religious system the triad of creation, preservation and destruction is represented by the Trimurti or triad of Brahma (principal deity), Vishnu (the world-preserver) and Siva (representing powers of reproduction and destruction).

20 Palmyra was site of a famous and notoriously rich and luxurious city in classical antiquity, located in deserts northeast of present-day Damascus, and centre of worship of the sun-god.

21 The 'Caaba' or 'Ka'ba' was a crude stone building housing various idols before Mohamed purged them and made the place the centre of Islamic pilgrimage, supposedly built by the patriarch Abraham.

22 The tabernacle was originally a religious sanctuary erected by Moses in the desert during the Jews' exodus from Egypt to the Holy Land, and was then used of the temple at Jerusalem.

23 Claude Marie Guyon (1699–1771) *Histoire des Indes Orientales* (1744).

24 Alexander Hamilton (d. *c.* 1732), *New Account of the East Indies* (1744).

25 An order of mendicant friars founded by crusaders in Palestine in the twelfth century; reform of the order in the sixteenth century was led by St Teresa of Avila.

26 In Hindu mythology Indra is a warlike god, represented as having four arms and hands; he is regent of the heaven of the gods and praised in many hymns.

27 John 12:12: 'see, your king is coming, mounted on an ass's colt', describing Christ's entry into Jerusalem, according to prophecy.

28 Properly, 'budgerow' – perhaps a misprint caused by Owenson's notoriously poor handwriting.

29 'Moultan', or 'Multan', is situated in the valley of the Chenab in Punjab in present day Pakistan.

30 Alexander of Macedon (356–23 BC), known as 'Alexander the Great', conquered much of the eastern Mediterranean world, and led his armies as far as northern India, at his death leaving a series of kingdoms that preceded the rise of the Roman empire; in eighteenth-century philosophy he was often used as a figure for the hero of destructive, rather than constructive and progressive, ambition.

31 Muhammad Firishtah, *The History of Hindostan, from the Earliest Account of Time, to the Death of Akbar; Translated from the Persian* (1768), translated by Alexander Dow (d. 1779).

32 'Formerly the Jesuits had an establishment in this city, performed their sacred offices, and offered to the eyes of Muslims and gentiles the pomp of their celebrations.', François Bernier (1620–88), *Histoire de la Dernière Révolution des États du Grand Mogol* (1670–1).

33 In one of Owenson's sources, Quinton Craufurd, *Sketches Chiefly Relating to the History, Religion, Learning, and Manners of the Hindoos* (1790), Saniassies are those who have given up family and worldly goods for a religious ascetic life; Owenson uses different spellings throughout the novel.

34 Jean de Thévenot, *Voyages de Mr de Thévenot, contenant la relation de l'Indostan* (1684).

35 A Hindu learned in Sanskrit and in Indian religion, philosophy and laws.

36 The *Musnavi* is a highly influential poem of over 50,000 lines in Persian by the sufi Islamic mystic Jalal al-Din Rumi (1207–73), and thus the 'Musnavi sect' is Muslim rather then Hindu in origin.

37 From the Spanish and Portuguese word for 'race' or 'breed'; here, a hereditary Hindu social class or group, originally comprising Brahmans, or priests; Kshatriyas, or warriors; Vaisyas, or merchants; and Sudras, or artisans.

38 Pierre Sonnerat (1748–1814), *Voyages aux Indes* (1782).

39 'Gazettes from the Delhi court, public news that mark day by day, and not in this bombastic style for which Orientals are criticised, important events at court and in the provinces – these are the gazettes spread throughout the empire', Abraham Hyacinthe Anquetil Duperron (1731–1805), *Tableau Historique de l'Inde* (1771)

40 From the Hindi word for 'teacher' or 'priest': a spiritual instructor or head of religious sect.

41 'Crishna', or 'Krishna' was the name of a deified hero, or incarnation of Vishnu, in later Hinduism.

42 A seat, usually canopied, on the back of an elephant.

43 'Kama-deva', god of love.

44 A cotton gown.

45 From 'mantra', Sanskrit for a sacred text used as a prayer or incantation.

46 From 'gayatri', an ancient twenty-four syllable metre used in hymns and other Hindu religious texts; one of these verses was held to be particularly sacred and was used as a morning hymn; Luxima recites it near the novel's end.

47 'Shaster' or 'shastra', from a Sanskrit and Hindi word for a sacred Hindu text.

48 The decorative and often elaborate religious mark put on the forehead to indicate the third (spiritual) eye and denotes a particular Hindu denomination.

49 Properly 'the Buddha' or 'a Buddha', i.e., 'enlightened one', usually taken to refer to Gautama, son of a king in the sixth- or fifth-century BC in northern India; he renounced a life of luxury for pursuit of spiritual enlightenment; Buddhist doctrine proposes pursuit of a middle way between self-indulgence and self-torture by avoiding the life of pain that results from desire, or craving.

50 'Faquirs' or 'fakirs', Muslim or Hindu religious ascetics and mendicants.

51 Possibly a reference to the Bhagavad-gita, an early didactic Hindu epic, or to the Bhagavata purana, a mystical text centring on Krishna, an incarnation of Vishnu .

52 The Ragamala is a series of structured and improvised musical pieces each expressing a particular mood.

53 From 'jinn' or 'jinneeyeh', a demon or spirit in Arabic lore and literature, but used here of spirits in Hindu lore.

54 Owenson here echoes Craufurd's *Sketches Chiefly Relating to the History, Religion, Learning, and Manners of the Hindoos.*

55 From a Hindi word for the part of a house in which the women are secluded.

56 Followers of the deity Ram; in parts of India unwanted girls and women would be given to temples ostensibly as pious offerings, but in effect to act as servants or even prostitutes.

57 H. T. Colebrooke (1765–1837) published a number of works on Indian laws, literature, philosophy, economy and culture.

58 Lakshmi is the Hindu goddess of fortune and beauty, the wife of Vishnu.

59 'Tap', pronounced 'tup', refers to a painstaking or onerous task undertaken for devotional reasons.

60 Temples carved from rock hills near Ellora in Hyderabad, central-southern India.

61 'Jaggarnauth' or 'Juggernaut', a title of Krishna as the eighth incarnation or avatar of Vishnu; at the god's festival at Puri, in Orissa, an image was dragged in a huge cart, under the wheels of which worshippers were reported to have thrown themselves in suicidal self-sacrifice.

62 The sacred major river of northern and northeastern India.

63 'Menu' or 'Manu', the Lawgiver, supposed author of the Manu-smriti, a code of Hindu law and jurisprudence, the effect of which was to give divine sanction to the caste system and to Brahmin supremacy.

64 John Henry Grose, *A Voyage to the East Indies, with Observations on Various Parts There* (1757, expanded 1766).

65 From the Sanskrit for 'the inaccessible'; Durga is a manifestation of the goddess Sakti and wife of Siva; she was created by the gods to slay the buffalo demon, and is often represented with ten arms, each holding a different weapon, and riding a lion or tiger; her festival is one of the greatest of northeastern India.

66 Sanskrit poetic texts containing the Hindu mythology.

67 'Soodar' or 'Sudra', from a Hindi word for a member of the lowest caste.

68 'Shanscrit' or 'Sanskrit', the ancient Indo-European language of India, in which the Vedas, or sacred scriptures, are written.

69 'Inns' or 'caravanserais'.

70 Here, characteristic of ancient and, presumably, simpler states of society guided by elders, or patriarchs.

71 Probably Dominique Bouhours (1628–1702), *La Vie de St. François Xavier*, published in French in 1682, translated by John Dryden (1688), and later abridged and translated by James Morgan (1764).

72 'This excess of warmth results from the situation of these high mountains found to the north of the route, stopping fresh winds, reflecting the sun's rays on the travellers, and leaving the country in burning heat.'

73 'He [Bernier] had no sooner ascended what he called the fearful wall of the world (because he regards Kashmir as an earthly paradise), that is, a high, black, bare mountain, than in descending the other side he felt a fresher and more temperate air: but nothing surprised so much in these mountains as to find oneself suddenly trans-

ported from the Indies to Europe'; Owenson is probably referring to *Histoire Generale des Voyages* (1746), ed. Abbé Prévost, *et al.*

74 Also 'cuscuss', or 'cuss'.

75 'Seringata' or 'seringa', a shrub also called mock-orange, known for its blossoms.

76 Probably Georg Forster, *Reise aus Bengalen nach England, durch die Nördlichen theile von Hindostan, durch Kaschemir, Afganistan, Persien, und Russland* (1796, translated into English 1798).

77 'Lories' or 'lorys', from a Malay name for parrot-like birds with brilliant plumage.

78 Silk-worms.

79 'Tibet'.

80 'Mangoostin-trees' or 'mangosteen-trees' (elswhere 'mangoostan-trees'), trees bearing an apple-like fruit.

81 'The Eternal, absorbed in contemplation of its essence, resolved in the fullness of time to form beings participating in its essence and its beatitude.'

82 'Ottar' or 'attar', from a Persian word for a fragrant oil obtained from roses.

83 From a Portuguese, and then Hindi, word for an open portico along the front or front and sides of a house.

84 The third incarnation of Vishnu was Varaha, a boar, who raised the earth out of the sea after a thousand-year struggle against a demon who had dragged the earth to the sea-bottom.

85 'Treemoortee' or 'Trimurti', see n. 19, above, p. 172.

86 'Nerekah' or 'naraka', a hell traditionally of seven regions, the last of which, Kakola, or naraka proper, is the bottomless pit, in utter darkness, where the damned are tortured in innumerable ways by demons.

87 'Kings' or 'princes'.

88 'Peasants'.

89 'These peoples need only refreshing foods, and mother nature has prodigiously furnished forests of citrons, oranges, figs, palms, and coconuts, and fields covered with rice.' François-Marie Arouet (1694–1778), pen name Voltaire, *Essai sur les Mœurs et l'Esprit des Nations* (1769), an abstract of world history; Voltaire was a leading figure of the French Enlightenment.

90 Elsewhere 'buchampaca', see above, p. 39.

91 From the Arabic, Persian and Urdu word for peace, also referring to an Indian gesture of greeting, a low bow with the right hand placed on the forehead.

92 From a Tamil word for lime or mortar made from oyster shells; according to early accounts, chunam was eaten with betel leaves.

93 Milton, *Paradise Lost*, III.346–7, describing the celebratory shout of angels.

94 Made of cane.

95 Milton's exhortation to himself, *Paradise Lost*, III.37–8: 'Then feed on thoughts, that voluntarie move / Harmonious numbers … '.

96 Rajini are also female powers of the night, or perhaps apsaras or heavenly nymphs; it is still given as a name for Indian girls.

97 François de Salignac de La Mothe-Fénelon (1651–1715), author of two influential education manuals and of various political and religious works.

98 From a Tamil word for a member of the lowest caste, then applied by Europeans to one of no caste.

99 'Bodily self'.

Volume II

1 'Saddi' or 'Sa'di' (*c.* 1184–1291/2), the great poet of Persia, born in Shiraz and educated at Bagdad, who spent much of his life wandering throughout the Middle East and northern India.

2 A European name for the Indian fig tree; its branches drop shoots that take root, enabling the tree to spread over a considerable expanse of ground, forming a temple-like structure.

3 'Tublea' is described later in the volume as the 'drum of condemnation', see above, p. 106.

4 Aurengzeb supplanted his father, the emperor Shah Jahan, against competition from his brothers, including Dara.

5 Shakespeare, *Othello*, III.iii.393.

6 'Poojah' or 'puja', Sanskrit word for Hindu rites of worship.

7 'Veidam' or 'Veda', one of the four sacred Hindu books (Rig-veda, Yajur-veda, Sama-veda, and Atharva-veda).

8 A Chandala is a person outside the order of castes, and therefore untouchable by those within the order.

9 Milton, *Paradise Lost*, IX.222, in which Adam explains to Eve that they must work apart in the garden of Eden, else looks and smiles may interrupt their tasks.

10 Catherine of Genoa (1447–1510), mystic and hospital matron, who inspired devotional writings then attributed to her.

11 Both the 1811 and 1859 editions leave unclear the correct placing of quotation marks here.

12 Knowledge based on experience, or what would now be called laboratory science; the reference anticipates the figure of Victor Frankenstein in Mary Shelley's novel of that title (1818), who turns his back on family and social life to pursue the secret of life in his laboratory. with disastrous consequences for himself and his family.

13 A similar phrases occur in two imitations of Milton's *Paradise Lost*: 'urges sweet Return' in John Hopkins, *Milton's Paradise Lost Imitated in Rhyme* (1699), IX.36; and 'urges a sweet return' in Richard Jago, *Adam; or, The Fatal Disobedience, Poems* (1784), II.ii.

14 'Kylausum' or 'Kailasa', the mythical mountain paradise of Siva.

15 In one of Owenson's sources, Nathaniel Kindersley's *Specimens of Hindoo Literature Consisting of Translations, from the Tamoul Language, of Some Hindoo Works of Morality and Religion, with Explanatory Notes; to which are Prefixed Introductory Remarks on the Mythology, Literature, &c. of the Hindoos* (1794), p. 2, 'the First Cause' is Paraubah-rah-Vushtoo, otherwise known as Brahma. According to Kindersley, pp. 42–4, in the Hindu cosmology there are seven upper worlds, regions of good and happiness, part of which humanity inhabits, and seven lower worlds, regions of evil and misery and the abode of demons and evil spirits.

16 'Vedas' and 'Shastras', Hindu sacred writings (see above p. 176, n. 7, and p. 173, n. 47).

17 The daivers are described in Kindersley, 'The History of the Nella-Rajah: A Hindoo Romance', p. 142, as the invincible guardians of the eight sides of the world; the land of the daivers is described there as Luxima describes it here.

18 'Madhucca' elsewhere.

19 Described in Kindersley, *Specimens of Hindoo Literature*, pp. 36–8, as the principal celestial liminaries, including Surian (the sun), Chudrai (the moon), Shevau (Mars),

Bouden (Mercury), Veeyauyum (Jupiter), Velli or Shoocra (Venus), Shunnee (Saturn), Rucca (head of the constellation Draco or Dragon), and Kaydoo (tail of Draco).

20 An Indian practitioner of yoga, a system of asceticism and meditation to achieve union with the supreme spirit.

21 Shakespeare, *Henry IV*, part II, III.i.6–8, spoken by the King: 'Nature's soft nurse, how have I frighted thee, / That thou no more wilt weigh my eyelids down, / And steep my senses in forgetfulness?'

22 'Awe-inspiringly'.

23 Siva; see above, p. 174, n. 65.

24 1 Peter 3:4: 'But let it be the hidden man of the heart, in that which is not corruptible ...'.

25 Site of eighth- and ninth-century AD cave temples with rock scupltures representing Hindu mythology, on the island of Elephanta (Gharapuri), near Bombay (Mumbai).

26 *Institutes of Hindu law; or, The Ordinances of Menu, According to the Gloss of Cullúca, comprising the Indian System of Duties, Religious and Civil* (Calcutta, 1794; reprinted London, 1796), translated by William Jones (1746–94), foremost British Orientalist of his time, colonial administrator, and leader of the movement to adapt colonial administration to local cultures in India.

27 'According to the testimony of all Kashmiris, several caravans are seen leaving their country each year.'

28 'One must above all consider that abstinence from animal flesh results from the nature of the climate.', Voltaire, *Essai sur les Mœurs et l'Espirit des Nations* (see above, p. 175, n. 89).

Volume III

1 The cow, the killing of which was punishable by death.

2 Elsewhere, 'lories' (see above, p. 175, n. 77).

3 'A wool, or rather hair, called *touz*, is taken from the chests of wild Kashmir mountain goats.'

4 Anna Letitia Barbauld, 'An Address to the Deity', l. 56, where the poet declares that she is prepared to submit to divine providence, 'While God is seen in all, and all in God'.

5 Nathaniel Kindersley, *Specimens of Hindoo Literature* (1794).

6 In Kindersley, *Specimens of Hindoo Literature*, p. 3, the Daivaudegoel are a race of demons invoked for protection from evil, and the Daivergoel are an order of spirits comprising ancient heroes and saints.

7 'It is in the Shastra that one finds the story of the fall of the angels.'

8 Mineral such as asbestos, supposed to resemble organic substances.

9 Elsewhere, 'Vishnu' and 'Vishna'.

10 Actually, 'vocal air', Milton, *Paradise Lost*, IX.530, referring to the serpent's ability to speak to Eve.

11 Milton's description of his situation as a republican and commonwealthman after the restoration of the monarchy, *Paradise Lost*, VII.26–7: 'On evil dayes though fall'n, and evil tongues; / In darkness, and with dangers compast round ... '.

12 'Seik' or 'Sikh'.

13 'Setlege' and 'Moultan', or 'Sutlej' and 'Multan,' in the upper valley of the Indus, now the Punjab region of Pakistan.

14 'Sindy' or 'Sind', the region of the lower Indus valley; spelled Scindi below.

15 1 Corinthians 13:1: 'Though I speak with the tongues of men and of Angels, and have not charity, I am become as sounding brass or a tinkling cymbal.'

16 Quintin Craufurd (1743–1819), *Sketches of the History of the Religion, Learning, and Manners of the Hindus*; in Craufurd, 'chancelas' is 'Chandarahs'.

17 'Officers of the Inquisition'.

18 John Joseph Stockdale (1770–1847), *The History of the Inquisitions: Including the Secret Transactions of those Horrific Tribunals* (1810).

19 Adapted from Luke 6:29, where Christ instructs his disciples and followers, 'When a man hits you on the cheek, offer him the other cheek too'.

20 Milton, describing Satan after being rebuked by an angel, *Paradise Lost*, IV.860–1: 'awe from above had quelld / His heart, not else dismai'd'.

21 'Caravansera' or 'caravanserai', a halting place for caravans.

22 Shakespeare, *Macbeth*, I.vii.35–6: Macbeth tells his wife he has decided not to murder the king because he is content with the success and 'golden opinions' of others that he already enjoys.

23 Milton, speaking of Lucifer, *Paradise Lost*, I.54–6 (of Lucifer): 'now the thought / Both of lost happiness and lasting pain / Torments him'.

24 Milton, describing the fallen angels, *Paradise Lost*, I.525–6.

25 Milton, describing the fallen angel Lucifer, *Paradise Lost*, I.593.

26 Santiago de Compostela, the familiar name of the apostle St James (d. AD 44), so called from Compostela northern Spain where his body was supposedly taken after his martyrdom and which became the site of the most popular pilgrimage in Europe; his feast day is 25 July.

27 'Catechuman' or 'catechumen', a new but as yet unbaptised convert.

28 From 1480 a special Inquisition was established in Spain, by permission of a papal bull issued two years earlier, to deal with the large number of non-Christians or recently converted Christians supposedly continuing to practise their former muslim or Jewish religion. After the Christian conquest of Muslim southern Spain in 1492, non-Christians were forced to profess Christianity or face expulsion; the Inquisition was used by Ferdinand and Isabella to assert their power throughout Spain.

29 *'Auto da fe'* or *'auto de fe'*, literally, 'act of faith', the term for display of those condemned by the Inquisition, after which they were handed over to the civil authority for punishments to be meted out.

30 'Messa di santo officio', means literally, 'mass of the holy office'; the holy office here is the Inquisition, and the procedure of the *auto de fe* was marked by celebration of mass, at which point sentences would be read out; until that point the accused were in ignorance of their fate.

31 'San Benito' or 'sanbenito', a corruption of the phrase 'saco bendito': a loose garment, bearing the x-shaped cross of St. Andrew, worn by penitents in the procession of the *auto de fe*.

32 A phrase explained by the insignia of the group: 'feugo revolto' is literally translated as 'upturned fire'.

33 'Alcaid' or 'alcayde': 'commander of a fortress or prison'.

34 From their weapon, the halberd, a combination of spear and battle-axe.

35 Milton, describing Satan, *Paradise Lost*, III.679.

36 'Executioner', from the bowstring used in Turkey to execute offenders by stranglulation; convicted heretics who converted at the stake would be strangled before the flames could reach them.

37 The tenth 'Avater' or 'avatar' is the last incarnation of Vishnu, who is yet to come.

38 The 'gayatra' or 'gayatri' (see above, p. 173, n. 46), which may be translated, 'We meditate on the glorious light of the divine sun; may he illuminate our minds.'

39 The Portuguese expulsion of the Spanish and coronation of the Duke of Braganza as Juan IV, re-establishing an independent Portuguese monarchy, in December 1640

40 Aurengzeb, one of the four sons of the Mogul emperor Shah Jahan, proclaimed himself emperor in 1658, see above, p. 176, n. 4, and subsequently conquered large parts of northern India; the events were made the subject of a verse drama, *Aurengzebe* (1675), by John Dryden, as a political allegory of the conflicts within the Stuart dynasty during the reign of Charles II.

41 In Owenson's day the term 'philosopher' had more the sense of intellectual and social critic, and had been made infamous in Britain by the self-styled *philosophes* who led the French Revolution.

TEXTUAL NOTES

3a THE MISSIONARY: / ... / 1811.] *1811*; LUXIMA, / THE PROPHETESS. / A
   Tale of India. / By / Sydney, Lady Morgan. / London: / Charles Westerton, Publisher, / 20, St. George's Place, / Hyde Park Corner. / 1859. *1859*

5a The Missionary.] *1811* The Missionary. / PREFACE. *1859*

   'THE following work has been greatly altered, and re-modelled by its highly-
   gifted authoress from her first production published upwards of forty years ago, in
   the shape of three volumes, under the title of 'The Missionary.' This tale of India
   received her last finishing touches only a few days before her decease, and she was
   engaged in superintending its revision through the press when that event took
   place. Since the period of its first appearance, a generation may be said to have
   passed away. The work will consequently come forth as comparatively new to the
   great mass of romance-readers of the present day.

   'Vividly portraying as it does the gorgeous scenery, the Manners, Customs, and,
   above all, the RELIGION of that portion of the great Indian Empire to which it
   relates – and these have been subject to little, if any change – the story of "Luxima," will, it is presumed, prefer no ordinary claims to public attention, and the
   more particularly on account of the recent melancholy occurrences[a] which have
   distracted a country with which we have so long had such extensive commercial
   relations.'

   [a The reference is to the Indian Mutiny of 1857–8, in which some Indian troops
   in Bengal and north-central India, incited by what they perceived as insults to
   their religious beliefs and practices, rebelled against their British officers, mas-
   sacred Europeans in several places, and tried to re-establish Indian rule. After
   the mutiny was quelled, administration of India was transferred from the East
   India Company to the British crown.]

6a votarists ... fault.'] *1811*; and simple votarists. *1859*

6b castle, ... are reflected, by] *1811*; castle. The whole pile was reflected in *1859*

6c uproar, ... Celebrated,] *1811*; uproar which was celebrated *1859*

6d Africanus.] *1811*; Africanus, illustrating the history of man. *1859*

6e What various epochas ... Hilarion!] *1811*; What epochs, what various states of
   human power, and such human degradation, did not such objects blend in one
   great picture! *1859*

6f sent, ... Hilarion] *1811*; sent in early boyhood by his uncle and the Archbishop of
   Lisbon, at the request of his grandmother, the Duchess of Acugna – the St.
   Helena[a] of her time and country – when he *1859*

   [a Reference to St Helen (*c*. 255–*c*. 330), mother of the Roman emperor Constan-
   tine; she promoted Christianity energetically.]

6g Francis.] *1811*; Francis, whom tradition reported to be a converted Hindoo, a
   Brahmin by descent, and long a professor of Indian learners. *1859*

7a the young ... surrounded;] *1811*; Hilarion, *1859*

7b and influenced ... emulated] *1811*; early learned to emulate *1859*

7c   until, his unregulated ... St. Francis.]*1811*; he resolved on taking the vows, and retiring into the order of the Franciscans. *1859*

8a   THERE is a dear ... what is not.' ¶ While] *1811* WHILE *1859*

10a Hitherto ... perfection.] *1811*; Hitherto the life of the young monk resembled the dream of saintly slumbers, for it was still a dream, removed from all those ties, which constitute the charm and the anxiety of existence, the spring of human affection, and the faculty of human reason lay still within him. Hitherto, his genius had exhibited grander sources of human good, but left him passionate and ambitious, and when the fervours of adolescence had subsided in the stern tranquillity of manhood, when the reiteration of the same images denied the same vivacity of sensation as had distinguished their original impression, then, the visions, which had entranced his dreaming youth, ceased to cheer his unbroken solitude; then, even Religion, though she lost nothing of her influence, lost much of her charm. Accustomed to pursue the bold wanderings of the human mind upon subjects whose awful mystery escapes all human research, intense collision with human opinions finally gave place to ceaseless meditation, and he became weary of conjecture. *1859*

10b determined on. ... permission] *1811*; determined on for the following spring. He passed the interim in profound study of the Hindoo language and the Sanscrit, and placed himself under the tuition of the learned converted Hindoo. Permission, too, *1859*

11a was,] *1811*; may be supposed to have been *1859*

11b Divinity. Nature ... genius.] *1811*; Divinity. *1859*

11c mortal ... man.] *1811*; human into a superhuman condition. *1859*

11d Jesuit, ... Franciscans,] *1811*; Jesuit, *1859*

12a sinless] 1811; sincere *1859*

12b insignificance, ... He] 1859: insignificance. But the Missionary

13a For the first time ... course:] *1811*; He endeavoured to shake off a train of thought so dangerous, convictions so foreign to his actual vocation. He quickened his steps as he paced the deck of the vessel and changed his mental meditations to more material objects. The sun was setting gloriously, *1859*

14a exterminated.] 1811; exterminated. He threw himself on the bare deck and 'weary of conjecture' slept. ¶ CHAPTER III[a] *1859*
     [a All subsequent chapters are renumbered accordingly.]

14b splendour ... air.] *1811*; charm of human beauty distinguished his form and motions. *1859*

14c so touching ... inspired.] *1811*; more devout. *1859*

15a saint; ... Heaven.] *1811*; saint, and left the man to self-consideration. *1859*

15b over it, ... belonged;] *1811* over it, *1859*

16a devotion. ¶ His eloquence ... passion!] 1811; devotion. *1859*

16b offered to his ... man.] *1811*; of the spectators. *1859*

17a while] *1811*; for every where religion, under some material form, proclaimed her influence over the mind or ignorance of man. Sometimes *1859*

19a cast'] *1811*; caste' *1859*

19b character of him who preached them.] *1811*; civilizing influence they were likely to produce. He was a Professor of Hindostani in the Jesuit College of Lahore, and some slight suspicion was attached to him of being the agent of their views, and a secret supporter of their doctrines, but this may have been a calumny of the Franciscans. *1859*

20a grace.] 1811; grace.*

* The mystic sect which Fénélon, A. B. of Cambrai, and the celebrated Mme. Guyon founded in Paris, was limited in its doctrines, and called '*The Religion of Love.*'[a] *1859*

> [a François de Salignac de la Mothe-Fénelon (1651–1715), archbishop of Cambrai and author of important educational manuals and devotional works, and Jeanne-Marie Bouvier de la Motte-Guyon (1648–1717) were proponents of quietism, a form of religious mysticism involving passive contemplation, extinction of the will, and self-abandonment to divine presence, thereby resembling elements in Hinduism.]

21a vestibule.'] *1811*; vestibule.' ¶ The Pundit looked earnestly on his listening auditor, and then added emphatically, 'but you must go alone, an ostentatious mission would destroy all hope of success and perhaps risk your life.' *1859*

23a devotion ... penetrate.] *1811*; devotion. *1859*

23b imagination.] *1811*; imagination. He had never been at Rome, and could make no reference with ceremonies not less brilliant or sensual. *1859*

23c respecting,] *1811*; respecting, and implicitly following in the track of his model, St. Francis of Xavier, *1859*

24a vast and mighty hall.] *1811*; vast hall. There was in this heathen congress composed of the most ancient creeds which time still preserves, something which, to the Christian Missionary, recalled the mystic rites and dogmas of his own faith. *1859*

24b Bhudda] *1811*; Bhudda*

> * Buddhism, which once possessed the minds of half the human race, and, still counts 220 millions of votaries, is historically one of the most mysterious of the Asiatic systems. Rising in the valley of the Ganges, two thousand years ago, it speedily flourished throughout India, though it is now extinct there, and it still reigns in Nepál, Tibet, Ava, Ceylon, Anam, Siam, Japan, and China; yet, filling such a space in the past and the present, nearly every great point in its annals is disputed. Many passages in classical writers as early as Herodotus, are supposed to bear reference to it, and its own records are vast, but it is impossible to separate the mythical from the veritable story. A single teacher, a body of disciples, a band of martyrs, a race of ministering kings, nobles and priests, persecution and victory, decline and extinction, – such is the history of Buddhism in India, where innumerable monuments attest to the immense dominion it once held. It was perfected from the idea of simple abstraction of the soul from all earthly care, to that of the threefold Intelligence, Creator, and Ruler. In the early stage, the power of meditation is illustrated by a story not to be surpassed by the ripest imagination of America. There was a man practising 'abstraction' on the edge of a tank, which some workmen were engaged in improving. They called on him to go out of the way, but so deep and devout was his meditation that he never noticed them heaping up the earth, and was buried without knowing it! In the same extravagant spirit is the curse denounced on him who shall strike a woman, even with the leaf of a rose. *1859*

25a brow, ... and] 1811; brow stamped with *1859*

25b decisive: ... understanding.] *1811*; decisive; and he imposed conviction on the senses. *1859*

25c him – he ... Avaratas,] *1811*; him; he passed rapidly over the religion of Buddha, of Avatars,[a] *1859*

> [a Incarnations on earth of a divine being.]

26a arguments: he] *1811*; arguments, and the command he had attained over their language. He *1859*

27a so.] *1811*; so, for it is difficult to combat mysteries with mysteries. *1859*

28a victim.] *1811*; victim. Among the most eminent women of this church, the most remarkable St. Theresa.[a] *1859*

    [a St Teresa of Ávila (1515–82), mystic and founder of many (reformed) Carmelite convents in Spain; her writings, especially her autobiography, were widely read and influential.]

30a Nun.] *1811*; Nun. He reflected, too, on the solemn and gorgeous form and rituals of his own religion, and thought the transition from one ceremonial to another might break the spell of her apostacy. *1859*

31a hopes, ... feelings,] *1811*; hopes, *1859*

31b orison.] *1811*; orison, and not on the Cross his eyes were fixed, but upon her. *1859*

31c apostolic] *1859*; apostolie *1811*

32a incredulity.] *1811*; incredulity; they believed him to be either a maniac or an impostor. *1859*

33a truth.] *1811*; truth, and when he proposed mystery for mystery each preferred his own. *1859*

35a tupesya] 1811; tupaseya *1859*

36a torrent, ... around,] *1811*; flinging, *1859*

36b shepherds,] *1811*; cow-herds, *1859*

36c girdle;] *1811*; girdle, and his small bible; *1859*

37a rocks with his dogs,] *1811*; rocks, *1859*

37b beauty, ... view,] *1811*; beauty, *1859*

37c mangoostin-trees ... dawn,] *1811*; mango-trees *1859*

37d bright ... already] *1811*; light and so aspiring in its attitude, that it appeared as if *1859*

37e sprite were enwreathed with beams, and] *1811*; sprite *1859*

38a figure, ... devotion.] *1811*; figure: she still remained. *1859*

38b which rosed her cheek with crimson hues, and] *1811*; which *1859*

38c shade. ... night.] *1811*; shade. *1859*

40a took ... subject of] *1811*; referred to *1859*

40b scene, ... waters.] *1811*; scene. *1859*

40c murva, ... fibres] *1811*; murva, *1859*

41a and casting up his eyes,] *1811*; but *1859*

41b earth ... beams,] *1811*; earth, *1859*

41c sparkled ... religion.] *1811*; she chanted the vesper hymn of her religion. *1859*

41d Missionary, ... profound.] *1811*; Missionary. *1859*

41e cheek, ... shaded.] *1811*; cheek. *1859*

41f woman, ... she] *1811*; woman. She *1859*

41g Missionary, with an air of dignified meekness,] *1811*; Missionary, *1859*

44a happiness ... perfection;] *1811*; happiness of such a feeling, *1859*

45a With eyes ... rise,] *1811*; As she threw her glances around, *1859*

45b grotto, and] *1811*; grotto before the monk had power to rise, and, *1859*

45c said,] *1811*; said in a caressing tone, *1859*

45d their dewy light,] *1811*; them, *1859*

45e position, ... bosom.] *1811*; position. *1859*

46a He perceived ... bashful] *1811*; She turned round, and a smile *1859*

46b again; for the pearl ... Priestess.] *1811*; again. *1859*

46c about to withdraw ... horizon,] 1811; sinking, *1859*

47a replied, ... word;] *1811*; replied, *1859*

47b yet the warm blush of sudden emotion,] *1811*; yet *1859*

48a soul.] *1811*; soul, and they worshipped together in the temple of nature's God. *1859*

48b apartment. ... air.] *1811*; apartment. *1859*

48c lattices, and ... light] *1811*; lattices. It *1859*

49a her eyelids ... feelings.] *1811*; and delightful visions seemed to absorb her whole being. *1859*

49b breathed ... and] *1811*; breathed *1859*

49c tender and impassioned] *1811*; tender *1859*

50a lovely] *1811*; young *1859*

51a feeling.] *1811*; feeling. The High Priestess of Cashmire converted, his work was done; he thus reconciled to himself his pausing in the progress of his mission, for the logic of the passions is always convincing. *1859*

51b bosom: ... worship;] *1811*; bosom: *1859*

51c this devotional ... earth.] *1811*; the pure blood mantling to her cheek, gradually suffused her whole face with radiant blushes, and a modest shyness, blended with the smile of pleasure lighted up her countenance as the Missionary stood wrapt in silent contemplation of her person, which he likened to the altar-portrait of St. Theresa by Murillo,[a] the treasure of his own convent in Portugal.

    [a Bartolome Esteban Murillo (1617–82), a Spanish painter favoured by the Franciscans.]

51d amazement, ... admiration.] *1811*; amazement. *1859*

52a boundless toleration ... excellence;] *1811*; indifferent toleration to the most obstinate faith; which resists all proselytism, and implores none; *1859*

53a and, with a crimson blush,] *1811*; and *1859*

53b conversion ... the man.] 1811; conversion, in proportion as it excited the admiration.

54a them, he fastened their glances on the earth.] *1811*; them, *1859*

54b Her sigh ... he] *1811*; He then *1859*

54c person, ... woman;] *1811*; person, *1859*

54d but still ... sought] *1811*; and *1859*

54e imagination. ... her.] *1811*; imagination. *1859*

55a repaid.] *1811*; repaid. This consciousness reconciled him to the inaction of his present ascetic life, and to his determination to remain some time longer in the solitary region where he then sojourned. *1859*

59a expectation. To contemplate ... ourselves.] *1811*; expectation. *1859*

59b fancy, ... mind.] *1811*; fancy. *1859*

60a Entombed ... itself.] *1811*; With all the despotism of a lofty spirit, which thought itself created equally to command others and itself, he gave himself up to meditation, and even to composition; for he was occasionally occupied on a life of St. francis, that he had begun during his voyage from Europe, but he could not command time, and waited for books from Lahore. *1859*

60b Sirinagur, ... infidel;] *1811*; Sirinagur, *1859*

60c He paused ... clustered.] *1811*; He paused as to contemplate its luxuriancy and its beauty. *1859*

60d Suddenly ... he] *1811*; He *1859*

61a body, as if ... impulse,] *1811*; body, *1859*

61b faculty ... imagination.] *1811*; passion of the Missionary's character – power. *1859*

62a knew] *1811*; had read *1859*

62b So slow ... notwithstanding] *1811*; Notwithstanding *1859*
62c mayana; ... repose.] *1811*; mayana, the thrush of Cashmire. *1859*
63a existence,] *1811*; happiness *1859*
63b breathed of] *1811*; recalled *1859*
63c His eye ... he] 1859: He
63d The Monk stood gazing ... tinctured by] *1811*; The Monk stood and gazed, and a
     convulsive exclamation, as it burst from his lips, electrified the soft and stealing
     sleep of Luxima. She started, rose, and beheld the Missionary near her, with a con-
     fusion in her look of *1859*
64a a short but touching] *1811*; a *1859*
64b Luxima made ... And] *1811*; Luxima remained silent, but *1859*
65a passions, and the human feeling;] *1811*; passions, *1859*
65b exclaimed, with softness and with energy,] *1811*; exclaimed, *1859*
66a tender ... opposed.] *1811*; repressive of a struggle between prejudice and confi-
     dence. *1859*
66b life; ... convinced] *1811*; life, suggested to *1859*
66c embrace.] *1811*; enjoy. *1859*
67a idolatrous: ... wept.] *1811*; idolatrous. *1859*
67b Chancalas!] *1811*; Chancalas!*
        * Outcast.
67c was secretly and] *1811*; was *1859*
68a languor of his manner; ... Confirmed] *1811*; gentleness of his manner. Early con-
     firmed, *1859*
68b evil; and ... equal.] *1811*; evil. *1859*
70a which habit had made so necessary to his happiness;] *1811*; to which he had been
     unaccustomed; *1859*
70b bestow. ¶ Dearer ... so lovely.] *1811*; bestow. *1859*
71a But when ... the] *1811*; The *1859*
71b As he approached ... to both.] *1811*; As he approached the Priestess and the shrine,
     his heart throbbed with feverish wildness; through the branches of a spreading
     palm-tree, he beheld her, leaning on the ruins of a Brahminical altar, habited in
     her sacerdotal vestments. Her brow crowned with flowers; her long dark hair float-
     ing on the breeze; she appeared a splendid image of the religion she professed –
     bright, wild, and illusory; captivating to the senses, and fatal to the reason. *1859*
71c eyes, which at once ... apprehension;] *1811*; eyes, *1859*
72a other, ... air.] *1811*; other. *1859*
72b doubts, ... agony.] *1811*; a doubt, vague, and embittered by suspicions. *1859*
72c peace.' With eyes ... truth,] *1811*; peace.' *1859*
72d evasive; which his heart ... distrust;] *1811*; evasive; *1859*
73a blushed; ... said,] *1811*; then added. *1859*
73b returned, seduced into softness by her tender air,] *1811*; returned, *1859*
73c He paused ... replied: 'I am indeed,] *1811*; he paused; and Luxima replied: ¶ I am
     indeed, *1859*
73d drop, which lurks beneath] *1811*; drop of *1859*
73e *passion*; ... thoughts?] *1811*; *passion?'* *1859*
74a Look ... speak] *1811*; Speak *1859*
74b repeated, throwing ... countenance:] *1811*; repeated;
74c enchant; ... light –] *1811*; enchant; *1859*
75a timidly taking his hand, and] *1811*; timidly *1859*
75b withdrew ... head,] *1811*; closed his eyes, and reposing his head on his hand, *1859*

77a disquiet and to agitate;] *1811*; disquiet; *1859*

78a moved, touched ... birth.] *1811*; agitated, and he not be the sole cause of her emotion. *1859*

79a When the heart ... Sheko.] *1811*; Thinking it some ornament of the sacerdotal vestments of the Priestess, he stooped to secure it; but it was no part of the insignia worn by the children of Brahma; it was the *silver crescent* of Islamism; the ornament worn at the centre of the turban of the Mogul officers; and deeply engraved in Arabic characters, was the name of the heroic and imperial prince Solyman Sheko. *1859*

79b suffocation, as though ... light,] *1811*; suffocation, *1859*

79c earth; ... action;] *1811*; earth; *1859*

79d This conviction ... wrath.] *1811*; Thoughts new and gloomy rushed on each other. That deadly sickness of the heart with which the most dreadful of all human passions first seizes on its victim, infected his whole frame. *1859*

79e loveliness ... operated.] *1811*; his estimation of the object and ardour of the character on which it, for the first time, operated. *1859*

80a innocence: ... setting;] *1811*; innocence and exquisite beauty; *1859*

80b love ... joys,] *1811*; love, *1859*

80c his sole, his solitary,] *1811*; his sole, *1859*

80d of Heaven;] *1811*; and servant of his church; *1859*

80e was moved and] *1811*; was *1859*

80f Throwing himself ... he] *1811*; He *1859*

81a them; for the affliction ... sleep.] *1811*; them. *1859*

82a course, ... Creator; –] *1811*; course; *1859*

83a He arose, ... resolution.] *1811*; He rose, agitated by a full consciousness of the cause of his misery. Knowing no solace but what he derived from the certainty that the secret of his weakness was known only to heaven and to himself, he resolved, before he debased the life which sin had not yet polluted, or broke the vows which were still revered, even when most perilled, to fly the scenes of his temptation, and to cling to the cross for redemption and support. *1859*

83b suspect. ... for ever.] *1811*; suspect. *1859*

84a He paused ... homage.] *1811*; He sighed profoundly, as he concluded an apostrophe inspired by his own humiliating convictions. At that moment, a gentle rustling in the leaves called his attention in the direction from whence the sound issued. The branches, thick and interlaced, slowly gave way, and thrown lightly back on either side, the Priestess of Brahma came forth from their dusky shade. *1859*

84b object – then pausing ... age!] *1811*; object. *1859*

84c Unseen ... the] *1811*; The *1859*

84d moment, thought ... passion;] *1811*; moment, *1859*

84e throbbed in its rapid] *1811*; raised its *1859*

84f audible; ... mind.] *1811*: audible. *1859*

85a He tembled ... abandoned.] *1811*; He trembled, and implored the assistance of Heaven. *1859*

85b solicit; ... it is] *1811*; solicit, but still as *1859*

85c Amidst the dreams of glory, amidst] *1811*; Amidst *1859*

86a taken her hand. ... There] *1811*; seized her hand, and there *1859*

86b indignation ... brow,] *1811*; indignation, and rage, *1859*

87a Luxima, ... reply.] *1811*; Luxima. *1859*

87b away with her long hair] *1811*; away

87c Luxima, whose loveliness … countenance,] *1811*; Luxima, *1859*

88a blushes; and chasing … tears,] *1811*; blushes; *1859*

89a those eyes … rays.] *1811*; her eyes. *1859*

89b at once … soul] *1811*; filled her *1859*

89c Missionary, in a faint and tender voice,] *1811*; Missionary, *1859*

89d head, sighed profoundly.] *1811*; head. *1859*

89e manner; … tenderness and] *1859*: manner. The instinctive

 89f could subdue, confine, and] *1811*; could. *1859*

89g love, enchanting and sublime,] *1811*; love, *1859*

89h and your soul,] *1811*; your ignorance *1859*

90a ought] *1811*; aught[a] *1859*

     [a 'aught' was the more usual form of the word.]

90b passion, … combated.] *1811*; passion. *1859*

91a eyes; … mind;] *1811*; eyes; *1859*

91b tranquillity of his conscience,] *1811*; self-confidence he had had faith in, *1859*

92a the Missionary … religion,] *1811*; Hilarion still lay silent, *1859*

92b scarcely accompanied … and] *1811*; resembling, in its *1859*

92c secret; … consecrated.] *1811*; secret. He felt the tears of love on his brow; he felt an affectionate hand returning the pressure on his own; and, if he was absorbed in illusion, it was an illusion which, though reason condemned, innocence still ennobled. *1859*

92d silence, … Fearing] *1811*; silence; fearing *1859*

93a act: it was … woman.] *1811*; act. *1859*

93b abandoned. … soul;] *1811*; abandoned; *1859*

93c amazement; … still] *1811*: amazement; *1859*

93d He trembled … he] *1811*; He *1859*

93e love.] *1811*; pity. *1859*

 93f The moon … echoes.] *1811*; The moon again shone out unclouded, rendering the minutest object visible: the stillness of the air was so profound, that the faintest sound might have been audible. *1859*

94a frame, … lips,] *1811*; frame, *1859*

94b Let me again … if] *1811*; If *1859*

94c terrific. … alone.'] *1811*; terrific.' *1859*

94d Luxima shuddered … support her;] *1811*; Luxima heard and shuddered, and seeming to awaken to a sense of her dangerous position, she shrank back from the arms still extended to support her; *1859*

94e back, … soul?'] *1811*; back.' *1859*

95a all the dazzling lustre] *1811*; the *1859*

95b look the brilliant, the blooming,] *1811*; look, *1859*

96a and form … woman.] *1811*; changed its expression. *1859*

96b He advanced … robe;] *1859*: She advanced and fell at his feet;

96c approached, and stood near] *1811*; approached *1859*

96d exquisite fondness on him,] *1811*; tender interest, *1859*

97a imagination, … mind:] *1811*; imagination; *1859*

97b a bigotry … influence, he] *1811*; it would be vain to attempt to reason with. He *1859*

97c to – and gazing … said,] *1811*; to. *1859*

98a 'Wondrous … thee.] *1811*; 'And wilt thou then, Luxima,' he exclaimed, 'thus suddenly, thus unprepared, abandon me? – now, that thou hast conquered my habits of feeling?' ¶ 'Oh, no!' interrupted Luxima, eagerly, 'oh, no! Part we cannot.

98b spoke. ... countenance.] *1811*; spoke. *1859*

98c intimation. ... emotions,] *1811*; intimation; and, after an affecting pause, she said, in a low but firm voice, *1859*

98d danger ... imagination.] *1811*; danger. *1859*

98e look of love ... will.] *1811*; look, tender and despairing. *1859*

99a lover.] *1811*; victim. *1859*

99b away. ... He saw] *1811*; away. *1859*

100a THE habit ... mind,] *1811*; THE human mind, when *1859*

101a listened. ... requisite.] *1811*; listened. *1859*

102a irresolution; ... happiness.] *1811*; irresolution. *1859*

102b sublimed and] *1811*; if not resigned, at least *1859*

102c altar. ... soul.] *1811*; altar. *1859*

103a He shuddered ... Yet he] *1811*; He *1859*

103b tresses ... calculated] *1811*; tresses, and the snowy vestments of the Brachmachira were replaced by the course habit of a Chancalas, or *outcast*, suited *1859*

108a too exquisite ... equal] *1811*; too profound to be expressed in words. Equal *1859*

108b meet ... words.] *1811*; enjoy thy presence and thy protection. *1859*

108c A thousand ... mind.] *1811*; Feelings, opposite to their nature and powerful in their influence, struggled in the bosom of the Missionary. *1859*

108d Indian. ... colourless.] *1811*; Indian. *1859*

109a touched ... mind.] *1811*; awakened her earliest associations. *1859*

109b spring, which fell ... cliff,] *1811*; spring, *1859*

110a seem to walk ... cares,] *1811*; seem *1859*

110b The Missionary stood ... 'the] *1811*; 'The *1859*

111a Nature's ... tears:] *1811*; a parent's tears; *1859*

111b silent: he sighed ... resist.] *1811*; silent. The appeal which the eloquent Indian made to his feelings, found an advocate in his own breast, as he glanced at the rosary, which hung from his girdle, the gift of a dying mother. *1859*

112a mean] *1811*; means *1859*

112b the shelter of his wing.] *1811*; his protection. *1859*

114a Eden; ... pilgrimage.] *1811*; Eden. *1859*

115a Outcast.] *1811*; Outcast. At night, the hut of a goala, or goatherd, afforded them rest and refreshment; his wife and himself, ignorant of their dialect, and taking their eleemosynary guests, for pilgrims, on their way to the shrine of the neighbouring pagoda, received with wonder the gratuity bestowed on them. When they arose, the twilight of the dawn conducted them to their respective bath, which innumerable springs afforded; and, when they again met, they offered together the incense of the heart to Heaven, and proceeded on their pilgrimage. *1859*

119a glen ... base,] 1811; glen *1859*

119b sensation ... feelings] *1811*; vigour to the nerves *1859*

119c had ever imagined to their minds. –] *1811*; could image. *1859*

120a He now beheld ... averting] *1811*; Averting *1859*

123a remained, involved ... 'Father!'] *1811*; remained. *1859*

123b a face ... Missionary] *1811*; her face, she joyously permitted him *1859*

123c wilds, ... tranquillity!] *1811*; wilds. *1859*

123d fortitude. ... empire.] *1811*; fortitude. *1859*

124a them. Having horizon. –] *1811*; them. *1859*

124b As it was ... Indian] *1811*; They now *1859*

126a these, which chilled ... and] *1811*; these, *1859*

126b tenderness, ... heart.] *1811*; tenderness. *1859*

126c they paused ... night;] *1811*; ere they proceed to encounter the pathless way, *1859*

126d but, ... pilgrimage,] *1811*; but *1859*

126e guide ... steps.] *1811*; give them shelter for the night, and guide their steps on the morning's dawn to the goal of their pilgrimage. *1859*

127a But the joy ... descending] *1811*; Descending *1859*

127b solicitude and anxiety.] *1811*; solicitude. *1859*

128a existence, ... life!] *1811*; existence. *1859*

130a in the disorder of] *1811*; in *1859*

131a The Missionary replied ... glance. Luxima] *1811*; Luxima *1859*

132a head ... exclaimed] *1811*; face in her veil, murmured, *1859*

132b Heaven – an outcast ... *kindred;*] *1811*; Heaven; *1859*

132c re-commenced ... difficulty] *1811*; proceeded on their arduous route. Hilarion, with difficulty, *1859*

133a But the Missionary, ... slowly, and] *1811*; But the Missionary gave not to her eloquent details the wonted attention with which he always listened to her. Her bigotted resistance to the aid offered her by the pariah, struck home upon his conscience; he felt it was thus he would have acted under the influence of his own religion, had some pariah of his own Church – the excommunicated victim, on whom the Church's thunders had fallen – ventured to cross his path, or pollute by his presence the air he breathed; the rites of excommunication were the same in both religions, equally terrible in their denunciation, and equally inhuman in their results; but he shook off these mortifying reflections, and turned his thoughts to the probability of soon overtaking the caravan *1859*

133b once, and at an immense distance,] *1811*; once, *1859*

133c to the moon-beams;] *1811*; in the setting sun; *1859*

133d remote] *1811*; remote and gigantic *1859*

133e mounted; – the moon,] *1811*; mounted. The twilight *1859*

134a The Missionary ... awakened it,] *1811*; Her Christian guide *1859*

134b protect her ... inherit!] *1811*; protect her. *1859*

134c Luxima, ... obliged] *1811*; Luxima, nearly exhausted by fatigue, required the arm of Hilarion *1859*

134d on whose ... wandered,] *1811*; gradually opened upon a sterile plain; *1859*

134e recovered ... permit,] *1811*; recovered, *1859*

134f passed: they then ... the] *1811*; passed. The *1859*

134g to the view ... splendour;] *1811*; above, *1859*

134h skies, ... relief;] *1811*; skies; *1859*

135a continued ... At] *1811*; proceeded despondingly in the desolate wild, until at *1859*

135b pain. ... abandon.] *1811*; pain. *1859*

135c by insupportable ... proceed.] *1811*; Luxima fainted in his arms. *1859*

135d but, in a moment ... . But] *1811*; but he had no power of utterance, and words would have proved poor vehicles to feelings so acute; and, *1859*

136a She lives, she] *1811*; She *1859*

136b in whom ... admiration.] *1811*; of another faith, Christian or Mohamedan, beheld them with sympathy and compassion. *1859*

137a Luxima] *1811*; the Cashmirian *1859*

137b confusion: ... Missionary] *1811*; confusion. It was now that the position of his proselyte, and her forfeiture of caste, for the first time appeared *1859*

138a *litter:* ... That] *1811*; *Litter*. His *1859*

140a Christianity;] *1811*; Proselytism; *1859*

140b ancient] *1811*; ancient of all known *1859*

140c confirmed] *1811*; amply confirmed *1859*
140d for I have ... good!'] *1811*; yet I have made one Proselyte:' he paused. *1859*
141a the beam ... loveliness.] *1811*; the glow of health and beauty. *1859*
142a affection,] *1811*; remorse, *1859*
143a *God*] *1811*; Religion *1859*
143b passions – and above all ... led;] *1811*; passions; *1859*
143c destiny, ... threaten her. At] *1811*; destiny with which he threatened her. ¶ At *1859*
144a love, ... art,] *1811*; love *1859*
145a thee, – who ... eyes. – Luxima,] *1811*; thee. ¶ Luxima *1859*
145b face, ... him. ¶ Silent] *1811*; face; he felt her tears on his hands, which she pressed alternately to her eyes and to her lips. Silent *1859*
145c pity, ... figure. It] *1811*; pity. ¶ It *1859*
145d sufferings, and situations: – he] *1811*; situation. He *1859*
145e him as creatures ... nature;] *1811*; him, *1859*
146a Amazed, confounded,] *1811*; Amazed, *1859*
148a God.'] *1811*; Heaven.' *1859*
148b He whom ... they] *1811*; They *1859*
150a insatiable desire of the] *1811*; insatiable[a] *1859*
    [a This deletion compromises the sense of the passage.]
150b behold her, ... sufferings,] *1811*; behold her, *1859*
151a the constitution ... himself to] *1811*; his natural tendencies than from the errors of those institutions which he blindly obeyed in ignorance or incredulity, and from *1859*
151b and unrivalled excellence,] *1811*; piety and virtue, *1859*
152a by the fatal ... affliction,] through the consequences of its failure! *1859*
152b mingled ... look] *1811*; combined to give his countenance *1859*
152c weakness; ... him.] *1811*; weakness. *1859*
159a heard. ... suppress.] *1811* suppress. *1859*
159b met] *1811*; was ready to meet *1859*
159c 'My beloved, I come! – *Brahma*] *1811*; '*Brahma* *1859*
160a him with a dignified and] *1811*; with a *1859*
160b human] *1811*; long-subdued *1859*
160c enthusiasts ... liberty,] *1811*; fanatics, for religion and vengeance, *1859*
161a unsettled; ... sorrow:] *1811*; unsettled; *1859*
162a The Missionary,] *1811*; Hilarion, *1859*
162b languidly] *1811*; wildly *1859*
163a bosom – ... boat –] *1811*; bosom, *1859*
163b the Missionary;] *1811*; Hilarion; *1859*
164a the Missionary,] *1811*; Hilarion, *1859*
167a glance] *1811*; look *1859*
169a character of / *A Christian Missionary*.] *1811*; character of A Christian Missionary. *1859*